Dreams
of the
Scottish
Highlands

BOOKS BY F.L. EVERETT

F. L. EVERETT

Dreams
of the
Scottish
Highlands

bookouture

Published by Bookouture in 2025

An imprint of Storyfire Ltd.
Carmelite House
50 Victoria Embankment
London EC4Y 0DZ

www.bookouture.com

The authorised representative in the EEA is Hachette Ireland
8 Castlecourt Centre
Dublin 15 D15 XTP3
Ireland
(email: info@hbgi.ie)

ISBN: 978-1-83525-984-9
eBook ISBN: 978-1-83525-983-2

For my mum and dad, with love from Scotland.

PROLOGUE

So this is how it ends. My life, my tentative hopes and dreams, romantic plans and schemes – all of it lies in tatters, somewhere in a wheelie bin in Kilburn.

I already miss the view from my little attic bedroom – the old London rooftops always make me think of Mary Poppins flying by with her parrot-head umbrella. I miss my best friend and flatmate, Alice, who makes me laugh more than anyone on earth. I miss Oliver, my boss... though I can't think about him right now. And my job. Not just 'job', in fact – the career I loved. Almost ten years of striving and proving myself, and it's all drifted to ashes on the breeze...

I stare out of the train window, but we're in a long tunnel and I can only see a stark, white image of my face that makes me look like a chain-rattling Victorian ghost. My hair is scraped back from my forehead because I couldn't face washing it this morning, and any make-up I'd applied has rubbed off, somewhere between the second Pret tuna baguette and the fifth chapter of *Overcome Your Self-inflicted Trauma and Waltz with Life* by Garett P. Eisenberger, pressed into my hands by Alice as the Uber drew up outside our flat.

'Try it,' she urged. 'It's a bit Californian, I know, but once you get past the inspirational guff, there's some genuinely useful ideas in there.'

Chapter one is entitled 'From Rubber Duckie to Smart Cookie!' I can't face it. Instead, I open the dust-dry article about the crisis facing the Scottish hospitality industry which I saved to my phone earlier, but the words dance before my exhausted eyes. I've barely slept in the five days since everything fell apart, and I can't imagine ever sleeping again.

It's another two hours to Iolair station, located somewhere in the far West Highlands of Scotland. The train now seems to be travelling at the pace of an elderly shepherd wending his way homewards. I think nostalgically of the roar and rattle of a Thameslink, honking traffic, angry cab drivers. But I've no choice. And as we pull into yet another tiny, deserted station with a name I can't pronounce, I lean my forehead against the cold glass and close my eyes.

It's time to face the truth. I've royally screwed up my life, I'm heading directly to the middle of nowhere and I have absolutely no idea how I can ever come back from this.

1

FIVE DAYS EARLIER

I glanced across the sweeping lawn to see Oliver enthusiastically air-kissing a woman in a skimpy gold evening gown. Behind them, the Cotswold stone of the hired manor house glowed in the late April sun, and music from the string quartet drifted over the crowd – Vivaldi, which made me feel I was on hold to a BT helpline.

I'd made an effort for the party and was wearing expensive wedge heels, actual lipstick and a red dress with a low neckline. I felt like RuPaul as I tottered over to where my boss stood, talking to the woman I now recognised as the pop star Bo'nita. Recently, she'd enjoyed a massive hit with 'If U Knew U Like I Do', the video of which involved a lot of writhing and finger-licking in a glittery bikini.

Oliver allowed his elegant, butterscotch-tanned hand to rest lightly on the small of my back as he introduced me. He had recently proposed to his PA, Antonia, and I'd had to grin through their engagement party at a Chelsea nightclub full of braying poshos crashing into towers of champagne glasses. It was a long night.

I'd always known he wouldn't choose me – Oliver was

Monaco, yachts, sports cars; I was Morden, rowing boats, and I didn't actually own a car. But that hadn't stopped me being obsessed with him since I'd joined Magnum Opus Events, Oliver's high-end company, three years ago. Every time he stepped out of his office to ask me a question about spreadsheets, every time we worked together at a wedding or a product launch, every time I looked directly into his turquoise eyes, or the sunlight caught his buttery golden hair, I was flooded with longing. Oliver never showed any sign that my feelings were reciprocated.

Perhaps that was because Antonia had a sheet of pale, shining hair and mine was a wild brunette tangle, or that she had slanting blue eyes and a St Moritz ski-tan, while I had large brown eyes and was generally pale as milk. Antonia was model-skinny, a Meccano assembly of clavicles, elbows and spine from which designer clothes hung like silken wings. I'd turned curvy at sixteen, and most of my online shopping involved typing 'disguise boobs' and 'small waist, wide hips' into Google.

Once – just once, a moment worn so thin with overuse in my memory I was no longer sure it had really happened – Oliver kissed me goodbye after a difficult corporate event that had taken weeks of late nights and early mornings to plan. We were flooded with relief after hours of tightly wound adrenaline, and as I turned my head to him and he leaned in, our lips met. Seconds later, my cab arrived and I rattled back to Kilburn flushed with unfulfilled desire and the creeping awareness that everything was now going to be infinitely worse. Neither of us ever mentioned it again.

I had briefly hoped, of course, but then Antonia turned up, and I had no choice but to focus on work and keep my inappropriate passion locked away. Only Alice knew, and she did not approve.

'I bet he kisses the mirror every morning,' she said. 'Doesn't bother with Antonia, just straight in the bathroom, big snog, runs a deft hand through his glistening waves... He's like Gilderoy Lockhart in *Harry Potter*.' She also insisted that his Pacific-blue gaze was due to coloured contact lenses – 'it's so obvious' – and spent a great deal of time attempting to distract me with online dating.

Unsurprisingly, it hadn't worked.

Oliver's hand was still on my back. Helplessly, I leaned into his touch, my skin tingling under his warm fingers.

'Cat's our indispensable head of organisation,' Oliver told Bo'nita. She smiled glassily. 'She can lay her hands on a stuffed ostrich or a speedboat with under four minutes' warning.' He glanced at me. 'Actually, she might be the *perfect* person to helm your wedding.'

I'd never been permitted to head up a celebrity wedding before, and Bo'nita was the sort of client who'd have a budget for stargazer lilies all over the roof and a team of synchronised drag queens twerking in the pool. Bo'nita's wedding could make my name. I could become a co-director of MOE, working with Oliver every day, flying round the world, forced by an administrative mix-up to share a minimal yet exquisite Tokyo hotel suite with him...

'I'm thinking old school,' Bo'nita was saying, as Oliver listened intently. 'Me and J-Ting don't want, like, a TikTok scene. More classic Insta vibes, like old time-y, 2017 energy.'

I nodded thoughtfully. I felt I should have reading glasses on a chain and a cardigan sleeve full of balled-up tissues.

'Like, not full early Kanye, obviously, but that feel. Maybe pink doves?'

'Doves sound great,' I said. 'I mean, there could be an animal rights issue if—' Oliver prodded me hard in the side. '*Great*,' I repeated, nodding emphatically.

She air-kissed my cheeks. 'I'll get my PA, Baby G, to set up a meeting.'

'Nice work,' breathed Oliver in his public-school tones as Bo'nita picked her way over the lawn towards her fiancé. 'Do you know how much that'll bring in for MOE? We really need this, Cat.'

He smiled down at me expansively. He looked the same as ever – thick, fair hair glinting in the late afternoon sunlight, that powerful jaw...

Massive chin like a shovel, Alice said in my mind. I ignored her.

Oliver lifted a full bottle of champagne from a table. 'Let's take this to the summer house. I want to talk to you.' He led me to a little stone folly with carved pineapples on its pillars and inside, a couple of wicker chairs surrounded by leafy, tropical plants.

'That haircut really suits you,' he said, as we sat down.

'Thank you,' I replied, startled. He had never before remarked on my appearance.

'I wonder.' Oliver leaned in thoughtfully. 'Is there anyone in your life? You're so professional, I feel I hardly know anything about you.'

'Well, my parents—'

Oliver laughed, his white teeth flashing.

Turkish veneers like war graves, said Alice in my head.

Shut up, I thought violently.

'I meant romantically.'

'Like you and Antonia?'

'Well, maybe with a bit less wedding planning.' He sighed heavily. 'It's all getting a bit much if I'm honest, Cat.'

'In what way?' I asked, when I should have said, 'Can I help?' or, 'It'll be fine.'

He settled back in his chair and handed the bottle to me.

'Toni's obsessed with having it at Chiverley, her family pile.

I mean it's massive, which is good, but that also means her bloody mother's involved in every single decision.' He adopted a shrill, excruciatingly posh accent. '"*You can't remove that tapestry, darling; it was Granny's, and Sotheby's are desperate for it.*" So apparently, we're getting married surrounded by thread-bare wall hangings of dismembered hares.'

'Love conquers all, though, right?'

'*Love*, yes.' Oliver broke off, staring into the distance. 'I wonder sometimes if...'

I tried to breathe steadily, despite the pounding of my heart.

'... well, if we're really making the right choice. Toni's dying to start a family and move to the country – buried alive in cottage-core.' He shuddered. 'I'm starting to wonder – have I been hasty?'

He turned to me, an anguished look in his Maldives-ocean eyes.

Champagne and adrenaline buzzed round my system like a swarm of wasps.

'The thing is, Cat, I look at you and I wonder—' he began, just as a shadow appeared in the doorway and a voice cried, 'Oliver, it's time for your speech!'

It was Vanessa, a perfectly pleasant colleague. I wanted to fling my champagne into her beaming face.

'To be continued,' Oliver murmured, and followed Vanessa's upright figure back down the lawn.

What had he been going to say? That he wanted me, after all? That he'd made a mistake? That it was all over with Antonia?

I took another long swig of Moët.

An hour later, I'd finished the bottle. I stood swaying at the top of the grand staircase in the elegant Georgian manor, blue carpet rippling below me like an unquiet ocean.

And I made the most stupid decision of my life.

2

Afterwards, I didn't get out of bed for twenty-four hours, until my mum rang.

I told her the bare bones of what had happened. 'All is not lost, pet,' she insisted, with her usual boundless optimism. 'I've got a proposal for you. Come for lunch.'

I reluctantly dragged myself out of bed and onto the Tube to Morden, and the comforts of the 1930s semi where I grew up.

My parents listened as I described my ocean-going mortification, Mum muttering 'self-satisfied little git' every time Oliver's name was mentioned and Dad ballooning with fury like a puffer fish when I got to the redundancy part of the Shakespearean tragedy that was now my life.

'You need to speak to your union rep,' he said. 'You could have justification for a tribunal.'

Dad was what used to be called 'a firebrand'. I'd spent a lot of my childhood stamping alongside him in my rainbow smock at human rights marches, while Mum distributed home-made badges.

'Dad, honestly, I don't want to. I just want to put it all behind me and move on.'

'It's the capitalist system, Cat – they think they can buy and sell human endeavour.'

'Shush, Gerry,' sighed Mum. 'Cat doesn't like to *dwell*.'

She turned to me, a look of suppressed excitement on her face. 'Do you remember my godfather, Alastair? We went up to visit him when you were young.'

I did remember – that brief weekend visit had remained branded on my mind for many years afterwards. I still thought of it instantly, whenever anyone mentioned teenage heartbreak.

'Vaguely,' I lied. 'Scotland?'

Mum nodded. 'That's right. Grandad Ned knew him from his Scottish fishing holidays, though of course, your grandad was a history teacher and Alastair owns a castle...'

'As you do,' murmured Dad bitterly.

Mum gave him a quelling look. 'Go and get the cheese, Gerry.

'I haven't heard from Alastair for years,' she went on. 'But I had a letter from him the other day. It could be the solution to all your problems.'

'How can some elderly Scottish laird be the—'

She held up a hand. 'Just read it.'

She went to the kitchen, and I heard her shouting, 'No, not the old cheddar! The *Comté*, Gerry! And the *sourdough* crackers!'

When she returned, she handed me a stiff cream envelope – it looked like the sort of thing a palace servant would hand-deliver in a pantomime. I unfolded the letter and scanned the looping black writing.

Dear Janet,

Firstly, I must apologise for being a dreadful godfather to you over the years. I am about to compound my lack of manners by requesting a most generous favour of someone whom I have only ever disappointed.

I looked up. 'Have we time travelled to 1865?'
'He's just posh. Keep reading.'

We now find ourselves in a rather impecunious position at Iolair, due to the gradual deterioration of the main building, and the increasingly vast sums required for its upkeep.

One of my sons had the felicitous idea of turning it into the sort of place which hosts events. The difficulty is, none of us have the slightest idea where to begin with this inspired plan, and I'm afraid Rory, who came up with the scheme, remains in America due to his work there.

If I recall correctly, Catrina works in 'events'. Do you imagine she might give up a week or two of her time to come and advise? We can offer accommodation, home cooking, and we do have the most marvellous surrounds for walking, stalking and grouse shooting, with fishing on the loch if she can spare the time to visit.

We should all be so very grateful.

With affection,

Sir Alastair

'Wait, is he, like, a *lord*? Or...?'
'A lord *and* a laird, I think. Cat, this could be a chance to take on a project of your own, one that's nothing to do with *Oliver and his events business,*' she said, in a tone normally reserved for '*plague-ridden black rats*'.
'You're famous for your organisation, Cat. Do you remember when you were tiny and you lined up all your teddies in alphabetical order?'

I snorted. 'My crippling childhood OCD? That's a nice memory.'

'Oh, Cat, it wasn't; you just liked routine and order.'

'Still do.'

There was a clatter as Dad returned carrying a tray of cheese and biscuits.

'But, Mum, it would take months – and it doesn't sound like they've got a budget to make it happen.'

'Then you can tell them that. I just think it's a good—'

'*Opportunity*, I know.' I sighed. 'What about my flat? I can't just abandon Alice.'

Actually, I could. Technically, Alice's very-well-off-but-neglectful parents paid for the flat, and I paid rent. She had already assured me I could have 'a money holiday' if I needed it.

A wave of panic crashed over me. 'I can't just rush off to Scotland. I've got to...' I paused. After years of pressing deadlines, it was quite terrifying to realise there was absolutely nothing I had to do.

Mum raised an eyebrow.

'... pack,' I sighed, defeated.

Mum smiled. 'Don't forget your waterproofs.'

3

'Iolair!' the ticket inspector bellowed, and I leapt to my feet, pulling my bag from the overhead rack. A Mr McTavish was supposed to be meeting me at the station, but as I stepped down from the train, legs weak from lack of use and food over the past few hours, I could see nobody waiting.

There were pots of spring flowers along the platform, a freshly painted green bench, and a small bookshelf of tattered paperbacks with a felt-tipped sign reading, HELP YOURSELF TO A GOOD READ!

The tiny station was surrounded by vast, pine-forested hills – or were they mountains? I had no idea, but in the distance, the highest peak was capped with snow, and there was a chill that felt more like winter than spring. The air smelled strange, and it took me a moment to realise that it was due to the lack of traffic fumes, rotting kebabs and burnt coffee beans that permeated the London streets. I gazed up and down as my train chugged away into the distance. It was after nine and still light, but I didn't love the idea of being alone in the middle of nowhere as darkness fell. I took my phone from my pocket, but it had no signal.

I was beginning to feel anxious when I heard a shout.

'Catrina Hardwick! Is that you?'

I looked over the track to see a sixty-something man wearing a woolly hat and a blue-and-red puffer jacket.

'That's me!' I called. 'How do I get over to you?'

He stared at me. 'I think it's generally assumed that you walk, lassie. Unless you'd like a fireman's lift, but the biceps are not what they were, right enough.'

'Aren't the tracks electrified?'

He guffawed. 'I very much doubt it or there'd be fried chicken all round every night.'

'Sorry?'

'The chickens,' he said, as if they were a girl band. 'They live at the station. Jock keeps them, names them all after Hollywood stars. Barbra Streisand hopped on the train last week, nearly got as far as Oban before someone spotted her. Over you come,' he added, beckoning me across.

No searing voltage ripped through me as I stepped across, so I had to assume he was correct.

He shook my hand with a wiry grip. 'I'm Donald McTavish; my wife Ishbel and I look after the castle. And its motley inhabitants,' he added, raising an eyebrow in a manner that didn't entirely reassure me.

'Now,' he said, leading me to a battered flatbed truck parked on the overgrown lane by the station sign, 'watch out for Hannay, there. He's extremely friendly.'

Hannay? Was he another son? I discovered my mistake when I clambered into the front seat and shrieked as a wet, hairy nose thrust itself into my ear.

I turned to see a vast Irish wolfhound slithering onto the back seat, endless legs spilling over the edge and shining brown eyes fixed on me.

'Hannay belongs to Sir Alastair,' said Donald, starting the

engine with a noise like an asthmatic walrus. 'But he likes a drive out wi' me. Ye're not scared o' dogs, are ye?'

'No,' I assured him. 'I love them.'

'Aye, just as well,' he said, rattling round a sharp bend. 'We're overrun wi' them. There's Hannay, we've got Douglas, a wee collie pup, then there's Arran and Alba. Spaniels, though I'll warn ye they think they're people. They belong to Himself.'

'Himself?'

'Young Logan,' amended Donald. 'Sir Alastair's eldest. Worries of the world on his shoulders, that one. He was forty when he was four.'

At the mention of Logan's name, a memory flashed through my mind. I shoved it away. I had vowed not to think about the last time I was here.

'Does he live there all the time?'

'Aye. Went to Edinburgh University. Came back full o' schemes and plans, but he's been unlucky these past ten years, I'll say that.'

I was warming to Donald – he was evidently an unstoppable gossip.

'Unlucky how?'

'This and that. The hydro-scheme green energy plan fell apart after someone complained, and DEFRA weren't happy with the rewilding idea – I'll admit I was a wee bit worried about the wolves meself – then he was set to marry, but she left him...'

'Who?' I asked, fascinated.

'Och, my big gob,' he said. 'I'll say no more, it's no' my business. This is Iolair village.'

We bumped over potholes past a handful of small white houses with grey slate roofs, a shuttered Post Office, a couple of shops and a pub called The Falls of GlennIolair, with a lone wooden table outside.

Hannay pushed his long, grey head between the front seats, and I stroked his wiry left ear.

'Tourists don't come up here these days so much, now there's the leisure park twenty miles down the loch – they've tea rooms this, log flumes that.'

'Is that why the castle is struggling?'

'I'd say no,' he said, compressing his moustache between his lips. 'I'd say that would be a simple case of running out o' money. Used to be a place like that would survive on inherited wealth, tenant farms on the estate, selling produce. But there's no call for that these days. I've told Sir A, he can sell up if he needs – Ishbel and I will move down to Dumfries, where our Flora lives, though he won't have it. Now, there's this new events scheme... I believe you're here to save us all,' he added. 'I wish ye luck, but I'll warn ye, it's no easy task.'

Ahead of us, the single-track road curved under arches of trees, and when it opened out again, I saw fields filled with sheep and large, hairy creatures with horns like bicycle bars.

'Highland cows!' I shrieked in delight.

Mr McTavish nodded solemnly. 'That'll be due to us being in the Highlands.' He turned up a small road and slowed. 'Here we are now,' he said. 'Welcome to Castle Iolair.'

My immediate feeling was one of disappointment. A detached stone house stood by the huge iron gates. Though it was admittedly pretty, with carved gables and pointed roofs and in Fulham would have cost at least three million ('with potential to develop basement gym'), it was not a castle. My heart sank as I realised we'd all be crammed together while I explained to dotty Sir Alastair that it was not possible to host paying events in a reasonably sized four-bedroom home.

I was trying to think of a way to express this subtly to Donald when I realised that he'd sped up again. We'd passed the house and were now travelling at a fair lick down a long road lined with trees. On our right was a wide river, shining in the dusk, and to the left, I made out a herd of spindly dark shapes by the base of a forested hill that must, I assumed, be deer. It really was like a fairy tale – one in which I was apparently being kidnapped.

'Where are we going?'

He half turned, puzzled. 'To the castle. You're expected.'

'No, but we just passed...'

He gave a bark of laughter. 'That's ma *hoose!*' he cried. 'The gatehouse! Ye thought that was the... Ah, dearie me. Ye're in for a treat, lassie. Any minute now.'

He drove further into the dusk, and as the road swept lower, I could see a vast, dark building. Lights glowed in the windows, pointed turrets pierced the sky, a shallow flight of stone steps led to enormous wooden doors. I expected a ragged Beast in a Regency frock coat to beckon me inside.

'Bloody hell,' I murmured inadequately.

Donald laughed. 'Aye,' he said, coming to a stop in front of the great doors. '*This* is the castle. If ye don't mind, I'll drop ye here – Ishbel's got a new season of *CSI Miami* cued up, and a bag o' Thai chilli crisps with my name on it.'

He handed me my suitcase, and Hannay leapt out after me.

'Don't let Himself bother ye,' were his last, alarming words as he drove off in a spray of gravel.

I stood on the stone step of Iolair Castle in the late evening gloaming. There was a vast, iron knocker in the shape of an eagle's head on the studded oak door.

I am Cat Hardwick, I said to myself as I lifted it. *I am organised and competent. It is the twenty-first century, and this door is not about to be opened by a vengeful magical creature—*

'Oh!'

The door was flung back and two whirling tumbleweeds shot out in a blur of golden fur. The step was suddenly the scene of riotous barking and wriggling.

And that was when I met Logan McAskill for the second time in my life.

4

'*Arran! Alba!*'

I stood paralysed in a maelstrom of whirling bodies and wild barking.

'You bloody little... DON'T BITE HIM! Right, no biscuits at bedtime...'

I stood in a ferment of indecision – should I help? Would I be injured? One cocker spaniel dashed past me, ears flying like ship's pennants, while the second, still wiggling and barking, was now clamped like a furious toddler under the arm of a tall, broad-shouldered man with untidy black hair, a straight nose, dark eyes and eyebrows knitted into a furious scowl.

'If you could use the side entrance to the left in future,' he said. His accent was somewhere between what Alice would call 'hot posh' and what I thought of as 'Hagrid Scottish' – Hottish?

'Sorry,' I said. 'I thought—'

'That bloody knocker drives them insane,' he said. 'There's no calming them now; the noise echoes through the entire castle.'

'I'm Cat,' I said. 'Sir Alastair wrote to my mum...'

'Oh yes,' said Logan, stony-faced. 'Didn't he just. *Events*. I'll apologise now for your wasted journey.'

'Wasted... how?'

He was still pinning the dog to his side, though it was making a noise like the demons in the vintage horror films Alice inexplicably enjoyed.

'Quiet, Alba! Look, it's all nonsense,' he said. 'Dad's got this bee in his bonnet, thanks to Rory.'

'Your brother?'

'Yup. Much use he is. Look, enjoy your stay, there's some good walks round the loch, but please don't think you'll be making a difference. Agatha's waiting for you in the kitchen,' he added, raising his voice over the dogs' wild growling. 'Second door by the stairs and along the corridor to the end. Leave your case in the hall. I probably won't see you again, so I'll say goodbye.'

He turned and strode back inside. He hadn't even said hello. If this was the sort of welcome provided by everyone at Castle Iolair, I'd be on the first train back to London tomorrow morning. In fact, I'd rather sleep on the green bench at the station.

Although... he was still handsome. Much older, more weathered and certainly angrier than the boy I'd once met. But I remembered his flawless skin, the black hair that shone like a raven's wing. Those things hadn't changed at all.

'You're Cat, then.'

A blonde woman who appeared to be in her late thirties was standing by a gleaming Aga. Large, cream-painted cupboards lined one wall of the kitchen, and an oak table which could easily seat twelve stretched the length of the room. In the corner, a black-and-white puppy lay on a matted dog-bed, chewing something unpleasant.

'Hello,' I said, 'I am. Are you Agatha?'

'Aye. And this is Dougie, the wee mite.' Her accent was a sing-song lilt.

'Logan sent me to the kitchen; he said there might be something to eat...' As I spoke, I inhaled the scent of herbs and rich meat gravy emanating from the pan on the hob and almost fainted with longing.

'Aye. I made a venison stew.' She ladled it into a blue pottery bowl, and placed a basket of home-made bread on the table. 'You sit, lassie. Eat. I'll show you your bedroom afterwards. I hope you run hot because it's no' warm.'

She volunteered nothing more. I was too tired to speak, so my meal was soundtracked by the noise of Dougie's puppy teeth nibbling his prize.

Afterwards, I stood and took my bowl to the sink to wash.

'No.' Agatha held a hand up. 'That's *my* job. Your job is to save the castle.'

'That's... well... I'll do my best.' I was all too aware that Logan had just told me in no uncertain terms that it wasn't possible.

I collected my case, and Agatha led me up the wide, shallow stairs overlooked by dark oil paintings of speared stags and looming forests. As I climbed, I couldn't help thinking I should have been carrying a flickering candle and wearing a muslin nightgown.

After a restless and freezing night, I sprang awake in shock as a sonorous male voice murmured into my ear. It took me a moment to remember I'd turned on the bedside radio alarm, and it was evidently set to a local station.

'Now, we've got Jack on the line, and he's saying there's a few stray sheep on the Oban road from Ballachford,' said the presenter in a strong Highlands accent. 'He tells us he's called round to Sandy's farm and they're bringing a trailer down right enough, but mind how ye go in the meantime...'

I sat up in bed and looked at my room. Morning light was filtering through a gap in the thick curtains, creating a glowing bar of warmth across the dark floorboards. It was the only heat source, seemingly – just as Agatha had warned me, it was indeed chilly, or perhaps a more accurate description would be 'a bit brisk for Scott of the Antarctic'. I'd slept under a duvet and two musty tartan blankets I'd found in the huge mahogany wardrobe, along with half the clothes I'd brought. I'd still shivered myself to sleep.

My bed was a high double with a wooden headboard, carved with fruit and flowers, and a mattress firmer than a cork-tiled floor.

Unlike my cacophonous London attic room, there was no noise at all penetrating the thick stone walls and it was unnerving. I could be entirely alone in this enormous castle. I hauled myself out of bed and over to the window, where I pulled open the heavy tartan curtains, peered through the leaded pane and found my breath trapped in my throat.

Outside, smooth green lawns dotted with yellow flowers ran down to a line of trees. Glossy shrubs bursting with pink and red blooms – rhododendrons? – lined the edge of the grass, and beyond the trees lay a vast silver stretch of shimmering water: Loch Iolair itself. In the distance, silhouetted mountains loomed, dove-grey in the morning haze, their jagged peaks piercing through wisps of sugared-almond cloud. I turned to fetch my phone and take a photo, catching a glimpse of myself in the tall, fly-spotted wardrobe mirror. I was wearing my shortie leopard-print pyjamas, a farewell gift from Alice, with a large, hairy brown jumper Mum had lent me, red knee-length hiking socks and a hand-knitted rainbow bobble hat, lovingly crafted by my auntie Margaret. 'I knew it'd come in useful one day,' Mum had said, stuffing it into my case.

As I returned to the window, I heard wild barking in the corridor. My bedroom door slammed back against the wall, and the spaniels shot in, hurtling across the bed in a whirl of shrill noise and mud.

'DOGS!'

Logan ran in seconds behind them. He looked furious, his dark curls unbrushed. His broad shoulders filled out a dark green cable-knit jumper, and his faded jeans were held up around his slim hips by a worn leather belt.

'For Christ's sake!' he roared. 'You KNOW not to do this... How many times...?' He grabbed both dogs by the collars as they cavorted through my suitcase, scattering knickers, and led them, still yapping, into the corridor, shutting the door on them.

He finally looked at me. 'That's an... interesting outfit,' he observed. 'We normally wear jeans and jumpers here, but do enjoy your stay in whatever feels comfortable.'

I opened my mouth to explain.

'Anyway,' he added. 'Good socks. Breakfast at eight, in the kitchen.'

As he left – 'Get DOWN, Arran, you lunatic!' floating from the stairs – I sank back onto the bed, weak with embarrassment. I was showing an awful lot of thigh, I realised, and my cheeks now matched the scarlet socks.

5

By the time I arrived in the kitchen, I'd changed into jeans and a clean jumper, with my favourite old Adidas trainers. Mum had said something about wellies, but they wouldn't fit in my suitcase. 'Anyway,' I'd told her airily, 'it's a castle – it's hardly going to be a pigsty.'

I may have been wrong about that, I realised, passing a tiled boot room which housed more rainproof jackets than a Norwegian fishing trawler and three neat rows of green, mud-encrusted wellingtons in various sizes. There was also a shelf of waterproof hats with wide brims, several enormous umbrellas shoved into – it looked like a withered elephant's foot, and I quickly looked away – and a pile of battered wicker hampers containing what I assumed was fishing equipment, as a rack of polished wooden rods stood beside them.

'There you are!' A cheerful voice assailed me as I rounded the huge, panelled door to the kitchen.

I found the long table already occupied by a wiry older man in a threadbare Fair Isle jumper and faded corduroys. He had thinning, tufty hair the colour of summer clouds and bright blue eyes, creased by his warm smile. Hannay the wolfhound was lying at his feet.

'You must be Sir Alastair,' I said, and he laughed.

'No need to call me Sir. It's lovely to meet you again, Cat. Have a seat. I hope you're hungry – Agatha's outdone herself.'

Agatha turned from the oven. 'I always outdo myself, Sir A,' she pointed out. I couldn't imagine Agatha ever suffering a moment's self-doubt.

She ladled bacon, sausages, eggs, beans, tomatoes and mushrooms onto plates, and set out a silver toast rack that looked as though it should be in the V&A. I looked up as Logan entered, and despite my perfectly sensible outfit, I felt heat flare through me.

'Changed your socks?' he murmured as he sat down opposite me. 'Shame.'

Agatha crashed a platter onto the table.

'Thank you, Ag,' said Logan, offering it to me. 'Lorne sausage, Cat?'

Rather alarmingly, the sausages seemed to be square.

'I've never seen...' I began.

'Oh, you must try a Scottish Lorne sausage!' insisted Sir Alastair. 'They're a genuine wonder of the world! When I was a little boy at boarding school, I used to dream of them – and butteries. They're a sort of Scottish croissant, made with masses of butter.'

'I used to dream of thrashing the first eleven with a single ball,' said Logan. 'I never did, mind.'

Boarding school and cricket. It made my own tedious years at Park View Comp seem almost bearable. I took a piece of the strangely angular meat and said, 'It's lovely to be here. I do hope I can help you.'

Logan snorted. 'I wouldn't count on it.'

I wanted to snap, 'Well then why let your dad spend money

getting me up here and waste everyone's time?' but I restricted myself to a simple, 'Oh?'

'As I told you last night,' said Logan, 'Dad's decided you're our last hope, but I'm afraid that ship has sailed. Events won't bring in the money we need to rescue Iolair.'

'You'd be amazed how much you can charge for celebrity weddings and things like that—' I began eagerly, through a mouthful of crispy bacon.

'*Celebrity weddings?*' Logan repeated. His cultured Scottish accent made it sound as though I'd said 'hardcore porn shoots', and his neat black eyebrows joined once again in horrified bafflement.

'That sounds very jolly, Cat!' Sir Alastair enthused, ignoring his eldest son. He poured me some coffee from the old-fashioned metal jug sitting on the table, and I sipped it gratefully. I needed a jolt of caffeine to deal with Logan's presence at this time of the morning.

'So you would... tell the celebrities we're available and they'd book, is that it?'

'Well, we'd need to promote it.' I smiled at the older man. 'Brochures, social media, a luxe-looking website – do you have an online presence? I couldn't find anything.'

'Online presence!' Logan almost choked on a fried mushroom. 'Only if you count Donald's Facebook chicken group. It's called Iolair Hen Husbandry; I'm pretty sure Madonna's a member.'

Sir Alastair shot him a glare. 'We don't currently have a website,' he said, 'but I'm sure that's something we could look into.'

'And we'd need to sort out a proper function room, something that can be a multipurpose space for conferences, weddings, corporate awaydays...'

'Dear God.' Logan gave a full-body shudder.

I was becoming increasingly annoyed. Why had I been dragged up here if I wasn't wanted?

Logan saw my expression. 'Look,' he said, in a marginally friendlier tone, 'we're miles from anywhere, as you've discovered, the roof's crumbling, there's leaks in every bathroom, the place needs a fortune spending to update it, we don't have anything like the catering facilities—'

'Am I Scotch mist?' demanded Agatha, who was sipping tea from a giant pink mug that read, 'THEY CAN'T DROWN EVERY WITCH'.

'No, no,' said Logan hurriedly. 'But even you can't cater for a hundred people from this kitchen.'

She shrugged. 'I've done trickier things. Starting with shopping my ex-husband to the police when he threatened to burn down the croft with my own ailing mother in it. He lived to regret *that*, aye.'

In the ensuing silence, I swallowed a piece of square sausage too loudly.

Logan sighed. 'I've told Dad over and over, it's not possible on our budget, and look, Cat, I'm sorry you've come all this way...'

'*Logan.*' Sir Alastair's voice snapped across the table like a rubber band. We all leapt to attention – even Hannay's ears were set to flight mode.

'I have invited Cat here as my guest,' he said icily. 'Iolair is still, unless you plan imminent patricide, my castle, and I will decide how we proceed. I suggest you get on with your own work, and Cat and I will begin ours.'

I almost felt sorry for Logan. It couldn't be pleasant to have your father publicly undermine you. The tips of his ears were scarlet, and he quickly swallowed his last bite of toast and stood up.

'Fine,' he said. 'I'm sure you'll let me know what you come

up with in due course.' He strode out of the kitchen, and Agatha rolled her eyes.

'Moody wee scone. Like a storm over Stromness,' she muttered.

'Sorry about my son, Cat.' Sir Alastair lifted another square sausage onto his plate. 'He's not famous for his sunny, even temperament, I'm afraid. We used to call him The Brooder when he was a small boy because he'd always be down in the henhouse, ruminating over some injustice.'

I smiled. It was rather sweet to imagine Logan as a little lad, stomping off to think amongst the chickens. Still, he'd turned into a thoroughly grumpy thirty-something.

'It's all right,' I said. 'I expect he feels he's being ignored, and nobody likes that. I've dealt with a lot of...' I was about to say 'egos' and changed it to 'reluctant participants in my work, so I'm quite good at being tactful.'

'That's why it's so important we sort this out,' said Sir Alastair, 'if only to pull my son out of this endless *funk* he's got himself into. He's got this mad scheme, you see...'

Hannay laid his long nose on my knee, and I absently fed him a bit of sausage. 'He's been in charge of the kitchen garden for years, and since the hydro-scheme failed to get funding, and then the wedding... well.'

I was dying to know more, partly due to my extreme nosiness, and partly because it was hard to imagine anyone turning down a man as handsome as the heir to Iolair. Then again, if she'd witnessed his temper...

'Anyway, now Logan's convinced we can raise money by becoming a market gardening enterprise, selling to hotels and restaurants in the West Highlands. I've seen the figures, and it's just not feasible,' Sir Alastair continued. 'What if there's a frost and the crops are ruined? What if there's a drought – or gales? Or floods!'

I felt I was suddenly talking to an ancient Aztec, but I

nodded, as if I knew anything about gardening or coastal weather systems.

'And besides, he'd have to factor in the vans and the upkeep, and the delivery drivers, and there's already Ross from Kinlear – he does fish and vegetables for the local area in his smart little van, comes every Thursday.'

'A very fetching man,' put in Agatha. 'Lovely teeth.'

Sir Alastair sighed. 'I've told Logan it can't work, but he's so damned stubborn. And of course, Rory's off in New York, living the high life, so he's no use to us.'

'I remember Rory,' I said. 'What's he doing over there exactly?'

'Oh, something enormously high-powered at Statler and Waldorf, or whatever they're called.' Sir Alastair shrugged. 'Investment banking firm. I don't think he enjoys it greatly, but by God, the money he makes.'

'Can't he...?' I began, and he shook his head.

'The castle can't survive on handouts from my younger son,' he said. 'Besides, Logan wouldn't hear of it.'

There seemed to be an awful lot of things that Logan wouldn't hear of, I thought bitterly. Like charm, good manners, open-mindedness...

'Look, I can see it all looks rather disheartening,' said Sir Alastair. 'But in time, he'll—'

In the distance, I could hear frantic barking.

'Those damn spaniels,' he muttered. 'Agatha, where's Dougie? They *will* come and terrorise him, and we simply can't have it.'

'Don't you worry, Sir A,' she said. 'I've made him a wee nest, in the cupboard.' She further opened a door that was ajar beside the fridge to reveal the puppy curled on what looked very much like the jumper Logan had been wearing last night.

Sir Alastair stood and brushed crumbs from his knees, which were swiftly gobbled up by Hannay. 'I have a little work to do, so I shall suggest Logan shows you round,' he said. 'Then perhaps we could meet in my study for a debrief?'

After Sir Alastair had gone, Agatha briskly patted my shoulder. 'I can see how you're feeling, lassie,' she said. 'Believe me, Logan is a good man. But he's very...' She paused. 'He's a darkness in him. Life isnae... sunshine and roses for the laddie.'

Well, it bloody isn't for most of us, and we don't all take it out on other people hovered on my lips, but I nodded. 'I'll bear it in mind,' I said. 'Thanks for a lovely breakfast.'

She raised a slim shoulder in acknowledgement, as footsteps, accompanied by excitable yapping, headed towards the kitchen door. I remembered Logan the previous evening, saying, *I probably won't see you again.*

He'd said the very same words the last time I met him. And it had taken me fifteen years to prove him wrong.

6

MAY BANK HOLIDAY WEEKEND, FIFTEEN YEARS EARLIER

'Come on, Jan,' shouts Dad. 'It's not as cold as it looks!'

He's wading determinedly into the freezing water, goose pimples stippling his pale legs. Mum looks at me. 'Do you want to go with him?'

'Not unless hell freezes over. Which is probably how it feels.'

She sighs. 'Fine. I'll go down, but I'll just watch from the shore. Unlike your father, I'm not *deranged*.'

She heaves herself upright and trudges over the pebbly beach to watch Dad splash his way to Svalbard. I get out my Motorola flip-phone, a recent sixteenth birthday present, and study the screen, but there are no bars. Back home, half of Year Eleven will be gathering at the park, and there's a very good chance Nathan Summers, aka Goldenballs, will be there, and so will Chloe Whittaker with her waist-length GHD-smooth hair and her Jane Norman crop top. I, however, am wearing Mum's ancient brown anorak and crouching on the wind-lashed shore of Loch Iolair, five hundred miles away, as the breeze whips my hair into stiffened candyfloss.

'Hey!'

I look up. Two figures are crunching down the beach, and as they approach, the silhouettes resolve themselves into teenage boys; one fair and stocky and about my age, the other at least seventeen, tall, darkly handsome and wearing an expression that suggests he's just swallowed a hornet. They are carrying fishing gear and heading for the small jetty near to where Dad is currently whooping and screeching in the water, churning up a whirlpool with his thrashing front crawl.

'Is that your dad?' asks the taller one. He sounds annoyed.

'No, he's my case worker.'

The younger one laughs. 'You must be Cat,' he says, in a soft Scottish accent. 'We're Rory and Logan; we've just got back from prison. I mean, school.'

I squint at him. 'But it's morning.'

'We're boarders. Dad just collected us after another joyous term at the Glenfinnachan Institute of Incarceration.'

'Oh, I see. Your dad's my mum's godfather. It's the first time we've been up here.'

'Look, can you get your dad to stop prancing about?' says Logan. 'He's going to drive all the fish away, if he hasn't already.'

'He's not *prancing*,' I say hotly. 'Your dad said we could come down and swim if we liked. Those were his exact words.'

'Well, *my* exact words are "can you do it somewhere else?"' says Logan. 'There are brown trout here, and he's going to disrupt the entire ecosystem—'

Rory glances at me and rolls his eyes. '*Sorry about him,*' he mouths.

'Excuse me!' Logan suddenly bellows, like a colonel summoning troops across the battlefield.

Mum turns. 'Hello there!' she calls cheerfully. 'You must be Logan and Rory. I haven't seen you since you were—'

'Yes, hello,' says Logan. 'Good to see you, Janet. Can I ask that Gerry swims somewhere else? The brown trout are—'

'Oh!' Mum looks horrified. 'I'm so sorry! Gerry! GERRY!' she shrieks. Dad begins an excruciatingly glacial crawl back to the jetty. 'The trout!' Mum screams.

Dad waves cheerfully and splashes on, as Logan silently monitors his progress, a young David Attenborough watching a doomed manatee.

'Lovely to have you here,' says Rory to Mum eventually, like a forty-year-old dinner party host. 'Some good walks up on the hills, and apparently we're going to have better weather this afternoon.'

I try to imagine Nathan 'Roadman' Summers holding this conversation with my mother, and fail.

Dad finally reaches the shallows and stands up, water coursing from his hairy chest like a 1970s movie poster of Poseidon. 'Woof! Refreshing!' he yells. 'Coming in, boys?'

In an agony of embarrassment, I slide in my iPod headphones and turn up the Lady Gaga album. I see Mum gesticulating and Logan solemnly explaining, while Rory smiles blandly at the view, evidently as mortified as I am.

Finally, Dad treks back up the beach, shakes like a Labrador and climbs into his clothes, exclaiming and shivering like a performance artist acting out 'being cold'.

'I've got some home-made baba ganoush in here,' says Mum, digging into her *Haringey Book Festival* 2007 tote bag. 'Want some, Cat?'

I shake my head, strangely unwilling to be seen eating North London aubergine dip in front of Logan. By now, he and his brother are standing at the end of the jetty, Logan demonstrating something to Rory – something unbelievably boring to do with fishing, no doubt, but I find I'm staring at him. He was rude and dismissive and unwelcoming, I remind myself, but for some reason, as I watch him, his shining dark hair ruffled by the wind, his slim, broad-shouldered frame bending towards his younger brother, my agonised thoughts about Nathan Summers begin to fade, and are instantly replaced by... oh no.

I put my head in my hands to hide my pink cheeks, and turn up 'Poker Face' to maximum volume.

I've only gone and developed a thumping crush on Logan bloody McAskill.

7

I stood in the entrance hall, eye to eye with an oil portrait of the fourth laird, who strongly resembled a haddock suffering acid reflux.

When Logan arrived, this time without the dogs, he gave me a smile that was more like a grimace of pain. Somehow, he still resembled a young Gregory Peck in *Roman Holiday*.

'Sorry about earlier,' he said. 'Dad and I don't quite see eye to eye on what's necessary, and I'm afraid you've ended up in the crossfire.'

'I understand,' I said, straight into professional mollifying mode. Did I? Only that Logan was stubborn and abrasive, no matter how fine his cheekbones.

'He said you had a plan about the kitchen garden...' I began.

'Oh, did he now? Did he also mention Ross the fish man and his smart little van?'

'Well...'

Logan closed his eyes and shook his head. 'It's hardly the same,' he muttered. 'Anyway. You don't need to involve yourself in that particular debate. I'll show you round, and then I'm sure

Dad will regale you with his plans for corporate entertainment packages and luxury petting zoos.'

'I know you're not keen,' I said, 'but perhaps I could draw up some basic plans for Castle Iolair and you could just take a look?'

'It's up to Dad,' he said tightly. 'He's made that pretty clear, so I'm afraid you don't need my signature to go ahead.'

As he turned his head away, the movement showed off the razor-sharp angle of his jaw. I wondered why artists weren't beating down the door to paint him. His portrait would be a whole lot easier on the eye than the fourth laird.

'It would be better if you're all in agreement,' I tried again. 'I don't want to cause a rift.'

'McAskill rifts run through our family history like the burns through the hills up there,' he said. 'It's nothing new.'

'Burns?'

'Scottish for streams. And by the way, for future reference, it's pronounced Castle Eye-oh-lare, not Ee-oh-lare. Look, I have to take Arran to the vet in an hour, so do you mind if we crack on?'

'Is he okay?' I was somewhat intimidated by the over-wrought spaniels, but I hoped it wasn't terminal.

'His anal glands need squeezed.'

I sensed my expression curdling into horror.

Something that was almost a smile passed across Logan's face. 'Well, you did ask.'

We began on the ground floor, in the main entrance hall. I longed to explain what a glorious greeting area it could provide to guests, with kilted waiters holding trays of whisky cocktails and a lone piper on the steps. Sadly, I suspected Logan would immediately abandon me if I so much as mentioned bagpipes, tartan or Scotch whisky.

'We tend to use the kitchen side of the main building,' said Logan. 'It's warmer so we all sleep up there, further down the

corridor you're on, and Dad's office and the spare rooms are on
the next floor. The attic's just storage and ancient servants'
bedrooms full of junk.'

'Does Agatha...?' I began, and he snorted.

'Agatha is not a servant. She's deigned to be housekeeper at
Castle Iolair for good money, but no, she sleeps on the next
corridor to us, overlooking the parterre gardens. She has a very
nice room which she keeps at the temperature of a tropical rainforest with fan heaters.'

I wondered which was Logan's bedroom and whether he
slept on an iron bedframe with a bowl of frozen water to wash
in. I couldn't imagine him enjoying anything so frivolous as a
duvet.

'This is the formal dining room,' Logan was saying, flinging
open a panelled wooden door. 'It was added by the ninth laird
in about 1760, so it's quite modern. We only use it at
Hogmanay, Burns Night or when Dad holds his salmon-fishing
association meetings.'

I peered in. The long room was painted a vibrant cobalt
blue which glowed like lapis lazuli in the morning sunlight. On
either side of the huge marble fireplace, carved and painted
panels decorated the walls with exquisitely delicate cherubs,
lions and heraldic flowers. A long, polished sideboard held a
silver punch bowl that a small crowd could comfortably use as
an emergency jacuzzi. Victorian oil paintings in weighty, gilded
frames depicted a set of angry-looking ancestors draped in plaid,
attended by spaniels who were presumably Alba and Arran's
long-gone relations. A gleaming cherry-wood table ran down
the centre of the room flanked by sixteen threadbare embroidered chairs, a glittering antique glass chandelier hung above,
and in the centre was a vast, silver vase in the shape of an eagle's
head.

'Iolair means "eagle" in Gaelic,' Logan explained. 'Those
ancestors went hard when it came to threatening rival clans.'

'This is... wow,' I said, inadequately, as Alba shot in and lifted a balletic back leg against the carved table base.

'For God's sake!' Logan sighed. 'Dad's mate Bill McDonald always brings his ageing pugs to meetings, and they pee all over the furniture,' he added to me. 'Alba's just reasserting his rights. Although you're *not allowed*!' he called, as the dog galloped back, having triumphantly overwritten the pugs' feeble messages.

'This is just amazing,' I said. 'It'd be perfect for meetings and conferences. We'd need tableware and so on, but...'

'Yes, IKEA tumblers leaving rings all over the table and laminated name badges,' muttered Logan. 'Here's the assistant regional manager of Data-Drone IT Solutions to bring you up to speed on the last quarter's sales figures, with a PowerPoint projection across some random ancestor who fought at Bannockburn.'

I laughed. 'It would be sensitively done,' I said. 'You wouldn't need to have anything to do with it.'

'Except for the fact that Barry and Nige from Sales would be ploughing through the honesty bar in the green drawing room, and crashing down the corridors looking for their bedrooms at 3 a.m., where they'd have "a cheeky fag" in bed and burn the entire castle to the ground...'

'As long as you're not catastrophising.'

'If I am, it's with good reason,' said Logan. 'There's no way of putting on events without throwing the whole castle open to all-comers. I do not want to be trying to sleep while a pissed-up hen party sings "Dancing Queen" and waves inflatable willies on the grand staircase. And what's more, it'll upset Hannay. He's old – he needs peace and quiet.'

I snorted at his childish use of 'willies', but he ignored me.

'We have fourteen bedrooms,' he went on, 'and only three usable bathrooms, all leaking. How's that going to work? Queues down the landing every morning? No hot water for weeks because Sharon from Strathclyde used it all up getting ready for her big day?'

'Don't be a snob,' I said crossly. 'We'd obviously have to look into the logistics.'

'Good luck,' he said. 'Unless you can cram forty guests into a stack of rabbit hutches in the attic and feed them on hay, I doubt there's a viable solution. As. I. Keep. Saying,' he added through gritted teeth.

He led me down yet another gilded, parquet-floored corridor lined with paintings of glum-looking Highland cattle and broken stone bridges over rushing torrents. At the end stood a pair of huge, carved wooden doors. I half expected a three-headed dog to present me with a riddle, but Logan flung them open and revealed a vast room with an arched wooden ceiling like a buttressed cathedral roof, studded with coats of arms and plaques.

There was an enormous Aubusson rug covering the wooden floor, and little else apart from a huddle of dark wooden chairs at the far end. Halfway up the wall was a minstrels' gallery overlooking the dance floor, where bands could play.

'The Grand Hall,' Logan said flatly.

'Oh, wow,' I breathed. I imagined Oliver's handsome face glowing with possibility at the sight of it. Often, we'd been to visit a proposed venue for an event and felt our hearts sink when the 'ballroom space suitable for a hundred' turned out to be a draughty barn with a concrete floor and no loo.

I wished I could call him, send photos of the space, invite him up to have a proper look, but I'd solemnly promised Alice that I wouldn't make the slightest attempt to speak to my ex-boss. That didn't stop me thinking about him, though, wondering what he was doing and whether he'd ever contact me again.

'This is the oldest part of the castle, originally built in about 1230.' Logan had reverted to 'efficient tour guide' mode. 'It was used for parties and local meetings, though during the last war, Iolair was requisitioned as a convalescent home for injured soldiers, and this was the main ward. Most useful thing that ever happened to it.'

'What do you use it for now?'

I gazed in admiration at the tall, mullioned windows with arched stone frames, which looked across the gardens to the loch.

'We don't,' said Logan. 'It was going to be used for my wed — well, it's not in use,' he corrected himself.

He had been about to say 'wedding'. Donald had mentioned love gone wrong, and I was dying to know what had happened, who had abandoned him and why – but Logan was now striding to the vast, stone fireplace, flanked by arrangements of bristling spears.

'This was where the lairds would parley, apparently,' he said. 'They'd come from across the Highlands to do business and discuss problems, and there'd be a semi-circle of wooden chairs, so everyone was equal before the fire.'

'Apart from the servants,' I said, imagining my dad's face (*And that's why we need trade unions, Cat!*).

'Yes, they lacked an equality and diversity charter in the sixteenth century, sadly,' said Logan. 'Though I'm sure, had they thought of it...'

I smiled. 'Even you must admit it's a perfect space for events. Imagine the bride—' I stopped. '... the *bright* evening sun, lighting up the room at parties...'

He gave me a quizzical look, and led me briskly through a run of smaller drawing rooms crammed with rose brocade chaises and antique side tables, and finally flung open a door to show me 'where we actually watch TV'.

This room was cosy as a hobbit's burrow, papered in a green William Morris print and crammed with mismatched tartan armchairs, higgledy-piggledy shelves of books, a battered velvet sofa with squashed tapestry cushions and coffee tables piled with dog-eared copies of *The Field* and *Horse and Hound*. There were several well-chewed dog toys lying on the faded hearthrug, including a mud-stained plush crocodile with three legs. 'That's Hannay's special friend,' Logan said. 'You must never move it.'

'I'll remember that.' I wandered over to a pretty rosewood console table, which was covered with framed family photographs.

The largest was a formal portrait. It showed a very attractive woman of around my age, with long dark hair and dark eyebrows. She was holding a small baby in old-fashioned white rompers and had her other arm around a solemn, black-haired little boy of about two, who was wearing red shorts and a *Thomas the Tank Engine* jumper and clutching a small wooden train.

'Is that you?'

Logan picked it up. 'It is,' he said. 'The tiny one is Rory, obviously – probably the quietest he's ever been – and that's our mum.'

I knew what had happened to her, of course, because my own mum had told me.

'Cancer,' Logan said, almost to himself. 'Swift and brutal. She didn't see her fortieth.' Logan must have been less than ten, I realised.

'I'm so sorry,' I said inadequately.

'It was a long time ago.'

He turned to leave, but my attention was snagged by a smaller picture pushed towards the back. It showed a tall, handsome teenage boy on a boat, with his arm around a beautiful girl. Her long red ponytail was lifted by the breeze, and she was laughing up at him, while he grinned at the camera. It was Logan as I remembered him. I felt an unexpected pang of sympathy for the teenager I had once been.

'I'll quickly show you upstairs, then I must get Arran into his harness for the car,' he said. 'He loathes it, so it's a lengthy job—'

His eyes fell on the photograph. 'Ah careless youth,' he said, raising an eyebrow.

'Was that your girlfriend?'

'We'd known each other all our lives, but by then... well, yes.'

'I wonder where she is now?' I said, gazing at the picture. It had been taken on a sunny, breezy day, white foam rising against the side of the blue boat. I could almost hear her laughter.

'Marina? Married, and living about a mile away.'

'Oh, that's nice...' I began, and he gave a mirthless laugh.

'She left me the night before our wedding to run away with a man I can't stand. So not all that nice, in fact.'

'Oh no, I'm so sorry—'

He ignored me. 'Anyway, I'll show you the rest, if you'd like to come this way.'

I didn't feel I had much choice.

8

It was a relief when Logan dropped me at Sir Alastair's study door after a whistle-stop tour of several sparse, unused bedrooms and two enormous, clanking Victorian bathrooms, one of which had a leak so dramatic it sounded like a glocken-spiel plinking in the corner.

Logan had become almost silent after the mention of Marina, and I suffered agonies of awkwardness as we marched along. In the end, I simply pretended he was a difficult client and pasted on my blandest professional smile. By the time we reached the door at the end of the east corridor, my cheeks hurt.

'Anyway, here's Dad's study,' Logan said. 'Off you go, to hold your summit meeting about corporate llama walks and rugby stag nights in the ballroom.'

Irritation shot through me. 'You haven't asked me about a single one of my ideas,' I said. 'You've made it very clear you're not interested, so I won't bore you with them, but please don't make ridiculous assumptions. My background is in large-scale, luxury event planning, not handing out vodka jelly shots aboard a sodding disco bus.'

At the back of my mind, I wondered why I'd never stood up

to Oliver like this. My heart was racing, but I felt perfectly clear-headed. How dare Logan belittle my career and dismiss my suggestions before I'd even made them?

'Fine,' he said flatly. 'I'll be sure to respect your professional opinion, but I can't say I'll go along with it. As I said, that's between me and my dad.'

He whistled for the dogs, who were racing up and down the corridor like excitable toddlers, and walked away.

I released a long breath, then knocked on the study door.

'Come!' called Sir Alastair, and I entered, feeling over-whelmingly relieved to be spending time with anyone who wasn't Logan.

'Cat! Good morning!'

Sir Alastair stood up, and Hannay rose, too, stretched and shook himself. I was surprised to see a woman sitting in the round-backed chair opposite the huge, oak desk piled with books about fish and botany. I noticed a paperback spy novel tucked discreetly beneath *Salmon Fishing in the Northern Waters*.

'Och, so you're Cat,' she exclaimed warmly, holding out a hand to shake. 'I'm Ishbel, married to Donald – I do all Sir Alastair's admin. We tackle the tech together, don't we?' She smiled at him.

'Infernal machines,' grumbled Sir Alastair. 'I'd be lost without her.'

Ishbel was tall, in her late fifties or thereabouts with a greying bob and a friendly, green-eyed gaze. She looked like a woman who could bake flapjacks with one hand and pull a child from an abandoned well with the other. 'Capable,' Mum would have said approvingly.

'It's lovely to meet you,' said Ishbel, smiling. 'I hear you're going to rescue Iolair!'

I wished people would stop saying that. 'I'll do what I can,' I said feebly.

Ishbel patted the chair she'd just vacated and hurried out. I glanced around as I sat down. Thanks to its position in the east turret, there were no corners to the room. Instead, shelves had been built in to fit the shape. They groaned with books, files and stacks of yellowing local newspapers. In between were slotted a moth-eaten taxidermied curlew, a stuffed pike in a glass case, a pair of Edwardian binoculars and several random pieces of tarnished silverware.

'Did you enjoy your tour?' Sir Alastair smiled at me.

'It's such a wonderful place,' I said, tactfully ignoring his question. 'I think people would be thrilled to come here for special events, weddings, parties...'

'Weddings,' said Sir Alastair heavily. He puffed his cheeks out. 'I rather wonder if that's why Logan's so set against the idea. Constant reminders of what happened to him.'

'It doesn't need to be weddings,' I said quickly. 'We could focus on the corporate side – any business that wants to impress clients would make a beeline—'

'Well, I suppose that's your department,' he said. 'Mine is scratching up the money to make it happen. Anyway, look.' Sir Alastair handed me a sheaf of papers. 'Ishbel's typed up my thoughts, so now you've seen the main rooms, perhaps you could let me know what you think, and come up with some sort of plan for how we might proceed.'

'Of course.'

'It's almost time for Hannay's daily constitutional down to the village,' he added. 'He likes to pop into the pub for a Scotch egg. Why don't you spend some time looking around the grounds before lunch while the sun's out, and have a squint at where we might put marquees and Portaloos and all that sort of thing?'

I was back in my safe place, planning and organising, and I

felt the weight of tension drop from my shoulders. I wasn't sure, however, if it was the stress of adapting to my new surroundings that had been troubling me or, as I suspected, the difficulty of spending time in Logan's presence.

Not least because every time I looked at him, I remembered what had happened all those years ago – and what an abject fool I'd made of myself.

The sun was warm as I strolled down the gravel path towards the gardens. In the distance, a breeze ruffled the loch into little white waves that sent spray arcing against the stone jetty. There were large wrought-iron gates closing the back of the castle off from the front, presumably to keep deer and day trippers out of the gardens.

I couldn't help thinking what a shame it was that the beautiful views and lawns remained private. So many places like this had opened up to the public, at least partially. I imagined a tea room, Ishbel guiding people round, signs pointing to car parking, Logan's face if I suggested any of it... but he'd have to wake up eventually. Sir Alastair was right: there was no way of keeping the castle unless they dragged it into the twenty-first century, and that meant letting people in, no matter how aristocratically furious Logan felt about it.

I had been wandering without looking where I was going, and looked up to find myself on the far side of the sweeping lawns, beside a rusting iron gate set into a mossy stone wall. I opened it, jiggling the latch, and stepped into a walled orchard with fruit trees in blossom, white and pink petals drifting across the grass.

Sparkling summer fruit cocktails in the secret orchard, I thought. *String quartet.* I closed the gate behind me and wandered round a box hedge to find another long lawn, bordered by a winding river that rolled over stones and boulders via several stepped pools and waterfalls, down to Loch Iolair. Further along I could see an old stable block, and the glint of sun on glasshouse roofs. I made my way down the pea-gravel path with a satisfying crunching sound, to explore further.

As I approached, a large tabby cat darted out of a shrubbery and came to wind herself round my legs. She had no collar, but presumably she belonged to the castle. She rolled on her back so I could crouch and stroke her tummy, then climbed onto my knee.

Eventually, she tired of my adoration and wandered off towards the stables. I rounded another stone wall to find an enormous, walled kitchen garden with a high wooden gate. I pushed down the latch and went inside. Here, there were poles separating the different beds and sections, netted fruit cages, rows of cold frames, trellises, raised beds, poker-straight gravel pathways between them, shining gold in the sunlight – and in the long, glittering greenhouses, I could see row upon row of leafy tomato plants in terracotta pots.

'*Get out!*'

Logan was striding across the garden, waving his arms violently.

'There's no need to be so rude!' I shouted back. 'Your dad said it was fine to come down here.'

'Not you, Tortoise!'

'Why are you calling me Tortoise?'

'The cat!' he yelled. 'The bloody stable cat, merrily relieving herself in my raised beds! Did nobody ever teach you to close a gate?'

I glanced behind me and saw the wooden gate hanging open as the cat streaked through it and away.

'And while I'm at it, if you think you're going to be holding soirées in my kitchen garden, with people tipping champagne into my cabbages and plonking their great arses on the cold frames, you can forget it.'

'I think nothing of the sort,' I said coldly. 'I'll leave you to it.'

'Arran's fine by the way,' he said to my retreating back. 'He only bit the vet once, but she did have a finger up his bottom at the time.'

I almost laughed, but my irritation took over.

'I'm glad he's all right,' I said icily, and stalked off to the kitchen, hoping that Agatha's lunch offering would be good enough to take my mind off Logan and his dog's troublesome rear end.

9

'Have you saved the castle yet?' Agatha demanded, as I ate her excellent pea-and-mint soup.

'I'm still making notes. Logan showed me round.'

She raised an eyebrow. 'Did he now? And are you single yourself, Cat?'

'Yes. But I've just come out of a very difficult... situation,' I said firmly. 'I'm most certainly not looking for a relationship.'

And if I was, it wouldn't be with Logan.

Agatha quirked her lips in the international expression for 'you tell yourself that, love'.

'I mean it!'

'All right,' she said. 'As long as you'll stay well away from Ross the fish man.'

'I can promise you I will,' I said, and she nodded solemnly, as though I'd taken a blood vow of sisterhood.

'Anyway,' I said, 'I'll just carry on with my notes...'

'Notes are no good,' Agatha announced. 'You must *do*. Sir Alastair and Logan – they're very decent folk, aye, but there's no *do*. Just talking and arguing, arguing and talking. Far too much thinking altogether.'

'I can see that,' I said. 'What do you recommend?'

'You'll be needing a swim in the loch. It makes your brain...' She shook her head so her blonde hair flew wildly back and forth. '*Awake*! The most awake you'll ever feel. I go most days,' she added.

'Wow. Even in winter?'

'*Always* in winter,' she said. 'It's so good for you, Cat. Go today. I'll leave my spare wetsuit in your room.'

'I don't know if...' I began nervously.

'Go.' Agatha fixed me with her azure blue stare. 'Just ten minutes to begin with and dinnae go out of your depth.'

'Okay,' I said weakly. 'I'll go when I've written up my notes.'

I couldn't feel my head.

My entire face had gone numb, and though I was apparently moving my arms and legs, swimming parallel to the shore, I was simultaneously having an out-of-body experience. I'd had no idea what cold really meant before this – I'd thought it was feeling a bit chilly at the bus stop, or bundling up for a frosty walk in Richmond Park, with a hot chocolate afterwards. I was a child, a naïve fool...

I looked up to admire the view of mountains and forests, appearing and disappearing above the churning water before my eyeballs iced over altogether and, as I did so, spotted a small black shape in the distance. It seemed to be moving towards me. Was it a seal? I thought of Nessie, giant sturgeon, ancient plesiosaurs rising to the surface... oh God, *eels*. I'd forgotten about eels, writhing in the dark beneath my legs. I was about to swim urgently to shore, when I heard a woman's voice calling to me.

'*Hellooo!*'

The approaching shape was now recognisably human, with

a neon-green swimming cap and strong arms cutting through the water.

'Hi there!' she called again, and I could see she was probably in her early thirties, with a round, pretty face. She wore a bright red swimsuit, with an emergency whistle tied to the shoulder strap.

'I'm Mel,' she said, swimming alongside me. 'Mel McCorran. I don't know if you've permission to swim off Iolair Castle shore, but the laird can be a bit funny about it, and I'd hate for you to get in trouble.'

'Oh, I am,' I said. 'I mean, I do. I have.' My teeth were chattering, and my words emerged as though a microphone was cutting out.

'Och, you poor love,' she said. 'You're frozen. Let's get out and warm up.'

We picked our way painfully over the stones in the shallows, and she grasped my towel and handed it to me. 'Get out of that wetsuit. I'll not look,' she said. 'You'll never heat up otherwise.'

My feet were the blue of the formal dining room, I noticed with interest, and I couldn't close my fingers tightly enough to undo the zip.

'Here, let me. You stayed in too long,' she said, admonishing. 'Classic schoolboy error. Mind you, it's such a gorgeous day, who could blame you? Don't you feel your head's had a spring clean?'

Mel talked a mile a minute in a musical West Highlands accent, and I was struggling to keep up.

'I don't know,' I said eventually, wiggling out of my damp, rubbery sausage casing. Thankfully, I'd put my swimsuit on underneath. 'I can't actually *feel* my head right now.'

She laughed. 'Sit on that rock, in the sun. I'd give you my fancy dryrobe but I left it two coves down, at Kincherrell. Have you been there yet?'

'No,' I said. My voice finally seemed to be working normally. 'I only arrived yesterday. I'm Cat Hardwick. I'm staying at the castle.'

'They're finally doing B&B?' Mel looked astonished. 'Nobody's mentioned this in the village!' She had pulled off her swimming cap to reveal wild brunette curls that snaked down her back. She reminded me of Moana in the Disney film, all strong curves and abundance.

'No, no – I'm vaguely connected to Sir Alastair.' I explained what had brought me to Iolair as the sun soaked into my chilled bones, though I left out the part about Oliver. I was cold enough, without that memory.

'Och, that's wonderful!' she cried. 'We must get together. I have *opinions* on that castle,' she added meaningfully. 'I just need someone long-suffering to share them with.'

Mel was a teacher at Kincherrell primary school, she explained – 'the wee bairns are bloody gorgeous. Can't say I'm not glad to get home, mind you. Glass of wine, reality TV session... though I swear I'm not always that boring.' She smiled. 'Sometimes, I actually make it to the pub.'

'Perhaps we could go for a drink while I'm here?' I suggested. 'Two single women together. Unless— sorry, I shouldn't assume.'

'Och aye, I'm single all right,' Mel said. 'My stepdad died a couple of years ago, so I moved back from Glasgow to be near Mum. I forgot the only men left at Iolair are Ross the fish man and Sir Alastair, wee poppet though he is.'

'I mean, there's Logan...' I began.

'That little ray of sunshine?' asked Mel, with a raised eyebrow.

I laughed, but at the same time, I couldn't help wondering quite how well she knew him.

. . .

I walked back up the lawn to the castle feeling positive for the first time since I'd left London.

Friends were everything, and Mel seemed great. Yes, I still felt distraught over what had happened, the misery of losing Oliver, knowing I had no job to return to... but Agatha had been right. The freezing water had shifted something, and even if it was only a passing handful of endorphins making me feel better, I'd take it.

I passed the kitchen garden again on the way to write up my notes, glancing in through the gate. Logan was at the far end, digging over a vegetable bed with a determined rhythm, stooping and straightening. As I watched, hypnotised by his steady movements, he jammed the spade into the earth and pulled off his shirt, slinging it over a fence post before continuing to dig. All the gardening had sculpted clearly defined abs, a broad chest and lean, well-honed biceps, I noted. Everything about him was hard and unyielding, unlike Oliver's sybaritic, soft-skinned charm. Logan was—

He looked up. 'Good swim?' he shouted, seeing my wet hair.

'Lovely, thanks!' I called, and hurried back towards the kitchen door before he noticed the deepening pink flush of my cheeks.

10

That evening, it was just me and Sir Alastair for dinner in the kitchen, eating Agatha's bacon-topped macaroni cheese. It might give me a heart attack, but I'd go happily, I thought, as Hannay stared imploringly at the dish. He was so tall, he could rest his long nose on the table, but Agatha flicked it gently with a tea towel, and he subsided to the flagstoned floor with a sigh.

'Poor old boy,' said Sir Alastair. 'Maybe we'll save a bit for you.'

Agatha muttered something that sounded like 'absolutely no discipline whatsoever', but Sir Alastair was addressing me.

'Now, Cat, you've had a look round, you've seen our situation... what's your view?'

I was glad Logan was elsewhere, though nobody had mentioned where exactly.

'I think the castle's best suited to smaller-scale corporate events,' I said. 'Weekend conferences, awaydays, that sort of thing. Weddings and private parties could be very complicated and expensive to host. Plus, there's the catering issue, all the dining options you'd need... With a conference, you can probably get away with offering a light lunch buffet.'

He clapped his hands together, startling Dougie, who was busily chewing his shoelace. 'Marvellous!' he said. 'Anything else?'

I thought of what Mel had said earlier.

'I know you wouldn't want to offer B&B in the castle for paying guests,' I said cautiously, 'but as a further income stream, is there anything we could do with the stables? I think people would love to stay on the estate.'

Sir Alastair sighed. 'We have thought of it, but the stables are in a dreadful state of disrepair. I genuinely don't think we can stump up the necessary – the roof's falling in and they're full of mice. Thank goodness for dear old Tortoise,' he added. 'She can't do everything, but she does her best. Sweet little thing. Do you know, she once caught a mole—'

'The bothy,' said Agatha, clearly tiring of Sir Alastair's animal-based tangents. 'That's where you could put guests.'

'Ah.' He nodded. 'There's a thought.'

I had no idea what a bothy was, or where it might be found.

'Shepherd's hut type of business,' Sir Alastair explained, noting my expression. 'There's been one up on the hills behind the castle for centuries, and various ancestors added bits, and it eventually turned into a sort of cottage with two rooms. It's very basic, but it's got an open fire and windowpanes. It needs looking over to see if it's worth doing up a bit.'

'I could go and see it tomorrow?'

'Go at the weekend,' said Sir Alastair. 'It's hard to find, so Logan will need to go with you. He'll be free then.'

'Free from...?' I didn't want to sneer, but surely he could take half an hour off planting tomatoes?

'From his job,' explained Sir Alastair. 'Didn't he mention? He grows all the fruit and veg for the Falls of GlennIolair pub; they're getting quite a reputation in the area for their menu. And three evenings a week he goes and cooks down there – he enjoys it, I think.'

'Logan's a *chef?*'

'It's just temporary – he was planning the hydro-scheme, but that fell apart, then we had a rewilding scheme, but DEFRA didn't approve, then the idea was that he'd marry Marina and they'd start a catering business together... Anyway, for the last eighteen months, he's been stuck here with me, trying to keep the castle functioning,' Sir Alastair went on. 'It's simply not working, and that's why we need you, Cat – to help us find a path forward.'

I nodded. I had to make this work, not just for my own reputation, but for the sake of Sir Alastair, and his miserable, jilted son and heir.

It was a few nights later, and I'd barely seen Logan in the interim. I'd been busy costing the idea of a conference venue, looking into insurance issues (extremely complicated when your venue was built in 1230) and coming up against endless problems – *where would delegates sleep? How would we provide food and drink? What about bathroom facilities?*

I was starting to think the whole thing was impossible, but I couldn't bear to let Sir Alastair down – or fail in my task, given the thankless job search that awaited me back in London. The weather had turned colder, and the iron-grey, churning loch looked a lot less appealing to swim in, while the rhododendrons had shed their petals in the wind, covering the lawn outside my window with wild confetti.

I was delighted to get a message from Mel suggesting a drink in the Falls of GlennIolair, and gratefully accepted a lift to the village from Donald McTavish.

'How're ye getting on, lassie?' he asked, as we headed down the drive past the deer herd, who all turned their heads in unison when we drove by.

'It's a wonderful place,' I said, smiling at him. 'Everyone's been so welcoming.'

'Have they *all*, now?'

I laughed. 'Well...'

'If ye're no' a spaniel, he's no' interested,' said Donald. 'After Marina... well, Ishbel worries about the lad. She thinks he needs to get away, get the weight of Iolair off his shoulders.'

'Can't he?'

'I know Sir A suggested that, after it all happened,' mused Donald, shifting Hannay's questing nose away from the gear-stick. 'But he's stubborn as they come, our Logan, and he was awful wedded to his schemes and plans... he takes everything very hard. Not like the other one. He's bottled sunshine, our Rory.'

'Shame he's not here,' I said, as we drew up alongside the glowing windows of the old pub.

'Aye. He's overdue a visit, right enough,' agreed Donald. 'Talking of visits, Ishbel reminded me to ask you down for a bite of tea at ours tomorrow night. Just casual, about six thirty?'

'I'd love to,' I said. 'Can I bring anything?'

'Just yourself,' said Donald. 'And don't let the wild rabbits in when you come through the gate. Ishbel's just planted out all her seedlings.'

'Shall we make it a bottle?' asked Mel. 'You can choose between a hearty red with echoes of long-ago goats, or a flinty white with a subtle aftertaste of loo cleaner.'

'Shall we do red? I like goats.'

Mel handed her card to the barmaid, and we carried the bottle and glasses to a velvet booth in the corner of the pub. The walls were hung with Victorian paintings of trout, while glass cases held further gloomy piscine specimens, surrounded by painted reeds.

'Fair to say it began as a fisherman's pub,' said Mel, following my gaze. 'But the evening menu is great, though a bit pricey on my salary.'

'Logan's food?'

'Aye.' Mel's green eyes shone in the candlelight. 'He really can cook, you know.'

I wondered again how intimately she knew him, but I didn't feel I knew her well enough to ask. Mel had no such qualms.

'So.' She leaned forward. 'What's the deal with you two?'

'There is no deal,' I told her. 'He does his thing, and I do mine – I'll only be here for a couple of weeks; we don't need to be the best of friends.'

'Is it the first time you've met him?' She topped up our glasses.

'Well, we came on holiday for a weekend when I was sixteen,' I told her. 'But he'd have been almost eighteen – we didn't have much to do with one another.'

It was only a small lie.

'Och, but he was a handsome lad,' sighed Mel. 'Everyone else had acne and all the Fourth Year fellas went to the Turkish barber in Oban and got those terrible tramlines shaved into their hair. Logan never bothered with any of that – he went everywhere in an old, checked shirt and jeans, and he slayed the girls just by ignoring them.'

I wanted to ask her if she'd had a crush on him, too, but I wasn't entirely sure how to put it without sounding weirdly jealous.

'I knew Rory a wee bit better,' Mel went on. 'Though they were away at Posh School and I was messing about at Kincherrell High, so we only met up in the holidays.'

'Was Logan dating Marina back then?'

'Ah, so you know the tragic tale?'

'Well, only bits of it...'

'He was,' Mel affirmed. 'They'd always been pals as kids,

dredging up treasure on the beach and running round the castle with Marina's wee brother, Cameron. When Logan's mum died, Marina's parents became a sort of auntie and uncle to him. They spent so much time together, people around here just assumed they'd get together when they were older.'

'And they did.'

'Yep – when they were about sixteen, they fell in love. They were just inseparable,' said Mel wistfully. 'That kind of first love when it's all pure and new and you've nothing to compare it with. Didn't hurt that they were both way out of anyone else's league, looks-wise.'

I nodded. 'She looked very beautiful in the photo I saw.'

'Wow, he's still got photos of her? I'd have torn every last one to scraps in his situation,' said Mel. 'He must have it bad, even now.'

I felt a pang of sadness. I had never triggered such passionate emotion in anyone unless you counted Gladstone, my childhood red setter, and he was anyone's for a malty biscuit.

'Did she really dump him the night before the wedding?' I asked.

The wine was going pleasantly to my head, and I wasn't above a gossip. Besides, I was genuinely interested. I also felt, in some rarely explored nook of my mind, a tiny bit jealous of Marina for having inspired such devotion from the worst-tempered man in the Highlands.

Mel glanced behind her, and leaned forward across the table. 'She really did. They broke up when they both went to Uni, then got together again a couple of years ago, when she moved back up here. The engagement was fast; we were all quite surprised, but it was all going ahead, invitations sent out, castle festooned with flowers – I'll be honest, I was looking forward to a massive knees-up; we had an invite cos Mum

knows Sir Alastair from years back – anyway, very late on, the
night before showtime, Logan rang round all the guests and said
he was very sorry, but it wasn't happening.'

Mel took a long swig of her wine.

'Go on,' I said, mesmerised.

'Well, I don't know Marina so well, but I saw an old school-
mate in here a week later, and he told me that Marina had been
having an affair with Jack Campbell all along – Jack runs the
chandlery, selling stuff for boats – and they'd run off to Gretna
Green together and married. They didn't come back for a
while...'

'I'm not surprised.'

'... but now they live just down the glen road, bold as brass,
running Jack's boat hire business and the chandlery together.'

'Does anyone speak to her?'

'Och, yes,' said Mel. 'You can't fall out round here – there's
not enough folk around to take sides. But I don't imagine poor
Logan does.'

As she spoke, the young barmaid approached, holding a tray
of small dishes, and began to lay them out on our table.

'Oh, we didn't order—' I began, but she smiled.

'Compliments of Logan. You've got local goat cheese and
heritage tomato puffs with basil, pan-fried new potatoes in a
delicate wild-garlic butter, new-season asparagus with a
marjoram drizzle...'

'Tell him thank you very much indeed,' I said, peering
greedily at the little plates. 'We really didn't expect anything.'

'He likes to try out new recipes on Thursdays,' said the girl.
'He says you're doing him a favour.'

'He should be cheffing in a Michelin starred restaurant,' I
said, when she'd returned to the kitchen. 'What's he doing
skulking about at Iolair?'

Mel shrugged. 'He's the heir. He feels responsible for the

place. Seven hundred years of history hanging round his neck. Rather him than me,' she added. 'I'm happy with my little cottage. Where do you live in London, Cat?'

I told her about Alice and our flat, and the grandly named roof terrace (in reality, a jerry-built flat section that required us to clamber out of the attic window).

'Invite her up here! We need some more women around the village.'

'Well, I don't know how long I'm staying...'

'Iolair's funny,' Mel mused, draining the bottle into my glass. 'People always think they'll just come for a wee while, and suddenly it's ten years later and they're married with three kids.'

She signalled to the barmaid, who hurried over with another bottle.

'Right,' I said to my new friend, 'tell me all about *your* love life.'

'Buckle up,' said Mel. 'Shall I start with the Arizona cowboy who owned no cutlery except a soup spoon, or the tattoo artist who wanted to etch gothic spiders onto both my knees?'

We laughed so hard that Logan came out of the kitchen to see what the commotion was about. He was wearing chef's whites, and while most men would have resembled the Muppets' Swedish Chef, Logan somehow contrived to look like a French restaurant owner, with his dark curls falling over one eye and a light dusting of stubble on his chin. I felt uncomfortably aware of the green scrunchie I'd used to tie my hair up, and the likelihood that mascara was smeared down my face from laughing.

'Food all right?' Logan asked, and I was astonished to see that he looked genuinely unsure.

'It was amazing,' Mel assured him, but Logan seemed to want approval from me, too.

'There aren't words to describe how delicious it was,' I told him.

'That's exactly what Alba said when I tried out my recipes on him.'

It occurred to me that this was the first time I'd seen Logan smile.

11

By last orders, I was pleasantly drunk, and Arran and Alba had wriggled out of the kitchen and were asleep on our feet like sentient hot-water bottles.

'I'll get a lift from the barmaid,' Mel said. 'She stays at Kincherrell. But how will you get back?'

'I'll walk with you,' said a voice from behind me, and I turned to see Logan changed back into his blue jumper and jeans, his hair sticking up in tufts from the heat of the kitchen. 'I like to come and go on foot – it gives the dogs a decent walk before bed.'

I was drunk enough to agree that was a good idea, and Mel gave me a very unsubtle wink as we gathered ourselves to leave.

Logan handed me Alba's lead, observing, 'He's slightly less likely to yank you into the ditch than the other one,' and extracted a large torch from his rucksack.

'It's okay,' I began. 'I've got my phone.'

'I like to see more than three inches ahead. Plus, a torch battery won't conk out halfway home.'

'Sorry I wasn't born and bred in the country,' I said, irritated. 'Me, with my idiotic city ways and my feeble light sources.'

'No need to apologise,' replied Logan infuriatingly.

We set off through the village which was now dark and sleeping; a single streetlamp shining onto the wet lane. It was only about a mile, a distance I thought nothing of walking in London as I passed neon-lit all-night shops and skinny foxes darting behind bins. Here, it felt like a lonely trek on an alien planet. Logan pointed the powerful torch beam directly ahead as we left the last cottage behind, lighting the branches of the pine forest on both sides of the narrow road, and the dogs trotted along, sniffing at strange animal smells in the overgrown verges.

It occurred to me that fifteen years ago, being alone with Logan late at night would have been my dream-come-true scenario. Now, I was just a bit pissed and trying not to break my ankle in a pothole.

'Don't the fir trees look lovely at night?' I said, to make conversation.

'Well, no,' said Logan, striding alongside me. 'Not really. They're not a native species, they were planted by the Forestry Commission, replacing the unique, ancient Caledonian rainforest. They're all the same, and they create a lightless canopy so nothing can live beneath them. They're just a commercial logging enterprise, and fatal for eco-diversity.'

I sighed. 'Thanks for mansplaining away my innocent delight.'

'I'm telling you the truth. If you'd rather live in a fantasy world of dancing unicorns and laughing pixies, good luck to you.'

'There's no need to be rude.' The wine and the darkness made me braver than I would have been in daylight.

'Sorry!' Logan sounded surprised and a little put out. 'I didn't think I was being rude; it's just how I talk.'

'Rudely,' I said, warming to my theme. 'Dismissively. As if you know everything and the rest of us know nothing. Maybe that's true, in my case, but I'm not a complete idiot. I know you don't want me here; I know you can't stand the idea of doing a single commercial thing with the castle when you could be funding it all by selling heritage tomatoes...'

'Now, who's being rude?' Logan asked calmly.

'... but it'd be a great help to me, and I'm sure to your dad, if you could at least pretend not to be in a permanent state of angry misery about every single thing,' I went on. 'It's exhausting and childish, and what's more, it's bloody demoralising for everyone else, including me.'

Logan began to speak, but I cut across him.

'You have no idea why I'm here,' I went on. 'Do you honestly think I'd just leave my very demanding career for weeks on end, to come and make pointless suggestions about your crumbling old castle for no reason? Or could it perhaps be that I've had my heart broken by Oliver, the boss who I've been in love with for three years, lost my job, and my entire life is currently swirling round the toilet bow— *Oh!*'

A vast, inhuman shape crashed across the path directly in front of us, torchlight gleaming in its black eyes for a moment, before it thundered back into the forest.

'What the hell...?' I could hardly breathe with shock, and I realised I was clasping Logan's forearm in a white-knuckled death grip.

'It's okay,' he said, over the wild barking of the dogs. Alba was tugging on his lead, desperate to follow. 'It's okay, Cat... it was just a deer. A female red – they're bigger than the roe deer we normally get at this time of year. Sometimes, they stray out of the estate into the forest.'

His voice was soothing, his words calmingly factual, and my full-body trembling began to subside as he spoke. 'There may be others with her, but they're not usually around at this time of night,' he went on.

Adrenaline still pounding, I leaned into his reassuring warmth for a moment, and he put a steadying arm around me. Under my ebbing panic, I was aware that his scent was familiar, a distant echo of memory – warm and spiced, like sandalwood on a campfire.

I was still holding his arm, and breathing in his clean, brushed-cotton shirt, feeling his broad chest beneath my cheek. I had once read that adrenaline spikes could lead to sex, that the surge of fear led to other urges, and for a moment, I understood it. Our faces were inches apart, the darkness cloaking our intentions, and if I'd never had to see him again after this, I'd have turned my face to his and kissed him – just because I could; because he smelled right, because he was there and safe and solid under my cold hand.

'Okay now?' he asked, dropping his arm. 'You'll get used to it. Deer are beautiful creatures, but not the sharpest tools in the shed.'

I removed my hand from his warm wrist, though my heart was still banging against my ribs. 'Sorry,' I said. 'When that kind of thing happens in Kilburn, it's a runaway Routemaster.'

Logan laughed, an unfamiliar sound. 'She was a surprise to me, too, to be fair,' he said. 'Better get these two home before they break free and give chase. Hang on,' he added, as we resumed our path. 'You were laying into me. Do you want to pick up where you left off?'

'No, it's gone,' I sighed. 'I think the deer cancelled out the drunken home truths.'

'Only if you're sure? I'd hate to block you in full flow – it's quite something.'

'I'm embarrassed now,' I said. 'You're my host, and you made us lovely little bits of food, and I just yelled at you.'

'It's fine,' said Logan, as we turned through the gate onto the long castle drive. 'You're right – I can be bad-tempered and dismissive. Things have been tough lately, but you don't deserve to be subjected to my moods. Seems you've had a hard time, too.' He paused. 'Besides, Dad's asked you up here, and I'm sure you're very good at what you do, so I'll let you get on with it.'

'Thanks,' I said. 'I appreciate it.'

We walked on, the dripping trees looming over us and the lights of the castle glowing up ahead. The unexpected intimacy of just minutes ago had been replaced by a polite formality, and I felt wrong-footed.

As we headed round to the kitchen entrance together in silence, I almost said, 'Do you remember the first time I came here?'

'What?' Logan asked, as I took a breath to speak and stopped.

'Nothing.'

He looked down at me, under the little light above the door, and our eyes met. In that moment, I was both my sixteen-year-old self, my heart pounding with longing and dread, and sensible, adult Cat, who was here to produce spreadsheets and draw up plans.

'Cat...' Logan began, but Arran plunged his face into the rain butt by the door and drank noisily, and the moment, whatever it might have been, was gone.

'Night, then,' Logan said. 'Good luck with your work here.'

He might as well have been an acquaintance at a conference, and as I climbed the stairs to my bedroom, I felt deeply relieved that I hadn't said anything more intimate.

12

I didn't sleep well. I lay in my chilly, ancient bed, staring into the darkness and thinking about what I'd almost said to Logan. He wouldn't have welcomed my memories – I knew that deep down.

The creaks and groans of the castle settling itself for the night were becoming familiar, but while I was beginning to feel at home, I was troubled by the scratchy relationship I seemed to have with him. It was clear that I was unwittingly dragging the way I'd felt so long ago into the present, that I was finding it difficult to see who he was as a man, rather than the handsome, troubled teenage boy he'd been back then. I was here to get over the mess I'd made of my life, and my unrequited feelings for Oliver, I reminded myself sternly – not to develop a sudden, flaring attraction to a bad-tempered bloke still in love with the woman who had jilted him.

I was looking forward to my 'bite of tea' with the McTavishes. I'd spent the day conducting a detailed assessment of loo facilities and drawing up costs for a compost toilet block near the stables – such was the glamour of my role. I wasn't sure it was even feasible, but I wanted to leave no stone unturned. I could see the worry etched on Sir Alastair's face, and Agatha had leaned into my ear at lunchtime and whispered, 'Don't say anything to the others, Cat, but I've emailed Rory.'

'Have you? Why…?'

'He's part of the family,' she said, as if it should be obvious.

'But if he wanted to be involved, wouldn't he be here? He must know what's going on?'

She shook her head. 'He's an awful busy man. It's easy to ignore what happens at home. I told him, "Come back. Castle Iolair needs fixed."'

'Did he reply?'

'Not yet,' said Agatha. 'New York's still asleep. But he will, right enough.'

As I wandered down to the gatehouse in the spring evening, I allowed myself a moment to enjoy my surroundings. Late afternoon sun filtered through the leaves of trees lining the drive, dappling the ground with slow, shifting light. In the distance, the loch glowed sapphire and a golden haze hid the mountains. The pure air smelled of promise, of earth and new growth. I filled my lungs and stopped to watch a rabbit darting across the field, a flash of brown and white as its tail vanished into a burrow.

'Evening.'

I looked up. Logan was coming the other way, holding an empty wooden crate with the dogs at his heels.

'I've just dropped off some vegetables with Ishbel,' he said. 'Donald's going to cook them for your dinner.'

'Thank you.' I paused. 'Will you not be joining us?'

'Me?' He looked startled. 'No, I'll eat with Dad, as usual.'

I wanted to say, 'I'd like to get to know you better,' or, 'I think we got off on the wrong foot,' but he showed no sign of wanting to engage in conversation.

'Well,' he said, after an awkward pause. 'See you.'

'Logan,' I said quickly, and he turned back. In the soft light, I could see the bracken colours in his eyes.

'I just... I'm sorry for what I said last night. It was rude.'

He looked at me. 'It's forgotten,' he said. 'Honestly, don't give it another thought.'

His eyes lingered on my face, and I felt unexpected warmth spread through my veins. The moment extended as neither of us spoke. It was only broken by the cacophonous honking of a skein of geese overhead, flying away from the loch, and we both craned our necks to watch them as my racing heart gradually slowed.

'They're migrating home for the summer,' said Logan. 'They'll be back in the autumn, when it turns colder.'

He smiled and raised a hand. 'Enjoy the veg,' he said, and turned back up the drive, the dogs gambolling alongside him.

It struck me that long before autumn arrived, I'd be gone from Iolair. I felt oddly melancholy, knowing I'd miss the return of the geese.

Ishbel threw open the bottle-green door as I raised my hand to knock.

'There you are!' she cried. 'We thought you'd drowned in the loch!'

Clearly in the countryside, six meant six, and not a London 'we left extra time in case you weren't ready' ten past. Besides, Ishbel was born ready. She led me through to a light, airy living room painted pale green, with family photographs on the walls and squashy dove-grey linen sofas. She thrust a glass of wine into my hand as Donald appeared in the doorway, drying his hands on a tea towel.

'Chicken pie,' he said, 'wi' a bit o' Logan's latest veg delivery. Hope that's okay.'

'It sounds lovely. Are you cooking?'

'Och, Donnie cooks every day,' said Ishbel. 'I can't make toast to save my life. My mother was a great feminist, spent all her time on women's lib marches down Sauchiehall Street in Glasgow, and she always told me never to learn.'

'Oh, mine was too!' I exclaimed. 'Though she loves cooking, as long as it's not for the patriarchy.'

We spent a pleasant ten minutes exchanging anecdotes about our politically right-on mothers, and Ishbel said, 'Fiona was a bit like that – always trying to drag Sir A into the modern world. She told me she was determined to bring the boys up believing in women's rights. That's what was so awful about her death. The boys were so young. Wee Logan took on the weight of the world after she passed. Sir A was grieving – he did his best, but he sent them off to boarding school as soon as he could, to give them stability, he said. I often wondered if they wouldn't have been better off here, with us and all their wee pals.'

'But Logan had Marina and her family, o' course,' put in Donald.

'He did, but... well, losing her again, in such a cruel way...' said Ishbel. 'It's been an awful blow to him, you can tell. He's a broken man.'

'Will she be there on Sunday, aye?' Donald asked.

Ishbel shrugged. 'I should imagine so, now she's back. The world and his wife are heading down there, right enough.'

I put my glass down. Were they all churchgoers? I hadn't gained that impression, over the course of my brief stay.

'Where is everyone going?'

'You don't know?' Ishbel looked shocked. 'It's only the Iolair Games, bonnie lass! The big event of spring round here – though I don't doubt they should have asked you to organise it because after the committee's chaotic efforts last year, it's a wonder people weren't chucking cabers into the tea tent.'

'Real Highland Games?' I asked. 'Kilts, tug of war, all the stuff off the porridge packets?'

'Maybe don't put it *quite* like that when you get there,' murmured Ishbel. 'They take it very seriously round here. Muir Strachan, the PE teacher at Kincherrell High, will be defending his five-year run of success.'

'And he'll let nothing stand in his way, the great prancing show-off,' guffawed Donald.

Ishbel gave him an admonishing look as a timer pinged.

'Ye must come, Cat,' Donald went on as we took our places at the pine kitchen table. 'Everyone from the castle always goes together, and we take a picnic. It's a grand day out.'

'Will I need to toss a caber?'

'No,' said Ishbel, reaching to top up my glass. 'But there's a good chance you might meet a few tossers.'

On Saturday morning, with only a slight hangover from Ishbel's generous wine-pouring followed by the whisky Donald had brandished after pudding, I realised it was time I updated Alice. She'd been begging for news, but I'd been too busy to go into any detail. Purely to show off, I FaceTimed her next to my bedroom window, so she could see the astonishing view of the loch and mountains behind me.

'I see it's a painful struggle up there.'

Alice was still in her fleecy spotted dressing gown, chomping through a family pack of Haribo Starmix.

'Sorry about the eating noises,' she said. 'Defcon One hangover. Now, tell me everything. Leave nothing out, however insignificant it may appear to the layperson.'

I told her everything – but for some reason, I couldn't bring myself to go into detail when it came to Logan.

'Is he hot?' Alice demanded, through a mouthful of jelly fried eggs.

'I mean, he's really good-looking, in an austere, Scottish way...' I began.

'Ooh!'

'But,' I added quickly, 'he's the grumpiest, gloomiest bloke – he's unbelievably snarky. We've already had a few run-ins because he doesn't want events at the castle.'

'Then why are you there?' asked Alice reasonably.

'His dad asked me, and Lairds trump heirs round here. Plus, it's better than sitting at home with no job, dying of embarrassment and grief about Oliver.'

'Oh!' Alice blurted, then caught herself. 'Sorry, no nothing...'

'What?' I narrowed my eyes. 'Tell me.'

I hoped Alice would never be arrested for murder because she'd find it impossible to lie to the police. 'You're right, Detective, he's buried by a lay-by on the M40...'

'Fine. That posh knob Tory-boy ex-boss of yours came round the other night, wanting to see you. I told him you'd fled to a castle in the far north...'

'*What?*'

'I made it sound like *Game of Thrones*,' added Alice gleefully. 'I might have thrown in some stuff about a tame eagle. And he said he needed to talk to you, and he left a letter...'

'A *letter*? Why can't he just ring or text?'

Just a week ago, bluebirds would have been circling my head while pink love hearts ballooned from my chest at the news. Now, I noted with some confusion, I felt both intrigued and irritated by Oliver's cloak-and-dagger behaviour.

'No idea,' said Alice. 'Because he's an entitled prick who wants to keep you on tenterhooks while he marries Nelly Smuggity-Poshparents in the golden drawing room?'

'Do you know what the letter says?'

'Er, no,' said Alice. 'I thought with it being private, I probably wouldn't steam it open. Although...' she added regretfully, 'do you want me to open it now and read it to you? *"Dearest Cat, Sadly, I have been diagnosed with terminal posh pillock syndrome and only have a few days to live..."'*

I snorted. 'Can you post it to me?'

'Or,' said Alice, almost choking on a foam heart in her excitement, 'I could bring it.'

She was now grinning like a maniac on my screen.

'I've got a couple of days off to take soon,' said Alice. 'I was thinking, I could do a road trip – come and see your castle, eat some haggis, flirt with the grumpy laird's son...'

'You won't want to – he's a nightmare,' I said quickly.

'Fair enough. Do you think there'd be room for me?'

I thought of the fourteen bedrooms. 'Oh yes,' I said, beaming at her. 'How soon can you come?'

13

Immensely cheered by the news of Alice's visit, I went to update Sir Alastair on events, and found him in his cluttered turret, gazing mournfully out of the window.

'Look at those damnable clouds,' he said, pointing to a swathe of grey rolling over the mountain. 'The Highland Games will be a washout.'

He turned to me. 'You are coming, aren't you, Cat? Agatha's making hot-water pastry for her miniature pork pies as we speak. It's quite an event. I used to be an absolute demon at the tug of war,' he added. 'Now, I'm the old duffer drafted in to give out the prizes. Probably for the best – wouldn't want to put my ageing back out. Logan can represent Clan McAskill.'

I had a sudden image of Logan in a kilt and vest, straining his arm muscles to hold on to a rope, bracing his thighs in the struggle, a light sweat breaking out on his brow... the vision wasn't entirely unpleasant, though it may have owed a significant debt to the Scott's Porage Oats packet.

'Rory always loved the games,' Sir Alastair added. 'Such a shame he's tied up with his job. Probably won't see hide nor hair of him till Christmas.'

I wondered if Agatha's email would do the trick. It seemed unlikely.

'Still.' He perked up. 'Should be a good turnout, and if it does rain, the tea tent will make a fortune.'

He smiled at me. 'I hear Logan's taking you up to the bothy this afternoon, for a recce. I'm interested to hear what you make of it, but I'd head up sooner rather than later with those clouds looming.'

I had pushed the bothy situation to the back of my mind. Several hours alone with Logan, coupled with a lengthy hike uphill, was not my idea of fun.

'I think he said some time after lunch,' Sir Alastair went on. 'It's rather a nice walk up along the river – the bothy's just by the bank where it widens out, a lovely spot.'

'Great,' I said brightly, though my mind was full of Oliver's letter – what did he want to tell me? Should I phone or text him? But if it was just about the jacket I'd left on the office coat hook, that would be mortifying. Perhaps I should wait...

Hannay stood up and shook himself, sending a drift of paper cascading to the floor.

'Time for your Scotch egg, old boy? Come on, then.' Sir Alastair heaved himself to his feet and opened the door for me.

I wished I could remain in his cosy turret all afternoon with a pot of tea and a spy novel. It seemed a far more enticing prospect than embarking on a long, uphill hike with Logan, no matter how handsome he may be.

By the time we'd eaten Agatha's practice pork pie and I'd got changed, rain was spotting the gravel by the kitchen door. Logan had left Arran and Alba with Donald – 'the wee lads can help me mend the fence down by the gate' – and he was apparently dressed for some kind of Olympic winter sport, bristling with Velcro straps and adjustable buckles.

'Is that what you're wearing?' he asked, studying my jeans and hooded jacket as if I'd turned up in a sarong and flip-flops.

'Sorry, I didn't get the memo about the entire team wearing sponsored kit.'

Logan was also wearing well-used walking boots, in contrast to the brand-new wellies I'd bought at the Iolair post office and general store that week. Mine were rainbow striped, and I suspected they might be for children because they were remarkably cheap.

'It's likely to rain harder,' he said doubtfully.

'And I have wellies! So... lead on.'

I had decided to be determinedly cheerful in contrast to Logan's endless gloom, if only to amuse myself.

'I've got a water-resistant, breathable shell jacket you can borrow...' he began.

'Honestly, I'll be fine. Let's go.'

He took a last, anxious glance at the sky and shrugged. 'Don't say I didn't warn you,' he said, as we crunched down the path towards the river. 'We'll go at a fair pace, too, if that's okay, as I don't like the look of those clouds.'

It was like being trapped in a particularly dull episode of *Countryfile*. I trudged after him as rain spattered on the border plants, the grey clouds now massing overhead, having drifted silently from the mountains like a game of grandmother's footsteps.

We went through an iron gate by the river, and the ground turned from man-made gravel to natural stone, passing just feet from the bank. Drops bounced off the water's surface, and a heron rose on origami wings and flew straight across our path. It was good to be out of London. Logan was hard work, but everyone else had been so welcoming, and the surroundings really were beautiful. Primroses lined the riverbank, and new buds turned the trees a vivid lime green that glowed through the drizzle. As we walked on, a family of ducks appeared, tiny brown-and-mustard balls of thistledown following their mother downstream.

I was lucky to be here, away from the stress of MOE and the ongoing misery of seeing Oliver every day. I hadn't realised quite how drained I was by my long, unrequited love for him. Now, at least, I could try to move on. Except the letter...

'Watch out!' called Logan as my foot splashed into a deep puddle, spraying my jeans with mud.

'How far is it?' I asked, shaking water off my leg and scuttling to catch up with his long stride.

'About an hour, hour and a half, tops,' he said. 'But it's quite a tricky walk in this weather – there's some rocky bits and a field that's effectively a bog, so we'll have to go round the edge. That's why I can't see how we can rent the place out – how are people going to get up there?'

'Quad bike?' I hazarded, having seen Donald zooming about the estate, with wee Dougie perched between his knees.

'Through a bog? And it's the other side of the river,' he said. 'There's a very old stone bridge, but it won't take the weight of a quad.'

It occurred to me that perhaps Sir Alastair was being excessively optimistic about the potential of this bothy.

'Well, how did they used to get up there?'

'Walked through a bog,' sighed Logan. 'I know I seem unduly negative about all your ideas, but Iolair just isn't designed for the comforts people expect nowadays. It would need absolute fortunes – millions – spending on it to make it welcoming to guests who object to being freezing cold or having DEFRA protected bats in the attic, or who want en-suite bathrooms and decent catering facilities.'

His dark curls were now plastered to his forehead, and raindrops quivered like crystals on his long eyelashes. Somehow, he still looked like a painting of a Georgian nobleman striding through a storm. I imagined I looked like a heftier version of the girl in *The Ring* emerging from her well.

We stopped to scramble over a stile set into a mossy drystone wall, and the hard, plastic sole of my boot slid on the wet wood.

'Careful!' Logan grabbed my arm. I could feel the grip of his fingers through the thin material of my jacket, and our eyes met as I turned.

His were the colour of autumn bracken in sunlight, unlike Oliver's glittering turquoise gaze. Logan was definitely not wearing tinted contact lenses. I almost laughed at the thought.

'I'm not sure those boots are up to the job,' he said, setting off again up what had become a densely forested slope. Above, rain beat on the branches, but despite the rushing river beside us, very little made its way through as we trudged across a soft bed of fallen needles.

'Shame we're walking through a lightless eco-disaster,' I remarked, and Logan laughed.

'Shame I'm right.'

The trees began to thin out, and I could see a steeper rocky slope up ahead, but the hill beyond was now wreathed in chill, damp mist and the rain was falling harder.

'I bet it's blazing sunshine in London,' I said. 'My friend will be on the roof drinking cocktails.'

'You don't strike me as an "afternoon cocktails on the roof" type,' said Logan, glancing at me.

'Why not?' I swept a hand from my damp jeans to my mud-spattered child's wellies. 'Look at me – the glamour never stops.'

'You just seem too sane,' he said. 'It's a compliment.'

'That's why the men fall at my feet,' I said. 'My extreme levels of sanity.'

I laughed, but I felt unexpected sadness shoot through me. Logan was right – I wasn't melodramatic or wild. I'd never be the sort of woman who threw plates and had men weeping with passion, or even the kind that handsome men would follow to the depths of Surrey to marry. I was sane, sensible Cat, happiest with a clipboard and a colour-coded spreadsheet, a woman who had alphabetised her Enid Blyton books as a child.

As we veered closer to the riverbank again, I saw the water was now thundering and crashing down the rocky hillside, and its level had risen. The rain was driving down in stair rods, and both my jeans and jacket were drenched, while a blister was beginning to form on my left heel.

'Are you okay?' Logan called over the noise. 'It's getting worse – the forecast said this wouldn't start till evening. We should probably turn back.'

I thought of the weary trek back down through the sheeting downpour, having to do it all again next week, Sir Alastair's disappointment...

'Let's just get there. Maybe I can dry out a bit.'

He hesitated. 'If you're sure. We can wait it out for an hour or so, and at least it's dry inside.'

'Lead the way,' I shouted over the sound of rushing water.

We spent another half hour tramping through deep trenches of mud at the edge of the wide bog. Staying upright was a better core workout than Pilates. At several points, Logan grabbed me as I threatened to topple.

'When we get back, I'll find you some decent wellingtons,' he said. 'I should never have sanctioned those ludicrous Barbie rain boots. You bought them in the post office, didn't you?'

'Might have done.'

'In the "you're not from round here, are you?" section?'

'Oh, shut up.'

He laughed. It was hard to see anything ahead now, as we seemed to be walking through a cloud. I rather fancifully mentioned this, and Logan snorted.

'It *is* a cloud,' he said. 'We're pretty high up.'

'Oh. I always imagined being inside a cloud would be quite pleasant,' I sighed, as hard pellets of rain battered my exposed face.

'Not in the Highlands, generally,' said Logan.

We scrambled up a slippery, rock-strewn sheep track and finally came to the small stone bridge. Logan was right – it had crumbled away with time, and while on a sunny day I felt sure it was charmingly picturesque, now, with white water rolling and churning just beneath and nothing to hold on to but wet, mossy stone, I felt a surge of anxiety.

'Hang on to me,' Logan shouted, seeing my face. 'And go slowly.'

I gripped the hand he offered, reassured by his firm hold. I had an urge to lace my fingers through his – there was a safety in his touch that made me long for something I'd never had. I'd spent my entire adult life being sensible, independent Cat, coping with whatever the world threw at me, hiding my true feelings, always the solver of problems and the calmer of storms. Logan's large, warm hand enclosing my small, frozen one made me feel reassured in a way I hadn't felt since I was a child. I knew without a shred of doubt that if I put my faith in him, I'd remain safe.

We inched across the bridge together. A sharp wind had sprung up as we'd climbed higher, and I shivered convulsively, pressing against his side as his body shielded me from the driving rain. At last, we stepped back onto wet grass, and I relinquished his hand, immediately missing its warmth.

'It's just up here.' He pointed to a small track leading towards the pine forest, and I followed him, until through the mist and rain we could see a low stone building, with a rough wooden porch and a single window. Logan banged on the door.

'Who's up here?' I asked, shocked.

'Nobody, probably,' he said. 'But rarely, climbers use it for a night on their way up to Ben Iolair. I don't want to burst in and give someone heart failure.'

There was no answer, and he rattled open the rusted iron latch and stood aside to let me in.

14

For a moment, I was so relieved to be out of the rain, I didn't
care what the bothy looked like inside. I sank back against the
wall, breathing in the delicious dry air.

'I'll get the fire going,' said Logan.

I unzipped my sodden coat, and hung it over a wooden
bench by the door.

Now the water was out of my eyes, I could see where we
were – a square room with whitewashed walls and a stone floor.
There were a couple of simple wooden chairs drawn up to the
empty fireplace, a stack of logs in the corner, and a splintered
table made from an old pallet, holding two enamel mugs, a tin of
sugar and a carton of UHT milk. In the opposite corner was a
bucket for water, and through the open doorway, I could see a
low, wooden bedframe supporting a single mattress and a stack
of faded woollen blankets.

'I think the pillow butler's having his fag break,' said Logan.

I smiled. 'I'm just glad to be out of that rain.'

I extracted my damp phone from my jeans pocket. There
was no signal, of course, and I felt a beat of discomfort. We were
up here with no way of communicating... Still, if anything went

wrong, I reasoned, I could just follow the river back down. I couldn't read a map, but how hard could it be?

Logan was unpacking his rucksack, and had laid out dry matches, candles, a Thermos flask, his 'better than your iPhone' torch, a handful of energy bars and a large bottle of water on the makeshift table. Finally, he dug into his inside pocket and extracted a silver hip flask, which he placed next to the water.

'How long are we staying? Should I book our sunloungers for tomorrow?'

'You weren't a boy scout, were you?' he said. 'Seriously, when you grow up around here, it's drummed into you to prepare for anything, weather-wise.'

As he spoke, the rain hammering on the slate roof seemed to surge in volume. It now sounded like a hissing pressure hose.

Logan glanced up. 'This wasn't forecast,' he said. 'We have to hope it's just a summer storm that'll be over before it causes any real damage.'

'What sort of damage?'

He shook his head. 'Let's have a cup of tea, and worry about that if we have to. If you can deploy the mugs, I'll sort the fire out.'

I gave the mugs a quick dust with the hem of my jumper, and poured the pleasingly strong tea. Logan deftly set a Stonehenge of logs in the fireplace, screwed up a sheet of old newspaper to tuck between them and lit the whole structure with a match.

As I watched him, I wondered if Oliver had ever competently laid a fire. The closest I could get was a recollection of him sitting round the firepit at a beach party we'd organised for a celebrity surfer. Everyone had Blue Juice cocktails, and the caterers' exquisitely rolled sushi was laid out on a fibreglass bodyboard, carried around by muscular waiters in open Hawaiian shirts. Looking back, it all seemed quite ridiculous.

'Right,' Logan said, standing up. 'That should help.'

The hot tea flowed through my veins, but I found I couldn't get warm. 'I feel frozen solid,' I told him.

'That's because you're wearing soaking-wet clothes,' said Logan. 'Look, take off your jeans. I'll get you a blanket from the other room.'

He looked at my expression. 'I'm more in paramedic mode than grand seducer right now,' he added, pointedly turning away.

I removed my ridiculous boots and pulled off the heavy denim. Instantly, I felt warmer.

'Here,' said Logan, ostentatiously averting his eyes as he handed me a scratchy tartan blanket.

It smelled musty but clean, and I wrapped it round my legs. He picked up my jeans and draped them over the edge of the table to dry by the fire. The flames were flickering strongly, drawn by the wind in the chimney, as he disappeared into the sleeping area and returned with an age-spotted glass and metal lantern case. Logan lit a candle and stuck it inside, then hung the lantern from a hook halfway up the wall.

'I remember me and Rory bringing that lantern up here when I was about twelve,' said Logan. 'Amazing nobody's nicked it.'

'Did you come up here much?'

'Now and then,' he said. The firelight was reflected in his dark eyes, tiny twin flames blazing as he looked at me. 'Mostly to go fishing in the pool by the bridge. It was a good place to sit and wait for trout.'

'Never sneaked up here with a girl?' I teased. 'Perfect hangout for the cunning teenage boy, I'd have thought.'

Logan glanced at me. 'Maybe once or twice,' he said, smiling. 'But seeing as I was pretty much living in my girlfriend's family home, we didn't really need to.'

Marina, I realised. Of course.

'Can you hear that noise?' he asked.

I'd become so used to the sound of the relentless, drumming rain, I'd almost forgotten about it. But now I listened, and beneath the downpour I could hear a much lower rumbling, growing in volume and strength, the sound of rocks and stones clashing together and bouncing apart, being carried at speed by a great torrent of water.

Logan shrugged his damp jacket back on and dashed outside. As soon as he opened the door, the noise doubled in volume to an ear-shattering roar. Rain sprayed wildly into the room, and the wind snatched at the door, so it slammed back against the wall.

I stood up and shuffled in my socks to the door, calling, 'Logan, what's happ—' and then I saw it.

The river had burst its banks, the old stone bridge had collapsed into the seething water and vast boulders were being flung downstream by the cascade. The river was twice as wide as it had been earlier, and it was clear that nobody could cross without being swept away. Overhead, thunder cracked and rumbled, and still, the rain pelted down.

Logan turned back to me, water streaming over his face, plastering his shirt to his skin, and his dark hair to his head.

'We're stuck, aren't we?' I asked, and he nodded.

'Until the rain stops and the water recedes,' he said. 'And I'm afraid it's impossible to say how long that might be.'

15

MAY BANK HOLIDAY WEEKEND, FIFTEEN YEARS EARLIER

'I wish Max was here.'

Mum looks at me in the rear-view mirror. 'That's nice. Most teenage girls don't want to hang out with their older brothers.'

'Don't say "hang out" – it's embarrassing. I've just got nobody to go around with.'

Mum sighs. 'Well, what about Logan and Rory? They seem friendly enough.'

She's returned to the Parent Zone, where apparently, striking up a conversation with handsome teenage boys is perfectly simple, and it's inexplicable that I wouldn't simply approach them with an interesting question about local birdlife and 'make friends'.

'Logan doesn't seem friendly at all.' Saying his name sends blood rushing to my cheeks, and I'm relieved I'm in the back seat where my parents can't see my throbbing face.

'He's only a bit older than you,' says Mum. 'I'm sure he'll be lovely if you let him know you're a bit bored. Anyway, Rory's more your age—' She breaks off. 'Ooh, Gerry, an oystercatcher! Look, with the little orange beak!'

I slump further into my hoodie and fruitlessly check my

phone screen again. We're heading back to the B&B, after a day of 'pootling' (Mum's word) round Glencoe, listening to Dad explain why the MacDonalds were 'the forgotten victims of history' and demanding to know what we'd do 'if the Campbells were coming for *us*, and it's *still happening today* in different guises, Cat, all over the world…'

I want to be back home, sitting in my friend Leyla's bedroom, borrowing her precious Black Satin nail polish and flicking through *Heat* magazine, not burning up with dread and excitement at the idea of Logan looking in my direction. Not that he has.

Mum's right about Rory – he's sweet, but I don't remotely fancy him, and I'm pretty sure the feeling's mutual. He asked if I wanted to go fishing with him earlier. I felt sick and my heart raced in case Logan might be there, but Rory added, 'It's just me, so more chance of catching something.' I would have said yes, for the company, but Mum was all excited about Glencoe and we're only here for another couple of days.

We're staying in a B&B in the village, which is a big disappointment. I haven't even seen the castle, but Sir Alastair said the boiler's packed up. It's freezing cold and his housekeeper's away, so he said we'd be happier at Glen View, which is so old-fashioned they haven't got duvets on the beds, just candlewick bedspreads and blankets, and there's still a dial-up modem if you want to get online. I've eaten all the free shortbread on the tea tray and had six baths in two days to use up the miniature bubble baths, and I'm bored rigid.

Sir Alastair's taking us out for dinner at the local pub later, so there's a slim chance Logan might be there. Disastrously, I only have jeans and hoodies with me – I might have to pretend I'm ill and not go, rather than let him see me dressed like a nine-year-old boy.

. . .

Logan is sitting directly opposite me, at the Falls of GlennIolair pub, wearing a heavy white cotton shirt, dark jeans and scuffed leather boots. His hair is unstyled but falling perfectly over his left eyebrow, and unlike Nathan Summers, who favours a ratty V Festival wristband and a gold chain from Elizabeth Duke at Argos, Logan is wearing no jewellery but a plain vintage watch with a battered leather strap. I'm trying not to stare at the lightly tanned wrist it's buckled round, feeling faint with longing.

'You all right, Cat?' says Rory, next to me. 'What did you make of Glencoe?'

'Oh...' I try to arrange my facial expression to 'politely sociable' and feel like a grinning Japanese theatre mask. 'It's amazing,' I say. 'So... vast.'

'Did you do much walking?' Logan asks, as if I'm an adult who does things like hillwalking, not a sixteen-year-old beset by GCSE revision and frozen with awkwardness.

'No... well, only to look at a waterfall,' I manage. 'It was good. You know, big. It's all huge.'

He smiles slightly.

The waitress brings bowls of soup that look suspiciously tinned, and sliced bread with the butter already on it. I immediately worry that I'm going to spill soup on myself. I borrowed a white top of Mum's that's not completely hideous, and she won't thank me for getting microwaved tomato and basil down the front.

I feel like a marionette, jerkily lifting my spoon, suddenly aware of all my weird movements in a way I've never been before. Logan, by contrast, looks supremely relaxed as he shells his prawns, and Rory's whacking pâté onto toast like he's grouting tiles.

'You around tomorrow, Loge?' Rory asks his brother, and my hair-trigger heart powers up again. 'We could show Cat the castle.'

'Not sure. I might be about in the morning,' says Logan,

plunging me back down the emotional log flume I've suddenly boarded. 'Depends if Marina's going to Oban or not.'

'Who's Marina?' I blurt, before I can stop myself.

'Logan's *special lady*,' says Rory, grinning. 'Joined at the hip, those two are.'

'Shut up, Ror,' says Logan wearily. 'And don't take my girl-friend's name in vain.'

A shadow passes over the sun, and suddenly my low-necked white top feels stupidly overkeen, my carefully waved hair a rigid, teased wig.

I put my soup spoon down. I doubt I'll ever eat again, the disappointment is so thick in my throat.

'Have you been together long?' I ask him, attempting 'casual curiosity'.

'I've known her all my life,' he says. 'But as a girlfriend, about a year.'

'Made for each other,' says Rory, cheerfully compounding my agony. 'They both like driving round country roads too fast and messing about in boats.'

So not only is Marina a vital, long-term fixture in his life, she can also drive and sail. What hope do I have, a visiting tourist kid with a faded Justin Bieber sticker on my homework file? I force a queasy smile as the waitress returns to take our plates.

'Actually,' I say stiffly, 'I've just remembered, Mum's got some plan to visit an art gallery near the coast tomorrow – I think we're supposed to be setting off early.'

'The Wee Art Sheds at Kilchullin? Oh, she'll love it,' says Logan. 'Really good café, too, if you like enormous cakes.'

I nod, struck dumb with misery. He clearly thinks I look like the kind of girl who enjoys 'enormous cakes'. Unlike sporty, slim, car-driving, yacht-wrangling, perfect Marina.

And we still have the main course and pudding to get through.

16

Logan pushed his entire weight against the door, battling the gale, and the latch finally gave in and clicked into place.

'So, this isn't great,' he said, running a hand through his dark hair. 'The way it's looking, it could rain like this all night. We might be stuck here till the morning, I'm afraid.'

I felt a smack of surprise at the unexpected news – but far less alarmed than I would have been with anyone else alongside me.

It had never occurred to me that when things went wrong in the countryside, sometimes, they couldn't be solved. I was so used to having emergency services and a phone signal and the AA to hand, I had no idea what we were supposed to do when we were plunged into this kind of medieval disaster. Except we didn't even have warm capes, or muscular horses that could wade through the rising waters and gallop us to safety.

'Will the bothy flood, do you think?' I tried to sound calm.

'It's unlikely,' Logan said. 'Obviously, the main force of the water is downhill – we'll only be in trouble if fallen trees and debris create a dam, and cause it to overflow up here.'

'Right.' I took a steadying breath. 'What if that happens?'

'Well, worst-case scenario, we'd climb on the roof,' said Logan. 'Have you got anything red? If it comes to it, we can listen out for the rescue helicopter and wave it when it passes overhead.'

I flushed, remembering the lace underwear I'd put on earlier.

'A bra,' I muttered.

'Sorry?'

'My *bra*,' I repeated crossly, and Logan snort-laughed in surprise.

'Well,' he said, 'let's hope it won't come to that. We should have enough candles to last us, but I'm afraid it'll be more energy bars for dinner.'

'And brandy?' I looked hopefully at his flask.

'If you like. Although, actually, it's Scotch,' he said. 'I'm like a St Bernard, I always carry a small barrel just in case. Good for shock, and sterilising cuts.'

'And for dribbling into my slack mouth, murmuring, "Wake up, Carruthers, it is but a flesh wound,"' I added. 'If we're going the full Victorian explorer.'

He laughed properly. 'And again, we must hope it doesn't come to that. I suppose Dad'll be worried when we don't come back, but Donald will understand what's happened and let him know,' he went on. 'If we can't get back before dark, the sensible thing would be to wait until the rain stops and hope we can wade across.'

'What's in the other direction?'

'A main road and a bus stop,' said Logan solemnly. 'Want to give them a try?'

'Why didn't you—' I saw his face. 'Oh, hilarious.'

'Sorry. But it's about twenty-five miles of dense pine forest, all of which looks exactly the same.'

'A lightless eco-disaster,' we chorused together.

I should have felt terrified, trapped by raging white water

with a man I barely knew and no electricity, phone or chance of rescue. But Logan had an air of such relentless competence, it seemed overwrought and silly to panic.

'I suppose this sort of thing happens quite often,' I said hopefully, sitting back in my chair.

He looked thoughtful. His hair was beginning to dry again, and I had a sudden urge to rake through his wild, dark curls with my fingers. I stared hard into the fire.

'Certainly not in my lifetime,' Logan said eventually. 'I remember Dad talking about the great storm of '87, but that was in the October. Lifted off half the castle roof, and apparently one of Jock McCready's Highland cows got blown into the orchard and was found happily eating all the fallen pears. Though that might have been Dad exaggerating to amuse us.'

'What a lovely image.' I smiled. 'Was he a nice dad when... after... well, when your mum died?'

'He was old-fashioned,' said Logan, looking at the fire. He had taken off his jacket to dry alongside mine, and was wearing a soft old, checked shirt, with the sleeves pushed up above his strong forearms. 'He didn't believe in grief therapists or talking it out, or any of that business we'd have nowadays. But he was very kind to us, and let us get on with our lives – I don't suppose he knew any other way to be.' He shrugged. 'And of course, we had Ishbel and Donald, who were lovely to us, and I had Marina and her parents.'

Unexpected sorrow shot through me, a distant echo of the hurt I'd felt at sixteen. Ridiculous how such things lingered.

'Do you still see them?' I asked. 'Her parents, I mean.'

Logan's mouth twisted in regret. 'Sadly not. They're good people, Rhona and Chris. They were kind to me when I needed it most. I wasn't great at expressing myself, back then.' He paused. 'Well, you still wouldn't call me Californian in my approach to emotion...'

I laughed.

'... but they understood that, and they gave me space when I needed it, and the chance to chat if I wanted. Albeit I didn't very often.'

He reached for the Thermos and refilled our empty mugs. 'May as well drink this tea while it's still warm,' he said. 'The question is, how are we going to fill the next fourteen hours or so?'

Illicit desire flamed through me, and I felt a searing heat in my cheeks. Yet Logan was so determinedly unflirtatious, I suspected he was simply expressing genuine puzzlement regarding the lack of entertainment available in our rain-swept bothy.

'We could play a game,' I offered. 'Word association.'

'Is this your belated attempt at Californian therapy? I assure you, it won't work.'

'No,' I said. 'Alice and I play it on long car journeys. Although Alice always cheats and says things like "Chris Hemsworth" for hot, instead of "oven".'

'What constitutes *not* cheating?'

'Being honest.'

Logan looked over at me, his expression unreadable. I assumed my hair was drying into a wild halo of frizz, and self-consciously pulled it back.

'Don't – curls suit you,' he said, then quickly added, 'Not that your hair choices are any of my business.'

'They will be when it's so bushy it fills the room,' I said, to conceal my delight at his compliment. 'You'll be battling through it to reach the door, like the prince in *Sleeping Beauty*.'

Logan added a log to the dwindling flames, and the water outside rushed and rumbled on.

'Rain,' I said.

'Flood.'

'Noah.'

'Animals.'

'Dogs.'

'Spaniels.'

'Trouble.'

Logan turned to me. '*Excuse* me?'

'Well, I haven't met many spaniels, but...'

'Are you dissing the lights of my life?'

'No! I'm just saying, they're quite... you know. *Lively.*'

Logan smiled. 'It's like having toddlers without having to join smug parenting groups and sing ridiculous songs. Although on occasion...'

'Do you really sing to them?' I found that hard to envisage.

'Might give them a quick burst of "Flower of Scotland", if I'm feeling fond,' he said. 'It calms them down.'

My treacherous heart was warming to Logan, aside from his compellingly good looks. I was just grateful for the company, I told myself. He was still rude and grumpy and intransigent, but he was evidently capable of being pleasant when it suited him.

'Have you always had spaniels?'

He smiled. 'We've had an absolute menagerie of all kinds of dog,' he said. 'That was the worst thing about living in Edinburgh – my landlord didn't allow pets, so I was reduced to stopping for a daily chat with every dog in Stockbridge. I generally ignored the owners, mind you. Much less interesting.'

'Did you come back here just for Arran and Alba?'

'Not solely,' said Logan. 'Dad's getting older, and I knew he was worrying about the future and needed a hand, and I'd done my master's, and was excited about getting the hydro-scheme up and running. It would have provided enough electricity to power the whole lochside, just from the waterfalls on the castle's land...' He heaved a sigh.

'Who do you think complained?' I asked boldly. It didn't surprise me that Logan had made a few enemies up here – I'd seen for myself that he could be belligerent and high-handed, but ruining his business seemed excessive.

'I don't *think*; I know who,' he said. 'Jack Campbell. Because he hoped if he ruined my business plans, I'd sod off back to Edinburgh and leave the path to Marina nice and clear for him.'

I was taken aback by the bitterness in his voice. I supposed it had only been eighteen months since he lost the real love of his life, whatever he might claim about the dogs. I felt an unexpected surge of fury on Logan's behalf.

'Why did they listen to just one complaint, though, if everyone else was behind the idea?'

Logan raised his eyebrows. 'Because Jack's bully-boy, weight-chucking father Bran is a councillor,' he said. 'In fact, he's the one in charge of processing applications for things like renewable energy sources. So that was that.'

'Couldn't you argue your case, though?' I began.

'Oh yeah, I didn't think of that. Tell you what, Monday morning, I'll be straight down the council offices.'

'Sorry.'

There was a brief silence between us, filled by the hammering rain, which still showed no sign of easing.

'So, what now, then?' I asked.

'I think a slug of whisky,' said Logan, deliberately misunderstanding my question. 'As country legend Jimmy Buffett once said, it's five o'clock somewhere. Actually, it's almost five o'clock here. Want one?'

'Why not?'

The hip flask wasn't big enough to get us drunk, I reasoned, so if we did need to climb on the roof, we'd probably just feel slightly warmer while we did it.

He poured a decent slug into our empty mugs. 'I'm not generally a big drinker,' he said, 'but I do find whisky is helpful at times like this.'

The silky, amber liquid glowed in the candlelight.

'I'm more of a red wine woman,' I said. 'But I agree.'

'You'll have to ask Dad to show you his wine cellar,' said Logan. 'He's been laying down bottles for years. He was going to give me some of the really good ones for the wedding, but... well, they're still there. Waiting for Rory's wedding, I guess.'

I sipped the whisky, its heat spreading through my veins like molten lava. 'Bloody hell,' I said. 'This isn't any old cooking Scotch, is it?'

Logan smiled and clanked his mug against mine. 'Actually,' he said, 'it was the one thing I liberated after the nuptial meltdown. My grandfather gave it to me on my eighteenth birthday and we were all supposed to drink a clan toast with it at my wedding reception. Quite glad we didn't, now.'

'Me too.' It was like liquid fire – every sip made me feel more invincible. 'Dangerous stuff,' I observed, putting the mug down.

'I'm not worried about you,' said Logan. 'Like I said, you're far too balanced to go on a drunken rampage.'

'That makes me sound extremely boring.'

He caught my look of irritation. The dim room was lit only by the fire and the wall lantern, and I could see the candle's tiny, steady flame reflected in his eyes.

'Cat, you're not remotely boring,' he said, so quietly I could barely hear him over the rain and the river. 'I'm the one who's dull. You have an exciting, ambitious life in London, with friends and fun and... roof cocktails.'

I laughed.

'I came home to live with my dad at the age of twenty-nine, and I'll probably end up dying here,' said Logan. 'I lost half my friends in the great wedding disaster, and now all I do is grow vegetables and cook them for pub customers and argue endlessly and pointlessly about how to save bloody Iolair,' he went on. 'I'm a man who sings to spaniels, for God's sake.'

'I think that's very charming,' I said, taking another gulp of the whisky. 'I used to sing to Gladstone, our family's red setter. I still miss him.'

'What did you sing?'

'Oh, he was a big fan of Bob Dylan,' I said. 'At least, that's what my dad always claimed.'

Logan laughed. 'I remember your dad,' he said. 'That time you all... well.'

Clearly, he'd suddenly remembered how our long-ago visit had ended, too, and neither of us were ready to go there conversationally. I doubted we ever would be.

'I'll go and check what's happening outside,' he said. 'Maybe get another candle lit.'

He picked up the matches and unlatched the door, standing just inside to scan the apocalypse beyond. He was almost as slim as he'd been as a teenager, but his shoulders were broader now, presumably from all the gardening, and his arms more muscular. He still had a great arse.

Calm down, Cat, I thought, dragging my gaze away. *You're still grieving Oliver, you can't go down another disastrous route...*

'Still bucketing, and it's coming down from Ben Iolair like Niagara,' he said. 'I think the water level's risen, but it's not breaching the bothy path yet. The gale's getting up, though.' The walls were rattling around us.

As he reached behind him to shut the door, there was a violent crash, and I screamed.

17

The old glass of the bothy's tiny window had blown in, and its shards now lay on the stone floor, glittering in the firelight that danced and wavered in the sudden wind.

'Oh my God!' I blurted. 'We'll freeze.'

Logan's expression was grim. 'Not in May,' he said, 'but it's not going to be a pleasant night.'

Bolts of rain, accompanied by a chill wind, were now driving in through the open space, drenching the floor and making me shiver.

'I can fix a blanket over the window frame to try and block the wind a bit,' he said, 'but it won't keep us warm.'

'I can't actually remember what warm feels like,' I assured him, 'so don't worry.'

Logan shook the wooden frame. 'Help me unstick this, Cat,' he said. 'We need to trap the blanket into the top.'

I tied the blanket that had been covering my legs round my hips like a sarong and stood. With a great deal of shoving and unseemly grunting, aided by a Swiss army knife Logan produced from his jeans – of course he did – we managed to crank open the frame and stuff the heaviest blanket into the space, before pushing it up again. Logan moved the bench into place to hold the bottom of the blanket.

'There,' he said. 'At least it's something.'

It was now dark as midnight in the room.

'Also, we now only have two blankets.'

He nodded. 'You take them. I have my jacket. I'll sleep in that, and I'll drag the mattress in so you can lie in front of the fire, but we'll have to eke the wood out.'

The alcohol was still buzzing in my blood, and I took a last swig of Grandfather McAskill's priceless whisky, for courage.

'Look,' I said, 'don't take this the wrong way, but wouldn't it make sense for us both to sleep on the mattress, with the blankets and your jacket? That way, we'd have each other's body heat, too. I don't mean...' I began, feeling my face blaze with heat.

'I mean... yes, that would be the sensible thing to do,' said Logan, as another violent gust billowed the wet blanket like a sail. 'But I don't want you to feel that... well, that I'm trying to turn it into something.'

'It was my idea,' I said. 'I won't think that.'

'Fine,' he said. 'I'll get the palatial bedding.'

He dragged the single mattress into the main room, pushed back the chairs and laid it by the fire. 'Not too damp, amazingly,' he said. 'I think it's best if we lie on one blanket, and pull the other one over us, and you wear my jacket.'

'It's a bit... buckle-y for comfort.'

He laughed. 'Fine. We'll put it over the top blanket then.'

'Take me for dinner first?'

I handed him an energy bar and took one for myself, and we sat in the chairs and ate them in comfortable silence, watching the flames. It was peculiarly intimate, as if we'd been married for years, and I had to remind myself that until this morning, I'd thought Logan a miserable, rude git. Perhaps he still would be one when we were in a less dramatic situation. Right now, it was hard to imagine being warm and comfortable back at the castle, with other people and the dogs milling around. In the dark, lit by the single candle and the fire, this bare, chilly room felt as though it was our whole existence – always had been, and always would be.

'We may as well get comfortable,' I said eventually. 'What time is first light?'

'It isn't, really,' Logan said.

'What?'

'Have you heard of the white nights?' he asked. 'We're so far north, it barely gets dark at this time of year. A few hours' dusk at most.'

'So we can set off back as soon as the river goes down?'

'Yep. I'll keep checking.'

I nodded.

'Logan,' I said. 'Slight problem – I need the loo.'

'Ah.' He stood up and began to unbuckle his trousers.

'Steady!' I said, alarmed. 'What are you...?'

'Taking these off so you have waterproof trousers to go outside in,' he said. 'Obviously.'

'Oh. Thanks.'

'Put my jacket on,' he added. 'Yours is like a soaked rag. And for God's sake, don't go anywhere near the river.'

'I'm not three, Logan.'

'I'm fully aware of that.'

I looked up from struggling into his trousers, and caught a full view of him standing by the fire in his navy boxers. I'd been wrong, his thighs were also rigid with muscle.

Jesus, Cat, get a grip. I turned and shuffled out in my enormous waterproof clown outfit. Never mind what I thought of Logan's body, my chances of seduction in this get-up were zero, even if I'd wanted to. And I didn't. Obviously.

Outside, the rain was coming down like iron bars, and the river was still a roiling cauldron. I spent my gale-blown penny, hanging on to the bothy wall, and staggered back inside, slamming the door. Logan was sitting up on the mattress, the blanket over his legs, and without allowing myself time to think, I shed his trousers and jacket, hung them over the chair backs and got in beside him.

Immediately, our thighs pressed together, skin to skin, and I felt a bolt of desire shoot through me.

He looked at me, sudden doubt in his expression. Had he felt it, too?

'Look, I know it's a bit intimate,' he said. 'Are you sure you're okay to do this?'

I was sure. I didn't want him to stand up and walk away, for that electric warmth to leave my side.

'It's fine,' I said, and my eyes met his. My breath, maybe my heartbeat, too, hung suspended for a moment. If he touched me now…

'Well,' he said, clearing his throat. 'We should probably try and get a bit of sleep, even though it's early. Give the rain a chance to stop.'

'Sure.' I lay down beside him, our bare legs now an inch apart. I could feel the heat of his body. Without pillows, my neck was at an awkward angle. Logan turned so he faced away from me, and I felt a pang of loss.

'Actually, you should be facing the fire,' he said. 'You're colder than me. Can you climb over, and I'll move back?'

He shifted as I tried to climb delicately over him, but my leg caught on his knee, and I lost my balance and slid against his chest.

'Sorry!'

'It's all right,' said Logan quietly.

I tried to arrange myself so we weren't touching, but on a lumpy, single mattress with a shared blanket…

'Look,' I said, 'if you lie facing the fire, too, we'll have more room to move.'

He rolled over. Now, his knees were against the back of mine, and the heat of that small contact was all I could think about. My heart was racing.

For a while, the only sounds were the rain and wind, the crackling of the fire, and the rhythm of our breath. I didn't want to analyse what was happening – more crucially, I couldn't. The world had shrunk to my acute physical awareness of Logan, the heat of his skin, the gentle whisper of his slow exhalations on the back of my neck. Shimmers of desire passed through me, and I hoped desperately that he remained unaware of my speeding heart rate.

'Put your arm around me, and we'll try and go to sleep,' I said.

'Sure? Okay.'

Logan tucked his arm around my waist, spooning me against his jumper. We lay, unmoving. All I could hear was the water outside, and Logan's soft breathing. He moved his hand slightly, and touched mine. Slowly, I closed my fingers around his. My stomach swerved like a car on an oily road at the contact, and I took a breath.

'Word association,' I whispered.

'Go on.'

'Bed.'

'Touch.'

'Stroking,' I said, as he moved his fingers over mine.

'Kissing,' he said, and I turned to face him, so our bodies were pressed together. His eyes were golden in the firelight.

'Kissing?' I repeated, and brought my hand to his face, feeling his stubble under my fingers, drawing his lips to mine.

That kiss. It contained everything I'd felt as a yearning sixteen-year-old, everything I felt now, a decade and a half later. Logan pulled me against him, his hands under my clothes, and weak with desire, I pulled off his jumper and T-shirt, running my fingers over his broad chest, then sat up and struggled out of my top.

'Is this the famous red bra?' he asked, lightly running a finger across its lace edge. I could hardly speak.

'Good job I put it on, in case of emergency,' I managed, and he laughed and pulled me back down to him. It wasn't on for much longer.

As his fingers traced my naked skin, I was nothing but sensation – mouth and hands, skin and warmth, and the sound of our quickened breaths. The blanket fell aside as he kissed his way down my body, and my eventual orgasm was loud and so intense, I trembled all over as electric silver rain passed through me.

A while afterwards, he whispered, 'Wait there,' and stood up. He walked, naked – everything I'd imagined – to the other room and returned holding an old tobacco tin. 'As I hoped,' he said, extracting a box of condoms. 'Good old Rory.'

'You're so beautiful, Cat,' he whispered, holding himself above me, slowly rocking against me, looking into my eyes, reaching to kiss me, again and again.

I didn't know how long it went on for – hours or days; we could have been in any place at any time – but eventually, we fell asleep, my head on his chest, his arms wrapped around me.

The rain on the roof had finally eased, and the gentle sound was like a lullaby.

18

I was woken by the noise of a sputtering diesel engine.

My cheek was on Logan's chest, his arm a warm weight around my back, and the fire had gone out. The room was bitterly cold, but daylight filtered through the edges of the blanket, illuminating the glass shards that still lay in the corner where Logan had kicked them. The rain had stopped.

The engine juddered to a halt nearby, and a voice called, 'Hello! Anyone there?'

In one fluid motion, Logan sat up from what had apparently been a deep sleep.

'It's Donald, on the quad bike!' He looked at his watch. 'Cat, it's eight o'clock – we slept right through. Hurry!'

It was as though I'd been drenched with a bucket of freezing water. I hadn't thought we'd suddenly be love's young dream after our night of passion – in fact, I hadn't thought at all, I'd only felt and touched and quivered. But as rude awakenings went, this was up there.

'Hi there, Donald!' Logan shouted. 'Give us a second!' He was standing up, yanking on his discarded trousers, pulling his T-shirt over his head, scanning for his boots. He threw my jeans at me – they were now only faintly clammy – and I retrieved my abandoned knickers from beside the fire and stayed under the cover as I pulled them on. My red bra was buried down in the blanket. In the cold morning light, as Logan shrugged on his jacket and unlatched the door, I felt nothing but embarrassed by its brazen scarlet lace, as if I'd tripped over a discarded tequila bottle on a work morning.

'I knew you'd stay put,' I heard Donald shout. 'Sensible lad! Cat all right?'

'She's fine,' Logan said. 'We made the best of it.'

We made the best of it?

As if our lovemaking – because that's how it had felt – had been a board game, a battered set of Yahtzee stuffed in a cupboard. And now the need to fill the empty hours was over and we'd go back to our normal life, and what – never mention it again? I had known it was only a physical connection, an opportunity to surrender to the sexual tension that crackled between us, but I hadn't expected Logan to be quite so dismissive. I'd hoped for a kiss, an acknowledgement that our night out of time had been... well, perfect – before we returned to our normal, separate lives.

It was foolish to feel hurt, of course. We were both adults, he still loved Marina and of course, I still loved Oliver. Logan was difficult and bad-tempered. I wanted a best friend, a partner in life, not a casual fling... and yet. I wished we could have gazed into each other's eyes, touched each other's warm skin just once more before it ended.

Logan turned back to me. I was dressed by now, folding up blankets and gathering the water bottle and hip flask. 'Okay, we can't both fit on the quad bike, so you go with Donald. But make sure you hold on tight – it's rough downhill through the forest.'

'But what about you?'

'I'll walk,' he said. 'Look, the river's gone down – we can

easily wade across now. We'll all be setting off for the Highland Games around eleven, so it's a good job he woke us.'

I felt as though something precious had been unexpectedly snatched away. I hadn't even had my usual cup of tea.

'Sure,' I said, attempting to match his brisk tone. 'I guess I'll see you down there.'

'Yup.'

Logan collected his rucksack, and I joined him on the bothy step. The morning air was soft, and a pearlescent white mist hung low over the forest. The raging river had dwindled to a gentle, steady flow, although the ripped branches and flung stones lining the banks remained a reminder of last night's chaos.

'Should we move the bed back?'

'The mattress? Nah, I'll deal with it next time I'm here,' said Logan.

No suggestion that I might be with him on that occasion, I noted.

He raised a hand to Donald. 'Cheers for coming,' he called across the river. 'Arran and Alba all right?'

'Aye, they're no problem,' said Donald, who this morning was wearing a tartan deerstalker hat with ear flaps. 'The wee lads are having their breakfast with Agatha and Dougie. Slept on our bed, the pair of 'em.'

'Well, I hope your night wasn't too disturbed,' said Logan.

I tried to catch his eye, just to see if there was any brief spark of acknowledgement regarding our own disturbed night, but he was already setting off down the little track to the water's edge.

'Morning, Cat!' shouted Donald. 'Wild night, eh?'

I flushed violently, before realising that he was talking about the weather.

'Yes!' I called back. 'That rain! Wow!'

Logan was striding through the shallows, holding his hand out for me to take.

'I'm all right, thanks.' I slithered my way across the wet stones unsupported, afraid that if I touched him again, I'd give myself away.

'Up you get,' Donald said, patting the seat behind him, and I clambered onto the quad bike and held on.

Logan saluted Donald and set off ahead of us towards the forest, as Donald steered the jolting machine in a wide circle and headed down the hillside, bumping over tussocks and rocks.

'Quite the West Highlands baptism of fire, eh?' he shouted above the noise of the engine. 'I hope young Logan was a gentle-man, and looked after you.'

'Yes, he was,' I said, ignoring the stab of sadness through my heart.

As we left the bothy behind, it occurred to me that last night's intimacy seemed to have dissolved faster than the morning mist.

Back at the castle, I headed straight to the kitchen for toast and strong tea. Today, Agatha was wearing a pink slogan sweatshirt that read, 'I'm too clumsy to be around fragile masculinity'.

'You were stuck in the wee bothy *all night*?' she demanded, her blue eyes narrowed in disbelief.

I nodded.

'None of my business, I know, but where exactly did you... sleep?'

I felt my cheeks redden. 'Oh, well, there's a mattress...'

'Aye, a single one.'

I focused on Dougie, who was systematically deconstructing something that looked suspiciously like Hannay's special crocodile.

'There were a couple of chairs,' I said vaguely.

'Chairs!' Agatha shuddered. 'I'd sooner sleep on a bed o' nails! I suppose you could have shared the bed without fear, Logan's a real gentleman, you know, Cat...'

'Is there any bacon?' I asked, desperate to get off the topic of sleeping arrangements and avoid the gleam of amusement I detected in Agatha's eyes.

'Nope,' she said. 'It's all about the big picnic today. There's cereal in the larder, but please, dinnae make a mess. I havenae time to clear up.'

I couldn't make one worse than I already had, I thought bitterly, fetching a bowl and going in search of Weetabix.

I felt marginally improved once I'd showered and changed. Having clean hair and jeans that didn't feel like a toad's skin helped, and as the sun had now broken through the mist, I put on my favourite scarlet top and my soft, vintage leather jacket – albeit I'd be wearing them with my mud-encrusted rainbow wellies.

I took a while over my make-up, peering in the mirror above the little basin, aiming for 'attractively outdoorsy, but not over-done', and by the time I returned downstairs to meet the others in the kitchen, I felt more optimistic that Logan and I would chat at the event, perhaps even sneak off for a drink to discuss what had happened.

Of course he couldn't have been loving towards me with Donald sitting there, I told myself. Besides, we were both adults, who had taken advantage of the situation – I wasn't some blushing ingénue he'd deflowered. Maybe it was just a one-off, and if so, it was probably for the best, but that was hard to remember when sharp thrills of physical memory were still running through my body.

It was decided that Sir Alastair would drive the car with me, Agatha and Hannay, and Logan would take the Land Rover with Donald, Ishbel and the two dogs.

'I'll pop back to check on Dougie,' Agatha announced as we scrambled in. 'Maybe twice. He's still awful wee.'

The not-at-all-wee Hannay draped himself across my lap in the back seat, and I found his wiry weight a comfort. I stroked his nose, and wondered if I was the world's biggest idiot as we drove in convoy down the loch road. Maybe Logan did this with every woman he met – if he lacked the charm, he certainly had the looks and the body to lure them. I took a deep breath, recalling his hands holding my hips as I straddled him...

'Everything all right, Cat?' Sir Alastair glanced into the mirror and caught my eye. 'Must have been quite a hairy night for you.'

I almost laughed. 'Yes, it was a bit... stormy,' I said. 'But Logan was very helpful, and we had some water and energy bars...'

'Always prepared for every eventuality, that one,' he said.

Not quite, I thought, thinking of the lucky condoms. Unless... surely Logan hadn't secretly brought them up there, confidently expecting me to fall at his feet? I stroked Hannay's ears, thinking. Whatever happened now, I decided, Logan and I definitely needed to talk.

It wasn't far to the fields overlooking the loch where the Iolair Games were taking place. The car parking area was hectic, with teenage lads in kilts beckoning cars to and fro, and excited dogs and children milling about. Sir Alastair helped Agatha with the food hamper while I dragged a large decorative box of bamboo cutlery and cardboard plates and napkins from the boot.

I spotted Logan heading towards us, and my heart skipped at the sight of his slightly unkempt hair. I'd run my fingers through it not long before. He was carrying a pile of tartan picnic blankets, and behind him, Donald and Ishbel had a spaniel each. Arran and Alba were leaping and twirling with excitement, rushing under passing feet and sniffing urgently at other dogs. Clearly, being away from their master hadn't left them too devastated. I assumed for them, a night at the gatehouse was like going to stay with adoring grandparents, involving endless indulgences and staying up late.

Eventually, we reached a space on the hill overlooking the main arena, a fenced-off section of playing fields, and we waited for Logan to unfold two enormous plastic groundsheets, then cover them with the thick wool blankets. Sir Alastair and Agatha lowered the basket down, and the McTavishes set up several camping chairs. Donald was wearing a red-and-blue kilt, long red knitted socks and hiking boots, while Sir Alastair's own kilt was green and navy, with a vast sporran that I suspected was made from real fur. Logan, by contrast, was wearing jeans.

'No kilt?' I asked him.

He shook his head. 'I prefer not to lord it about at these things,' he said. 'People are always coming up to Dad asking about the castle, and I'd rather be fairly anonymous.'

'Yeah, life's tough for celebrities,' I joked, and he half smiled, then turned to ask Agatha where she wanted the wine cooler. Logan was very much not behaving like a man who'd apparently been bewitched by me a matter of hours ago.

Come on, Cat, I told myself, as I tore my eyes away from his muscular forearms. *You knew the score – a physical crush, a one-night stand – it happens all the time. He's hardly going to declare his love for you in the cold light of day. You wouldn't want him to. And besides, you can't simply get over Oliver by rolling under Logan.*

Though even as his familiar face passed through my mind, I realised I hadn't given my beloved ex-boss a thought since I had turned over in the firelight and looked into Logan's eyes.

19

The ground was ringed by tents and stalls, and a group of small, chatty children in matching green kilts was gathering in the rather muddy arena.

'Look, the Highland dancing's starting!' cried Ishbel. 'Come down with me – we'll watch the opening ceremony.'

A skirl of bagpipes cut through the noise of the crowd, and people began to make their way with more determination to the showground. I stood to go with Ishbel, and was puzzled to see Logan heading off in the opposite direction, with a tense set to his shoulders.

I couldn't help myself. 'Does Logan seem okay to you?' I asked Ishbel as we passed rows of excitable families and large men in kilts doing warm-up exercises on muddy grass.

'Och, well.' She glanced over her shoulder as we walked. 'Word is, Marina's here with Jack Campbell. So...'

'Logan didn't see her here last year?'

Ishbel shook her head. 'She's no' been back that long,' she said. 'There's been no contact between her and Logan, so this'll be the first time they've met since the wedding that never happened. He's been dreading it for weeks, I'd imagine.'

'I see.'

I saw all too well. His great lost love, the beautiful ex who jilted him – and he'd just happened to fall into bed with the only available woman in Iolair, the night before he knew he was going to see her again.

Of course Logan had been using me to make himself feel better – I'd been nothing more than a human shot of whisky to get him through the night. But, a stern and unyielding voice inside my head asked, hadn't I been doing the same – throwing myself at another attractive man to try and get over Oliver, giving myself an ego boost because Oliver had rejected my charms and Logan had not?

Perhaps in the middle of the night, with the rain lashing down and the firelight flickering over our bare skin, it had briefly felt like something more – but it was a foolish woman who tried to turn a one-night stand into something meaningful. It was over now – and I wouldn't make the same mistake twice.

We stood by the roped-off area and watched the children whirl into the Highland fling – they were adorable, but I couldn't focus on anything but berating myself. I didn't even like Logan much, I thought, as tiny children twirled and bagpipes keened. He was set against all my ideas for the castle, he was bad-tempered, rude, dismissive…

The music piped to a halt, and the children filed from the field to vast applause and whooping. To my surprise, I saw it was Mel who was leading them away, and I waved. She grinned, and pointed to what I assumed was the drinks tent, judging by her dramatic 'tippling' hand-motions. I hoped the proud parents hadn't seen that.

The children were swiftly replaced by adult pipers in full Highland regalia, and regimental drummers. They launched into a rousing 'Flower of Scotland', which of course made me think of Logan singing it to his spaniels.

When the last note had died away, I made my way to the

drinks tent, a large, white structure like a wedding marquee. *I wouldn't have put it there,* I found myself thinking. *Too many people trying to get inside from a narrow pathway, only one entrance and the bar's at the far end, which is idiotic planning...* Even when I wasn't working, it seemed it was impossible to switch off my events brain. Perhaps a Pimm's would help the process.

I joined the milling queue, scanning the crowd for Mel, and saw her at the rear, talking to an older woman. I waved frantically, and she shoved her way through the broad backs and scratchy kilts towards me.

'Hey, you!' she said. 'I'm so glad you're here, I'm gasping for a drink. I was up at six, ready to drill the tinies – they're all back with their mums and dads now, chucking TVs out of hotel windows after the big gig.'

I laughed. 'We're set up on the hill, although everyone seems to have wandered off for now.'

'Och yes, I just saw Logan by the gun-dog trials field,' said Mel, her eyes widening. 'Top gossip – you'll never guess who he was talking to!'

'Marina.'

'Aye, the very same! Heads together, deep in discussion, no sign of Jack...' She nudged me in the ribs. 'This could be his big play to get back together with her.'

'She's married,' I said, more coldly than I'd intended.

'Never stopped anyone,' Mel observed wryly.

'Was that your mum over there?' I asked, to change the subject.

'Yep. She's looking after wee Belle for me, while I relax after my big choreography moment.'

'Belle? Is she your dog?'

Mel looked embarrassed. 'Look, I should have said – I'm sorry, I just didn't want to make a thing of it...'

'Of what?'

'She's my daughter,' Mel said. 'She's just turned six. Folk were a bit funny about it when I moved back up – all the old gossips, wittering away – so I don't tend to talk about her till I'm sure I won't be judged.'

'Mel! Why on earth would I judge you?'

'Och, you wouldn't, I know,' she said, shaking her head as if to shift her mindset. 'But it was a one-night stand, she's never had a dad and people gossip, you know. I can't bear them to think bad things about my lovely wee lassie, so with new people, I tend not to talk about her.'

'Was her dad—'

Mel shook her head. 'Don't be offended,' she said, 'but I *never* tell anyone who that was. I have my reasons.'

I was suddenly assailed by the realisation that Logan could be Belle's father. Mel had always thought him so handsome... he wasn't with Marina six years ago... Maybe they'd had a fling, and she'd never told him the truth. For a moment, I wondered whether Mel's friendship with me was genuine – or whether she was simply using me to get closer to Logan now it was all over with Marina. I felt an unexpected urge to lay claim to him.

'You're not the only person to have had a one-night stand.' I raised an eyebrow.

'You didn't!' she breathed.

'I actually did.'

'Oh my *God*!' Mel almost shouted. Several people turned round. 'When?' she asked, at a more normal volume. There was no jealousy in her eyes so far as I could tell – only amusement and mischief.

I smiled. 'Last night.'

We had reached the front of the queue, and I broke off to order a jug of Pimm's and lemonade which came with a herbaceous border bobbing on top. Once served, we retreated to a table outside.

'So go on – what happened?'

I gave her a heavily edited, PG version – the flood, the bothy, the mattress by the fire.

'Blimey, you don't mess about.' She clinked her glass against mine.

'It's not something I'd normally do,' I said. 'But I wanted to get over Oliver...'

'By getting under Logan?'

I raised my eyebrows. 'How do you know I was under him?'

She shrieked with laughter. 'Cat!' she said. 'You've livened this place up like a bottle rocket. I forbid you to go back to London.'

'I think Logan would like me on the next train south. I'm pretty sure he was just getting back at Marina because he knew he'd see her today.'

'I don't think he'd—' Mel stared over my shoulder. 'Well, speak of the devil...'

20

I followed Mel's gaze, and saw Logan walking towards us, beside a grown-up version of the girl I'd seen in the picture.

Marina was beautiful, of course, but I hadn't expected her to look quite so exceptional among the ordinary crowd. She was almost as tall as Logan, athletically slim and with a face like a pre-Raphaelite painting: wide-set blue eyes, winged cheekbones and that great tumble of shining auburn waves down her back. No wonder she'd entranced Logan.

Heads turned as they passed – perhaps because they made a beautiful couple, but also, it occurred to me, because locally, this was like seeing Brad Pitt with Angelina, years after the split. It was front-page news.

'Hi, Mel,' Logan said, as she raised a hand. 'You know Marina, obviously.' He waved a vague hand towards me. 'Marina, this is Cat. She's helping Dad out with plans for the castle.'

Nice to be relegated to a functionary, I thought. A vivid image of him gently cradling my face as he kissed me flashed through my mind. That was what, fourteen hours ago?

I smiled and shook her pale, cool hand.

'I hope you can pull the place into the twenty-first century, Cat.' She had a low, musical West Highlands accent – of course she did. 'It's a wonderful building, but it needs a bit of attention.'

'Well, Cat's planning to turn it into a corporate conference venue,' said Logan flatly.

I wanted to chuck my unfinished drink over his head. He knew it was Sir Alastair who'd asked me to come – why was he painting me as the villain here?

'Not quite,' I said. 'We're just looking at what might work to secure its future.' Suddenly, I was talking like a lifeless drone, too. Any minute, I'd say, 'If you all can turn to the infographic on page fifteen...'

'Anyway,' said Logan shortly. 'Good to see you both.'

Marina raised a casual hand in farewell, and they walked away together.

Mel looked at me. 'What in the name of hell was that?'

Unshed tears of embarrassment burned my eyes. The man who had whispered endearments in the dark, who had trailed a hand down my spine and made my entire body shiver with longing, who had... I shook my head to dispel the images flooding my memory.

'I have no idea.'

'If he's thinking he's getting Marina back, he's off his head,' said Mel angrily. 'And the way he spoke to you...'

I shrugged, in an attempt to recover a shred of pride. 'That's a one-night stand for you.'

'Amen to that,' said Mel fervently. She drained her drink. 'Come and meet Belle. She'll cheer you up, if anyone can.'

Gratefully, I followed her away from the tent, back towards the main arena where kilted men were assembling for the 'stone toss', whatever that was. It would be nice, I thought, if someone very large could accidentally toss one at Logan's arrogant head.

. . .

The spectators' field was filling with enormous, bearded men holding plastic pints of beer, cheering on their mates. It transpired that a stone toss was exactly what it sounded like – a man whirling a stone on a chain round his head, and seeing how far he could chuck it.

'It's all a bit medieval, isn't it?' Mel murmured, leading me over to the striped tea tent as the tannoy roared, 'And big Niall Fergusson holds the record!'

She waved at the woman I'd seen her with earlier, who was sitting with a small girl. Belle had Mel's curly dark hair – or was it Logan's curly dark hair? – and a sweet, round face with big brown eyes.

I smiled at Belle as we approached, and she thrust a paper bag towards my ear. 'Would you like some of my brownie?' she asked politely. 'Granny says I have to share it, but I don't really want to.'

I laughed, as Mel said, 'Belle! That's not what you say to people.'

Mel's mother rolled her eyes. 'Honest to a fault, my granddaughter,' she said.

If Logan was her father, that was a direct genetic link right there.

'I'm Lorna,' she added, extending her hand to me. 'It's lovely to meet you.'

Like Mel, Lorna radiated warmth. Her greying hair was cut short, and red-framed reading glasses hung on a cord around her neck. She also wore a denim jacket, patterned cotton trousers and a Sex Pistols T shirt.

'I think I'd better head back to the others,' I said. 'It must be getting close to picnic time.'

'Och, the Iolair picnic is famous,' said Lorna. 'The rest of us make do with hot dogs from Ewan's wee stand, while the lairds eat roast swan.'

'Mum!' Mel laughed. 'She's joking,' she said to me apologetically, dragging Lorna away.

I was smiling as I headed back up the hill, warmed by my encounter with Mel's little family. I wasn't by the time I reached the site of the Iolair picnic, and found everyone sitting rigidly silent on camping chairs, pretending to watch the caber toss while Logan argued a few feet away with a man who must, I assumed, be Jack Campbell.

'I'm afraid I'm not prepared to leave Iolair simply because you find it inconvenient,' Logan hissed. 'It's my ancestral home, and—'

'Oh, and don't we all know it,' sneered Jack, who was shorter than Logan, with a face that reminded me of a fox – small, bright-blue eyes, a pointed nose, slicked-back sandy hair – the sort of 'cheeky wide-boy' looks I'd always run a mile from.

'What's that supposed to mean?' Logan asked, instead of walking away, as he should have done.

'Exactly what I say.' Jack leaned back, surveying him. 'That you seem to think being millionaires' – Sir Alastair snorted quietly – 'gives you the right to do whatever you want around Iolair, and what's more, that it gives you the right to play the big I am with *my wife*.'

'We were having a civilised conversation!' Logan snapped. 'Which, God knows, is more than you've managed in eighteen months. You've ruined her life, yet I don't hear a word of apology to her.'

I wondered if I should intervene before someone threw a punch.

'I've nothing to apologise for!' Jack shouted. 'She was bloody grateful to be rescued from a bloke with a stick up his arse who didn't give a crap about her.'

'How dare you say that to me?' thundered Logan.

Donald was rising to his feet, glancing nervously at Ishbel, who was mouthing, '*Say something, Donnie!*'

Sir Alastair was now muttering, 'Uncouth young idiot,' under his breath. But Agatha rose from the blanket, where she'd been crouched feeding bits of sausage roll to Hannay.

'You!' she said. She poked Jack hard in the back, and he whipped round, furious.

'You shouldnae come here, to the Iolair picnic,' she said, her voice rising, 'that has taken me three days – *three days* – to make, and say such things!'

'Back off, lady. I'm not saying them to *you*,' Jack began rudely, but she prodded him again – this time in the chest – with the hand that wasn't holding a sausage roll.

'You're saying them to Logan, laddie, so you're saying them to everybody here,' she said icily, her pale blue eyes flashing in the sunlight. 'We're his family. If you insult him, you insult every one o' us.' She folded her arms and glared at him.

'Look, things have got a bit out of hand...' Jack began feebly.

'Yes,' said Agatha. 'Because you've damn well made them out o' hand. So you'd best leave.'

'I just...'

'Wheesht. Be off, back to your wee boats. You're not wanted here.'

Logan was shaking his head, a strange expression on his face. If I hadn't known how angry he was, I'd have thought he was suppressing a bark of laughter, as Jack released a pent-up huff of fury and stamped off down the hill.

Logan glanced around the group. 'Sorry about that, everyone,' he said. 'Ill-mannered little eejit.'

To my surprise – and slight envy – he hugged Agatha tightly. 'You are a star, Ag,' he said quietly. 'I shouldn't need you to fight my battles for me, but I'm very glad you did.'

She shrugged. 'It's nothing. He's always been an absolute roaster.'

'Hear, hear,' murmured Sir Alastair. He gestured hopefully

towards the picnic basket. 'Those marvellous pork pies aren't getting any younger. Shall we?'

Admittedly, as we ate, I still felt a carousel of negative emotions towards Logan. I was embarrassed by the unguarded heat of last night's passion, hurt by his brisk description of me to Marina and, if I was honest, envious of his beautiful ex-fiancée's clear hold over him. It was just a one-night stand, I knew, and clearly there was no future for the two of us, with me soon heading back to London, and him still bitterly resistant to all my plans for the castle.

Besides, I'd spent years deep in unrequited love with Oliver. That was hardly going to change overnight, I reminded myself, although having had my vague fantasies of five-star Tokyo hotel suites superseded by one night of wild sex in a flooded bothy, it was odd how much less heartbroken I now felt about my ex-boss.

'You can't just get over somebody; you have to replace them,' Alice always said. 'Find a better version, and it'll happen automatically.'

Was that what I'd done? Or perhaps I'd just ensured that now I could feel bad about two entirely different men – neither of whom had the slightest interest in me.

21

'The hill race is about to begin...' The announcement crackled over the tannoy. 'The legendary Iolair hill race... We have two dropouts, ladies and gentleman, two places to be filled urgently... Come on up, support your clan, help us out...'

'Support your clan, Donnie, go on!' Ishbel prodded Donald in the side. He was eating a slab of game pâté on an oatcake, and almost choked.

'My hill-racing days are long gone, love,' he said through a mouthful of crumbs.

'What about Logan?' I asked. In part, I felt he should represent the castle – mostly, I still felt annoyed enough to send him up a fairly large hill in inadequate clothing.

'Oh, excellent idea!' Sir Alastair clapped his hands together. 'Come on, Logan – bring glory back to the name of Castle Iolair!'

Logan looked irritated. 'I'm wearing jeans.'

'They're selling shorts with an embroidered Nessie logo down in the crafts tent!' said Ishbel excitedly.

Logan looked at her. 'You want me to wear some kind of handcrafted garment with a *Nessie logo?*'

She shrugged, her eyes alive with mischief. 'Go on, Logie,' she said. 'Remember the Iolair lairds' family motto?'

'What is it?' I asked, intrigued.

'He may not win, who never struggles,' said Sir Alastair. 'But in Gaelic, I think it's something like *cha bhuanaich esan nach dean stri*.'

'Oh that's pretty good,' I said. It certainly resonated for me – lately, life had been nothing but struggle.

'Fine.' Logan gave in. 'I haven't run up a hill since we did cross-country at Glenfinnachan and stopped for a Marlboro halfway, but if it'll shut you all up...'

We cheered as Logan made his way down to the registration tent, and, presumably, to buy his Nessie shorts.

Agatha decided to return to check on Dougie – 'to make sure the wee man hasnae got himself stuck in the cupboard' – and Sir Alastair took charge of the spaniels, who were full of stolen sausage rolls and had fallen asleep on a picnic rug, leaving me to lead the well-behaved Hannay down to the starting line.

People were gathering at the roped-off area, and several men were doing stretching exercises, along with a couple of very athletic-looking women in vests and running shorts. One, with a model's figure, was bending to retie her shoe, and as she stood, I saw her blaze of auburn hair, now gathered into a ponytail that streamed like a pennant in the breeze. Marina. Of course she'd be competing – she was the perfect example of an outdoorsy type, the sort of woman who swam across Hebridean whirlpools cavorting with seals, and sprinted up mountains to blow away the cobwebs.

I thought of my last 'run' with Alice. We'd managed a kilometre and a half at the pace of a motorised Zimmer frame, then given up and gone for coffee and croissants to celebrate our newfound fitness.

Marina was jogging on the spot to warm up, and as I watched her long, shapely legs move in perfect rhythm, I saw Logan walking up to take the place next to her. He was wearing a white T-shirt and black shorts. Annoyingly, the cartoon Nessie logo was invisible under the hem of his top.

Considering he'd spent most of the previous night rolling around with me in a freezing hut, he looked incredibly energetic; muscular thighs tensed and ready, broad shoulders straight and his unruly hair pushed back from his forehead, giving him the look of a noble 1930s sportsman.

I didn't want to be hopelessly physically attracted to Logan. I didn't want to feel a sick swoop of envy watching Marina leaning across to speak to him, or a lurch of desire as he laughed. I wished I was back in the cosy castle kitchen, cuddling Dougie while Agatha raged about men. Better still, back in London – but I couldn't give up and head home, because until I made a success of the castle, I had no job, and very little chance of getting one.

I'd painted myself into a corner in a moment of weakness – and now I'd simply have to live with the consequences.

'One more place to fill!' boomed the tannoy. 'Don't be shy, ladies and gents, we're almost there – we need ten competitors to fire the starting pistol!'

'Why can't they do it with nine?' I asked Ishbel.

'Ah,' she said, 'Ewan's hot-dog van sponsors the prize, and unless there's at least ten runners, he won't provide six months' free hot dogs on request.'

'How do the winners claim their prize?' I was genuinely curious.

'Well, he only opens his stall up for events. The rest of the time, I suppose it'd be in his wee kitchen, down in the village.'

'So... the winner would just go round and demand a hot dog when they fancied one?'

'I imagine that's what likely happens. Ewan prefers to have

his television on at all times, so you'd be eating your free hot dogs watching repeats of *Take the High Road.*'

I nodded, looking at the competitors earnestly limbering up. 'No wonder they're taking it so seriously.'

As I spoke, the tannoy came to life again. It suddenly occurred to me why the announcer's voice was so familiar – it was the presenter from Radio Iolair, who woke me every morning.

'Get ready, ladies and gents, we have a late entry! He and his lovely wife have recently returned home to Iolair, so put your hands together for our local chandler, the man of note with the mended boats, *Jack Campbell*!'

There was a thin scattering of applause as Jack, now wearing rather skimpy white shorts and a rugby top, waved confidently at the crowd.

I looked over at Logan, who was eyeing Jack with contempt. Marina was staring at her husband, too, her perfect brow slightly creased.

'On your marks...' the announcer shouted.

Seconds later, a small child in a kilt let off a party popper, coloured streamers flew through the air and landed on somebody's straw hat, and the race began.

'Come on, Logan!' screamed Ishbel.

Logan set off in the lead with a long, loping stride, just ahead of Marina and a wiry bald man who was furiously pumping his arms.

'That's Muir Strachan, the PE teacher I told you about,' said Ishbel. 'He'll be absolutely enraged if he doesn't win.'

The hill was dotted with clumps of reeds and tussocks of grass, still wet from last night's torrential rain. A couple of the runners slithered on mud as they began the ascent, and I hoped nobody would break an ankle in their desperate attempt to win the chance of compressed tinned meat and telly.

As the crowd bellowed encouragement, a cloud slid over the

sun, and the hill was cast into shadow. The runners were now well on their way, and Marina had pulled level with Logan. *Well matched in every way*, I thought. Why on earth had she run off with Jack Campbell? He seemed to have very few appealing characteristics, based on his strutting bantam display earlier. Was there something Logan hadn't told me?

I wanted Logan to win, purely so I could enjoy the idea of him eating tepid hot dogs on Ewan's sofa, but as a light rain began to fall and people groaned and raised colourful umbrellas, I looked up and saw that Jack was now overtaking him as the runners headed to the rocky crest of the hill. He was sprinting almost diagonally, as if he was trying to get closer to his wife – or to Logan. The three of them disappeared over the top, as the rest straggled towards the summit.

Just as I was wondering if there'd be time for me to nip and get another Pimm's before they all returned, there was a distant, panicked shout.

'Man down!'

Concern rippled through the crowd, and the front runners put on a burst of speed to see what had happened, while those at the rear looked uncertainly towards the showground, clearly wondering whether to come back.

Muir the PE teacher reappeared over the hill, waving his arms. 'Paramedics!' he shouted. 'We need help!'

Fear shot through me. Was it Logan? Had the further exertion after last night caused his heart to fail? Had he fallen from a concealed cliff?

I clutched Ishbel's arm. 'What can have happened?'

Her eyes were fixed on the hill, where now, the other runners were trailing back down, the race abandoned.

'I don't know, but dear God, I hope it's not— och, there's Jack!'

He was jogging back over the brow, shouting, 'We need a

stretcher!' and to my horror, seconds later, Marina appeared behind him, waving her arms.

My heart galloped with anxiety. Logan was invincible – I had put all my trust in him last night, knowing he wouldn't allow me to be harmed. He radiated competence and physical ease. It couldn't be him who was hurt; it must be someone else... I closed my eyes.

'There's no team of paramedics here,' said Ishbel, in horror. 'We'll have to call an ambulance from Oban – it'll be a half hour at least.'

Even as I extracted my phone from my pocket to dial 999, part of me was thinking, *What kind of idiot organises an event of this size without public liability insurance and a team of trained medics on stand-by?* The rest of me was experiencing chills of genuine terror at the idea that Logan was badly hurt.

By the time I was off the phone, a man in a green boiler suit clutching a first aid bag was haring up the hill.

'That's Pete,' said Donald. 'He's the local scoutmaster; he's done a first aid course.'

'But there's no stretcher?'

'I'll go and get the picnic blankets,' said Donald. 'Just in case.'

'You can't carry a casualty in a picnic blank—' Ishbel began, but he was already pushing through the crowd, Hannay at his heels. Sir Alastair was helplessly clutching the rope that separated us from the starting line. Ishbel put her hand over his, and as I followed their gaze, I saw two small, racing dots travelling at speed up the hill, the sound of barking drifting back to us on the breeze.

'Arran! Alba!' I shouted. There was no sign they'd heard me. There was nothing else for it – I ducked under the rope, and set off up the hill in pursuit, as fast as I could manage in my hopeless rainbow wellies.

It was higher than it looked, and Arran and Alba had skittered over the rocky hilltop long before I'd panted my way up. It was raining properly again now, and I almost fell several times as I scrambled towards the summit. I could hear the dogs barking much more clearly as I clambered the last few feet, and finally looked down to the ridge just below me.

Logan lay still, his eyes closed, his face white and streaked with rain. I stood paralysed with horror – how could this be the Logan who had held me above him with such strength and grace, who had pushed back my hair so he could kiss my burning neck?

Pete was bending over him, murmuring, 'Logan, come on, pal, can you hear me?' The dogs stood by their master, barking and keening an eerie lament, like canine bagpipes. Jack was standing nearby, watching – but not Marina.

Marina was kneeling in the mud by Logan's prone body, tears mingling with the rain on her pale cheeks, her white-knuckled hand gripping his – and she was sobbing.

22

For a moment, fear stopped my voice in my throat. 'Is he...?' I managed.

Pete looked up. 'Aye, he's alive, right enough. Slipped in the mud and smashed his head on a rock. He's out cold, though – we need that ambulance.'

'They said they'd come as fast as they can,' I said, hurrying to cuddle Logan's dogs in an attempt to quiet them. Arran slumped against me, quivering, but Alba maintained a steady, alarmed yapping.

'What happened?' I asked Marina, as Jack jogged back up to the summit, perhaps to scan for an arriving ambulance – or to get away from his wife, given the look of contempt she was directing at him.

She took a shuddering breath and wiped a muddy arm across her eyes.

'Jack,' she said, 'he was trying to get across to run with me, and they collided, hard. Logan slipped on a patch of mud, and I saw him smack his head as he went down.' Another sob escaped her. 'And it's all my fault because I only entered the race so I could talk to Logan properly! I didn't know Jack was going to join at the last minute and trip him up!' She glared at her husband's damp back. Jack didn't appear to have a scratch on him.

'I'm sure it wasn't your fault,' I said inadequately, ruffling Arran's damp ears. But it was almost certainly Jack's, I thought – and perhaps it had been deliberate.

'Come on, Logan, mate,' urged Pete again, a note of panic entering his voice. He looked up. 'He needs airlifted off this hillside. If he's got a brain injury...'

Marina's crying intensified, and I felt a tilting sensation at the horror of Logan's accident. It was impossible to think that so recently, I'd fallen asleep in his arms, my entire body aware of him, his scent, his warm skin against mine. I was glad of the rain as hot tears spilled down my cheeks. Pete took Logan's pulse and checked his airways again, and the wail of a siren cut through the noise of the crowd below.

Minutes later, three burly paramedics were jogging up the hillside with a stretcher and enormous bags of medical supplies on their backs. I felt an overwhelming sense of relief that Logan would soon be in safe hands. *But brain damage*, whispered an insidious voice in my head. *Spinal paralysis... tetraplegia...*

Pete explained to them what had happened, as Marina continued to clutch Logan's hand and weep, and I tried to keep the spaniels from climbing onto his prone body to investigate further, though Alba ignored my instructions.

As one of the medics crouched to examine Logan, his eyes blinked open.

'Hello, mate,' said the bearded paramedic. 'How are you doing? You had a fall.'

Logan's gaze moved slowly around the gathered onlookers. His face was still a deathly shade of mushroom, but he was awake.

'Hello,' he said quietly. 'I fell. I did not "have a fall". I'm not eighty-five years old.'

'Logan!' Marina cried. 'Thank God!'

I wanted to cry with relief, too, but felt it wouldn't be good for his ego to witness more than one woman sobbing with joy at his recovery.

'Why are the dogs here?' Logan murmured, reaching a hand to Alba's quivering nose.

'They ran up to find you,' I said, and he finally focused on me. 'They really do adore you,' I added, but the paramedic spoke over me – 'Can you lift your arm for me, Logan, mate?' – and all that was audible was 'adore you'. He shot me a quizzical look and returned his attention to the professionals.

After checking him thoroughly, they agreed that Logan's knee was sprained, not broken, and that his head injury needed checking at the cottage hospital.

'Oh, come on,' I heard him muttering. 'I'm fine. I can count backwards from a hundred, I can tell you who the Prime Minister is, I can say, "Excuse me, where is the duke's piano recital?" in French...'

'Can you?' I asked. 'Why on earth, of all the phrases?'

'Very old-fashioned textbooks at Glenfinnachan,' he said, and smiled for the first time since he'd come round.

The men and Pete gently rolled him onto the stretcher – 'I'm fine – I can walk!' – and set off on a careful trek downhill to the waiting ambulance, with Marina in hot pursuit.

'Marina!' Jack shouted. '*Marina!*'

She spun round. 'This is *your* fault, you jealous prick!'

Jack pantomimed astonishment. 'Why's it *my* fault?'

'Because I saw you knock into him!' she yelled. 'You could have killed him!'

'It was an accident...' began Jack, but Marina, now soaked through, with her blazing red hair escaping and trailing round her pale face in ringlets, pointed at him like a vengeful ghost.

'I saw you.'

She turned away, following the odd little procession down

the hillside, and I walked after them with Arran and Alba dashing ahead, leaving Jack standing on the summit, still loudly protesting his innocence.

Back at the starting line, all was chaos. As well as the competitors whose run had been truncated and their outraged supporters, half the showground was milling about, gossiping and spreading rumours – 'Three people've died up there,' I heard a teenage boy confidently tell his girlfriend, who gasped in horror.

Sir Alastair was marching to and fro with Hannay, barking, 'Why will nobody inform me of my son's condition?' as Donald stood by, anxiously clutching his pile of picnic blankets.

I hurriedly gave the good news to Sir Alastair, who loomed anxiously at my shoulder. 'Oh, thank heavens,' he said, pressing a hand to his tweed-clad chest. 'I've been imagining the worst. One hears such dreadful stories of athletes suddenly conking out...'

'No, I'm afraid Jack cannoned into him trying to reach Marina,' I said. 'Though according to her, it was deliberate.'

'Wouldn't surprise me.' Sir Alastair looked thunderous. 'That cocky little barrow boy would crush his own grandmother into the mud if he thought it'd improve his prospects.'

'Well, Marina didn't seem very happy with him.'

Sir Alastair shook his head. 'No, indeed,' he muttered. 'Marry in haste, repent at leisure.'

Was that what Marina had done? But why in haste, I wondered, if she'd left Logan almost at the altar? She could have dated Jack – there was no need to rush down the aisle.

Once again, I wondered if there was something Logan hadn't told me.

23

Ishbel and Donald took charge of the three dogs, and Sir Alastair and I made our way back to the Land Rover and set off for the hospital – Logan's father needed support, I reasoned, and if I was being brutally honest with myself, perhaps the thought of Logan lying in pain while Marina tended to his every need was too much.

'I do hope he's all right,' fretted Sir Alastair, as we juddered over potholes. 'Head injuries can be such a danger.'

'He seemed in good spirits,' I said, then wondered why people only ever said 'in good spirits' when someone was unwell. If true, it was also a very unfamiliar state for Logan to enter, and I should probably warn his doctors.

I looked out of the window as we passed grazing Highland cattle, their calves trundling behind them like benign floor mops, and glimpsed the grey, rain-swept loch through the trees lining the single-track road. I was beginning to feel so at home here in this ancient, peaceful valley, although it was increasingly difficult to separate my feelings for the landscape with my feelings for the far less peaceful heir of Iolair.

'Cat, I do hope this isn't intrusive,' Sir Alastair said, after a period of silence.

I froze – surely he didn't suspect anything about last night?

'I just wanted to ask,' he went on, his eyes fixed on the wet road ahead, 'whether you're enjoying your time here? I'm concerned that we've very much thrown you in at the deep end, and while, clearly, you're doing wonders with your plans and costings, is it all a bit much? I know Logan isn't the most amenable chap when it comes to challenging the status quo...'

'Oh, no, you mustn't worry!' I said, relieved. 'I love it here, and Logan's... well, it's fine. It's not surprising he's annoyed with me – I mean, you know, a bit worried...'

Sir Alastair laughed. 'I am under no illusions about my beloved eldest son,' he said. 'He doesn't want anything about the castle to change, and frankly, nor do I. But as I've told him, sadly, we have no choice.'

'I don't know that I'm much use,' I began.

Sir Alastair shook his head. 'You have an outsider's perspective. None of us can see things as they truly are – we're too bogged down in our love for Iolair, nostalgia, a yearning for the good old days. We need you to wake us up a bit, show us what can be done and help us move forward into a new era.'

I suddenly felt as though I was at an inspirational TED talk.

'Well, I'll do my best, but I'm not sure I have that much power,' I ventured.

He huffed a small laugh, narrowly avoiding a red squirrel that darted across the road ahead.

'Cat, you have far more power than you assume,' he said. 'Particularly when it comes to Logan.'

I felt numb with shock. Surely Sir Alastair hadn't guessed...? I longed to ask, 'In what way?' but now we were heading into the hospital drive, approaching a long, modern building where an ambulance was parked beside a glass door marked 'Accident and Emergency'.

'Ah yes, Logan McAskill,' said the receptionist, once we were inside. 'He's been taken up to the wards; I believe he's in Thistle.'

'Thistle?' I asked, as we made our way to the lifts.

'There's only three wards,' said Sir Alastair. 'Thistle, Gorse and Bramble.'

'They named all the wards after spiky Scottish plants?'

'You haven't met the nurses,' he said with a small smile, as the doors closed.

Upstairs, signs directed us to a small, yellow-painted ward with six beds. In one, an old man was fast asleep, snoring like a honking goose. In the only other occupied bed, Logan was lying propped up on three pillows wearing a blue-and-white hospital gown, looking slightly less pale than the last time I'd seen him and still extremely handsome. There was no sign of Marina, and I felt a wave of relief.

'Hello, son,' said Sir Alastair. 'Nasty business.'

Logan gave him a faint smile. 'Thanks for coming. Jack Campbell is a nasty business all on his own.'

A nurse came in. 'Visiting Mr McAskill?' she asked, unsmiling. 'I'd ask you to keep it brief – Doctor's just checking the CT results for contusions. Internal haemorrhaging after a head injury can often be fatal.'

'I'm fine,' said Logan. 'Well, a headache like I've been trampled by Jock's herd, but otherwise I'm fairly sure I'm okay.'

The goose-snorer gave a startled yelp and subsided into a worrying silence.

'He does that a lot,' said Logan. 'I thought he'd died at first, but it seems to be just another dream stage. He'll emit a sort of eerie wail in a minute, then the snoring resumes.'

I laughed. 'I'm so relieved you're okay,' I said. 'You were deathly pale up there.'

'What exactly happened?' Logan asked me. 'I know you

were there when I woke up, and I've a vague feeling that Alba was standing on me, but that can't be right.'

'No, he really was.' I explained what had happened, Muir Strachan's yell, how Marina had been sobbing over Logan's prone form. I tried to sound sympathetic to her as I recounted it, though I longed to sit on the bed, take his hand, check he really was all right. Was that Marina's job again now?

'Marina?' Logan looked puzzled. 'Last thing I remember, she was talking to me when I was trying to save my breath for running, then I saw Jack thundering up on my right, and it was lights out.'

'So she didn't come to the hospital with you?'

He began to shake his head. 'Ow! No, it was just the cheery paramedics asking me about days of the week and politicians.'

Sir Alastair patted the blanket over Logan's feet. 'As soon as we get the results, we'll spring you out of here,' he said. 'I'm sure there's nothing wrong with you that the dogs and Agatha's lentil soup can't fix.'

Logan looked at me. 'He'd say that after a nuclear bomb.'

'And I'd probably be right.'

'Actually, Dad...' Logan looked up at him. I suddenly imagined him as a little boy, leaning back on his pillows asking for another bedtime story. 'Do you think you could get me a cup of tea from the machine?'

'What if you need an operation?' I asked, but Logan ignored me.

'It's just in the foyer,' he told Sir Alastair. 'This water she's brought me tastes like iron filings.'

'Of course!' Sir Alastair seemed thrilled to have a job to do.

Once he'd left, Logan pointed at the chair next to his bed. 'Come and sit down.'

Surprised, I did as he asked. Close to his side, I could still smell the grassy mud on his skin, mingled with that faint echo of smoky sandalwood.

'Look,' he said, 'I just wanted to say that I'm sorry for how I was before – when I saw you and Mel,' he clarified.

'When you were with Marina?'

He nodded. 'Ow. Mustn't move head, note to self. Yes – I mean, it's no excuse, but... things are a bit...' He trailed off.

'Look,' he tried again, 'last night was... unexpected and lovely...'

I looked away. I knew what was coming – *but it was a one-off*... and it was exactly what I'd have said, too, if he'd asked me. So I wasn't sure why I felt I was about to be miserably dumped, when I was fully aware of all the reasons Logan and I could never work.

'It's all right,' I said, before he had to say it out loud. I still had some pride. 'It was just one night out of time, and nobody but us will ever know. Let's just keep it that way, and we can be friends, or whatever we are.'

His face was still pale, and pain flashed through his eyes as he turned his head towards me. 'I hope we're friends, at least,' he said quietly, and closed his eyes.

I was about to reply when Sir Alastair returned, holding a flimsy plastic beaker of tea by its rim.

'Infernal machine,' he said. 'Chuntering and spitting away at me, and for some reason, this so-called tea smells of cocoa. Why one can't simply ask a nurse to make a proper pot...'

'I think they've better things to do, Dad,' said Logan, as the nurse came back in.

The man in the opposite bed had indeed resumed his shuddering poultry noises, and she twitched his blanket up irritably, before crossing to us.

'The doctor needs to discharge you,' she said. 'The CT results aren't showing any cranial damage or obvious bleeds on the brain. As far as we can tell, at this stage of recovery,' she added ominously.

I caught Logan's eye and almost laughed.

'So I can go home?'

'As soon as Doctor has been.'

'And that will be...'

'When she's free. This is a very busy working hospital, Mr McAskill.'

'Actually, it's Himself, not mister,' I said.

'I'm sorry?' She turned to me irritably.

'This is the incumbent Laird of Iolair,' I said, indicating Sir Alastair's back view, in his heathery tweeds and kilt. He was now gazing down at the car park, clearly eager to be gone. 'This is his eldest son, Himself of Iolair. I'm his sister, Herself of Iolair, and we'd very much appreciate it if you could use the correct forms of address from now on.'

She drew herself up. 'Apologies,' she said stonily. 'I shall make sure to inform Doctor.'

After she'd stalked from the ward, Logan let out a bark of suppressed laughter. 'What was that absolute nonsense?'

I smiled. 'She was annoying me. Brain bleed this, busy hospital that. I've been to dolls' hospitals with more drama.'

'I really must remember not to get on the wrong side of you,' he said. 'I have no idea what you'll say or do.'

I raised an eyebrow with a smile. 'Best if you never find out.'

Fifteen minutes later, when Sir Alastair was wondering aloud whether we should wake up the snorer – 'Can't be good for the chap, creating that sort of racket' – Dr Lizzie Gillespie finally arrived. She was in her thirties, with a friendly face and her cardigan on inside out.

'So sorry,' she said. 'There's a child with a nasty tummy ache – the parents were convinced she's at death's door. Turns out she ate seventeen mini rolls when they weren't looking. Anyway, which of you is Himself?'

Logan shot me a look. 'Just "Logan" is fine,' he said.

After a brief consultation, Dr Gillespie signed him out, offered him a crutch for the knee sprain – 'I'll manage,' said

Logan firmly – and we were back in the car park, arranging Himself in the front of the Land Rover while I sat in the back.

Every time we bumped over a pothole, he winced, and by the time the car crunched to a halt on the gravel by the main steps, Logan was quite white again.

'Come on, son,' said Sir Alastair, proffering his arm. 'Let's get you up to bed. Can you manage the steps?'

Logan surveyed the three wide stone stairs as if he was at the base of Rome's Spanish steps.

'Here,' I said. 'Lean on me, too.'

He reluctantly placed a hand on my arm. I was aware of the warmth of his fingers through my sleeve – it still hadn't been twenty-four hours since we'd spent the night together, and I felt the memory of his touch in every nerve as we slowly progressed towards the castle door.

As we reached the top, it flew open. First came the dogs, leaping at Logan in wild excitement, then Agatha appeared, apron askew, looking more excited than I'd ever seen her.

'Logan! You're alive, you daft wee scone!' She glanced behind her. 'You'll never guess who's here to see you.'

'Who?' Logan asked warily.

A man appeared behind her in the entrance hall. Light shone on his blonde hair, and his expression was sheepish. As we stood on the step, he raised a hand in greeting.

'See,' Rory said, stepping forward. 'I told you I'd be back.'

24

The last time I'd seen him, Rory had been just sixteen, slim as a whip with floppy, boy-band fair hair and a tendency to hide behind his fringe. Now, he was huge.

Years of punishing Manhattan gym workouts had given him shoulders like hams and thighs that could crack nuts. His nose had been broken at some point, I realised, and his youthful tan had faded into the pallor of a demanding office job. He was still very handsome, his blue eyes retained the feline slant echoed in Logan's dark ones – but now his hair was pushed back from his forehead and I could see the deep V between his eyebrows. He smiled at me, showing perfect Upper East Side dentistry.

'Thought I'd surprise you all,' said Rory cheerfully. 'But my flight from JFK was delayed, so I missed the Highland Games. I was going to go in for the caber toss, and give you all a horrible shock.'

'You see!' said Agatha triumphantly. 'I emailed and here he is! He'll help us save the castle now, won't you, laddie?' She squeezed his shoulder, and threw her other arm open in a flourishing gesture, as if she'd just led a prize cow into the ring.

'Well, this is marvellous!' said Sir Alastair. He looked more thrilled than I'd ever seen him. 'Come and have a drink, Rory, and tell us all about life in New York!'

Rory hugged Logan. 'Great to see you, bro! How's the Ministry of Homegrown Tomatoes? And what the hell have you done to yourself?'

Logan mumbled something about the hill race. I noticed he didn't mention Jack or Marina.

'Hello, Rory!' I said, smiling. 'It's been a while.'

He shook his head. 'Must be... what, fifteen years? More? Last time we met, you were eighty per cent hair and twenty per cent attitude.'

I laughed. 'Happy days.'

'Shame you never came back after that one time—' Rory began, and I saw Logan shoot him a warning look.

'Anyway. Great that you're here,' Rory added quickly. 'I'm going for a shower, then I hope we'll all catch up properly over dinner.'

'Ah.' Sir Alastair looked regretful. 'I'm afraid the shower in your room is more of a rusty trickle. I've been meaning to get it looked at...'

'Use mine,' said Logan. 'I'm not lying down, now my brother's made his prodigal return. I'll take the dogs for a hobble round the lawn.'

'You will not!' said Agatha hotly. 'You've a head injury, and you need stayed put!'

'I'm afraid Ag's right, old boy,' said Sir Alastair. He looked at me. 'Cat, could you give the dogs a quick go round the grounds? It's nearly their teatime, so not for too long.'

Logan looked mutinous. 'Be careful, Cat,' he said. 'Arran won't come back unless you...'

'Oh, Logan. Still the Great Worrier,' said Rory, slapping him on the back and making him wince again. 'If she can cope with you, I'm sure Cat can handle a couple of small spaniels.'

He herded Logan towards the stairs – 'Here, lean on me, we

could do with an elevator here...' – and I followed Agatha down the corridor to the kitchen door, Arran and Alba trotting after us.

'A welcome feast!' murmured Agatha to herself. 'Venison from the cold store, potatoes, cream...' She hurried off to the outbuildings, and I took the chance to slip out to the lawns, before I was forced to help her lug a dead deer back inside.

The dogs pranced ahead, and I breathed in fully, for what felt like the first time in that long and peculiar day. The rain had stopped and a late afternoon sun was glittering on the green-house roofs and transforming the stretch of loch I could see to flickering shades of sapphire. The lawn was glowing an almost unearthly green, the rhododendrons freshly rinsed, pom-poms of red and pink flowers releasing their scent across the long gardens, as a thrush fluted carelessly from a branch. It was ridiculous, I thought, that anywhere so perfect could exist.

I heard my dad's voice in my head – *It's easy to buy perfection if you've got money...* – but for once, I disagreed with him. Castle Iolair was a relic from Scotland's long and bloody history, and it was pure luck for the McAskills that they were still clinging on. Soon, if we didn't manage to save it, the whole place would be sold off and turned into boxy apartments or a luxury hotel. Perhaps that wouldn't be such a terrible solution – the McTavishes off to Dumfries, Sir Alastair making the best of a cosy flat full of battered hardbacks and taxidermy... But I thought of Logan, and of how much Iolair meant to him – to all of them. I would do my utmost to save the castle, and perhaps now Rory was here, we could look properly at the finances.

Strolling along, lost in my thoughts, I reached the walled orchard and stopped to admire the frothing white blossom, backlit by the sun. It was only when Alba gave a sudden bark that I glanced round and realised there was just one dog behind me.

'Where's Arran?' I asked him, scanning the lawn beyond the gate. Alba barked again, more urgently.

I hurried from the orchard, calling for the missing spaniel – but remembered, too late, that Logan hadn't finished his sentence.

'Arran won't come back unless you...' What? Emit a war cry? Sing a Gaelic ballad?

I broke into a run, Alba at my heels, as I called wildly into the shrubberies that edged the lawns. Perhaps he'd gone back to the kitchen door? I was about to retrace my footsteps and check, when I glanced over to the loch and froze. A small shape was splashing out into the deeper water, determinedly swimming after a duck. As I gazed in horror, the bird took off and skimmed away towards the island, leaving Arran adrift and uncertain.

'Arran!' I bellowed, as Alba increased his wild barking. 'Come back!'

I sprinted past the trees, and down the little path to the pebbly shoreline by the jetty. Arran was now dog-paddling wildly on the spot, using up energy and warmth as he splashed, but showed no sign of having heard me. The loch water was like ice, and he was only a little dog... I thought of Logan's face if I returned without him.

Without stopping to think, I pulled off my boots and jeans and waded in, still yelling, as Alba anxiously danced up and down on the shore.

The water gripped my bare legs like iron bands. The sensation was such agony it could have been white heat engulfing me. Trying to breathe steadily, already trembling with cold, I launched myself towards Arran in a ragged front crawl. Freezing loch water washed into my face, and I gasped in shock, but kept my eyes on the sleek little head and flailing paws ahead of me. I had no idea how much time had passed when I finally reached him, but I grabbed his thrashing body before he could swim further away in panic.

Now, I was frozen, exhausted and one arm down as I clamped him to my side, desperately trying to keep his small head above the roiling water.

What a bloody weekend, I thought, as I turned to swim back to shore. The sun had been obscured once again by iron-grey clouds, and a bitter wind was now skimming the loch surface as I swam against rising waves that slapped black, ice-cold water against us.

I could hear Alba's distant barking from the beach, but my entire head was numb, and I could no longer feel the arm holding Arran. I swam on, yet the shore seemed to be getting no closer. If anything, it seemed further away – my world was swiftly reduced to the unforgiving, rolling water and the piercing cold. I had been terrified that Arran might not make it back. Now, I was becoming afraid that I wouldn't, either.

I swam on, but my energy was draining away. I was working on pure adrenaline, and I could no longer see the shore. The waves were higher now, breaking over and around us, and I battled rising panic, unsure whether I was swimming back or further out into the loch. I had to save Arran, no matter what. I risked a glance. He was still with me, but his eyes were drooping with exhaustion, and he'd stopped wriggling.

I was beginning to hallucinate. For a moment, the rocking of the water convinced me I was in a sunlit train carriage, my head leaning against the warm seat as we sped onwards, and now I knew we were genuinely in trouble. Why had I been so stupid as to run into a freezing body of water, instead of phoning the castle to ask for help? Why was I so horrified by the idea of letting Logan down that I'd sooner risk mine and Arran's lives than let him know I'd lost sight of his beloved dog? *This is such an idiotic way to die, Cat.*

Oliver's blandly handsome face passed through my mind, but it didn't give me any comfort. Instead, I thought of Logan –

his austere, perfect cheekbones, his kindness, how he'd held me so tightly all night in the bothy, how he loved his family and his dogs, and sang to them.

It was almost as if I could hear his voice, I thought vaguely, as the churning water carried me onwards.

25

'Cat! Stay where you are!'

The words seemed rather specific for my frozen brain to have come up with.

'Cat! *Stop swimming!*'

For a moment, the waves dropped, and I turned my head towards the sound. The shore was a long way off, but in that second, I saw a brief, diagonal image of Logan, Alba, a blue rowing boat... but Logan was in bed; he'd been hurt...

'*Cat!*'

The shout sounded nearer, but my ears were filling with water as I struggled to keep Arran aloft, and I was losing strength – soon, I'd go under. I could only see the mass of dark clouds overhead and feel the relentless roll and push of the water.

'Give him to me!'

I refocused and saw a pair of hands reaching out, a blue jumper cuff. I used the last of my strength to thrust the dog towards rescue. As soon as the weight of him had gone, I felt myself begin to sink. The water filled my eyes and nose and drew me into its darkness, and I no longer knew which way was up or down.

And then a hand closed around my wrist and pulled so hard I gasped as my head broke the surface. Powerful arms lifted me, though I couldn't move my own limbs to help, or ease the struggle to drag me into the boat. I was a dead weight, so cold the air felt like knives on my skin.

'Bloody hell!' Logan kept saying, as he wrapped me in his jacket and rubbed my blue limbs violently. 'Bloody hell, Cat, you could have died.'

I couldn't speak, but I was distantly aware of splashing oars. The dog had stopped barking, and gradually I realised that something warm and dry was lying beside me – Alba. Logan had brought him out on the boat with him.

'Is Arran...?' I tried to say, but it emerged, 'Id Allan...?' through my knocking teeth.

'Arran will be fine,' said Logan. 'You saved his life.'

'Wa... my... faul...' But that was all I could manage.

Already, we were back in the shallows, that grey, pebbly shore the most welcome sight of my life. Logan climbed from the boat and towed it onto the beach, limping as he did so. He picked me up, his hands supporting my legs, my arms around his neck. I was now shivering in wild spasms. 'The dogs...' I began, but as I spoke, I saw a tall figure sprinting from the house, waving his arms.

'Rory! Take Arran,' shouted Logan. 'Get him into a warm bath. Quick as you can.'

Without speaking, Rory scooped up the soaking-wet spaniel and ran back up the lawn, followed by Alba.

'I can walk,' I said. 'Your knee... your head...'

'Shush.'

Logan was clearly in pain, but I couldn't walk, and we both knew it. I could barely think. He stumbled up the lawn, my head against his shoulder, and we burst through the kitchen door.

'Sit,' panted Logan. 'I'll get Agatha. She has first aid training.'

'Dear God!' she said when she saw me. 'You might have drowned! I gave you a wetsuit, but I didnae expect you to swim across the bloody loch!'

'No, no... it was... it wa...' My teeth were still clamped together, and I couldn't stop quivering. My hands were pink claws. I reminded myself of a lobster, and suddenly laughed hysterically.

Agatha looked sternly at me. 'Are you seeing things that dinnae exist?'

I thought of the rocking train carriage. 'Not now,' I said soberly.

'Top off,' she instructed.

Logan, lurking in the kitchen doorway, cleared his throat. 'I'll head up to check on the dog.'

I almost said, 'It's nothing you haven't seen before,' but instead I managed, 'Thank you for rescuing me.'

'Well, I could hardly leave you out there,' he said. 'Or Arran, more importantly,' he added, as he closed the door behind himself.

Agatha wrapped me in a large hairy blanket, which I belatedly recognised as Dougie's. She spread another over my knees, and placed the puppy on my lap, who turned round three times then settled down. 'Hold on to that puppy,' she said. 'He'll warm you up a wee bit. And when you can speak, you can tell me why you attempted to drown yourself in the depths of Loch Iolair.'

'I didn't mean to...' I was shaken by another spasm of shivering. 'I was tr... trying... to... I lost A... Arran,' I said. 'He swam...'

'He chased a duck, aye?'

She rolled her eyes, pressing a cup of tea laden with sugar

into my hand and helping me to close my stiff fingers around the handle. 'Lassie,' she sighed. 'Wee Arran loves ducks more than anything. You must *never* shout and run because then he swims farther away.'

'What should I have done?'

'Whistled. Always take the whistle. The dogs are trained to return when they hear it.'

I closed my eyes. 'What bloody whistle?' I whispered.

'It hangs on the back door. Logan didnae tell you?'

'I think he was about to...'

I leaned my head back, holding Dougie, who was warm as a freshly baked loaf. He tentatively licked my wrist before settling down to chew the ends of my wet hair, and I thought about how close I'd come to the end. If Logan hadn't seen me from his bedroom window, and run down, despite his injuries... a deep shudder ran through me. He had saved my life – and I'd never be able to thank him enough.

It took over an hour to get the feeling back into my limbs, and as I sat in the warm kitchen with Agatha bustling around me, making dinner with a Niagara of double cream, I felt a growing sadness.

I was starting to love life here at Iolair. Despite everything – the complications of my night with Logan, the worries about the castle's future – hell, the fact that I'd just nearly died in a freezing loch – somehow, all the frantic concerns of my London life seemed to be hovering somewhere far away.

It seemed surreal that just a couple of weeks ago, I'd been hopelessly in love with Oliver, ordering matching aqua-blue napkins and camellias for a high society wedding, meeting butterfly suppliers to ensure there were no animal rights issues when they were released at the Nova Perez album launch, brainstorming whether we could really serve canapés via remote-controlled drones at a secret AI software reveal in The Shard.

I almost laughed, thinking of the frustrating hours junior executive Mandeep and I had spent weighing balls of panko-crumbed rare goats cheese to ensure they were of uniform size. My job was ludicrous. My London life – apart from Alice – was ludicrous. And when a fairy-tale castle in the middle of nowhere felt more real and important than my actual career and love life, maybe it was time to make a change.

When I could speak, move my fingers and stand up, Agatha sent me for a bath. As I made my way to my room, I could hear the rumble of Logan and Rory's voices further down the corridor. It seemed to be an intense discussion.

'Can't expect to simply...' I heard Logan say, and then Rory – 'It's not as if we haven't...'

I paused, eavesdropping, though I knew I shouldn't. Straining to make the words out through the thick oak door, I heard Logan say, 'If only my wedding hadn't...' and then he evidently walked away because his words became an indistinguishable mumble.

It shouldn't matter. Of course he had been devastated, his fiancée had dumped him in the most humiliating way possible to run off with Jack bloody Campbell. It would be strange if Logan didn't still feel distraught, particularly after what had happened earlier.

And yet, our shared night was still so recent and had been so passionate – or at least, I had felt that way. It was hard to separate my emotions from my treacherously yearning body, and while my head knew there was no future with Logan – that he was, in fact, arrogant, bull-headed, bitterly resistant to change and hopeless at discussing anything that wasn't ecology, dog or compost related, as well as not interested in a relationship with me – my nerve endings were singing a different tune, as I headed for my hot bath.

It was just a physical chemistry thing, I told myself. *Because of what happened when you were sixteen, and his gardening muscles – and now you've had your chance, and you've had your fun. Sort out the castle, go home, and think about the rest of your life and what to do with it.*

I went to the large, clanking bathroom beside my room, locked the door with its stiff, tarnished brass key and ran a deep bath with water as hot as I could bear. Then I climbed in and let the entire past twenty-four hours steam away, thinking only about the sound of the birds outside, and the steady drip of the leaking pipe.

26

Dinner was a gathering of the walking wounded.

Rory was suffering from jet lag, Logan was limping and wincing at loud noises, and I was dressed in three jumpers, thermal leggings and jeans with thick, hand-knitted Fair Isle socks that Agatha had made me wear. The core of me still felt like liquid nitrogen, but the rest had warmed up thanks to the long bath and a reunion cuddle with Arran, who was now wearing a small red jumper and seemed entirely recovered.

We took our places at the long kitchen table, the dogs slumping on the flagstones beneath, and Sir Alastair gazed around the little group.

'My goodness,' he said, at last. 'What a day it's been.' He raised his glass, the red wine glowing in the light of the tall white candles that Agatha had lit.

'To reunions,' he said, smiling at Rory. 'And recoveries.' He nodded at Logan and me.

'Rory, what's really brought you back so suddenly?' Logan asked, as we began to eat. 'Future's looking alarming? Shares plummeting?'

Rory smiled. 'Agatha sent me a very sensible email, laying the situation out clearly.'

'What *situation?*' Logan's tone was suddenly icy. He drained his wine glass. He shouldn't be drinking after his head injury, but it seemed a bad moment to point that out.

'Well, I assume Agatha means the castle's parlous finances,' said Sir Alastair regretfully.

'If parlous means "very bad", then aye, I do,' said Agatha, with some passion. She set her glass down.

'I grew up with my five brothers and sisters in a wee croft on Orkney, and our auld dad left us when I was just three, to marry Sexy Mhairi from the fisheries. So our mam had a great deal to cope with, and we never had a penny between us. I know folk say happiness is what counts nowadays, but they dinnae *ken*.' Agatha's cheeks were flushed. 'Money *matters* – and it's the only way to save this castle. So I got Rory back to help us.'

'I mean, I can't afford to pitch in...' Rory began nervously. 'I've my rental apartment in Manhattan, and—'

'No, no,' Agatha said impatiently. 'We just want ideas, and that's your job, is it not, laddie?'

'Well, I'll do my best,' Rory said, clearly relieved. 'Maybe we should sit down tomorrow, I'll have a look at the spreadsheets...'

'Spreadsheets?' Hannay lifted his head at his master's alarmed tone, and Sir Alastair absently fed him a breadstick.

'I can't believe you're still feeding that hound from the table,' said Rory. 'If you did that in NYC, the police would probably taser you for health and safety violations.'

'Well, Hannay understands perfectly well that it only happens on special occasions,' said Sir Alastair guiltily, over the noisy crunching from beneath the table.

'And yes, Dad. Spreadsheets. You've got the entire estate; Logan's vegetable business; Agatha, Ishbel and Donald's wages, plus the casual staff; the actual running costs of this place, which must be enormous – surely you've got some kind of system to keep track of it all?'

A silence fell. I glanced at Logan, who looked mutinous, his hand resting on Arran's silken ears – for comfort, I realised. Whenever Logan was sad or angry, he turned to his dogs, never to humans.

'Well,' said Sir Alastair eventually, 'it all just comes out of the trust, so...'

'You've no idea what it all costs, have you?' Rory shook his head in disbelief. 'No wonder we're in trouble.'

'Hang on a minute,' said Logan. 'You're the one who hared off to Manhattan years ago and left us to deal with everything here. It's all right for you to come swanning in with your criticisms, but Dad and I manage just fine, even if it's not with the latest *financial software*.'

'I hardly think a simple *spreadsheet—*' began Rory hotly, but Agatha slammed down the wooden spoon she'd been using to stir the casserole.

'No!' she said, in a voice that would stop traffic on the M1. 'You willnae argue when I cook!'

Logan and Rory glanced at one another.

'Sorry, Ag,' said Logan, and Rory added, 'Apologies.'

'Cat.' Sir Alastair turned to me kindly. 'Are you sure you're all right? You've barely said a word.'

'Sorry – I'm fine, thanks.' I smiled at him.

I could hardly tell him that I found myself unable to tear my eyes away from Logan, no matter what we'd agreed about just being friends.

27

MAY BANK HOLIDAY WEEKEND, FIFTEEN
YEARS EARLIER

The art gallery, a huddle of long, weather-beaten sheds, is quite good, it turns out – Mum's in boho heaven, exclaiming over seascapes and admiring driftwood sculptures of otters. Dad enjoys the coffee and carrot cake afterwards and the sun's out, so the three of us go for a stroll down the beach as gulls wheel and shriek overhead.

'Last day today,' says Mum sadly. 'Feels a bit too soon to be heading home tomorrow.'

'Well, Year Nine won't teach themselves. Or let anyone else attempt to, for that matter,' mutters Dad.

I say nothing, but I'm aware of a rising desperation within me. Last night, when we got back to our B&B, I lay awake until 3 a.m., thinking about Logan – the soft hairs on his forearm above the elegant leather watch strap, the angle of his perfect dark eyebrows, the cool way he half smiled when Rory was being excitable.

The idea of never seeing him again feels like physical pain, an agony I don't know how to cope with. Yet I also know he's almost two years older than me, and he has a beautiful, sophisticated girlfriend. Besides which, he hasn't shown the slightest flicker of interest in me beyond basic politeness.

I was tired and quiet over breakfast, and Mum placed the back of her hand to my forehead and asked, 'Are you coming down with something?'

Unrequited love, I thought.

Now, as we wander back to the car, she says, 'I saw a poster for a jumble sale at Iolair village hall earlier. You like vintage stuff, Catrina – maybe you'll find a bargain.'

'Great,' I say, imagining it'll be a pile of musty kilts and moth-eaten jumpers... but you never know. Besides, a good rummage through old knitwear might distract me briefly from my relentless thoughts of Logan, and the unsettling swooping sensation I experience whenever I imagine kissing him.

Dad puts on Radio Two for the drive back to Iolair village, which, although it cuts out regularly, seems to be dedicated to ruining my life further, with an endless stream of yearning songs about tragic love.

When they drop me off, I'm glad to jump out of the car and make my way down the narrow street to the little white hall with a scout hut symbol over the door.

There's a grey-haired woman in a tartan skirt taking 20p on the door – 'Bag yourself a bargain, dear!' – and I feel briefly uplifted by the thrill of the hunt as I turn into the hall that smells of warm dust and rubber mats, and see rows of tables heaped with clothing, books and bric-a-brac.

Fifteen minutes later, I have a pile of dresses, tops and jeans draped over one arm, two pairs of glittery 1960s dance shoes in the other hand, and I'm in serious need of a large carrier bag so I can put it all down and carry on shopping.

'Shall I take that for ye?' asks another woman, who must be at least eighty-five. She's bent almost double with a face like a walnut, and I immediately feel guilty as I hand over the pile for her to count.

'Jean!' calls another of the volunteers. 'This *Reader's Digest* dictionary set doesn't have a price; can you take a look?'

'Och now, do excuse me a moment,' she says. 'I'll just get someone to help ye...' She creaks off in search of a volunteer, and seconds later, I look up, straight into the mesmerisingly dark eyes of Logan McAskill.

'Cat! Hello there.'

'Why are you... what... You don't seem the jumble-sale type,' I say, simple words suddenly foam blocks in my mouth.

He gives me a puzzled smile. 'What's the *jumble-sale type*?'

'I just mean... you know, the castle and everything...'

'Still our local village, though,' Logan says mildly. 'Dad's always been keen on me and Rory helping out. Anyway, it's fun. Or are you assuming we're living like Little Lord Fauntleroy up there, with butlers bringing us platters of Turkish delight and fanning us with palm fronds?'

I try to imagine Nathan Summers speaking like this and fail. His usual opening gambit is 'all right, losers?'

'Sorry.'

'No need to apologise.'

Logan swiftly flicks through my pile of seventies dresses and fifties beaded cardigans. 'Call it two quid the lot.'

'Really?'

'Unless you'd like to donate even more to the church roof appeal. Get your name on the plaque.'

I smile uncertainly.

'I'm joking. What are you up to after this?'

The world instantly reduces to the invisible pinprick that is the correct answer. I don't know what I need to say to unlock the prize. Might he offer to accompany me somewhere? Is he going to invite me up to the castle? Is he just being polite? I stare at him, like a person trapped behind glass as oxygen is pumped away.

Logan frowns. 'I'm not trying to chat you up or anything,' he says. 'I was just going to say, I'm heading down to the loch a bit later to take the boat out. Thought you might like a trip round the island.'

Oh my God.

'Yeah – yes. That'd be great, thanks. Yeah, cool.' I turn away, my face burning.

Logan calls after me, amused. 'Four o'clock, on the jetty? If your mum and dad are okay with it, of course.'

He might as well have said, 'What with you still being a little kid.'

'No, they'll be fine!' I insist. What they don't know can't hurt them.

I wander blindly out of the hall like someone leaving the scene of an accident. Logan is taking me out in his boat. Just the two of us, on the loch, in the sunshine. I need to run back to the B&B, dump my purchases and commence a two-hour makeover.

And most importantly, I need to hope that somehow, he and Marina will have split up by four o'clock this afternoon.

28

The conversation picked up over Agatha's delicious food, as Rory told us about life in New York. Although I'd travelled abroad a little for work at MOE, I'd never been and I was curious.

'Is it like being on a film set?' I asked. 'All yellow taxis and WALK/DON'T WALK signs?'

'Yeah, pretty much,' agreed Rory. 'When I first arrived, we drove down Fifth Avenue in the cab and I felt like Mr Big in *Sex and the City*.'

'You wish, mate,' said Logan. 'How's your very own version of Carrie?'

Rory put his fork down. 'Ah,' he said. 'I was waiting for a good moment to tell you, but... well, the truth is, Stacey and I are over.'

'Oh, bro.' Logan reached over and patted Rory's shoulder. 'I'm sorry. What happened? I thought it was forever. *To the moon and back*, as she used to write on Instagram. *My rock. My big guy.*'

Rory blinked at his plate. 'Yeah,' he said. 'Me too. Let's just say her friendship with the bloke in the apartment upstairs wasn't as innocent as I'd fondly imagined.'

'Oh dear,' Sir Alastair looked distressed. 'Was she... well...'

'Cheating on me? Yes. For months. I only found out when I came home early on her birthday, at six o'clock, and discovered them. The worst thing was, she didn't even look embarrassed.'

'Did you treat her right?' Agatha asked, pointing a forkful of potatoes at Rory.

'What? Yes! I did everything I could to show her how much I—'

'Aye, you worked like a wee packhorse, and left your woman lonely.'

'No, I didn't!'

She shook her head. 'You think six is *early* for coming home. It isnae, Rory, lad. She's bored, she needs loved, she's getting a wee smidgen of attention from the laddie upstairs – that's how it goes. You snooze, you lose.'

Agatha shrugged and popped the potatoes into her mouth, while Logan shook with laughter and Rory stared at her.

'It's not as simple as that...'

Logan recovered himself. 'I think it's entirely as simple as that, you know. When you love somebody, you put them first. Always.'

'I'm not taking romantic advice from someone who—'

'*Don't.*' Logan's tone carried a serious warning, and Rory subsided.

'So, it's all over? I think that's a great shame, but it will be very good for you to spend some time back home,' said Sir Alastair.

'Well.' Rory pulled a face. 'It may be a bit longer than "some time".'

'How d'you mean?' Logan asked.

'Okay.' Rory drew in a deep breath. 'I may as well tell you.

Now Stacey's dumped me, I've quit my job and given notice on the apartment, too. I've had enough of big city life.'

We gazed at him, like uncomprehending sheep watching the farmer tap-dance.

'What I'm saying is,' said Rory, 'I'm back for good. The prodigal son has returned to Iolair. And I'm absolutely determined to sort this castle out, once and for all.'

There was a cacophony.

Agatha cried, 'Wonderful news!'

Sir Alastair bellowed, 'Good lad! Delighted to hear it!'

And Logan demanded, 'How, exactly, are you intending to do that, Ror?' while all the dogs barked at once in response to the sudden excitement.

I felt happy for the others, and Rory had been kind to me, all those years ago – but I wondered how the dynamics of the castle would change with his arrival, and whether I'd be needed at all, now the New York whizz-kid was back.

How I wished I could have found Rory attractive – he was single, solvent and seemingly stable. All the good S words. He was also perfectly nice-looking, well-built, fundamentally kind and had a decent sense of humour. He just wasn't his difficult, foul-tempered, intransigent, sexy brother. And that was the only problem.

Over pudding, we managed a desultory chat about Rory's flight and what had delayed it (a child had forgotten its toy walrus) and ate Agatha's light-as-a-cloud lemon meringue pie, then, to my relief, Logan pushed his chair back and said, 'It's been a long day. If you don't mind, I'll head up.'

'I'll knock during the night to be sure you're not dead,' said Agatha briskly.

'Nonsense,' said Sir Alastair. 'I shall do that.'

'No, my room's next to his,' said Rory. 'I'll do it.'

I took a deep breath. 'I will,' I said. 'Logan saved me from drowning – it's the least I can do.'

'No, you can't...' began Rory, but he petered out. 'To be honest, I'm absolutely done in from the flight. It would be great if you could.'

'Yes,' agreed Agatha, 'I'm listening to my audiobook of *Invisible Women* in my bed. I might not hear the alarm.'

'Well...' Sir Alastair pulled a troubled face. 'I do so hate to wake Hannay once he's settled on my feet...'

'God's sake, all of you,' said Logan. 'I'll be fine; I'm not going to drop dead!'

'You're supposed to do it for any head injury, though,' I insisted. 'I'll only tap lightly on the door, and you say, "I'm alive," and I'll go away again.'

He groaned. 'Alive and wide awake when I don't need to be, but okay. Not every hour, though, I beg you.'

Afterwards, as I settled in bed and set my alarm for midnight, I noticed that my heart was racing. Just last night, I'd been cradled in Logan's powerful arms. If I visited him in the darkness, tapping on his door, then slipping inside and under the covers beside him, even just to hold him, would that be so bad?

Though I'd suggested that we should just be friends for so many sensible reasons, not least my fragile heart. It had been crushed by Oliver's smooth indifference – I wasn't going to hand it over to an arrogant sod who was seemingly still in love with his ex, no matter how much chemistry sparked between us. I had warmed up now, and I was exhausted after the insanity of the past twenty-four hours, but sleep was a long way off.

At midnight, I turned off the alarm before it sounded, pulled on my warmest jumper and clicked open my door as quietly as I could. I half hoped Logan would be asleep when I tapped the door – that way, my heated thoughts might be extinguished by the dash of cold water they so badly needed.

'Logan?' I tapped again, sudden fear slithering through me. If he didn't answer this time, I'd go in and check. One of the spaniels emitted a squeaky little snore, but there was no reply. I turned the handle and opened the door a crack. 'Logan, are you okay?'

There was a rustle of blankets as he turned over. 'I'm fine. Still alive.'

My panic subsided, leaving me feeling foolish. 'That's a relief. Do you need anything?'

'Sleep.'

'Okay, but is your head...?'

'I'm going back to sleep now. Night.'

The bed creaked again. I quietly closed the door and returned to my room, feeling exiled.

At three, I knocked again.

'Sleeping. Go 'way,' he groaned, as I retreated.

I went back to bed, bleak with rejection, and told myself I was being ridiculous. By five in the morning, as the dawn brightened further, I almost believed it.

29

Having slept straight through Iolair FM, I was woken at nine by a pinging WhatsApp message. It had been sent the previous night, but Wi-Fi at Iolair was like wartime radar, coming and going as the fancy took it.

> *Guess what? I'm heading to the Far North this Thursday! Turn down the four-posters and have the tame eagle ready to greet me. I've stocked up on Starmix. Road triiiiipppppppppp!!! A xxx*

Part of me was thrilled that I'd be seeing my best friend so soon. But underlying my excitement was the horrible realisation that I hadn't actually *asked* anyone whether such a visit would be acceptable. Was there room at the castle? Would Logan immediately dismiss my beloved best mate as irritating and irrelevant? Worse, would he fall for Alice's big blue eyes and white-blonde bob? Although based on the weekend's revelations, his heart still lay with Marina...

I threw off the blankets. I'd go and ask Sir Alastair now, before my courage failed.

I found him poring over an article in the paper headlined

'WARNING FOR SCOTTISH HOSPITALITY AS TOURISTS HEAD ABROAD', and he sighed as he looked up.

'Hello, my dear. Quite recovered after your dunking in the loch?'

'Yes, fully restored,' I said. 'I feel extremely embarrassed and very grateful to Logan.'

He peered at me over his reading glasses. 'You look pale. I know you must be exhausted after keeping the lad awake all night.'

My cheeks burned. How could he possibly have known? Had Logan told him? I wanted to die on the moth-eaten Persian rug, or, failing that, call a cab to the station without speaking to anyone ever again.

'Every two hours, wasn't it?' he continued. 'Though of course, one can't be too careful with a head injury...'

'That's right,' I said, almost gasping with relief. 'But he seemed fine.'

'Jolly good. I was hoping you and McAskill Minor might be able to have a chat today,' added Sir Alastair. 'I rather think the disastrous end to his relationship has been quite the blow for poor Rory. He could do with some discussion of our plans to take his mind off things. Oh yes, and there's something else happening on Friday...'

'I have something I need to ask you,' I said, before he could roll on any further. 'It's... my friend is... well, she's coming on holiday to Scotland, and I wondered whether she might be able to drop by... well, stay. The night. Maybe two... but of course, she can stay in the village if you'd prefer. It's not a problem!'

Sir Alastair regarded me. 'You young people,' he said. 'You do seem to have terrible trouble expressing yourselves. Of course she may stay. I'll ask Agatha to make up the bed in the Queen's Room.'

'The...?'

'Ah.' He chuckled reminiscently. 'One story has it that Mary, Queen of Scots once stayed in the old section of Iolair Castle. Every castle in Scotland seems to have hosted her at one time or another, so I doubt it. But it's a nice story.'

'It will be a fabulous story when the castle opens for events, either way,' I said. 'People will be queuing to see the Queen's Room.'

'Perhaps ask one of the boys to show you later,' he said. 'We don't use them much as they're bloody draughty in winter, but your friend should be fine in May. When shall we expect her?'

I hesitated. Hannay gave an enormous yawn, and rolled onto his back, knocking over a small, precious-looking vase with one flailing paw. It was like living with a chaotic Shetland pony.

'Well, she did mention Thursday,' I said, somewhat downplaying the wild excitement vibrating from Alice's all-caps messages.

SHOULD I BUY A VIV WESTWOOD MINI-KILT ON VINTED?

IS LOGAN HOT?

WILL I HAVE TO EAT HAGGIS BECAUSE THAT'S AN ACTUAL WORLD OF NO.

CAN WE HAVE COCKTAILS ON THE CASTLE ROOF?

She had added a string of 'pina colada' emojis. I imagined Logan's face at the idea of serving coconut-based booze smoothies as we clung to the turret in a gale, and almost laughed out loud.

'Ah, yes, now, that might work out rather well,' said Sir Alastair. 'I was about to say, on Friday, our friends Harwood and Annabel Giles-Patton have invited us to their annual

Corryvreckan sail. We all go along for the afternoon, and it's rather marvellous. One can quite often see porpoises!' he added, his eyes alight with childish glee. 'Or should I say porpi? No, that can't be right... anyway!' He clapped his hands together, and Hannay twitched in his sleep. 'Invite your friend along. We leave from Ardanachan harbour at around ten and sail back after lunch. It would be a lovely introduction to the West Highlands for your visitor, don't you think?'

'It sounds wonderful.' I had a sudden recollection of Alice telling an anecdote about being violently ill on a choppy school trip to Calais. In my case, I'd been on the ferry to Roscoff and back on holiday, and an ex had once rowed me splashily round the Serpentine, explaining why he thought I could stand to lose a bit of weight. We'd only been together for three weeks, and by the time we pulled up back at the boathouse, we no longer were. And of course, I had been in a boat with Logan – twice, counting yesterday.

I had a sudden, horrible thought.

'Will Marina be there?' I asked, attempting a tone of cheerful curiosity. 'I remember Logan saying she was something of a sailor.'

Something of a sailor? Which 'golf club small talk' filing cabinet did that emerge from?

'Ah, no.' Sir Alastair blinked. 'I'm afraid the Giles-Pattons and the Campbells are rather... well, let's just say they don't get on. Old family feuds,' he said vaguely.

I longed to know more, but I nodded. 'Understood,' I said, still in hearty golf-club mode.

There was a brief rap on the door.

'Come!' called Sir Alastair, and Arran and Alba hurtled into the room like a whirling dust storm, followed by Logan.

Electric fish swam through my stomach as he gave me a brief, distracted smile. His hair was ruffled and he looked tired, but no exhaustion or concussion could extinguish the beauty of that bone structure. He was like a haughty, quivering racehorse next to Rory's chunky, cheerful roan pony. Again, I wished I could find Rory attractive – if only I was drawn to ponies, life would be so much easier – but he had never appealed to me in that way. Then again, Alice might feel differently... I wondered whether I should attempt a bit of meddlesome matchmaking during her visit, like a bored Jane Austen heroine.

'Morning, Dad,' said Logan, leaning against a rickety-looking bookshelf that held a cracked phrenology skull and a Victorian stuffed otter.

'Feeling better, son?'

'Much, thanks,' said Logan. 'Despite being woken every five minutes.'

'Two hours,' I murmured.

'It very much felt like five minutes. I've been talking to Rory and he's desperate to see the finances, such as they are. I said we'd all meet in the office at ten to go through everything.'

'So, you're happy to listen to his ideas?' I asked tentatively. I'd assumed Logan would be dead set against any of Rory's go-getting plans.

'Of course.' Logan looked surprised. 'I only ever dismiss ideas that I know from experience can't work.'

He looked at me steadily, and for a moment, I was certain he wasn't just talking about the castle. I looked away, irritated. There was no need to hammer it home – I'd already agreed we were better as friends, or passing acquaintances, or whatever we now were.

'Where's the office?' I asked flatly.

'Oh, didn't you show Cat?' Sir Alastair looked surprised.

Logan shrugged. 'I didn't think she'd need to see it. It's in the east wing; it's basically a converted dungeon. We use it when we need space for a meeting, that kind of thing.'

'A converted...?'

'It's not the conference suite at Canary Wharf, basically,'

said Logan. 'We may as well head down there, and prepare for the Wall Street Thermal. He was so cold last night, he borrowed my woollen long johns.'

'How very seductive,' I said, forgetting that Sir Alastair was listening.

'You'd be amazed. Arran! Alba!' he called. 'Come on.'

Arran reluctantly lifted his nose from the waste-paper basket, and Alba guiltily inched backwards from under the desk, making alarming gagging noises in her hurry to swallow evidence.

'I'll join you shortly,' said Sir Alastair. 'I just need to finish the cryptic crossword. *Rejected Grecian receptacle was fast.* Seven letters, begins with S.'

'Spurned,' said Logan heavily.

I didn't look at him as we left the room together. Was he thinking of Marina's rejection of him – or his own feelings of indifference towards me?

30

I silently followed the dogs and Logan down the main staircase and along the corridor, where he sent the dogs to the kitchen, opened a door I'd assumed was a cupboard and ushered me through. We were in another long, whitewashed corridor, with doors lining each side and, above us, a long row of brass bells marked in painted letters with the rooms of the castle.

'Servants' bells!'

'Clearly, we no longer use them. I can only imagine what Agatha would say if we tried.'

I smiled. 'Do they still ring in the rooms if you ding one?'

'No,' Logan said, 'Mum had them taken out – she didn't want to be constantly reminded of the "upstairs, downstairs" side of things. Despite living in a castle,' he added. 'She wasn't like that, though – she thought everyone was equal. She just fell for Dad, and ended up here.'

I thought about Fiona, so beautiful and happy, snuffed out so young. 'What was her background?'

'She wasn't a gold-digger, if that's what you're implying,' Logan said coldly.

'Of course I'm not implying any such thing!' I felt as though I'd been slapped. 'Why on earth would I think that?'

'Some people do. Boys at school did, because Mum was normal, not the nineteenth generation of Fotherington-Thomases, like their own parents. That's why I didn't talk about her much when I was young.'

'Kids can be cruel.'

Logan shrugged. 'I learned to deal with it. To answer your question, Mum was from Edinburgh, and her parents were anti-quarian book dealers. She met Dad when he came into their shop looking for Edwardian books on salmon fishing. Appar-ently, it was love at first sight, and they were married six months later.'

'Wow, how romantic.'

'Well,' he said. 'It worked for them. But it's not for everyone.'

He fell silent, and I remembered once again that Marina had broken his heart. Clearly, I was not the woman to mend it – I knew that, so why did I feel a powerful pang of jealousy? Perhaps because of what had happened so recently with Oliver, I reasoned. I needed a partner who wanted *me* – not one who was engaged to somebody else, or still in love with his beautiful, wild ex.

Logan cleared his throat. 'Right, the dungeons are this way.'

'Not a sentence I expected to hear this morning,' I observed brightly, following him through a smaller oak door which opened onto an alarmingly steep spiral of stone steps. I trailed one hand against the rough wall to steady myself, feeling increasingly dizzy as we continued to descend.

'Is this a dungeon or a well?'

Logan laughed. 'Almost there.'

We rounded the last curve, and entered a small, stone-walled room, with a low ceiling and a single door opposite. I felt a sudden wave of claustrophobia, and clutched the wall behind me.

'It's just through— Cat, are you okay? You're pale.'

'Sorry.' I took a deep breath. 'This hasn't happened since I visited the Blue John Mines on a school trip in 2006. Miss Hampsey had to guide me out while the others went to look at stalactites. It was mortifying.'

'We can go back up...'

'No, honestly – I can't face all those steps again. Let's just carry on; I'll be okay in a sec.'

He looked at me doubtfully, and I attempted a smile, waiting for the nauseated panic to ebb.

Logan shook his head. 'You're a brave wee lassie,' he said jokingly. 'You never let anything stop you.'

'My mum would say it's my need for control in a chaotic world. Did I mention she once did a psychotherapy course?'

'Keep her well away from me. She'd have a field day. Look, come here.' To my surprise, Logan grasped my cold hand, sending a treacherous shot of desire through me as our palms touched.

'Hold on tight,' he said. 'It's just through there.'

The door opened, and Logan flicked a light switch. Glass wall lights illuminated a wide, whitewashed space, with colourful, framed paintings of sea life on the walls. On the stone floor there was a huge, blue-and-orange Persian rug, and in the middle of the room was a long, modern beech-wood table with ten matching chairs. A little drinks trolley held a kettle, mugs and a biscuit tin.

'It's freezing down here,' said Logan. He dropped my hand and went to switch on a silver wall heater. 'Should warm up pretty quickly when the others arrive. Are you feeling okay?'

I sat down along one side of the table. 'Fine now,' I said cheerfully, though I could still feel the warmth of his fingers on mine. 'Sorry about that. I hadn't realised it was still an issue – funnily enough, I don't spend much time underground, day to day.

'I like the paintings,' I added, gesturing towards one of bright red and blue sea urchins, floating in soft, jade-green water. It was so unlike all the other art in the castle, with its fusty landscapes and dead stags, it was like being in a different place altogether.

'Oh – those are Mum's,' said Logan. 'She was good, wasn't she?'

'I love them,' I said, 'but why are they hidden away down here?'

'Well, she did up this room,' he said. 'She thought Dad should have somewhere to take business types that wasn't his mad turret full of dust and owl pellets. Plus, I think looking at them made him too sad, for a long time.' He sighed. '*The McAskills, unlucky in love.* That should be our Gaelic motto.'

As he spoke, I heard footsteps clattering down the stairs, and Rory exploded into the room, panting and steaming like a bull facing down a matador.

'Morning,' he gasped. 'Just been for a run down the lochside. Much tougher than my air-conditioned Manhattan gym.'

He wiped his flushed face with the small towel he was carrying, then draped it round his neck and flung himself into a chair.

'Don't suppose Ag would make me a green juice, do you?' he asked Logan, who was regarding his brother as if an unruly dog had scampered into a lecture hall. 'It's really easy – you just throw a handful of organic spinach in with some diced kiwi and ginger...'

'Good luck finding kiwis at the village shop,' said Logan, unsmiling.

As he spoke, slower footsteps crossed the stone floor outside.

'My goodness,' said Sir Alastair. 'Those stairs will prove the death of me.'

He sat at the head of the table, Hannay throwing himself to the rug alongside. I wondered how he'd navigated his endless wolfhound legs down those stairs.

Sir Alastair placed three large, dusty box files on the table. 'This is most of it, I think. Bank statements, outgoings, that sort of thing. Oh, hold on...' He extracted the desiccated carcass of a large beetle from the top file and brushed it to the floor. Hannay promptly ate it and went to sleep.

'Dad, seriously?' Rory looked horrified. 'You don't have online banking, or spreadsheets, or... This is how they managed their finances in Victorian times!'

Sir Alastair bristled. 'This system served my ancestors perfectly well.'

'I can leave for this part,' I suggested. 'It feels a bit private.'

'Not at all!' Sir Alastair cried. 'Cat, you are essential to this operation. You need to know where we stand before we can agree to any plans.'

Logan distributed the overflowing files between the three of us. 'Dad, if we go through and you explain anything that doesn't make sense...'

'Good luck with that,' murmured Rory, and Logan shot him a quelling look.

Sir Alastair nodded benignly. 'As long as we're finished in time for Hannay's Scotch egg.'

An hour later, my brain felt as though it had been through a mincer.

Every few seconds, Rory would say, 'Four hundred pounds to Jed McCavity every *month*?' And Sir Alastair would say brightly, 'Oh, Jed's the mole man! He's essential to keep the lawn free of molehills. He tells the most marvellous stories about his time in the SAS,' or Logan would ask, 'Lifeboat Crew Veterans?' and Sir Alastair would argue, 'I like to bung them a bit of cash; it's a wonderful charity.'

Whatever the expense, Sir Alastair had a good reason for it, from boiler lagging to rolls of premium chicken wire ('Donald insists it keeps the pine martens out of the hen coop') to Agatha's food bills ('£154 at the Oban delicatessen?' 'We eat a lot of chutney,' he said defensively).

I had discovered that Donald and Ishbel were collectively paid more than I could ever dream of earning as an events executive, and there were enough purchases from the antiquarian bookshop in Edinburgh to fill a public library. It was not my place to question Sir Alastair's finances, of course, but Rory certainly thought it was his. He had been neatly jotting down figures as we went along and adding them up.

'Dad,' Rory sighed, when all the papers and spidery notes had been stuffed back into their boxes. 'I'm going to be straight with you. If you keep going as you are, the castle trust will run out in around eighteen months, and there's absolutely nothing coming in to replace it, bar seasonal courgette sales.'

Logan looked up. 'Eighteen *months*? I thought the trust was guaranteed for Dad's lifetime, at least.'

'Not any more. It's all but gone.' Rory sat up, his hands flat on the table. 'I have a possible solution, though, and I'd like you to hear it.'

Logan raised his eyebrows. 'What do you suggest?'

'Angels.'

We all stared at him. I wondered if he'd gone entirely mad and that was why Stacey had cheated on him with the man upstairs.

'Angels?' Logan repeated gently, apparently reluctant to give Rory any kind of sudden shock.

'I'm not sure *praying*...' began Sir Alastair.

Rory laughed. His teeth really were dazzling. 'Angel investors. Venture capitalists. Business people who like the idea of having a share in an ancient Scottish castle. People. With. Money.'

'Well, that's all well and good,' said Sir Alastair, 'but where do we find these unlikely people? I hardly think Morag Bains at the post office will be shovelling her hard-earned pension our way. And nor should she,' he added firmly.

'Dad, I have a contacts book full of these people. It's what I did in New York, matching VCs with start-up businesses that need funding.'

'And what do these "angels" get in return?' asked Sir Alastair, now agitated enough to feed Hannay a pink wafer. 'Half the castle? All of it?'

Rory waved his hand irritably. 'They'll only take any repayments when we're up and running as a tourist venue and events business. Plus, we put their name on the brochure, maybe a photo of them on the south lawn. Billionaires love all that ancient stuff – it makes them feel legit.'

'So we're looking at helipads and endless gratitude?' Logan demanded.

'It's better than us all being homeless,' snapped Rory. 'Or do you want to give Ag, Donald and Ishbel notice, and rot away in your crumbling castle till one day you're found face down in the onion patch?'

Logan glared but subsided.

'So, as time is of the essence and we don't have capacity to meet with fifty VCs individually, I suggest we host one massive event to introduce them all to Iolair,' Rory continued. 'A summer weekend, drinks on the lawns, a seven-course sit-down dinner... But how will we fit them all in...?'

'If I may,' I said, 'this is very much my area, and I can tell you now that a dinner like that will be a nightmare to arrange without fleets of staff and teams of cooks. And they don't come cheap, plus they'd all need overnight accommodation.'

'Then what do you suggest?' Logan asked.

'A ceilidh,' I said promptly. 'Dancing, reels, a live band...' I thought of Mel's tinies. 'We could even have Scottish dancing and bagpipes! Then for the food, what about a Highlands-themed buffet with the best local produce, haggis, all Logan's veg... and whisky cocktails. You could all wear the McAskill tartan, and perhaps we could offer boat trips on the loch?' I rattled on. 'Really showcase everything the castle has to offer.'

I glanced up. Logan looked as though I'd suggested a ritual sacrifice of all four dogs on the lawn.

'All wear tartan?' he repeated slowly. 'Haggis and Scottish dancing?'

'Well, I know it's a bit obvious, but—'

'It's not just obvious; it's an *insult*.'

I felt both foolish and hurt. Keeping everyone happy was already impossible, and I didn't enjoy being the target of Logan's hot temper.

'Oh, for God's sake, Logan,' said Rory, 'I think it's a great idea. The Americans will love it. Cat's right – we need to show-case the place, demonstrate what's possible.'

'If what's possible is a humiliating mimicry of every cliché in the *Scotland for Beginners* book, then why stop there?' said Logan. 'Why not have an inflatable Nessie on the jetty giving rides to the kiddies, and oh wait, I know, we could all dress up as Bonnie Prince Charlie and make the dogs wear tam o'shanters...'

'It doesn't have to be naff,' I said. 'We can make it elegant and classy, with gorgeous food and a decent band...'

'And then what?' Logan glared round the table. 'They decide to invest, and suddenly they're telling us they want to rename it Tartan Towers and open a gift shop in the Queen's Room selling orange wigs, and we have to go along with it

because we're up to our ears in debt to some Texan "angel"
whose great-great-grandfather once visited Fife?'

'Or we could carry on as we are,' said Rory coldly. 'Let the
castle fall down around our ears, while we cling on like snipers
who don't know the war's over. Wait until the bailiffs sell off the
ancestral furniture at the Barras market in Glasgow.'

'Surely it won't come to that?' murmured Sir Alastair
faintly.

Rory slammed a hand on the table, making me jump. 'Wake
up! That's *exactly* what it will come to, by Christmas next year!'
he almost shouted. 'Logan, unless you want Dad to be cele-
brating in the Bide-a-Wee rest home overlooking the ring road, I
suggest you both start listening to me and Cat.'

'Perhaps he has a point, son,' said Sir Alastair.

Logan shook his head. 'Or we could reapply to build the
hydro-scheme, but you're too scared of the Campbells causing
us problems to risk it,' he shot back. 'Or we could invest in
kitchen garden sales to hotels all over Scotland, which I
researched in depth and proved could succeed, but you didn't
want to invest in the vans we'd need "just in case it fails". If
you'd taken your head out of the sand two years ago, Dad, we
wouldn't be in this situation! And now we're reduced to some
kind of *Highlands cosplay* to amuse a bunch of one-percenters
who wouldn't know nature if it bit them on the *arse*. And I
bloody well hope it does.'

He shoved his chair back. 'Do what you like,' he said. 'I'm
out.'

The door swung shut behind him, and Hannay gave a small
whine of concern.

'Well, I was going to suggest a show of hands,' said Sir Alastair sadly, 'but under the circumstances... I suggest you and
Rory forge ahead, Cat, and we'll have to hope Logan will come
round.'

'He won't,' said Rory bitterly. 'He never does.'

As we stood and headed out in silence, Hannay's claws clicking on the stone floor, I felt another wave of nausea – but this time it wasn't claustrophobia.

It was the realisation that I'd truly burned my bridges with Logan this time, regardless of whether I was ready to do so or not.

31

I spent the afternoon walking the castle again, this time accompanied by Rory. As if Logan's earlier outburst was too toxic to be mentioned, he maintained a strictly professional façade.

'What about accommodation?' he asked, as we headed up the grand staircase. 'We can't expect guests to share rooms.'

'I think the best thing might be to try and get a deal with the nearest decent hotel,' I said. 'The whole thing is going to cost us dear, but it's do or die, based on the figures.'

'Speculate to accumulate,' agreed Rory, nodding.

I felt suddenly as though I was talking to Oliver, walking the floor before a celebrity launch. Normally, that would have given me a pang of sadness – now I just felt amused by how seriously we'd taken it all. I had a sudden memory of Oliver urgently saying, 'It all hangs on whether Kensington Palace will allow can-can dancers inside the building,' and I almost laughed out loud. At the time, I'd felt only helpless desire, gazing at my boss in full professional flight.

'I think drinks down by the jetty early on, to showcase the loch,' Rory was saying.

Showcase the loch? repeated Logan in my head.

'As you say, perhaps a boat trip – we can ask Harwood about hiring the *Jaunty Anne.*'

'Named after Annabel?'

'Hard to believe when you meet her, but yes. She must have changed dramatically with age,' said Rory, and I laughed.

'Then we can have a buffet in the dining hall,' I went on, 'and the ceilidh in the Great Hall. Do you know any good bands?'

Rory paused by a marble bust of a furious-looking laird. 'Actually, Mel might,' he said thoughtfully.

'Mel? From Kincherrell?'

'Yes!' He smiled. 'We were great friends when we were younger. Haven't seen her for years, but I remember her brother was in a ceilidh band called Weave the Willow. Have you met her yet? How is she?'

'I met her soon after I arrived,' I said. 'In fact, she was at the Iolair Highland Games, with her daughter.'

Rory paused, his hand on the polished banister. 'Her *daughter?*'

'Yes, Belle – she's six now. Adorable.'

'Six! Is Mel married?'

'Single mum. She seems to be doing an amazing job.'

'Yes, Mel was always so determined. Brave.' Rory shook his head. 'I can't believe she's a mum. Seems so grown-up.'

'It does,' I agreed. I refrained from mentioning my suspicions about Belle's paternity. 'I can barely take care of a pot plant.'

'You seem perfectly organised to me,' said Rory, snapping back to professional mode. 'In fact, you're also the only person apart from Agatha who can see there's a giant problem here that needs solving fast.'

'Don't Donald and Ishbel know?'

Rory sighed. 'They'd follow Logan into battle with a Shetland pony and a water pistol. They'd never go against his wishes. He spent a lot of time with them growing up – they're like his surrogate family.'

'Not yours?'

He shrugged. 'I was younger when Mum died – a bit more resilient maybe. I think it hit Logan hardest in some ways – being the "heir to Iolair" and all that. He takes it very seriously.'

'I suppose it *is* serious.'

'Yeah.' Rory gazed down the long corridor hung with portraits ahead of us. 'I guess that's why I ran away to London, then New York. I wasn't much use here, it was all "Logan's birthright" stuff. I didn't want to spend my adult life watching him succeed while I failed.'

'I'm sure that's not...'

Rory shrugged off my well-meaning reassurance. 'It was how I felt. But now, I've grown up, and I think I can be useful. The main problem is getting my bloody brother on board.'

I nodded. 'I don't think Logan is easily persuaded.'

Rory glanced at me. 'Well,' he said, 'if anyone can, you can.'

I was startled by his echo of what Sir Alastair had said on the way to the hospital, and was about to ask Rory what he meant.

'What are you two doing?'

Agatha was approaching, carrying a large laundry basket full of sheets.

'We're looking round to see where we can put people,' I said.

'You can't put them here,' she said dismissively. 'They'll need put at the West Iolair Hotel down the loch. They'll do you a deal. It's where my mother stays when she visits.'

I had never thought of Agatha as having a mother. She seemed so independent and self-assured, it was as though she'd sprung from a mountainside.

'Will she be visiting soon?' I asked, curious.

Agatha shook her head briskly. 'She cannae. She's needing a wee spot in the sheltered housing, but we cannae afford the decent place and she won't leave the croft till we can. We're all six of us saving up for her.'

'Can we help?'

Agatha looked at me, a challenge in her eyes. 'Make the castle work,' she said. 'That way, I can keep my job.'

Two hours later, we had agreed that she was right – there was no way the VCs could stay in the unused bedrooms. The old silk wallpapers were often in threads, the lumpy mattresses stained by ancient stone hot-water bottles, and the long velvet curtains home to colonies of silvery moths. It would take months, and fortunes, to turn them into the sort of smooth, luxury-heritage spaces these people would expect.

For a moment, surveying the water-stained brass taps of the bathrooms, and the cracked red floor tiles, I treacherously wondered whether it might be easier simply to sell off the whole place and have everyone move to a nice modern house with working plumbing.

'Just the Queen's Room now,' said Rory. 'I think we've seen everything else.'

I was dying to see it and find out whether Alice would be thrilled or horrified by her accommodation on Thursday.

I followed Rory down long corridors, up and down small flights of carpeted and uncarpeted stairs, through a hidden door in the wall to the very oldest part of the castle, where the ceilings were lower and the walls rougher, and eventually, we arrived at a large oak door with a dark and gloomy portrait of Mary, Queen of Scots hanging beside it.

'What a welcome for her,' I said. 'It was probably her passport photo. I bet she was gutted when she saw they'd picked that one.'

Rory laughed. 'She probably never even visited.'

He depressed the stiff iron latch and opened the door for me.

'Oh my God!' I jumped violently as a dark form moved from the window.

'Sorry.' Logan emerged from the shadows of the large room. 'Are you all right, Cat?'

I nodded, still unable to speak.

'I was just... I come in here to think sometimes,' Logan said quietly.

'Rest of the castle, with its daylight and modern comforts, not good enough?' asked Rory, irritated.

Logan pulled open a pair of heavy crimson curtains, and a thick drift of dust shone in the bar of light.

'It's nice and peaceful. Anyway,' he said, 'I'll leave you to it.'

He looked wretched, and I noticed his limp seemed to have worsened.

'Or you could help us,' Rory said.

'Help you do what? Carve up the castle and sell off chunks to the highest bidders?'

'Well, it's that or have the bailiffs take it for nothing, Logan.'

They glared at one another.

'If anyone would listen to my plan,' Logan said coldly, 'perhaps we could save Iolair without all this corporate frenzy. But apparently, it's too late.'

'I'll listen,' I said. 'I'm sorry you feel overlooked.'

Logan shook his head. 'Thanks, but it won't work without everyone on board. Listen, I won't be around for a couple of days. I need some space to clear my head and think about my future.'

'Where are you going?' I blurted. I felt an unexpected sense of emptiness.

Logan shrugged. 'Not decided yet. Depends on a few things.'

He raised a hand and trudged away down the corridor.

'Fine,' said Rory. 'Easier without him drifting about like an odourless gas, anyway.'

I wanted to defend Logan, but I didn't want to raise Rory's suspicions regarding my true feelings. And besides, perhaps he had a point.

I quickly understood why the Queen's Room was so appealing to Logan. There was a sense of deep calm here, despite the dust, and a vast, carved and gilded four-poster with faded silken bolsters and an embroidered counterpane. Dark wooden beams crossed the ceiling, and the long leaded windows with their tiny panes of warped, ancient glass threw wavering lozenges of light around the room.

'Do you think we should do anything with it?' Rory asked.

'We should probably have some information or something on the wall,' I suggested. *'"We aren't sure if Mary ever visited, but let's say she did."'*

Rory laughed. 'Yeah, though Logan wouldn't approve of fudging it. My morally righteous brother.'

'Where do you think he's going?' I asked, trying to sound casual.

'Dunno. I'm slightly wondering if the divine Miss Marina has anything to do with it.'

I felt a lurch of jealousy. 'But she's married to Jack.'

'Not for long, I suspect,' said Rory. 'And good riddance. Maybe she and Logan will soon be holed up in the Iolair Hotel's honeymoon suite, ordering champagne on room service and making up for lost time.'

He laughed and turned to leave the room. I felt relieved that he hadn't seen the sudden desolation on my face.

32

The rest of the day passed at a glacial pace. I found myself wondering constantly where Logan was, and who he was with.

I spent the late afternoon holed up with Rory in the cellar office, going through his list of invitees. 'There'll be a few last-minute guests, too, I expect,' he added. 'These types always know other people they want to bring along. But as long as they're rich, eh?'

I nodded. 'And as long as the budget doesn't spiral out of control.'

'It won't,' said Rory. 'I'm off to the Iolair Hotel in the morning to do a Del Boy-style deal. I used to... know... the owner's daughter.' He gave me an unsubtle wink.

'Charm away.' I smiled. 'We need all the help we can get.'

After hours of tortuous budget spreadsheets and buffet discussions, I was delighted when as we headed back upstairs, my phone pinged with a message from Mel.

Fancy pub tonight? I HAVE GOSSIP!

My spirits lifted. I might be inexplicably pining for Logan's touch, but at least I could get drunk with a friend while I did so.

'I got Prosecco.'

Mel arrived at our table, banging down a silver bucket. I remembered how snobbish Oliver had always been about our clients who ordered crates of Prosecco rather than champagne.

'Bridge and tunnel people,' he had called them, despite living in Belsize Park, rather than the Upper East Side.

'Lovely,' I said, smiling at her. Mel looked particularly vibrant in a red flowered dress that showed off her strong legs, her wild curls clipped up and falling round her face.

'So,' she said, after pouring us two glasses and glancing round to make sure nobody was paying attention to us. 'What's happened with Logan since yesterday? Tell me everything.'

'Nothing to tell. Apart from me nearly drowning and him saving me.'

'*What?*'

Several customers turned round at Mel's shriek. I outlined what had happened.

'Oh, for the love of God! Is wee Arran all right?'

'He's fine. He's gone away with Logan and Alba for a couple of days.'

'Where?'

'I've no idea,' I said. 'He's all upset about the plans for the castle, now Rory's back.'

'Wait, what? Rory's *back*?'

'I forgot you didn't know. Yes, apparently, he's split up with Stacey, and he's come back to "save Iolair".' I made air quotes. 'Good luck with that.'

She seemed speechless. 'Wow,' she said eventually, and drained her glass, immediately pouring herself another.

'What's your gossip?' I asked her, curious.

'Well.' Mel lowered her voice. 'I was chatting with one of the school mums who knows Marina, and she told me they've split up!'

'Marina and Jack? Are you sure?' For some reason, I felt I had to be certain. If it wasn't true, the plummeting weight in my stomach might rise back up again.

'My friend said she saw Jack throwing his stuff into the car and roaring off.'

'Just a row, maybe?' I said hopefully.

'Doesn't sound like it. She went to check Marina was okay, and apparently, it's all over. Not surprising after yesterday...'

I nodded. 'Wonder where he's gone?'

'Och, I expect he's got a girl in every port, that one,' said Mel. 'Marina should have stuck with Logan—' She broke off. 'God, sorry. I forgot you're having a thing.'

'We're not!' I said, trying to laugh. 'It was one night, that's all. I think we're both keen to pretend it never happened.'

But for very different reasons, I thought. The sooner I got over Logan, and headed back to London, the better. Strangely, that was exactly what I'd told myself fifteen years ago – and I'd made a complete fool of myself back then, too.

Mel and I got mildly drunk, and laughed over her stories of daft teen escapades with Rory and a bunch of others. 'Logan was too sensible to join in,' she added. 'He was always a grown-up, even when he was sixteen, with his serious girlfriend and his big responsibilities.'

'Do you think that's why he's so against the castle plans?' I asked her. 'Because he thinks it's his responsibility to fix it and he feels like he's failing?'

Mel smiled at me. 'For someone who hasn't known him long, you sure do understand him well.'

I wondered how well Mel herself understood him – and

how Logan would feel if it turned out he had a daughter living a mile away. From what I knew of Mel, she'd do anything rather than be thought a gold-digger. Was that why she'd kept the identity of Belle's father a secret? I couldn't think of a way to ask – and I very much doubted she'd tell me, even if I did.

I didn't stay too late, partly because Donald came in around nine. After a chat with a few of the locals at the bar, he headed over to our table.

'Do the two of ye want a lift home?'

It hadn't occurred to me that without Logan, I'd be walking back along the forest road without company or a decent torch, and we clambered gratefully into the truck.

'How's Rory?' Donald asked. 'Full o' schemes?'

'Seems so.' I told him about the ceilidh we had planned for all the potential investors.

Donald compressed his moustache, a sure sign of doubt. 'I take it Logan's none too happy about this?'

'That would be a wild understatement.'

Donald shook his head sadly. 'He's gone off for a day or two, I believe.'

'Do you know where?'

Mel caught my eye in the mirror. I reminded myself not to sound too concerned.

Donald shrugged as we passed the castle drive and drove on to Kincherrell down the tree-lined single-track road.

'He's maybe headed for Auld Reekie – Edinburgh, his old haunts,' he clarified. 'Get a bit of smoky city air, a few bright lights. A change is good for the soul sometimes.'

'Where does he stay there?' Mel asked.

'It'll be his old place, little attic up in the New Town, with a very bohemian artist landlady,' he said. 'She still lets him stay when it's free. Terrific view of Arthur's Seat. I helped him take some stuff up there once, years ago. Surprisingly tidy for a young lad.'

As we dropped Mel off at her little white cottage, and headed back to the castle, a country music CD playing, I thought about Logan's cosy little attic, and who might be joining him there. Even if Marina was nowhere near Edinburgh, she'd left Jack, and who else was she going to turn to but her old love? I imagined her porcelain skin against his, her red curls blazing across the pillows like fallen autumn leaves.

I had to get a grip, I realised. One night of passion didn't make a relationship, it didn't make us accountable to one another, and Logan had made it very clear that he wanted things to go no further with me. Frankly, I wasn't sure I did, either. What future did we have? I couldn't imagine Himself of Iolair trekking up and down to London while I tried to set up a boutique events business for celebrity launches, and the idea of Logan ever attending such a party was like parachuting Hannay into a cat's home.

I needed someone fun and laid-back, someone who didn't take life too seriously and shrugged off problems. Logan was the opposite of that.

No, I thought, as we finally rolled up to the castle steps, and Donald chivalrously got out to open the door for me. I'd had my fun, and now I'd leave Logan to whatever his future held.

The only certainty was that it didn't contain me, and it never would.

33

Over the next couple of days, I slept badly and spent my waking hours throwing myself into work.

The weather had turned to a set-in drizzle that shrouded the mountains with an impenetrable mist and turned the drooping petals brown on the rhododendrons.

'The bluebells will be out soon,' said Sir Alastair, passing by as I gazed through the hall window at the damp lawns on Wednesday afternoon. 'By mid-May, everything's blooming all at once – it's a floral paradise. But of course, that means the midges are out, too.'

'Are they really as bad as everyone says?'

He laughed. 'Worse. But I'm grateful for them because if we didn't have the buggers, we'd be overrun with tourists night and day.'

The castle could do with a few more of those, I thought, but I didn't say so.

Agatha had made up the ancient bed in the Queen's Room for Alice, dusted, hoovered and left jugs of wildflowers on the table. I found myself feeling genuinely excited about her visit, and spent the evening making plans for what we might do while she was here. Friday, of course, was the boat trip – and while part of me hoped Logan would be back in time so I could introduce him to my friend, I was also aware that if he didn't make it, I'd feel a whole lot more relaxed.

I was early to breakfast, and smiled as Sir Alastair poured coffee into his favourite mug. It was the size of a large plant pot and covered in multicoloured spots. Just the sight of it cheered me up.

'Now, my dear, have you and Rory confirmed a date for the ceilidh?'

That was the one thing we hadn't settled on, though we'd been discussing late June as an option, to give us enough time to plan.

'Well, not quite yet...' I began as Rory hurried in. Dougie, who had taken a great shine to him, scuttled over to flop on his feet, leaving him immobilised.

'Cat,' he said. 'We need to talk.'

'Is everything okay?' I was alarmed by his fixed expression.

'Yes, all fine.' He glanced at Sir Alastair, who was obliviously spooning up porridge and leafing through *The Herald*. 'But it's kind of urgent.'

I put my toast down, and followed him into the corridor.

'What's up?' I hissed.

'We need Logan to come back, right now. It's not possible without him.'

'What's happened?' I felt a flutter of panic.

He leaned against the wooden table where Agatha stacked the post, and a small cascade of bills in brown envelopes slid to the tiled floor. 'I've just got back from the hotel,' he said. 'I thought I'd go early, and get my pitch in. Jillie was there – my old friend.'

I raised an eyebrow and nodded.

'She said she could do a deal on twenty rooms, but the only two nights they have free is... well...'

'*Tell me.*'

'Next weekend,' said Rory very quickly.

I sighed, disappointed. 'Oh dear. Well, back to the drawing board.'

'You don't understand.' He shook his head. 'It's the only luxury place for miles that can accommodate that many guests. They're booked up till September after that.'

'You aren't seriously suggesting...'

Rory swallowed. 'I said yes. We've got just over a week to get everything ready.'

Three hours later, I was waiting on the steps for Alice, my excitement at her imminent arrival somewhat crushed by the heart-pounding stress I now felt. But when I heard an engine racing up the long drive, I ran down the steps, ready to fling my arms around my friend. I slowly returned them to my sides as I realised it was Logan's car speeding into view and slewing to a stop on the gravel.

'Where's Rory?' He strode towards me, the dogs jumping at his heels. 'I got his message, and in the name of—'

'*Hello, Cat, how nice to see you,*' I said. As usual, I felt a jolt at his presence, a sensation of being magnetised towards him that I couldn't explain.

'Yes, sorry, how have things been?'

He was wearing a thick blue roll-neck jumper, and looked like a handsome actor playing a fisherman. I bent to greet Arran and Alba, who rolled on their backs for tummy tickles. Despite everything, I'd missed them.

'As of this morning, pretty stressful,' I admitted. 'Rory's up in the turret, breaking the news to your dad that we have a week till C-Day, and then he's got to tell Agatha.'

'I don't envy him that.'

As he spoke, we heard another engine. This time I was

thrilled to see the familiar scarlet of Alice's red Mini jerking up the drive, *The Best of Tina Turner* blasting from the open window.

'Oh, for God's sake,' snapped Logan, and before I could speak, he was sprinting down the drive, shouting, 'This is a private residence, not a tourist attraction!'

'Logan, she's my friend!' I yelled, as he made furious 'turn round, you fool' gestures, but Arran and Alba were now barking wildly with excitement and drowned me out.

Alice performed a lurching emergency stop, turned off 'What's Love Got to Do with It' and leapt out. My best friend was wearing pink Converse boots, small denim shorts and a satin bomber jacket with 'Queen Bitch' embroidered on the back. She was clutching a sharing bag of Revels.

'I think you'll find I'm an invited guest!' Alice said in her poshest accent, as I jogged urgently towards them, the dogs tumble-weeding alongside.

'Nice try,' said Logan scornfully. 'There's a B&B in the village, and I suggest you make your way—'

'Alice is my best friend,' I interrupted Logan crossly. 'She's invited.'

He fell silent as we looked at him.

'I do apologise, Alice,' Logan said eventually. 'We have a lot of trouble with tourists coming to gawk in the summer. May I take your luggage?'

'You may,' said Alice, smiling at him, her blonde hair lifting in the breeze. He picked up her enormous, flowered suitcase, leading the way inside.

Alice dug me in the ribs. '*That's him?*' she hissed loudly. '*He's* Himself of Iolair? You didn't say he was *gorgeous!*'

Logan half turned, and I felt my face flare with heat. He hefted the suitcase up and down the stairs and round corners to the Queen's Room, walking ahead while Alice exclaimed over every portrait and marble bust.

'Oh my *God*!' she shrieked when, finally, Logan flung open the oak door to reveal the historic four-poster.

Alice flung herself backwards onto it, her legs in the air.

'If you could be quite careful,' Logan murmured. 'That bed dates from the sixteenth century, and I'm not sure it's insured.'

'Is it haunted?' demanded Alice. 'Please say it's haunted.'

Logan sighed. 'If you'd like to believe it's haunted, let's say the ghost of Mary, Queen of Scots drifts from the cupboard at 4 a.m. every morning, wailing, "The throne shall be mine," in Old French.'

Alice stared at him. 'Really?'

'No.'

He turned to me. 'I'm going to find Rory and get to the bottom of this new fiasco,' he said. 'See you at dinner.'

When he'd gone, Alice performed a silent scream, hands by her face like a 1920s Pierrot.

'He's *so* handsome and brooding,' said Alice. 'GSOH – Grumpy Scottish Old Heathcliff. Can I have a crack, or have you snogged him?'

'Actually,' I said, and paused. 'I've done more than snog him.'

This time, she screamed out loud.

It was a great relief to pour it all out to my best friend, leaving no stone unturned. We played Revels roulette as we talked – 'Coffee!' spat Alice horrified, halfway through my long description of the night in the bothy – and by the time I'd finished, she was staring at me.

'Well, what's stopping you?' Alice asked eventually. 'Why aren't you riding him like a cowgirl night and day, pausing only to say, "Hi, Alice, get yourself a drink," between naked Twister positions?'

I sighed. 'Because it can't work. Obviously. He's here and I'll be in London, he's bad-tempered and serious and ecologically minded, and I'm cheerful and fun and bad at recycling...'

'You're not *that* fun,' put in Alice. 'Ugh, orange flavour.'

I ignored her. '... and he's already said we're better off as friends, which we obviously are, and then there's the Marina factor...'

'Who?' asked Alice, her eyes narrowed.

'The woman he was going to marry.'

I explained all I knew, but for some reason I didn't mention that Logan had probably spent the past couple of days with her.

'You're making her sound like some kind of mystical Scottish mermaid,' said Alice. 'She can't be that amazing. And why did she marry that Jack Campbell if he's so awful?'

'She was in love with him, apparently.'

'Pah,' said Alice. 'Love is just a social construct to justify our feelings of lust and formalise the raising of children.'

'Bad date?' I asked, and she nodded. 'He took me to a chicken shop and asked if I'm polyamorous.'

When we'd stopped laughing, I offered to show her round. The rain had stopped, and the loch was spangled with sunlight. It was hard to remember that I'd almost drowned in its freezing black depths just a few days earlier.

34

As we strolled down the lawn and Alice pretended to be Lady Mary in *Downton Abbey* twirling a parasol, I heard the sputtering engine of a quad bike, and saw Donald and Dougie motoring purposefully towards us.

'I've heard the news,' Donald said grimly, after I'd introduced Alice. 'I've no idea what Rory thinks he's playing at, but it's not possible.'

'I know, but I don't think we have a choice.'

'Well, Sir A's having litters of kittens over it, Agatha's shut herself in her room and is refusing to come out, and Ishbel's rosacea flared up the minute she heard the word "buffet".'

'I can do all that side of things,' I said. 'We can book caterers if we need to.'

'Aye, Morag's niece Elvira does a lovely cheese-and-pineapple hedgehog.'

I had never heard Donald being sarcastic before. It was a worrying development.

'As for young Logan,' he continued, 'I doubt he'll stay on after this. He says he's heard about a job he might apply for, and then Sir A will be left all alone, and the castle will be sold from under him!' He glared round at us as if we were fist-shaking bailiffs.

I felt deeply troubled at the idea that Logan might leave Iolair for good. It would be like the ravens leaving the tower of London.

At dinner, the others were discussing the boat trip as Sir Alastair had sensibly imposed a 'no ceilidh talk at the table' rule.

'Will it be very choppy?' Alice asked. 'I'm not scared; I'm excited,' she added hastily.

'Shouldn't be,' said Rory. 'I've not been for a few years, but last time it was like a millpond. What do you think, Logan?'

'Well, with the Corryvreckan whirlpool, it always depends on the timing,' he said.

'Whirlpool?' repeated Alice faintly.

'We don't sail into the actual whirlpool,' Logan told her. 'Just round the edge.'

I looked at him pouring wine, and an unexpected physical memory of our night together shot through me like a bolt of electricity. I took a deep breath, and tore my gaze from his elegant hands, my thoughts from what they could do.

'Right.' Alice glanced at me unhappily.

'We don't have to go...'

I desperately wanted to, mainly because it was a chance to be near Logan and he'd have no opportunity to escape me. I knew the coming week would be a nightmare – we'd all be working eighteen-hour days to get the castle ready in time, and my chances of speaking to him at all would be slim. Soon after the ceilidh, my time at Iolair would come to an end. There would be no more events planned, and no convincing reason to stay in touch with Logan. Besides, if there was any chance he was back with Marina, why would I want to torture myself? I'd go home, and start my life again as a single woman.

Alice read my face in an instant.

'Of *course* we're going,' she said.

After dinner, we headed up to the Queen's Room again, and Alice extracted a bottle of champagne from her rucksack. 'I forgot to ask Agatha about glasses,' she said, 'but Mary, Queen of Scots's tooth mugs will do.'

We settled on the bed, and I was about to give a toast when Alice shouted, 'Wait!'

'What?'

'I forgot! It's in my suitcase – hang on...' She dived under the bed and extracted a battered envelope, which she handed to me.

'It's the letter from Oliver,' she explained. 'Please open it – I was really good and didn't steam it open, even though I easily could have done.'

I put my glass down on the Jacobean side table, and slit it open.

Just a few weeks ago, a letter from Oliver would have made my heart pound, as unicorns of romantic fantasy danced the tango in my imagination. Now, I felt an unwelcome tug back to the past, when everything within me longed to move on.

I scanned the handwritten page, taking in his familiar, looping writing.

'The man writes like a ten-year-old ballerina,' Alice muttered.

'Wow,' I murmured.

'What? Tell me!'

'*Dear Cat,*' I read out loud, '*I have thought long and hard about reaching out to you...*'

'Are you a BT helpline?'

'*... and I'm sorry it's taken me a while to process everything. I want to let you know how sorry I am about the way things shook down...*'

'As if he was just an innocent bystander to your trauma.'

'... and I apologise for my part in that, however small and inadvertent.'

Alice hooted.

'While I can't offer you your old job back (and I'm sure you've since moved on to better things!), I'd love to take you for lunch when you return from your holiday oop north...'

'I hate *oop north* people,' said Alice. 'So patronising.'

'... and discuss what you shared with me in greater detail. With all my best, Oliver.'

'So, he wants to discuss the fact that you love him?'

I still couldn't bear to think about what had unfolded on the night of the party.

'*Loved*,' I corrected Alice. 'Past tense. And looking back, I probably only thought I did. It's not as if I ever had time to meet anyone else – he was the only man I ever saw apart from Mandeep, and they're gender-fluid.'

'Will you go for lunch?' asked Alice.

I sighed. 'What would be the point? So he can boast about his wedding to Antonia and revel in my undying admiration? No thanks.'

Alice high-fived a portrait of a seventeenth-century clansman. 'You're over him! The glorious day we thought would never come!'

'Well, it did,' I said. 'And thank God for that. I'm finally free.'

But even as I said the words, I wondered if I was being entirely honest – or whether I'd emotionally tied myself to someone I could genuinely fall for, who cared for me even less than Oliver had.

35

The rain had eased the next morning when we assembled in the main hall to drive to the little harbour a few miles away.

'We should see red deer on Jura,' Logan was telling Alice. 'Maybe we'll even spot a sea eagle or a pod of dolphins.' He looked particularly handsome in his blue jumper and jeans. His jaw was shaded with dark stubble, and I fought the urge to touch it.

'Will there be puffins?' she asked him feebly. 'Say yes – I've always wanted to see a puffin.'

We had laid into the thermos of alarmingly strong G&T she'd fished from her suitcase as soon as the champagne was finished. As a result, I'd woken at six feeling as though goblins were drilling into my skull and demons were pouring toxic waste into the holes they'd made. Alice was now leaning against a suit of armour, looking whiter than Agatha's laundry pile and breathing heavily. I didn't feel much better myself, despite a large fried breakfast.

At the harbour, the sky had cleared and the whole scene looked like a cheerful jigsaw puzzle with gleaming white boats bobbing gently, masts reflected as eccentric squiggles in the sparkling blue water. Sir Alastair waved from the jetty, and as he did so, I realised that the enormous MTV-video yacht moored alongside was our craft. A woman in a pink linen dress was waving from the deck.

'This is your motley crew is it, Alastair?' she called, in a voice bred to carry over six fields.

''Fraid so!' he shouted cheerfully. 'All the reprobates!'

I wondered why upper-class people were always jokingly demeaning themselves and their families. Perhaps it was to ward off jealousy, although that didn't seem necessary with Annabel. My parents, mortifyingly, had my A-level certificates framed in the downstairs loo. Posh people were more likely to say, 'Not entirely the ignoramus we all assumed, then.'

We boarded the yacht via a wobbling gangplank, Alice clutching my arm and looking pistachio green.

'Hello, hello, hello!' boomed a crimson-faced elderly man wearing a sailor's cap with a double-breasted white jacket, pink Bermuda shorts and deck shoes. 'Who do we have here? You're a sight for sore eyes, my dears!'

He leaned in to damply kiss our cheeks, and I almost choked on the whisky fumes. I hoped he wasn't captaining the boat.

'Harwood Giles-Patton,' he said, pumping our hands. 'Welcome aboard, lovely ladies!'

Alice cast me a horrified glance, and I shrugged. It wasn't as if Harwood was going to grope us with Annabel's piercing gaze fixed on him.

Close up, Annabel had skin like a crocodile handbag, a bouffant blonde bob, and was so tanned and wiry she looked as though she should be clinging to a twig inside a glass tank.

'Come through to the poop deck,' she said briskly. 'We're having sea breezes as we set sail.'

We followed her past polished teak and brass, glinting glass and acres of white leather seating to the back, where Sir Alastair, Logan and Rory were already chatting to a huddle of pink-faced men in expensive sailing gear and wraparound sunglasses. Their wives sat a little further away, wearing pale linen and Penelope Chilvers espadrille wedges. One was saying, 'The real trouble with Antigua at this time of year is the absolute *invasion* of tourists,' while the others nodded indignantly.

Rory was holding forth about the history of Iolair. 'Of course, it's claimed the fourth laird had the second sight, and predicted the Battle of Bannockburn,' he was saying. His slight Scottish accent had intensified to a rolling burr. Logan saw me watching, and rolled his eyes, making me smile.

I looked over the rail to see more couples boarding and felt relieved that I'd had so much 'small talk with rich people' practice in my career. There was some shouting below, the gang-plank was moved away and the boat swayed, as if it was glad to be free. So did Alice. As we pulled away from the jetty, I noticed she was gripping the rail with pure white knuckles.

'Al,' I said quietly, 'do you need to lie down?'

She nodded, her eyes closed. 'Might be sick.'

I spotted a steep flight of wooden stairs, and half carried her down them. We staggered through a small corridor hung with compasses and brass instruments and found a seating area with a coffee table displaying a glass-encased map of the Windward Islands. 'Sit me,' gasped Alice.

I lowered her onto the long white sofa, and she immediately turned so her face was buried in a cushion.

'Look, love, if you really think you're going to be sick, I need to get you a bucket.'

'Mmhm.'

'You do think you are? Or...'

She whimpered. The boat had picked up speed; we were bouncing over the waves. Stuck down here, I was beginning to feel slightly queasy, too.

There was a swing door with a round porthole opposite the

door we'd come in by, and I pushed through it, into a tiny galley kitchen made from stainless steel. It was like being inside a cheese grater, but that wasn't the most pressing issue facing me. Because standing at the far end, gazing through a porthole at the rolling waves, was a tall, slim woman with a tumble of red curls down her back.

'Sorry!' I said, as she turned. 'I didn't mean to startle you.'

'Oh, hello,' she said politely. 'I'm Marina.'

I was both shocked at her presence and irritated that she clearly found me so forgettable.

'Cat. We met at the Highland Games.'

'Oh yes, of course, I remember now. Poor Logan. Thank goodness he's on the mend,' Marina said. 'That knee's been giving him all sorts of trouble.'

It sounded as though she'd been spending a significant amount of time with him.

'I didn't know you were coming on the boat trip,' I said, aiming for cheerful rather than accusatory. Surely Sir Alastair had mentioned the Giles-Pattons' deadly feud with the Campbells? I suddenly remembered that she had left Jack after the Highland Games and was, unofficially at least, no longer a Campbell.

In fact, she was single, and in close proximity to Logan, whose heart she had broken not long ago. My smile felt strained and unnatural.

Marina laughed. 'Why would you? I was only asked at the last minute. Do you need something?' She glanced enquiringly round the pristine kitchen. I explained about Alice.

'*Cam!*' she yelled, and a large, copper-haired man in chef's whites pushed his way through the swing door, carrying a bucket of something that smelled like an evaporated rockpool.

'That's... pungent,' I murmured.

'Roasted langoustine shells for the lobster bisque.'

'Cam, she needs a sick bucket,' said Marina.

'Do you need to sit down?'

'No, it's for my friend.'

'Caaaat!' Alice's cry was a desperate wail.

Cameron deftly tipped the reeking shells into the spotless sink, and hurried in the direction of her voice, holding the empty bucket.

'What the hell is that smell?' I heard Alice say, swiftly followed by demonic horror-film noises.

'Oops,' said Marina. 'I'm afraid my little brother is an act first, think later kind of guy. It runs in the family,' she added wryly.

The boat veered to the left, and I too experienced a sudden wave of acute nausea. 'I need to go upstairs,' I managed.

'Ah.' Marina nodded. 'It can get you like that, when you can't see the horizon. I'll come up with you.'

'But Alice...'

'Cameron has a first aid certificate,' she said. 'She's in good hands.'

Vowing to return as soon as my stomach permitted, I followed Marina back up the wooden stairs and into the glorious, ozone-breezy fresh air. I clung to the deck, watching the still horizon as the boat climbed and dropped over the waves. We were now passing a series of uninhabited islands, where crowds of squawking cormorants perched on the seaweed-stained rock, and wild goats foraged on treeless cliffs.

As we skimmed past another rocky outcrop, I heard a voice shrieking, 'Seals!' I whipped my head round, to see a pile of animals like long, furry party balloons on the shore, their liquid eyes watching us pass.

'Oh my God,' I said to Marina, who was now standing nearby. 'They're *wonderful!*'

'I suppose I've got used to them, but they're lovely, aren't they? Sometimes, when I swim in the Corryvreckan, they swim alongside. Being bumped by one of those big, furry bodies is quite an experience. Though they smell terribly of rotten fish. Oh, sorry,' she added, as I blanched.

'Marina, darling!' Annabel swept towards us, now in giant sunglasses that made her look even more like an earwig. 'So glad to see you!' She air-kissed her on both cheeks. 'I hear you've left the dreaded Campbell clan!'

'News travels fast.'

'Oh, somebody always knows somebody who knows somebody, don't they?' tinkled Annabel. 'Far better off without him. Awful family. If I were you, I'd get out of Iolair altogether for the foreseeable.'

'I have been away for a few days, actually,' Marina said. 'I took myself off to Edinburgh. Looked up a few old haunts.'

By 'old haunts', I assumed she meant Logan. So they had been together, after all. My heart felt leaden in my chest.

36

'Super,' said Annabel. 'Anyway, darling, lunch on the fo'c'sle – sorry, you're a landlubber, aren't you, Cat? It means the front deck – in an hour or so. Help yourself to cocktails.'

I was enjoying this luxury trip entirely at the Giles-Pattons' expense, so I tried not to find her entirely obnoxious as she wafted a hand and drifted off to speak to the huddle of expensively kitted out sailors. They were now drinking champagne, and roaring with laughter at Rory's jokes.

Now we were through the long chains of islands, the sea was calmer, and the wind had dropped. I felt almost physically normal again as I descended the vertical steps to rescue Alice.

To my surprise, I could hear her shrieking with laughter and the low rumble of Cameron's voice.

'And what's this one?' she was asking as I pushed open the swing door.

'Ah, that's a wee mermaid,' he said. 'Got her when we moored in Chiang Saen. I was half-cut, and the guy didn't really speak English... Looks more like Marilyn Monroe with the body of a trout, eh?'

Cameron was sitting close to Alice. There was no sign of

the bucket, but she had a steaming cup of tea in front of her, and her face was no longer green. She appeared fascinated as Cameron detailed the tattoos all over his enormously muscular arms.

'Are you okay?' I asked, and she pulled her gaze away from his left bicep.

'So much better. Cam gave me a ginger biscuit and tea, and I feel amazing.'

'Cure for all ills, that,' he said, smiling at her. 'She'll be back up in a minute,' he added to me. 'I need to get on with lunch for you lot.'

Alice shot me an eloquent look that said 'go away, Cat' in neon. I nodded, and backed through the swing doors. This time I thought I'd explore further, and headed up another set of steps and down a narrow passage, which led to the deserted deck at the front of the boat. On a higher level, a long table was laid for lunch, with white cloths and yellow-striped cushions set along the benches, and I was about to go and admire it properly when I heard voices.

'Because I just can't,' I heard Logan say. I dodged behind a pillar as they came nearer. 'It's not what I want any more,' he went on. 'You of all people should understand that.'

'So you're just going to walk away?' asked Marina. 'Leave without a backward glance?'

Logan shrugged. 'Yes.'

'Well, you can always come back if you miss it too much,' she said.

The breeze blew his next words away.

Marina said, 'You know I'll always be there for you,' and she put her arm around his shoulders and leaned to kiss his cheek, her wild, windblown hair concealing them both as effectively as a dropped stage curtain.

I turned away, aware that I was effectively spying. Had Marina been talking about the castle, or their relationship? My heart was bumping unpleasantly, and I was aware of a wild, all-consuming sadness rising through me. I had thought my night with Logan was just a physical reaction to a remarkably attractive man, and that scratching the itch would help me move on from Oliver. It had done so – but not in the way I'd intended. Logan now occupied those parts of my mind instead – but Oliver's romantic life had largely taken place offstage, at home with Antonia. I'd only ever had to see him in work mode. Logan was everywhere, and so were his lost loves, still circling him like wraiths. *Does nobody ever move on in this place?*

I backed through the door where I'd come in, and made my way to the other deck. I gazed at the rolling hills of Jura as we approached the misty island. Seabirds skimmed alongside us, and the air was salty and damp. I watched the dark, forested shore slide closer as seagulls circled overhead, crying mournfully, and there was great excitement when someone thought they might have spotted a sea eagle roosting in a Scots pine tree. On the other hand, it might have been a very dense clump of twigs. Rory pointed to a herd of red deer strolling in the bracken, nervous, elegant heads lifted to watch the yacht pass. Their vivid colour and wide eyes reminded me of Marina.

'Marvellous shooting last year at the McDuff estate up in Perthshire,' I heard someone say. 'Great fun!'

I turned away, thinking of what my parents would make of these people. This wasn't my world – but was it Logan's? We were so very different... Perhaps he'd be better off going back to Marina, if she was offering.

Harwood stood up, swaying slightly though the sea was smooth. 'I hope you all have champagne,' he called loudly. 'I wish to propose a toast. Here's to us! Who's like us?'

The group raised their glasses and chanted, 'Damn few, and they're all dead!'

Logan now stood alone, his back to the group, gazing at the seabirds that followed us. Perhaps he wasn't one of them – and instead, he was dreaming of his freedom, longing for the day he could turn his back on the whole lot of them – including me.

After a lavish lunch of lobster bisque, roast chicken salad and raspberry mousse, which Alice put away as if she'd been on wartime rations for months, I went to sit down on the lower deck. Harwood had been holding court, telling endless stories about sailing round Cap d'Antibes in a gale and bemoaning the trouble with finding a 'decent crew' in Essaouira, and I needed some peace and quiet. Alice had sneaked back down to see Cameron again.

For a while, I leaned on the rail watching the deep blue mountains of Jura and Scarba pass, and looking out for seals lying on the flat rocks of the little coves we passed. Cormorants flew low on the water, and skeins of soft mackerel clouds laced the sky over the horizon.

This place hadn't changed in centuries – perhaps millennia. What I saw as I watched the angular cliffs and wind-ripped trees of these deserted Hebridean islands slide by was what any sailor of the past would have seen. How could Logan bear to leave behind so much timeless peace and beauty?

Lost in my reverie, I looked up to find him standing beside me. I jumped as if I'd manifested him from the waves.

'How long have you been there?'

He smiled. 'Not long. Sorry I startled you.'

'I'll come back up in a minute,' I said. 'Just needed a break.'

'Don't blame you. This is when I miss smoking,' he said, leaning on the rail next to me. 'It was such a good excuse to escape. Now, you have to say, "I'm so sorry, I can't stand another moment of your company, do excuse me."'

I laughed. 'I find it hard to imagine you smoking.'

'I used to do all kinds of things,' he said. 'Drink till I fell over, dance all night...'

'*Dance?*'

'Only if The Fall came on at Bodega, the Edinburgh night-club we used to frequent. Or "Bods" as we used to call it. Aren't students hilarious?' he said morosely. 'And it wasn't really dancing, more sort of flinging about and trying not to get your eye poked out.'

'Marina said she's just got back from Edinburgh,' I said, before I could stop myself.

'Did she?' said Logan flatly. Clearly, he was not willing to discuss whatever relationship he was having with her. She and Jack were still technically married, of course, and Logan would hate any lochside gossip. I felt hurt that he didn't trust me – and the realisation that they'd been together was like a stone sinking to the silty floor of my stomach.

'Look!' he suddenly said, and pointed. I scanned the waves, but could see nothing beyond a couple of terns gliding by.

'No.' Logan gently put a hand on my cheek and turned my head further, so I was looking back towards the island. I felt the heat of his fingers and caught my breath, then I saw what he was looking at. No more than thirty feet away, a pod of dolphins was breaching the water. As I watched, two leapt into the air, twirled once and disappeared under the waves.

'Oh...'

Logan put his hand over mine on the railing. 'Keep watching.'

Seconds later, more appeared – huge, gleaming creatures performing a spontaneous marine ballet, their turns and dives making rainbows in the sunlit arcs of spray. I had no idea how long we stood there, mesmerised with joy – or at least, I was. I'd never seen anything like it. We waited after they stopped surfacing, but Logan said, 'I think they've gone now,' and as he spoke, I saw their dark blue shadows skating past the boat and away to the deep sea beyond the islands.

'That was the most magical thing I've ever seen,' I told him.

Logan smiled. 'Me too. I've seen them before, but not so close, or for so long.'

His hand was still on mine. Now the spell was broken, I didn't know whether I should move it, but I could feel the pulse beating through his palm against my skin, and I couldn't bear to pull away.

He turned to look at me. 'Listen, Cat,' he said, 'I know I've been so bad-tempered about the ceilidh idea, and I just want you to know that my feelings about it are nothing to do with you.' He sighed. 'I don't think whatever the castle turns into, even if we do get investment, is something I want to be a part of. I love Iolair because of its history, and because we grew up there, and Mum was such a part of it – but if Rory's right about the figures, and I think he is, it has to change dramatically. I'm thinking I might get a job somewhere else for a while.'

'Yes, Donald said.' I didn't mention that I'd overheard him talking to Marina.

'I've an old Edinburgh mate, Jamie, who went back home after he graduated,' Logan went on. 'Now, he runs a restaurant by the shore that's getting incredible reviews. He messaged me to say he's looking for someone to run their market garden – they grow all their own produce, amazing herbs you can't get here. They use seaweed and foraging in their cooking, too, and... well, anyway, I'm thinking it might be worth giving it a shot for a few years.'

'It sounds great,' I said, trying not to imagine Castle Iolair without Logan. 'Where is it?'

'New Zealand.'

I paused. 'Sorry, I thought you said New Zealand.'

'I did.' Logan half smiled. 'It's a long way, I know.'

'But... what about your dad? And...' I wanted to say 'me', but an image floated into my head of Marina running down a flight of sandy steps, carrying an armful of foraged greenery and holding the hand of a small child with Logan's dark eyes and her blazing red curls...

'There you two are! Lurking about in the bowels of the yacht!'

Logan snatched his hand from mine, as Annabel came round the corner clutching another glass of champagne, light bouncing off her enormous sunglasses. She strongly resembled Anna Wintour after a night in a dehydrator.

'Come up – we're about to enter the Corryvreckan whirlpool,' she commanded. 'It's so much *jollier* when we're all there to see the tide change.'

'We'll talk later,' said Logan quietly, and I nodded.

Though what was there to talk about? He was going as far as it was possible to go, with or without Marina, and I'd just have to get over it. I'd got over Oliver, I told myself. I could do it again. Although Logan was absolutely nothing like Oliver. He was an infinitely better person.

Up on the deck, there was still no sign of Alice, but everyone else was crowded to one side of the boat.

'You can see how the tides are now changing,' bellowed Harwood, delighted to have an audience again. 'Observe the crossing of the waves – a sign that the whirlpool is beginning to run.'

I peered over, between two of the linen-draped women, and saw what he meant. Two sets of waves were racing towards each other, crossing and swirling. As we watched, the jade-green swell became more noticeable, bumping against the rocky outcrops in a spray of foam, and sending seabirds soaring and crying into the air.

'The roll of the water looks almost muscular, doesn't it?' I asked, fascinated. 'As if it's alive.'

'Oh yes,' Marina spoke. 'It's a very strange feeling when you're in the moving water, as if someone huge and strong is pushing and pulling you.' I thought of her with Logan, and had to close my eyes to dispel the vivid image.

'Aren't you scared?'

Marina laughed. 'I would be if I was caught in the whirlpool, but we know when to get back into the boat. And I don't come alone. I swim with Cam sometimes, or..." she hesitated. 'I used to go with Logan.'

'Wouldn't recommend jumping in now!' boomed Harwood. 'It's really getting going.'

He was right. The boat was now lurching up and down like a car on the waltzers, and I was beginning to regret the lobster bisque.

'I think I'll just go and sit inside...' I said feebly.

'Cameron's got ginger biscuits,' called Marina as I wavered down the steps.

I pushed through the swing door again, and instantly reversed.

In the brief flash I'd witnessed, Alice was pressed against Cameron, his hands were in her hair and they were kissing passionately on the white leather banquette. I hoped they hadn't heard the door swinging. I retreated to the deck, and saw Logan looking at me, confused.

I shook my head. 'They're... Alice is...'

'Cameron?'

I nodded.

'Ah, the Swordsman of the Glen strikes again.'

'He's not a blushing virgin, then?'

Logan snorted. 'I just hope your friend doesn't fall for him,' he said. 'Either she'll be left high and dry when he sails off into the sunset, or she'll end up travelling the world with him – but either way, it would make things a bit awkward for me.'

'Things?'

'Well, he's Marina's brother.'

He turned as Rory called over. 'Loge! What was that chap's name at school? Used to hide all his tuck in a locked box?'

'Robin Neilssen,' Logan shouted back.

Rory beckoned him over. 'Come and tell Johnny here what you did in revenge...'

As we sailed out of the pitching waves into the calmer waters that would lead us back to Ardanachan harbour, I wondered what Logan had meant. Awkward because he didn't want any romantic connection to Marina in his life – or awkward because he'd have an ongoing connection to me?

Either way, it didn't matter. Soon, Logan would be thousands of miles away – and I'd almost certainly never see him again.

37

I spent Saturday showing Alice the rest of the castle and taking her down to the loch 'to show me where you almost drowned'.

She had taken a great shine to Sir Alastair, and after losing her for an hour, I finally tracked her down in his turret, chatting to him. She had a stuffed badger on her knees, and they were deep into a discussion on Victorian taxidermy.

'I might take it up,' said Alice earnestly.

I thought briefly of the pottery, tae kwon do and poetry slam hobbies which Alice had picked up and discarded over the years. ('I didn't know "slam" meant I had to perform! I thought it meant you wrote fast!')

'Well, if you do, I know a lovely little chap in Perth, remarkable skill,' said Sir Alastair. 'Let me know if you ever make it back up here.'

'Oh, I hope to quite soon,' twinkled Alice.

As soon as I'd managed to extract her, I turned to her beadily. 'What do you mean by "*quite soon*"?'

Alice shrugged as we headed back to the Queen's Room. 'Couple of weeks?'

'Al, I probably won't even be here by then.'

'I wasn't entirely thinking of you,' said Alice. 'Cam WhatsApped me this morning, inviting me on a foraging picnic. He says we can sail to this little unpronounceable island and pick our lunch, then he'll cook it over a charcoal grill...'

'You, foraging?' I said. 'You won't even buy a Pret salad in case there's something weird in it.'

'I'd stir-fry deadly nightshade for the chance to fondle those arm muscles again.'

'So it wasn't just a snog?'

'No, I really like him. He likes me, too,' Alice added. 'He's exactly my type, and he made me laugh. Plus, he's definitely not polyamorous because I asked.'

'But, Al,' I blurted without thinking, 'he's Marina's brother, and that's weird.'

'Why? You're not dating Logan – are you?'

She let us into the room, and we flung ourselves onto the historic bed as if it was a bunk at Center Parcs.

'Well, not really... I mean, we couldn't even if we wanted... It won't work...' I trailed off.

'Ah,' Alice said. 'You're mad about him.'

'I am *not*.'

'You are. And I know because of the way you reacted to Oliver's ridiculous letter. A month ago, you'd have framed it and kissed it every night.'

'Can't a woman just be happy to be single?'

'Of course she can. But after Bothygate, I don't think you are. Look, I'll tell Cam it's not going to happen.'

Alice picked up her phone, and I snatched it from her.

'You will not! Because your love life has nothing to do with anyone else, including me, and he'll tell Marina and she'd tell Logan and then I'll have to move to Bratislava and live in the witness protection programme, being called Olga and running a cigarette kiosk for the rest of my life.'

'I'm pretty sure they have events companies in Bratislava,' said Alice thoughtfully.

'Look, can we drop it? I feel embarrassed and ridiculous, and I'd rather just forget it ever happened. And anyway, Logan's moving to New Zealand.'

'Come off it... you can't be that bad in bed,' said Alice, and I threw a stray Haribo fried egg at her.

I explained what he'd told me, and she nodded. 'It makes sense, though. It's beautiful there, none of this so-called weather we get here, lots of jobs, low crime...'

'Because Iolair is such a hotbed of county lines drug trafficking?' I snapped.

'You *really* don't want him to go, do you?' asked Alice.

I shrugged childishly.

'I've no idea why I even like him,' I mumbled. 'He's arrogant and foul-tempered and bores on about ecology all the time...'

'You love ecology,' said Alice. 'Remember when your mum made you go on that "save our trees" vigil and you were in the local paper hugging a sapling?'

I sighed. 'I could be riding on the back of a blue whale waving a Greenpeace banner, and it still wouldn't work with me and Logan.'

I didn't mention the moment when he'd placed his hand over mine as we'd watched the dolphins. I didn't want Alice to feel sorry for me in my romantic delusions.

That evening, Alice and I went to the Falls of GlennIolair pub.

I half hoped Logan would be there again, cooking, but a flame-haired teenage boy seemed to be doing everything single-handedly, and the menu was reduced to a ham taco special or deep-fried cheddar and pickle balls. We ordered both, more out of curiosity than hunger. At nine, Donald came in for his usual pint.

'You live in the gatehouse, don't you?' Alice asked, and Donald nodded.

'Then I did you a favour earlier!' She looked delighted.

'Did ye, right enough?'

'I saw your sign that says PLEASE SHUT GATE DUE TO RABBITS, and I spotted some that had escaped,' she said. 'It took me ages, but I rounded them up, and now all six are back in your garden! So cute,' she added. 'I love that you let them be free range, hopping about.'

Donald, for once, was speechless. Slowly, he put his pint down.

'The sign,' he said carefully, 'is to keep the rabbits *out* o' the garden. Because, ye see, lassie, they eat the plants.'

Alice's face fell. 'Oh!' she said. 'I thought they were pets. So they're...'

Donald nodded. 'Pests,' he said flatly. 'That's right.'

My shoulders were quivering.

'If ye'll excuse me,' he said, 'I'll need to be getting back to rescue Ishbel's seedlings. Though it may be too late, o' course.'

He turned, and trudged wearily to the door, leaving his half-drunk pint on the table.

'You're not from round here, are you?' I asked Alice, and we collapsed, laughing so hard that at one point, I couldn't breathe.

'Good luck with the rural foraging,' I managed, and we were off again.

There was no lift home from Donald, but it transpired there was an occasional taxi service run by Morag's cousin's boy, Hamish, who could be persuaded to take us for double fare after 8 p.m. We crammed into his wheezing Fiat Punto, singing along to 'Love Machine' on his crackling radio as we bumped over potholes.

'You'll be staying at the castle, aye?' he shouted over the music.

'Cat is,' said Alice. 'I'm just visiting.'

'So you'll know Himself, Cat?'

'Aye,' I said, and quickly changed it to 'yes' before my friend could mock me.

'Bad business, that,' said Hamish, swerving violently to avoid a small animal. 'Leaving the love of his life on the eve of the wedding. Auntie Morag had her new hat sent down from Oban on the train; she was in bits.'

'No, wait – Marina left him,' I said, puzzled.

'She didnae!' Hamish looked outraged. 'If that's what he told ye, he's a liar as well as a laird. He dumped her, and she ran off wi' Jack Campbell because she couldnae stand folks' pity and the man'd been banging down her door for a decade.'

'Are you sure?'

'Aye, I'm very sure. Marina was my wee sister's best pal for years. Beside herself, she was. White dress hanging on her wardrobe, best day of her life about to happen – then it's all over with a few hours' notice.' He warmed to his theme. 'I'm surprised folks have been so pleasant to Himself since, if I'm honest. But if he's telling everyone she left him, no bloody wonder. The great, posh snake,' he muttered to himself.

We drew up at the castle, and I paid Hamish.

'Hope you didnae object to my bit o' gossip,' he said. 'But ye should know what's gone on, I reckon.'

He nodded and drove away, his engine rattling into the distance.

'Wow,' said Alice. 'Are you going to ask him about that? Or should I, now I'm soon to be marrying her brother at Edinburgh Castle?'

'I have to,' I said, opening the kitchen door. My heart was bumping uncomfortably. 'I need to know why he lied to me.'

'Did he actually *lie*, though?' asked Alice, always inclined to be kind, as we made our way down the corridor.

'Well... yes,' I said reluctantly. 'He said she'd left him just before the wedding. I thought that's why he was gloomy. Why would he tell everyone she'd jilted him if it wasn't true?'

'I don't know.' Alice's face looked troubled in the dim light of the kitchen corridor. 'That's why you should ask him – as long as you're absolutely sure you want to discover the truth.'

That night, I lay in bed, thinking in circles. If Logan had left Marina, perhaps he wasn't still in love with her. And if not, where did that leave me – other than twelve thousand miles from New Zealand, and hopelessly ill-suited?

As the long, white night began to brighten towards dawn, I had firmly decided, once again, that there was no future for me and Logan – and that the best thing I could do would be to make a success of the ceilidh, then head home to London and embrace the single life.

Alice left early on Sunday, Billy Joel's 'Piano Man' blasting from her speakers.

After waving her off, I decided I'd better go and apologise to Donald and Ishbel about the rabbits, although every time I thought about Alice's good deed, I found myself snorting with laughter. I was also profoundly relieved that my friend hadn't performed her rabbit whispering in Logan's vegetable garden. I doubted he'd ever descend from that particular pinnacle of rage.

As I made my way down the long drive in the sunshine, I saw a tall figure walking towards me, two prancing dogs at his heels, and realised with a jolt of nerves that it was Logan.

'Morning!' he called. 'Off for a walk while it's nice?'

He was wearing a soft green T-shirt and old jeans, and I found myself focusing on his lightly tanned arms. I also wondered why he was speaking to me like a vicar greeting a parishioner.

'No, I'm going to see Donald and Ishbel to apologise,' I said. I explained about the rabbits, and Logan laughed.

'It might not be a bad thing that Alice has gone home,' he said. 'Then again, Cameron seems awfully taken with her.'

'Have you spoken to him?'

'Marina mentioned it. He's hoping Alice'll come back up for a visit soon, apparently. Perhaps the old rake's finally reformed.'

I felt bleak suddenly. Me back in London, no more Logan, Alice becoming best mates with Marina up here... I couldn't help myself. I needed to know.

'Logan, are you and Marina friends now?'

He looked startled. 'Well... of a sort, I suppose. Yes, I hope so.'

'Even though she left you hours before the wedding?'

I held my breath, afraid I'd gone too far.

Logan closed his eyes and sighed. 'That's not exactly what happened.'

I waited, but he glanced at his watch.

'I'm late for a meeting with Dad,' he said. 'But look, meet me in the kitchen garden in a couple of hours. I've got a kettle in the potting shed – we can have a cup of tea and a chat.'

I nodded, gave the dogs' heads a ruffle and went on my way.

'And don't let any rabbits in!' Logan called as he headed back towards the castle.

38

Two hours later, having apologised profusely ('Och, the lassie wasn't to know,' Ishbel said over her home-made shortbread, 'besides, I've netting over the strawberries.'), I walked back up to the vegetable gardens, skirting the front of the castle.

The old stones shone in the sun, bluebells were just beginning to colour the south lawn a soft, spectral purple, and the thought of leaving this magical place tugged painfully at my heart. But if investment didn't come soon, they'd all have to go, and the castle would be sold off to the highest bidder.

Tortoise was lying on the warm stone path as I reached the kitchen garden gate, and I bent down to stroke her tummy. She was waving her furry trousers in the air, and I was crooning endearments, when I looked up to see Logan standing beside me.

'No cats in the potting shed,' he said, in a warning tone. 'I'm not as forgiving as Ishbel.'

'You're not coming, are you, Torty?'

'Do not cheapen her name,' Logan said solemnly. 'She deserves her full title: Miss Tortoise McAskill, Chief Rodent Operative.'

I laughed, although my heart was bumping unpleasantly. Would Logan reveal that he and Marina were back together? Worse, would he admit that he'd lied about who called off the wedding? Because while Logan had his obvious faults, I had always felt him to be implicitly trustworthy. If he wasn't, I'd be forced to question my own judgement – again.

He led the way through the neat beds and bean rows to a substantial wooden shed with little glass windows and a green-painted door.

'Coffee?' he asked, lighting the Calor gas ring and holding up a cafetière.

'That's very fancy.'

'I spend a lot of time in here. Might as well have decent coffee.'

I looked around. The shed smelled pleasantly of dry wood and fresh earth with an undertone of creosote. Tools, garden forks and spades hung neatly on the walls, and two old, chipped bentwood chairs were placed by a table made from wooden vegetable crates. It reminded me of childhood Sunday morning visits to my grandpa Ned's cheerful allotment, and as I took a seat, I felt the tension leaving my body like a cloud of wasps.

'So...' Logan handed me a striped mug and sat down in the other chair. The door was open, the air warm, and birdsong drifted in. 'What was it you wanted to know, exactly?'

I looked at him. Those bloody cheekbones of his. It was odd that they were simply versions of the same dull facial bits and bobs we all have – but only Logan's made me want to trace a fingertip over them, marvelling at their exquisite symmetry.

'I know it's none of my business,' I said. 'But I thought... I had the impression that Marina had left you. I thought you still had feelings for her. Then someone said it was the other way around. I mean, obviously you don't have to tell me; you hardly know me really...'

Logan's face was unreadable.

'There's no reason why you shouldn't know, I suppose,' he said eventually. 'Yes, it was me who called off the wedding. I changed my mind the night before.'

I felt profound shock – both at the news, and at his lie. '*Why?*'

'I didn't love her. As a friend, maybe, but not in the way I should have done if we were going to spend our lives together. I did when we were young; we were inseparable...' He caught my eye and looked away, perhaps recalling my visit long ago. Even now, I hoped he wouldn't mention it. '... But I'd fallen back into the relationship because I was lacking direction, I suppose, and she was here and everyone said it was meant to be, and I was so fond of her and nostalgic for what we'd once had that I convinced myself it was love again.'

'But you asked her to marry you?' I felt angry on Marina's behalf.

'No. She asked me. Never say I told you this, but we were walking on the beach up at Kilcrossan, and she took off her rucksack, and unpacked an entire picnic with china and a bottle of champagne. Then she got down on one knee in the sand, and asked me.'

'But you could have said no?'

He shook his head. 'I couldn't. It would have broken her heart, and I thought maybe I could reignite all my old feelings for her if I just tried harder. I said yes. She was so happy, everyone was so thrilled for us, and if I was going to stay in Iolair, as I planned to, I thought it made sense to have someone I knew and trusted beside me. But...'

'But you didn't realise you couldn't go through with it till literally hours before the wedding? Bloody hell, Logan. I think I'd have killed you with a ceremonial sword, never mind run off with Jack Campbell.'

'I know. It's the worst thing I've ever done, and I felt like absolute shit about it. Still do, actually. But it was Rory who made me see sense.'

'*Rory*? Why, what did he say?'

'He was going to be my best man,' said Logan. 'Despite disagreeing over how to save the castle, we've always been close – maybe because of losing Mum. And he sat me down the night before and poured me a very large whisky. He said, "Logan, I need you to be honest with yourself. Because after tomorrow it'll be too late. Do you really, truly love her?" And I hesitated before I answered him.' He looked up at me, his expression haunted. 'And that was when I knew I couldn't go through with it.'

'Oh my God,' I whispered. 'What did you do?'

'I went to see Marina,' he said quietly. 'It was ten o'clock at night, the Grand Hall was all decked out with flowers and gold chairs, most of the guests had arrived and were bedded down all over the castle – it was a complete nightmare, and it was all of my own making.'

He took a long breath. 'Sorry, this isn't pleasant for me to talk about...'

'You don't have to,' I said, desperately hoping he'd carry on.

'Might as well tell you the rest,' he said, taking a swig of coffee. 'Maybe it'll be cathartic. So, Cameron answered the door, and said Marina wouldn't come downstairs because it was bad luck to see the bride the night before the wedding...'

I winced.

'I know. But I said it was urgent, and he went to get her. She was pissed off that I was there at all, but she took me into Chris's study and asked what was wrong. I said I couldn't go through with it, we weren't right for each other, and it wouldn't be fair to marry her, feeling as I did...'

'I hope she brained you with a desk lamp.'

He gave a twisted smile. 'She thumped me quite hard, actually. Then, understandably, she had hysterics. Rhona and Chris came in, and I think they were both in shock. They didn't believe me at first, but once it was clear I wasn't going to change my mind, Cam told me to leave in no uncertain terms, so I did. I spent the night dismantling chairs and tables, and unravelling flower garlands so we didn't have to look at it all in the morning. Rory helped me.'

'Bloody hell.' I shook my head, trying to imagine the way Marina must have felt. 'Then what?'

Logan sighed. 'This is like speed therapy. I don't think I've actually told this story in full since it happened. Then all hell broke loose. First, I told Dad, and I thought he was genuinely going to disinherit me. But once he understood my reasons... well, he accepted it. But he was furious it had taken me so long to wake up.'

'But everyone else?'

'Here's the thing,' Logan said. 'Marina was too upset to speak to me – of course she was. But Cameron came over first thing and he told me that I must tell everyone it was her who'd called it off.'

'Why?'

'Because she couldn't stand the pity,' Logan said sadly. 'Marina's always had great pride, and the idea of everyone feeling sorry for her, wondering why I'd changed my mind – she couldn't have borne it.'

'So that was why she ran off with Jack?'

'That little *cretin*,' said Logan bitterly. 'He took advantage when she was at her most vulnerable, and he offered her a simple way out of all the gossip and rumour: go away with him, then everyone would believe she'd called off the wedding to be with Jack.'

'Having met him, it does stretch credibility a bit,' I murmured.

Logan laughed. 'I agree. But his awfulness made me feel

even worse. When I heard they'd gone, I felt sick. It was all my fault, and she deserved – no, deserves – better. Anyway, Dad made me tell all the guests, quite rightly, and we paid off the caterers and the band and stood down the registrar, and they all went home, some more peacefully than others.' He shuddered. 'It was the worst day of my life, by a country mile. But not a patch on what I put Marina through, I'm sure. I wrote to her and called and messaged, but she blocked me. I hadn't heard a single word from her till recently.'

'Do you wish you'd gone ahead with it now?'

'God, no. It was entirely the right thing to do. I was just an absolute idiot for leaving it so late, for not asking myself the right questions.'

'What *are* the right questions?'

Logan looked at me again. His eyes caught the sunlight, and I saw the green and gold flecks in his dark irises.

'I've thought about this a lot since. I suppose they're: Do I love this person so much I can imagine getting old with them? Does the idea of one day not being with them feel agonising? Would I give up anything to save our relationship?' He put his head in his hands. 'For me, the answer to all of them was "no". Oh, and one more,' he said, muffled. 'Do we make each other laugh?'

I thought of Oliver. He had never once made me laugh, other than politely, in all the time I'd known him.

'That's an important one,' I said.

Logan nodded. 'Vital. And Marina is lovely and kind and clever – but she never made me laugh. I don't think she found me very funny, either.'

'Certainly not on the wedding morning,' I said, and he snorted.

'Nobody was laughing that day, trust me.'

'So Agatha and Donald and Ishbel – they don't know the truth?'

'Agatha does. She took one look at me, and she knew. She had me drink a triple whisky and made me a ham sandwich, and then she said, "It's no' for us to judge the hearts of others, laddie." She is a wonder,' he added. 'But much as I love him, Donald is a talker – and I couldn't risk betraying my promise to Marina.'

'So wait – you weren't in Edinburgh together?'

'What? No! I was back at my old attic flat, trying to make major life decisions. The only person I spoke to for two days was Bernie, my old landlady, who wanted to heal my moth-eaten chakras with a rose-quartz crystal. Marina still has tons of mates in Edinburgh, though,' he added. 'She was probably drowning her sorrows with them in the White Hart.'

'And at the games?' I asked. 'You seemed quite friendly.'

'Jack was boiling with rage about that,' Logan said. 'As you witnessed. The truth is, Marina finally replied to me a couple of months ago. She said she'd been too hurt and humiliated at first to think about whether we were really suited forever, but since being with Jack, she'd been considering what she needed in a relationship. She wanted someone who... well anyway, what she wants is her business,' he said quickly. 'And it's not me any more. But basically, she was thinking of leaving Jack, despite his possessive adoration of her, and she wanted to let me know she would forgive me for calling it off the way I did.'

'Would? Not *had*?'

'No. She said she needed to see me again to see how she felt. Whether we could be friends.'

'Fair enough.'

'So, when we met at the games, that's what she was doing. You see why I didn't want to highlight the fact that we'd just spent the night together.'

My face flared with heat. 'Of course – I completely get it.'

'Not that it wasn't... well, wonderful. In fact.'

I gazed at him in shock. 'Really? You thought that?'

He nodded. 'Didn't you?'

I found I couldn't speak, as he reached out to touch the side of my face – and then his mouth was on mine, and my arms were around him – and I realised that no matter what I told myself, I wasn't over Logan McAskill at all.

Perhaps, in fact, I never would be.

39

MAY BANK HOLIDAY WEEKEND, FIFTEEN YEARS EARLIER

There's a little blue rowing boat bobbing at the jetty, and Logan is already waiting beside it, his dark hair ruffled by the breeze.

My own hair is as perfect as it's going to get, via my GHD rip-off straighteners and half a bottle of John Frieda serum, and I'm wearing my best jeans. I can hardly breathe or speak with nerves, but Logan raises a hand in greeting, and says, 'Be careful in those boots – the jetty's quite slippery.'

I'm wearing ankle boots with a little chunky heel because they make my legs appear marginally longer. Also, I look less like a golf club side-on than I do in trainers. 'Steady,' he says, and takes my arm as I wobble into the boat.

I'm trying to commit the sensation of his hand touching me through my jacket to memory, so I don't look where I'm putting my feet and stumble sideways as a wash of water tips the boat slightly.

'Watch yourself!'

'Sorry.' I lower myself onto the wooden seat, my face hot, and very aware that so far, our communication has consisted largely of warnings and apologies.

'Don't worry.' Logan seats himself opposite me. 'I'll just take you round the island and back. Are you sure your mum and dad are okay with it?'

I feel like an eight-year-old on a school trip. Any minute he's going to say, 'Did your mum sign the permission slip?'

'Yeah, totally fine,' I lie. Mum and Dad would have several litters of kittens each if they knew, but I told them I was going to walk up to the castle, which I still haven't seen.

Logan digs under his seat and produces an appalling neon-orange garment. He hands it to me. 'Here, you'll need to wear this,' he says casually, as if he hasn't just sounded the death knell on my romantic hopes.

The square, padded life jacket smells of mould and has more straps and toggles than a six-person tent. 'I mean, I'm honestly fine,' I say. 'I'm not going to fall in.'

'No jacket, no boat,' says Logan, like a teacher. 'Sorry, Cat, but it's non-negotiable.'

'Why aren't you wearing one?'

'Because bloody Rory left mine somewhere and now, we've only got one,' he says. 'Plus, I know I can swim in the loch. I don't know if you can.'

'I can! We had swimming lessons, like, every week in Year Seven...' I begin, then realise how childish I sound. I want to cry with frustration – this isn't how the boat trip was supposed to go.

Sullenly, I pull on the life jacket and allow Logan to tighten straps and adjust clasps. I feel like a Lego person made of blocks.

'Right,' says Logan. 'I think we're all good. Off we go.'

He dips the oars into the water, and I watch his biceps tighten as he pulls us away from the jetty. A monochrome bird skims by.

'A sandpiper,' says Logan. 'They nest on the shore, just by the woods.'

Mum would be thrilled with all this ornithology chat, I think. The surface of the water is calm, and I reach down to trail my hand in it, thinking I might make a pretty romantic picture.

'Wouldn't do that,' Logan says. 'Your hand'll go numb, plus it causes drag on the boat.'

'Sorry.' I snatch it back and instead watch the passing scenery, desperately trying to think of cool, witty things to say. Logan seems quite happy to row in silence.

'Is it nice, living at the castle?' I ask, when the silence begins to feel like a third person, crouched in the boat alongside us.

Logan raises an eyebrow. 'Nice? I don't know. It's special and historic and makes people judge me and think I'm an entitled prick. I'm not sure if it's *nice*.'

'You don't seem like an entitled prick,' I venture feebly.

Now we're out on the water, a stiff breeze has sprung up and my carefully smoothed hair is whipping over my face, sticking to my coral Juicy Tube lip gloss. I try surreptitiously to pick it off.

Logan smiles. 'I should have warned you. Marina always ties her hair back when we go out on the loch – she can't stand it blowing into her face, and there's so much of hers.'

For a brief moment, I feel a terrible urge to pin down this paragon of lush curls and good sense, and chop it all off.

'Do you see her a lot?' I ask. 'I mean, with you being away at school?'

'As much as I can,' says Logan. 'I stay over at her parents' house quite often when I'm back. They're cool.'

I nod, as if staying over at a boyfriend's house is something I'm casually familiar with. I can't even imagine it.

'Look.' Logan glances over his shoulder as he steers the boat towards the rocky shore of a tiny, tree-covered island. 'There's part of a ruined castle behind the trees,' he says. 'Want a quick look? Oh, but your boots...'

'No, I'd love to!' I exclaim, almost leaping into waist-deep water in my eagerness to disembark.

'Let me get the boat up on the shore,' he says.

I stay still, as he jumps down and begins to pull.

'You could get out, too,' he says pleasantly. 'Makes it a bit easier to drag.'

That's it. Logan thinks I'm a dead weight, in the wrong boots, with vain, stupid hair that sticks to me. I want to go home and cry, but he's leading the way up the beach, so I chuck my life jacket back into the boat and follow him. Logan pushes through some thorny branches, holding them back for me. We emerge into a mossy clearing where the stone ruins of an ancient castle stand, covered in ivy and creeping moss.

'This is the old Kincherrell castle,' he says. 'Rory and I camp out here sometimes.'

'Did you ever come here with Marina?' I blurt, and instantly wish I could rewind time to a moment when I hadn't just said something profoundly stupid.

Logan looks at me curiously. 'Once or twice,' he says. 'Why?'

'No reason.' I stare blankly at the rocks in front of me.

'Cat,' Logan says gently, 'has anything upset you? Have I done something wrong?'

To my horror, I feel tears pressing.

'Hey,' says Logan. He crosses the rocks again and puts his arm around me. He smells of outdoors, clean cotton, expensive spice – not a hint of the cheap body sprays the boys at my school wield like olfactory weapons.

'Tell me what's wrong,' Logan says firmly.

I lean my head against his warm chest, blinking furiously. 'It's just... I just...' I'm never going to see him again. What have I got to lose?

'I just think that I'd really like to kiss you,' I say helplessly.

There is a pause that feels eternal.

'Ah,' says Logan.

His arm drops away, and he turns to look at the blue boat resting on the shore.

'Shall we head back?' he asks.

Unable to speak, I follow him, leaving my pathetic hopes behind me in the ruins.

40

Logan pulled away first. We were both breathing heavily, and the straps of my top had fallen from my shoulders when he'd bent to kiss my neck.

He looked at me, and I could see his pupils were still dilated. 'Cat,' he whispered, and cleared his throat.

'Logan.' I smiled tentatively at him.

He reached out, and brushed a strand of hair from my face, then he stood to put the kettle on again. It seemed a humorously domestic task, in contrast to our sudden display of passion in the potting shed.

'Are you okay?' I asked.

He laughed. 'I have no idea. Are you?'

'Yes. If a little confused.'

Logan sat down beside me again, and took my hand. 'I'm sorry,' he said. 'I don't mean to blow hot and cold, it's just... I really like you, Cat. Obviously. I mean... you're beautiful and sexy and clever and brave, and everyone else here thinks the world of you, too.' He paused. 'You're wonderful, actually.'

Joyful relief flooded through me, and I opened my mouth to reply.

'Wait,' he said. 'The thing is, I really have decided that I'm leaving. The job in New Zealand is everything I've tried and failed to do here, with a much higher chance of success. And now Marina's back and single, everyone'll be trying to get us back together, and the Campbells are lurking around, and Rory's set on turning Iolair into a conference centre... well, the decision's pretty much been made for me.'

'But it's your inheritance,' I urged. My last roll of the dice.

'I suspect it'll be sold off long before Dad goes. And if not, I'll leave it to him and Rory to decide what happens next.'

'You won't stay and fight for it?'

Perhaps I really meant 'fight for the relationship we could have'. I felt sorrow creeping through me like mist rolling over the loch.

He shook his head. 'I'm a lover not a fighter,' he said. 'But I shouldn't even be a lover. Honestly, Cat, I don't want to mess you around – you deserve the best. Plus, you'll be going back home soon after the ceilidh, and I've told Jamie I'm ready to fly out as soon as I get my work visa.'

'Does your dad know?'

'Not yet, but he soon will. Not looking forward to that conversation,' murmured Logan.

'So you wouldn't stay and... well, try it? See what happens?'

I meant between us, and it was clear he understood that. He stroked the back of my hand with his strong, tanned fingers.

'It wouldn't be fair on you,' he said. 'I hate cities, and I don't like parties – I couldn't spend time in your world for long. And I can't expect you to trek up here all the time, to watch me trying to fit into some corporate scheme and being miserable. I think we've just... missed our moment.'

He sighed, and I gently withdrew my hand. He was right, of course. We didn't belong in each other's worlds, and all my organisational skills and problem-solving experience couldn't fix that.

'So that's it,' I said. 'That was our last kiss.'

'No. *This* is the last one.'

Logan touched my jawbone with infinite delicacy as he drew my face towards his. He kissed me as though I was precious to him, and I kissed him back in the same way.

'Another coffee before you go?' he asked, finally pulling away again, and I shook my head.

'I need to get back to the castle. Continue my evil scheme to turn it into a soulless business park.'

He smiled. 'Friends, though?'

'Always.'

He kissed my hand and watched me leave, making my way through the sunlit vegetable beds and bean rows. Tortoise watched from the warm flagstones, but I didn't stop to pet her. If I paused, there was a chance I'd turn and run back to the shed, throw myself into Logan's arms, beg him to stay, to move to London, take me to New Zealand... No, that was never going to happen.

The thought of being so far from family, Alice, home, was impossible. Logan was right. We were like travellers from distant planets who had briefly connected – but there was no future together. It squeezed my heart in an iron fist to acknowledge the truth, but that didn't make it any less real.

In the shadow of the east turret, I stood for a moment, took a long breath and told myself that I'd always have the memories – the night in the bothy, that kiss just now... even when I was very old, I wouldn't forget how I'd felt, held in Logan's arms. I remembered my mum watching *Casablanca*, her favourite film, as tears hovered in her eyes, whispering, 'We'll always have Paris,' along with Humphrey Bogart.

Logan and I would always have the bothy.

. . .

Reality intruded the moment I walked through the kitchen door. Rory was at the table, his laptop open in front of him, and Agatha was making tea with Dougie draped over her shoulder, nibbling her ponytail.

'Ah, Cat.' Rory glanced up. 'We've had some RSVPs – so far it's all been yeses, and I'm delighted to say that Ryan Clough is coming, too.'

'Who?'

'Sorry, I forget you don't automatically know everyone in the world of high finance,' he said apologetically. 'Runs a hedge fund, one of the big beasts of the Square Mile, plays golf and likes the idea of having Scottish ancestry, though he's probably about as authentically Gaelic as an orange wig. Just married his fourth wife...' Rory shrugged.

'Men,' said Agatha darkly. Her tea mug today read, 'May you have the confidence of a mediocre white man'.

'Rory, we need to talk about food,' she said. 'Logan's on vegetables, and I'm all prepared to make three or four muckle great stews. Ow, Dougie! Get off!'

'Ah.' Rory looked pained. 'Agatha, I was actually thinking we'd hire caterers.'

I was puzzled. 'Is that wise? It'll blow a massive hole in the budget, and I'm not sure it'd be any better than what we can offer.'

I tried to sound efficient, though my heart was still racing from my encounter with Logan, and I could sense my cheeks were flushed.

'These are very demanding, very successful people with high expectations,' Rory said. 'They're the kind of high-flyers who go from VIP lounge to yacht to penthouse. They're used to private chefs, diets tailored to their individual microbiome, the best of ev—'

He jumped as Agatha slammed her mug down on the wooden table.

'I dinnae cook for folks' *microbiome*,' she said, her blue eyes blazing like gas rings. 'I cook good, plain fare that people like to eat. If you dinnae need me, I'll head off back to Orkney for the weekend to visit my ailing mother. See how you get by without me.'

She placed Dougie gently in his cupboard, then stalked from the kitchen, slamming the door behind her.

We were silent for a moment.

'You might want to go and apologise...'

Rory looked anguished. 'But what I'm saying is true, Cat. If we want millions in investment, we can't give them a cauldron of home-made stew and expect them to pony up. We're going to need the big guns.'

'What big guns? Iolair hog roasts, coleslaw fifty pee extra?'

'There's a high-end catering firm in Edinburgh, The Refined Palate, that does amazing buffets. It's pricey, but they offer baked whole trout with caviar, and...'

'Rory, we can do whole trout for nothing, Logan can catch one—'

He set his jaw, and I caught a glimpse of the mutinous little boy within.

'I just think we should all focus our efforts on the actual ceilidh and schmoozing,' he said. 'Can you get Mel's brother's number, please? And we need to sort out flowers, blazing torches to light the entrance; we'll need to hire agency staff for the waiters and cleaners, a bus to bring everyone from the hotel... No, wait, a boat. Better if they can sail down to the jetty and have cocktails on the shore...'

Rory rattled on, and eventually, I got my phone out to take notes.

Twenty minutes later, I had a list of things to do longer than a wizard's scroll, and first on the list was 'appease Agatha'. I also needed to speak to Donald about boat hire and flaming torches, and Ishbel about guest lists and RSVP admin... already, the kiss with Logan felt as if it had happened in a parallel universe. How could we have such physical passion between us yet such a clash of dreams, plans, personalities?

With Oliver, I had been in love – or perhaps infatuated was a better word, I now realised – partly because our dreams were so similar, and so work-oriented. We were both focused on the same goals; the fact that he looked a bit like a young Robert Redford was just a bonus. But with Logan, there was no such unifying drive. He was the heir to an ancient castle; I'd get half the equity on a crumbling 1930s semi when my parents died. He'd been to a famously high-achieving boarding school; I'd trudged through the local comp's key stages, rolling up my school skirt and flirting with Nathan Summers.

Now... well, now, Logan was going to grow rare herbs in New Zealand, and in just over a week, I'd be back in London, setting up a minuscule events business from Alice's kitchen table. We had nothing in common.

So why did I feel so achingly sad?

41

To cheer myself up, I decided to undertake the most pleasant task first, an old habit from my MOE days. I sat down in the cosy living room, and phoned Mel to ask about her brother.

'Actually, he's here right now,' she said. 'The wanderer has returned from the high-level international ceilidh circuit. Do you want to come and meet him? I'll stick the kettle on.'

'I'd love to.' At that moment, given the various tensions clogging the air at the castle, the idea of sitting in Mel's cottage garden with a cup of tea sounded like an invitation to paradise.

An hour later, I was in a lawn chair eating one of Lorna's excellent scones with fig jam, and laughing at Duncan's jokes. Mel's brother was a man mountain, six foot four and with a chest like a seafarer's trunk. He had Mel's dark curly hair and green eyes, and I felt quite relieved that Alice hadn't managed to scoop him up during her brief visit, too.

'We're free on Saturday,' he confirmed, to my great relief. 'That private concert for the Dubai prince fell through, so...'

Mel rolled her eyes. Belle was pottering about with a watering can, and watered his feet. 'You don't want those to grow any bigger, love,' he said. 'I can already row out to sea in one of my trainers.'

'*Can* you?' she asked excitedly.

'Trust the favourite uncle,' said Mel, smiling. 'He swoops in, convinces her we're setting sail in a pair of shoes and leaves me to deal with the crashing disappointment.'

'That's what uncles are for,' he said cheerily.

I wondered how Mel coped without a dad for Belle, and once again, the idea flashed through my mind that her father might be living under a mile away. If it really was Logan, Belle would be the heir to Iolair, I realised – so surely he ought to know, and have the chance to build a relationship with his child? Mel's pride may be admirable, but she was potentially standing in the way of Belle's inheritance. I had to find out for Logan's sake, I realised – and it was only the smallest voice at the back of my mind whispering, '... *and if he is her father, then perhaps he won't go to New Zealand.*'

Dinner that evening was a tense affair – I could barely look at Logan, and he seemed equally keen to avoid my eye.

Agatha was engaged in a violent ballet of plate-slamming and spoon-clanking whenever Rory spoke, and Sir Alastair had entered the 'paralysed with fear' stage – one which I recognised from many past clients, who were full of enthusiasm until their event drew close enough to become inevitable. Then they turned into silent, rocking waxworks of terror.

'Have we thought this through?' he kept saying, picking at his cauliflower cheese as if landmines were hidden in it. 'Are you sure, Rory, about this caterer business?'

'I have enough vegetables and fruit to make a buffet for five hundred,' said Logan. 'And you *know* Agatha's a fantastic cook, and Ishbel would help.'

'Logan.' There was a warning note in Rory's voice. 'I know

what these people expect. It has to be way beyond anything we could manage. Plus, I thought you wanted no part in it.'

'I don't,' said Logan crossly. 'I just don't like to see Dad's money being spaffed up the wall.'

'Please don't argue over supper,' said Sir Alastair wearily. 'Look, about this boat hire... I could ask Harwood if they can get the *Jaunty Anne* onto the loch. That might save us a bit.'

Rory's eyes lit up. 'That would be perfect! They get picked up from the hotel, sail down to the jetty, cocktails on the shore, a lone piper serenading them up through the gardens, then a castle tour, drinks, dinner and the ceilidh, before it sails back on the stroke of midnight. It's dramatic, it's Scottish, they'll love it.'

'*It's Scottish?*' queried Logan. 'We are technically *in* Scotland, which renders it Scottish by sheer force of geography.'

'You don't understand!' Rory jabbed his fork in the air. 'Some of the VCs coming are Americans – they're absolute suckers for the full misty isles, skirling pipes, eighty-seven types of whisky, tartan, haggis-neeps-and-tatties Scotland. We have to provide it.'

'I can go to the post office,' said Agatha flatly. 'I'll buy fifty fluffy Highland cows in tartan hats for their going-home gifts.'

Logan snorted, but Rory slapped his forehead. '*Gifts!*' he said wildly. 'They'll expect a keepsake! Something they can use, or put on their desk, but it has to be classy, and it can't be big if they're flying home... something better than fridge magnets or baseball hats... Snow globes? Cake?'

'*Cake?*' I repeated. 'Is there a particularly Scottish sort of cake that won't fall apart in transit?'

'There's tablet,' said Sir Alastair hopefully. 'Pure sugar, but so very delicious.'

Rory shook his head. 'Some of these people are very into well-being,' he said despairingly. 'No, it won't do.'

'I've an idea,' said Agatha. 'But Rory doesnae think I'm useful, so perhaps I'd best keep it to myself.'

'Please tell us,' I begged. The last thing we needed was Agatha turning into a tragic martyr.

She brightened. 'Back home on Orkney, I had a wee hobby. I made soaps and bath bombs.'

Sir Alastair looked baffled.

'Body scrubs, face masks...' she went on. 'I used local herbs and flowers that I picked myself, and I sold them in the market. People loved them – they went down a treat with the tourists.' She paused. 'We could do that, with a wee logo, gussy them up in gift bags.'

'Agatha,' I said, 'I think that's a completely brilliant idea. Think about it, Rory – she can use herbs from Logan's garden, and we can make a little "Castle Iolair" logo and get stickers made for the wrapping. And the VCs can use them, and take them home, and be constantly reminded of the castle... You're a genius,' I told Agatha.

She nodded. 'Aye, I'm aware. I'll pop to the chemist tomorrow.'

'That is superb,' Rory said. 'Ag, you're brilliant. I'm really sorry about the food thing; it's just...'

'I know.' She made a flicking gesture with her hand. 'Doesnae matter. This is better. I'll be doing your fancy guests a turn.'

She turned to Logan. 'I'll need large steel buckets, a source of heat, access to the stables,' she rattled off. 'I'll need a wide selection of herbs and flowers – maybe oats, maybe some grains for scrub, and I'll be up in the top field first thing, so you'll need to draw me a wee map of where the bogs are.'

'This is me not being involved, is it?' Logan asked, but he was smiling at her. 'Fine. We'll go round the garden, and you can show me what you need.'

I promised to organise the logo and wrappings, and Rory nodded. 'Not *too* pretty,' he warned. 'These are very alpha men, so give them something traditionally Scottish they can use in their private gyms.'

Logan caught my eye, and I almost laughed.

'Well, it all sounds marvellous,' said Sir Alastair. 'And what can I do to help?'

'Actually, Dad,' said Rory, 'I thought you could make a speech. You know, welcome them all to Iolair, talk a bit about the history, why it's so vital to preserve it for future generations to enjoy, all that.'

'Oh, good Lord!' He looked pale with fright. 'I don't know if I can... I've never...'

'You're always addressing lairds!'

'Yes, but that's different.' Sir Alastair shook his head. 'They understand everything already, and it's usually just about fishing. I don't have to... what do you say? *Big it up.*'

'Or Logan could...?'

'No, Logan could not. Why don't you do it?' he asked Rory.

'Because I'm not the bloody heir! Plus, they'll want a real live laird who's walked the walk. Dad can do it, he'll be fine.'

Sir Alastair swallowed. 'All right, I suppose I shall,' he said. 'Anything to save Castle Iolair.'

The next few days were among the busiest of my life.

I caught occasional glimpses of Logan in the garden, pushing wheelbarrows of herbs to the stables, and I knew Agatha was getting up at five daily to work on her products. She had decided to make scented candles, too, and dispatched me to the craft shop in Oban first thing.

I longed to stay and watch ferries sail into the harbour from the misty Isle of Mull over the water, sit in a shorefront café with a decent flat white and browse the bookshops, but we were all on a strict timescale. Agatha had scrubbed out the stables, and Logan had given her a stack of pallets to dry her soaps on. The entire place smelled like a wood of bluebells in the early morning, with a delicious undertone I couldn't name.

'Bog myrtle,' she told me. 'All from the fields up the hill.'

I'd bought bright pink tissue paper and navy ribbon that I'd found at an art shop tucked down a side street, and I was going to create a logo of the castle silhouetted by a circle of herbs, and make labels.

'*The Castle Apothecary,*' I said to myself, trying it out.

I liked it. I snapped a few images of Agatha at work, and then wandered into the vegetable garden to take some pictures of the herbs and lavender bushes. We should have an Instagram account, I thought, so the VCs could tag us if they posted anything about the ceilidh, and we could show off images of the castle...

Rory's enthusiasm for 'Scottishing it up' was causing some trouble, however. Every time I walked through the entrance hall with my clipboard, I'd spot a new polyester tartan tablecloth slung over a sixteenth-century sideboard, or a tatty jug of dried thistles where there'd previously been a beautiful silver candlestick.

'I'm just reminding them they're in Scotland,' Rory argued when I confronted him over the framed cartoon of Nessie he'd hung in the downstairs bathroom – a prime example of what Logan witheringly called 'plastic Gaelic'.

'There's a loch and a bloody great mountain outside the window,' I reminded Rory. 'I think they'll know.'

By Friday evening, the *Jaunty Anne* was bobbing by the jetty, captained by an overexcited Harwood.

'Annabel's gone to a health spa in Perthshire,' he said, glowing pink with delight. 'Nobody to police me!'

The first guests had begun to arrive at the Iolair Hotel,

according to Rory's ex, who was seemingly in constant contact as if they were both on a police stake-out.

Donald had trimmed the lawns to a perfect emerald carpet, and Agatha had surpassed herself with the soaps and candles. Even wrapped and labelled, they perfumed the small room we'd requisitioned off the Grand Hall with a heavenly, wild scent. She had made the candles in Victorian teacups she'd found piled into an old crate in the stables, and washed and polished to a gleam. When we turned one over, we found it had a 'Castle Iolair' stamp on the bottom, which delighted us all.

My spreadsheets were checked off, my timeline was high-lighted in seven different colours and almost everyone was accounted for. 'Though there'll be a few turning up who haven't bothered to RSVP,' said Rory.

'How rude.'

He shrugged. 'That's high rollers for you.'

The only remaining problem was Sir Alastair's quivering terror at the thought of giving his speech, most of which I'd written for him – and my looming sense of dread.

It wasn't the ceilidh. Things had gone remarkably smoothly so far, and I knew we'd done everything we could to make it a success. I'd overseen far trickier projects than this one, with far less helpful clients.

No, the gleaming clan sword hanging over my head wasn't fear of failure. It was the simple fact that once the event was over, there'd no longer be a reason for me to stay. I'd be heading back to London, and Logan... Well, Logan would be going much, much further away.

And whenever I caught a glimpse of him in the garden, or passed him a dish over the kitchen table, or smiled at him as we crossed on the stairs, despite all the common sense I could summon, I felt as though my heart might break in two.

42

Saturday morning dawned warm and cloudy.

The loch was a dark mirror reflecting the overcast sky, and the lawn was damp. By seven we were all at breakfast, dividing up our tasks – even Logan, who had consented to decorate the tables with flowers from the gardens.

Agatha and I spent the morning checking the rooms, replacing dead lightbulbs, putting soaps into gift bags, and once the caterers and staff arrived, showing them round and directing them. The waiters were all wearing kilts, and I had to admit they looked marvellous, while the cooks were in chefs' whites and gleaming toque hats. I remembered Logan in his own chef's whites, and had to clutch the banister for a moment as longing pierced me.

'We'll need to use the catering fridges for the whole sea bream, the quiches, langoustines and the desserts,' said Gavin, the largest chef, in a booming Glaswegian accent. 'If you can just point me to them...'

'We don't have catering fridges,' I said, puzzled.

He looked thunderous. 'Then, lassie, we'll be contravening

several laws on the safe preparation of food, and we'll lose our licence. I was told ye were a castle.'

'We are.' I swept my arm towards the vast windows and huge oil paintings. 'Obviously. But we don't have catering fridges because we aren't a catering business.'

'Then what the hell am I supposed to do?' bellowed Gavin. 'Right team, pack up. We've been misinformed.'

'No!' I shrieked. 'Don't go! We can sort something out!'

'No, ye cannae,' he said. 'We've three professional fridges' worth of food on ice blocks in the van, and once it melts, we're looking at salmonella, *E. coli*, campylobacter...'

'We can divide it between our fridges,' I said desperately. 'Maybe Mel could squeeze in the desserts – I could run them down to her cottage—'

'Lady.' Gavin glared at me. 'That is no' how we work. We're used tae dealing with celebrities.'

'I have dealt with more celebrities than you've made hot buffets,' I said. 'And nowhere in your contract did it mention catering fridges.'

I had entered what Alice called my 'ice queen' mode. I'd developed it over years of being yelled at by frantic clients, and it was reasonably effective – but it didn't work on Gavin.

He picked up a vast metal dish and set off back to the van, and his team dutifully followed him. Ten minutes later, they were gone.

There was only one person I wanted to talk to about this unmitigated disaster, and I found him placing small, neat signs in the vegetable beds which read, PLEASE DO NOT DISRUPT THE LETTUCES.

Arran and Alba set up a volley of excitable barking as I approached, and he raised a hand.

'How's the buffet?' Logan asked. 'I saw them unloading roast swan for fifty with a gold-leaf dressing.'

'If only.' I explained what had happened, attempting to

keep the spiralling panic out of my voice. '... and so, the thing is,' I finished, 'we're going to need to do it ourselves, and we've got six hours.'

Logan stared at me. 'Cat, it's not possible. They'll have to eat at the hotel and come here afterwards.'

'They can't! The restaurant's shut for repairs, Rory said, and besides, we've promised them a dinner. Any vegetables you've got, bring them to the kitchen and we'll see what we can do. I'm going to beg Ishbel to drive to the big Tesco in Oban, and Agatha and I'll start cooking.'

'Cooking what?'

'I don't know!' I almost shrieked. 'Whatever we can make for fifty VIPs who are expecting roast swan.'

Logan heaved a sigh and ran a hand through his hair. 'I'll help,' he said. 'I can do some big, fairly fancy salads and trays of roast potatoes – I'll use the ovens at the pub. I think there's some trout from Dad's last fishing expedition in the freezer; get Ag to run cold water over it till it defrosts, and perhaps phone Mel and Lorna, see if they can come down.'

His calm, reasoned approach was helping me to rediscover mine.

'Right,' I said, putting a hand on Arran's silky ears to steady myself. 'I'll go and marshal the troops, prep the kitchen and talk to Rory. Maybe Donald could help you get the veg up to us on the quad bike.'

'On it.' Logan smiled at me. 'It'll be okay, Cat. We'll make it work.'

'But you didn't even want this to happen,' I said, worried.

'I absolutely didn't,' he agreed, 'but you're in big trouble, and I'm not going to stand by and watch you suffer out of spite.'

'I could kiss you,' I said, then realised quite how inappropriate that was.

'Maybe a firm handshake,' he said, laughing at my expression. 'Go on, and take the dogs with you. I don't need their questionable help digging up potatoes right now.'

By one o'clock, Ishbel had texted to say she was on her way back with several litres of double cream and a raft of haggises, and Logan had requisitioned Agatha's soap-making buckets, lined them with cling film and was chopping neat piles of salad to throw into them.

Agatha had made enough pastry to build a brutalist house and was violently rolling it into rectangles to make venison pies, and Donald was on potato-peeling duty with his shirt sleeves rolled up, wearing Agatha's favourite apron which read, 'Fragile Like a Bomb'. Mel and Lorna were on their way, leaving Duncan to watch *Finding Dory* with Belle, and Rory was herding a flock of teenage waiters away from smoking in the orchard towards sorting out crockery.

I was flitting between the various factions, and had just dangled three enormous trout in the river wrapped in carrier bags, because tap water wasn't defrosting them fast enough. We'd serve them with a hollandaise sauce, which Agatha insisted she knew how to make, after the haggis bonbons, and then we'd do the pies with potatoes and roasted vegetables, with a mushroom wellington for the vegetarians and salads on the side... none of it was quite what the VIPs would be used to, and the words 'traditional' and 'rustic' would need to be heavily employed in our descriptions.

'We'll put so much whisky in the dessert, they'll no' remember what they ate,' promised Agatha.

Time seemed to have speeded up horrifically – and while the castle kitchen was large by normal standards, we lacked the raft of catering equipment available in any professional set-up. There was a lot of 'Who stole my knife?' and 'I need that pan!', and with the humidity outside and the Aga blasting out heat, it was like working in the red-hot core of a furnace. At one point I took my jumper off, revealing the spaghetti-strap vest I was wearing underneath. I saw Logan glance at my shoulders, linger for a moment, then look away. I found myself smiling for the first time that afternoon.

At five, Logan began to take trays down to the Falls of Glen-nIolair pub in the Land Rover, and I ran down to check the welcome at the jetty. I found three white-cloth-draped trestle tables, fifty sparkling glasses and several jugs of whisky cock-tails. Sir Alastair was peering into them, looking worried.

'Cat, do taste this,' he said. 'Have I made it too weak, d'you think?'

He handed me a glass, and I sipped. The roof of my mouth was instantly stripped away, heat coursed through my blood-stream, and I felt both invincible and woozy.

'If anything, perhaps a little strong,' I gasped.

Sir Alastair looked delighted. He leaned forward confid-ingly and murmured, 'My plan is to get them all squiffy before my speech, so they won't care what I say.'

I laughed, but felt a small twinge of apprehension – drunken VIPs bashing into the statues and sliding down the bannisters wasn't on my agenda for the evening. I hadn't exactly mentioned the food fiasco to Sir Alastair, either. It was obvious that he was already a bag of nerves about the whole thing, and I couldn't bear to make it worse.

'By the way, Cat,' he said, as I turned to go. 'I haven't thanked you for your sterling work getting Logan involved.'

'I'm afraid I didn't even try to persuade him...' I began, and Sir Alastair smiled gently at me.

'Perhaps not directly,' he said, 'but women have their subtle ways, don't they?'

. . .

In the kitchen, Mel and Lorna were making an enormous cranachan, the traditional Scottish pudding with cream, raspberries, toasted oats and honey – and judging by the heady aroma, Agatha had indeed sloshed half the drinks cabinet into it.

'It should really be served with shortbread,' Lorna fretted. 'Mel's granny used to make one that just disappeared in your mouth...'

'Mum, there's no time for that,' Mel began. She glanced up as Rory came in.

'Mel! You're here!' He bounded over and hugged her, and they immediately launched into conversation, as though it had been minutes, not years, since they'd seen each other.

'Mel,' Lorna said eventually. '*Melissa!* Those oats will burn to a crisp!'

'Sorry.' Mel extracted herself. She returned to the Aga, but I saw her turn and glance back at him, just once – and that was when it finally clicked into place.

It was now almost time for the evening to begin, and as I dressed in the low-cut white silk frock and tartan sash I'd ordered online, looking down to where the *Jaunty Anne* prepared to set sail on the still water, my stomach roiled with nerves. If the evening was a disaster, I felt it would be entirely my fault.

I made my way down to the jetty, wobbling slightly in my wedge heels – Rory had pointed out that dancing a ceilidh in stilettos was like trying to knit with tagliatelle. I would stand beside Sir Alastair to welcome the guests as the *Jaunty Anne* returned.

Rory was there, fully kilted and booted, but I wished Logan was standing with me. Although the others had been so appreciative of my efforts, I sensed that only Logan knew what it was like to be a perfectionist, to feel the weight of everyone else's expectations on your shoulders. Logan, however, was lurking somewhere else in the castle, having agreed to make a brief appearance during dinner. I wondered if, like his brother and dad, he'd be wearing a kilt. Admittedly, most kilted men had knees like squashed ham baps, but in Logan's case I could see how it might work.

'Here they come!' Sir Alastair took a swig of whisky and straightened up, while Rory raised a hand to wave at the yacht slowly rounding the curve of the shore.

As it approached, I felt a sudden sting on the back of my neck. The loch was glass-calm, but watching the boat tack towards the jetty, I noticed a strange seething in the air, as if it was shimmering. I turned to ask Rory what it was, but Harwood was now bellowing hearty greetings, and the gangplank was coming down.

I thought of the slightly lumpy pies awaiting the guests, and felt a spike of dread. Sir Alastair was pale and clammy with nerves, but Rory was striding down the jetty, crying, 'Ryan! Betsy! So amazing to welcome you to Iolair!'

Soon, almost everyone was assembled onshore, and had been given a whisky cocktail – or, 'Just water for me,' said several of the VCs, who clearly had plans to live forever by existing on spirulina juice and the sort of facial 'tweaks' that make everyone look like a half-melted waxwork. A couple of people were still to arrive. I could see their shadows chatting to Harwood as he boomed on about the spec of his yacht, but finally, they too were picking their way down the gangplank to the jetty. I raised my hand to greet them, and froze.

Making her way towards me was global pop star Bo'nita, last seen on the most humiliating night of my life. She was wearing a silver mesh dress and heels like rapiers – and on her arm, sporting a panama hat perched on his golden hair and a perfectly fitted cream linen suit, was the man I'd assumed I would never see again.

43

'Oliver,' I managed. 'Bo'nita! I had no idea...'

'Last-minute decision, babe,' she said, lifting her glass to me. Her nails today were painted Black Watch tartan. 'I've never been to Scotland, and when Ollie asked me, I thought, *Why not?* I might do a whole routine on the next tour with topless male dancers in kilts and leather harnesses... I feel like it'd totally work for my next single, "Pump 'n' Grind Me (All Night Long)",' she added thoughtfully.

Sir Alastair was gazing at her as if a mermaid had burst from the loch and was talking to him in a strong South London accent.

'Lovely to have you here!' he said eventually. 'I'm the Laird of Iolair. Gosh, that's rather tricky to say. Cocktail?'

'Oliver Corman-Blaize, Magnum Opus Events.' Oliver pumped his hand briskly, then turned to me. 'Cat,' he said, in a low voice, 'you didn't reply to my letter.'

'There was nothing to say.'

'Oh, there's plenty to say, believe me,' Oliver said. He touched me lightly on the arm. Once, that contact would have set off an entire heavenly orchestra, but not any more. Now, I just felt irritated.

'I didn't know you were friends with Rory,' I said.

'He arranged the loan for me to start the company,' said Oliver. 'Always stayed in touch. Actually, I thought you might have had a word... made sure I was on the guest list?'

I shook my head, and he chuckled.

'Well, I believe you, thousands wouldn't.' He raised an eyebrow. 'I need to talk to you. Things have changed.'

He turned to Bo'nita. 'All right, darling?'

'So are you two a... couple now?' I asked.

She shrieked with laughter. 'Hell no, babe!' she said, whacking my arm with her talons. 'I'm deep in my lesbian phase. Might have just leaked a certain story to the tabloids about me and Sadee CC.'

'The DJ?'

She nodded. 'We're giving it a go, but she's in Tokyo right now.'

As she spoke, I felt another vicious sting on my neck, then more on my face.

'Ow,' shrieked Bo'nita, flapping her hands. 'Something bit me!'

All around us, VIPs were flapping and swearing, spilling drinks as they batted violently at the air.

'Midges!' roared Ryan Clough, lurching past with his jacket over his head. His wife followed, screaming and slapping at her tanned bare legs.

There were clouds of minuscule insects now engulfing the party on the shore like a vicious rain, and the still air was dense with whirling, biting mayhem. Guests' exposed skin was swarming with black dots, and still more midges descended, until the air was thick with them. A well-coiffed woman staggered into the trestle table and sent several cocktails flying in her bid to escape, and Sir Alastair was waving his arms like a wizard whose spell has gone wrong.

'Follow me!' Rory yelled, and I dashed behind the yelling, furious VIPs, herding them up the lawns towards the castle, coughing and spluttering as we inhaled the tiny insects.

'The piper!' Rory shouted to me as we ran. 'He's supposed to be playing "Flower of Scotland" as we approach!'

'Postpone him!' I bellowed.

Logan needn't worry about his lettuces – there wasn't going to be any garden tour. Ahead of me, Oliver was using his hat to wildly sweep the air ahead of him. Bo'nita had taken her shoes off and was holding them as she sprinted.

Finally, we reached the castle entrance, where flaming torches and two puzzled waiters holding trays of champagne greeted the panting, bedraggled guests. As we made our way up the steps into the darkness of the hall, a shadowed figure stepped into the light.

My first sensation was one of relief – then I realised Logan was wearing the full, traditional dress of the McAskills, with a sage-green tweed jacket, white shirt and kilt in the clan colours, with woollen socks and lace-up leather boots. I almost blushed at how devastatingly handsome he looked.

'You look stunning, Cat,' he said quietly, taking in my white dress. It occurred to me that until now, Logan had only seen me in jeans and jumpers – or naked.

Now is not the time for that thought.

'Problem?' he murmured, nodding at the guests, who were gulping down flutes of champagne and brushing themselves violently. One woman was picking at her hair like a distressed bonobo.

'Midges.'

'Oh *hell*,' said Logan. 'They always turn up in mid-May. I should have reminded Rory.'

'They arrived with the boat,' I said. 'New plan just dropped – drinks in the formal drawing room.'

'Got it.' He raised his voice, dialling up his accent to somewhere just below Hagrid.

'I'm Himself of Iolair,' he called, 'Logan McAskill, brother of Rory and son of the laird. It's a pleasure to welcome you all to Castle Iolair, and I do apologise for the uninvited guests who've flown in specially to be here with you tonight.'

There was a murmur of laughter. The guests were decompressing, emanating relief that they were now in safe hands.

'If you'd all like to follow me to the drawing room,' Logan went on, 'traditional canapés will be served overlooking the lawns.'

I exchanged a glance with Rory, whose expression clearly read, 'Where's all this come from?'

Soon, we'd assembled in the drawing room, waiters were handing around haggis bonbons, and Rory had taken over the small talk. Sir Alastair was draining another flute of champagne, and I wondered whether I should gently ask him to slow down when I felt a damp hand on my bare arm.

'Cat,' said Oliver, his voice low. 'I need to speak to you – is there somewhere private we can go?'

'I'm working.'

I also didn't want to hear whatever he had to say – red flags were waving, alarms were sounding and a large sign was being nailed up reading, DO NOT ENTER. I'd only just got over my years of madness regarding this man, and no part of me wanted to return.

'It's important.'

Oliver stroked a finger down my bare arm, which tickled aggravatingly.

'Two minutes,' I said.

Everyone seemed to be chatting, the waiters were circulating, and Bo'nita was telling Sir Alastair a long anecdote about losing her tour luggage in Dubai and wagging a tartan-tipped finger at him. He was smiling gamely.

I led Oliver to the corridor outside. We were followed by Hannay, who was finding the crowd stressful. He flopped down at my feet, and I scratched his back with the pointed toe of my shoe.

'What is it? I've only got a second.'

Oliver smiled gently at me, the way you'd smile at a precious, adorable child. 'Oh, Cat,' he said. 'At last.'

'"At last" *what*?'

He chuckled fondly. 'At last, I've woken up. It was when you said what you did... I couldn't stop thinking about it. I had to make you redundant to give myself a chance to understand how I really felt, without seeing you at work all the time...'

'What?'

'Don't get me wrong, we did need to cut back on wages. But I thought, well, if she's not around and I *still* feel this way, it means something.'

I felt blindsided. 'You took away my entire career to *see how you felt*?'

Hannay rose to his feet. He growled at Oliver, who backed off with a fey little skip.

'Can you get that bloody Hound of the Baskervilles away from me?'

I laid a hand on Hannay's neck, and he subsided, grumbling.

'No, I didn't "take your career away",' said Oliver. 'Besides, I knew you'd fly, far away from the shackles of MOE. And once I realised you had such strong feelings for me... well, it clarified a few things.'

'What things?'

A door opened further down the corridor, and Logan emerged, saying to someone behind him, 'Could you check on the dogs? I've got to get the salads dressed.' He turned and took in Oliver and me, heads together, speaking in low voices. I saw a flash of something in his eyes, but it was hard to tell whether it was despair or derision.

'Antonia and I have split up,' said Oliver, oblivious. 'It wasn't right, Cat, and it took your courage in speaking up for me to see it. I ended things last week. Of course, her mother's distraught, all the gilt-sprayed chairs are going back and the flower people are keeping the deposit, but you have to be true to yourself, don't you?'

'I imagine Antonia's more distraught.'

'Cat.' Oliver lifted a hand and traced a thumb down my cheek, much as I imagine he'd seen Colin Firth do in period dramas. It felt like a fly crawling on my face, and I jerked away.

'It's not about Antonia now,' he said. 'It's about us. You and me.'

Down the corridor there was movement, and I looked up to see Logan's retreating back. I had a strong sense he'd heard our exchange. Every part of me longed to follow him, but Oliver put a hand on my arm, and murmured intimately, 'To be continued, somewhere more private.'

But I was over him. It was as though my feelings for Oliver had been a dead weight, pinning me down for years, and now, the burden had suddenly been lifted and I was free. I remembered Alice once talking about instantly falling out of love with her first long-term boyfriend. 'He pouted like a child one night when I didn't want to have sex,' she told me. 'My vagina slammed shut like a trapdoor, and that was it. Feelings gone.'

Now I'd been exposed to the powerful Oliver antidote that was Logan, I couldn't remember what I'd ever seen in him. I suddenly understood Alice rolling her eyes as I insisted 'you just don't know him', and my mum pursing her lips as I banged on about his 'buttery hair'.

I went back into the drawing room with Hannay, aware that the food needed to be served very soon. I was keen to get some roast potatoes into Sir Alastair to absorb the booze, though judging by the roar of noise, most of the guests were already well on their way. There was no sign of Logan. Ishbel and Agatha had been in charge of laying out the buffet in the vast dining room, and a table of fine wines was supposedly being manned by one of the kilted young waiters.

I hurried down the corridor to check, and found everything in place – the salads had been decanted into huge decorative tureens, the trout was on a vast silver platter surrounded by watercress, Agatha's sauce stood beside it and enormous trays awaited pies and potatoes. Lorna's cranachan was in several crystal bowls in the fridge, and the band was already setting up in the gallery of the Grand Hall. If you didn't count the midges and Harwood being too drunk to sail anyone back to the hotel later, it was going swimmingly.

I didn't know how much Logan had heard of Oliver's confession, but I suspected most of it. I experienced a burning urge to find him and explain that I had no feelings whatsoever for my ex-boss. Admittedly, Logan was heading to the other side of the world soon after this, and though every time I thought of him so far away, I experienced an aching sensation in my chest, I knew we had no future.

Regardless, I didn't want him to leave thinking I was still in love with someone else.

44

I herded the guests down the corridor towards the dining room.

Rory had decided that the piper would now accompany the procession, but within the echoing stone chambers of the castle's long passageways, the pipes sounded like a grief-stricken banshee wailing for her lost love. It was a relief when the final vibrating note died away and gave my ringing ears a chance to recover.

Still, there was no sign of Logan. Oliver was sticking close to me, gazing in my direction with cow-like eyes, and Bo'nita was talking to Donald about livestock husbandry. 'I would literally die for a set of fancy chickens,' she was saying. 'Them ones that look like cute little hats.'

'Frizzles.' Donald nodded. 'Or ye may be thinking o' the Buff Orpington, a fine bird and a great layer, unless she becomes egg-bound...'

VIPs were beginning to approach the buffet, the waiters standing by with serving tongs, and I felt a spike of nerves. Perhaps the food really wasn't up to scratch – it was the sort of tasty, rustic offering you might get at a summer wedding where enthusiastic aunts had pitched in to help, not the exquisite delicacies these people had been trained to expect. We were serving supermarket yellow-sticker baguettes, for heaven's sake.

When most of the guests had sat down, I strolled casually round the white-clothed tables, checking everyone had drinks, and eavesdropping. Rory was speaking to a very sleek-looking man who had a strong Greek accent. He was saying, 'I hear you, Rory, but a helipad is non-negotiable for our clients. We'd need to site it on the lawn for their comfort, view or no view.'

I hoped rather desperately that he'd decide against investing.

I passed a table where a very tanned woman with frosted blonde hair was saying, 'I adore Scotland with my *heart*. Did you know my ancestors came from Aberdeen? We're hoping to visit there tomorrow morning, before our lunchtime flight.'

I didn't point out that Aberdeen was a good four hours' drive away. Bo'nita was now sitting beside Sir Alastair, encouraging him to down a shot of tequila she'd poured from a silver hip flask concealed in her Dior micro-bag.

'Settles the nerves a treat, Sir A,' she said. 'I always do a slammer before a big show. Like, if we're opening with "Touch You Up", it's a big dance number, so it massively gets me in the headspace.'

He nodded bemusedly and downed it in one. Hannay, beside him, looked alarmed.

Oliver was sitting with a couple of businessmen he evidently knew. 'Cat!' He waved. 'Come and work your charms on my pals. This is Sven Lackberg, who owns Wyzass Software, just floated on the stock market, and Darko Bix, a serious player in the Bitcoin space.' Oliver winked.

I imagined what my life would be like as his partner. Endless flesh-pressing events with overgrown teenage hackers. I envisaged them all wearing hoodies in darkened rooms, banks of flickering screens turning their pale faces an aquatic blue.

An image of Logan, bare-chested and digging the vegetable patch in the sun popped into my mind. Where *was* he?

'Hello,' I said. 'I'm afraid I can't stay – I'm working – but I do hope you're enjoying the traditional Scottish dinner.'

Darko, who looked about twenty-three, nodded. 'I'm loving the concept of cheese and fish. So, like, fully random.'

He waved a hand at the sauce liberally covering his plate. On closer inspection, it did seem to contain a great deal of grated cheese.

'Excuse me a moment,' I said.

Agatha had seated herself amongst a coterie of well-dressed wives. In her black dress, with her hair up, she looked beautiful, imposing and more than equal to them.

'It's such a braw opportunity,' she was saying. 'Dinnae dismiss the idea of a wee swimming pool. Maybe a Turkish spa doon the auld dungeons.'

Champagne seemed to have made her even more Scottish than she already was.

A woman whose face was rendered egg-smooth by Botox was nodding earnestly. 'And so much Instagram potential,' she said. 'Influencer retreats are a must-have.'

'Agatha,' I said quietly. 'Can I have a quick word?'

She looked up from where she was mapping out a labyrinthine spa complex on a napkin.

'It's going awful well, Cat,' she said. 'They're loving the food. Shame Rory didnae listen to me in the first place.'

'That's great.' I lowered my voice to a whisper. 'Why is there cheese in the Hollandaise sauce?'

She looked puzzled. 'D'ye no' like it?'

'I haven't tasted it yet. But... it's not meant to have cheese in. Did you use a recipe?'

'I dinnae need a recipe,' said Agatha, with scorn. 'I make sauces every day. You said Holland, so I used Dutch cheese. It's got two whole Edams in there, and it's delicious.' She turned back to her audience. 'I think the best use of the attics is for a wee state-of-the-art games complex,' she said.

As I returned to check on the buffet, where waiters were now serving up the pies, I noticed a commotion was breaking out at the door.

'You can't come here, throwing your weight about!' Logan was snapping at someone concealed by the large door frame. 'We don't want your cash!'

I skidded over, almost breaking my ankle on a dropped roast potato, and saw Logan, in his full Scottish regalia. He was towering over Jack Campbell, who was accompanied by a bald, older man with the same beady blue eyes.

'I don't imagine you have a choice, pal,' said Jack. 'Everyone in Iolair knows the castle's on its uppers, and we're offering to bail you out, McAskill.'

'It's not as if this scout-hut fundraising buffet's going to cut the mustard,' snapped the older man, evidently Jack's equally unpleasant father, Bran. 'A bit of old fish and a pie? I'm surprised you've not put out a bowl of crisps and set up a tombola.'

'You're no more welcome here than your son is, Bran,' said Logan, ice crackling through his tone. 'I'd like you both to leave. Now.'

'I think that's up to Rory, actually,' said Jack. '*He* invited us.'

'I think you'll find he didn't do any such thing.'

'The invitation was to Marina Campbell plus one,' said Jack. 'Marina being otherwise occupied, my father and I are exercising our right to attend. When we own Iolair, I'm sure we can find a bolthole somewhere in the grounds to keep you in.'

'Excuse me,' I said. 'Logan, may I have a quick word?'

He turned to me, his face still rigid with anger as I drew him away.

'Just let them in,' I whispered. 'It's better than making a scene, and they can't invest in Iolair without your dad's permission.'

Logan shut his eyes, common sense wrestling with fury. 'Fine. As long as I don't have to look at the free-loading gits. I'm going to fetch the puddings.'

I returned to the two grinning men. 'Please, come in,' I said formally. 'I hope you enjoy the ceilidh.'

'I will if you dance a reel with me in that dress,' Jack said lasciviously, and my desire to slap him was only tempered by the fact that I'd just urged Logan to calm down.

I turned away and went to speak to the band, who were missing a vital cable for their amp. By the time I'd tracked it down under a table, being experimentally nibbled by Alba, the guests had almost finished their pudding. The drunkenness level had risen another notch thanks to the whisky it contained, and it was time for Sir Alastair's speech.

I hurried to alert him, but was alarmed to see an empty chair and crumpled napkin where he'd been sitting.

'Bo'nita,' I said, 'have you seen Sir Alastair?'

'He was here... a while ago?' She drummed her tartan nails on the tablecloth thoughtfully. 'Actually, he looked a bit pale, he's been knocking back the slammers.'

The waiters were collecting plates, and people were beginning to flock round the wine table again. I needed to find the missing laird before they all started drifting away to poke round the castle, and there was no audience for the vital speech.

In the corridor, I ran into Logan.

'Where's your dad?' I hissed. 'He's vanished.'

Logan shrugged. 'Probably hiding from the bloody Campbells. Cat, listen, who on earth was that guy you were talking to in the corridor?'

'Oliver.' I was about to explain further, but Logan's face stiffened.

'As in your ex-boss Oliver, who you were in love with? The one who then sacked you?'

'Yes, but—'

'You invited him here?'

'No! I had no idea – Rory did!'

'Right. So he's thinking of investing? Or has he come to beg you to return? Because from what I heard of your conversation, it sounded very much like the latter, and I'd prefer not to be an unwitting party to some classless interloper's declaration of—'

'Why are you talking like Mr Darcy?'

'I'm not. I simply think that—'

'Oh, shut up,' I snapped, before I could stop myself. 'I haven't got time to justify myself to you, and I don't need to. I need to find your AWOL father, so he can make his damn speech before it's too late. Unless you'd like to do it? No, I thought not.'

I stalked away, a prickling at the back of my neck suggesting Logan was staring after me.

There was no sign of Sir Alastair in the sitting room, nor was he hiding in any of the downstairs rooms, though I did stumble on a couple who were snogging urgently under a bust of the seventh laird. From the way they sprang apart, I assumed they hadn't arrived together.

Increasingly worried, I made my way to the turret, and banged on the door, then flung it open. Hannay was lying on what looked very much like Sir Alastair's formal tweed jacket, and as I peered over the desk, I heard light snoring. The Laird of Iolair was lying spread-eagled on the window seat, fast asleep and still clutching Bo'nita's silver hip flask.

'Sir Alastair!' I shook his arm lightly, and he emitted a gusty, rattling snore, then sat up, wild-eyed.

'Whass happ'nin'?'

'It's time for your speech,' I said loudly. 'To the VIPs, before the ceilidh?'

'VI fleas,' he mumbled, closing his eyes again. 'Stoopid.'

I felt genuine panic.

'They're all waiting for you,' I said firmly, 'and you promised Rory you'd do it!'

'I promised him a green bic'cle once,' said Sir Alastair faintly. 'Nice l'il m'chine. I dunno if he ever...' He was asleep again.

I looked at Hannay, who raised an ear and closed his own eyes, burrowing further into the jacket. 'You're both useless,' I muttered, and left them to it.

Back downstairs, guests were milling about. Many had left their tables, as I'd feared, and were wandering off.

I beckoned Rory, and he hurried over. 'Where's Dad?' he hissed. 'It's all running late. He—'

I explained, and Rory swore so loudly, several people, including Agatha, looked across, although she was the only one who rose to her feet and came over.

'What is happening?'

'Sir Alastair's drunk and asleep. He can't do his speech.'

'No speech?' Agatha looked horrified. 'But then nobody will understand why they need to invest!'

'Agatha, I know! Rory, could you...?'

He blanched. 'Oh God, Cat, I can't. I've had too much to drink.'

'Logan?'

'Not in a million years.'

Agatha nodded decisively. 'Then I shall speak.'

'But you haven't written a speech...' I began.

It was too late. She was already banging her knife on a glass, and clambering onto a spindly gold chair.

45

'People!' she shouted. 'I need your attention!'

Heads turned, and mild surprise rippled through the crowd, before a hush fell.

'I am Agatha McBrae,' she announced. 'I'm divorced from a shiftless wee eejit, and this castle has given me *life*. I do everything at Iolair, except for the odd jobs and the lawns, that's Donald. And admin is Ishbel. Logan does vegetables. But the rest.'

People were now listening, rapt.

'Now, Sir Alastair is a bit peely-wally,' Agatha went on. 'I suppose you'd all say *indisposed*. He was going to tell you all about Iolair castle, how old and special it is...' She made a 'pah!' gesture with her left hand and wobbled slightly. 'But old and special is no use if it's falling apart! You should see the bathrooms, those ancient pipes are held up by rust alone. As for the roof, we've no' been able to touch it for years, though it's falling down about our ears, because there's a protected colony of bats in there. That's why we need your money, and plenty of it.'

Uneasy laughter from the crowd. I wondered if I could step

in and lift her off the chair. I caught Rory's panicked eye – he was evidently having the same thought.

'Ancient, beautiful, och aye,' Agatha went on, wagging a finger. 'But all the bills come in a lovely scarlet print now, and if we dinnae get investment to turn the castle we love into a luxury hotel or events centre, by Christmas poor Sir Alastair will be biding in a poky flat on the ring road. One that smells of tinned soup because I'll no' be cooking for him.'

People were glancing at each other, unsure how to respond to this tirade of hard truths.

'Now look.' Agatha dropped her voice to a confessional murmur. The room was silent. 'My wee mother needs a care home. She *longs* to move to Strathan View Lodge – they have classic karaoke on Tuesdays and all-comers chair yoga. But it's no' cheap. My wee sister Mary gave up her annual holiday to Stranraer at Easter to save up, and *I cannot lose this job!*'

People were now staring, mesmerised. Rory took a subtle step towards her, like a zookeeper wielding a tranquiliser dart.

'We cannae open to tourists,' Agatha went on, her voice rising with passion. 'Everything's too auld and broken, it cannae be insured. The beds are like concrete, the carpets are full of moths...' She pantomimed horror at a rising cloud of imaginary insects. 'No double glazing. Even my mother's turf-roofed croft is warmer in winter!'

She paused for a moment, like a great orator waiting for the crowd to settle.

'But,' She raised a fist in triumph, 'I havenae given up yet, even if Himself thinks it's all a waste o' time. You'll invest! We'll open for events! Sir Alastair will be saved! The bats will have a new roof!' Agatha paused before the climax.

'*And my mother will have her karaoke!*'

At last, she stepped down, to thunderous applause and cheering.

I looked across the room, to see Logan in the doorway. He

was moving oddly, and at first, I couldn't work out what was wrong with him – until I realised that his shoulders were shaking with laughter.

The ceilidh came as a great relief, despite the fact that I'd never danced a step of a reel in my life.

Weave the Willow made a joyously Celtic noise, with fiddles and accordions, and the 'caller' shouting out the steps at top volume from the gallery. It was fair to say the circles we made were somewhat ragged, and the tunnels created by raised hands for others to skip through were more like drifting wind-socks, but it was wild, breathless fun.

Logan had rejoined the crowd, and, to my surprise, had contradicted his earlier vow not to dance. His limp was now barely noticeable and as I galloped down a row of couples, holding hands with a red-faced sixty-something hedge-fund owner, I saw that he was my next partner. He grabbed my hand firmly, and whirled me into a spin.

'Having fun?' he shouted into my ear.

With his warm hand on my waist and my chest pressed against his tweed jacket, I really was enjoying myself at long last. As we whirled, I almost laughed at Logan's extreme compe-tence. He knew exactly where to go, how to lead and when to release me so he could raise my hand and spin me. It was like being tumbled by a very precise washing-machine cycle.

The music and steps were finally falling into place together and as I spun back into his arms and he held me to him, I allowed myself a brief fantasy that we were a couple, and that if I wanted to, I could simply reach up and kiss him. I did want to, very much, and judging by the way he was looking at me, I realised, he did, too.

'Mind if I cut in?'

Oliver, flushed with champagne, his blonde hair damp with

sweat from unaccustomed exercise, was standing beside us, reaching his hand out towards me, as if I was a parcel the neighbours had taken in.

'Yes, I do,' said Logan pleasantly. 'Unless you'd like to dance with him, Cat.'

'No, I don't...'

'For God's sake, Cat!' Oliver's voice rose. Logan and I had stopped dancing, and he'd steered me to the edge of the dance floor as Oliver trotted after us. 'I've come all this way to tell you how I feel...'

'Perhaps she doesn't want to know,' said Logan coldly.

'Oh, but she does.' Oliver smirked, his gaze raking my cleavage. 'Has she not told you?'

'Told me what?'

My face flamed. Dancers wheeled and spun around us, but the three of us stood still, tension crackling.

'That she's been in love with me for years.' He slung a proprietorial arm around my shoulders.

Logan shrugged. 'We all make mistakes.'

My mind raced – I needed to let Logan know I'd been deluded, that it wasn't true, if it ever had been, that...

'I was still engaged at the time, but that didn't stop you, did it, Cat?'

He gave me a little, amused squeeze.

'No,' I said frantically. 'It was a mistake – I don't know what I was thinking.'

As I looked into Logan's puzzled eyes, I finally allowed myself to remember everything.

I'd got extremely drunk – weeks of sixteen-hour days preparing for the party had exhausted me, and Oliver's cliffhanger chat in the summer house had propelled me into a state of do-or-die recklessness. I had to resolve the way I felt, one way or another,

I couldn't spend another year working alongside him, sick with unrequited passion.

After wandering the manor swigging champagne, I made my way down the stairs and onto the dance floor, weaving under the coloured lights. Oliver was dancing with a couple of young TV presenters – in my memory, they'd melted away after seeing the alarming determination in my eyes.

'Oliver!' I shouted over the music – Taylor Swift, singing 'Blank Space'. 'I need to talk to you.'

He looked down at me. 'Fire away.'

That was what he always said in meetings, and I laughed. He smiled, took my hand and whirled me round with the music.

'What is it?'

I crashed against his chest, dizzy, drunk, euphoric with adrenaline, knowing this long, painful chapter of my life was about to be resolved.

'I just need you to know...' I shouted.

The DJ stopped the chorus for the crowd to sing along.

'*I love you!*'

My words rang out across the silent dance floor. Oliver took a step back, and I almost fell. I heard gasps, laughter, and just before the music crashed back in, a voice rang out from the edge of the dance floor – aristocratic, crystal clear.

'Shame it's me he's marrying, Catrina.'

Two days later, Oliver called me in and explained that Bo'nita had called off her wedding to J-Ting, and he needed to make urgent budget cuts.

Sadly, I was the main one.

46

Now, just a few weeks later, Oliver smiled down at me. I was still pinned to his side, and it was unpleasantly clammy.

'You were right, Cat. We should have been together all along.'

'*No!*' I blurted, horrified.

I pulled away, leaving his arm dangling. 'I wasn't right – I was lonely and overworked and I created something from nothing...'

'For God's sake!' Oliver's voice rose. 'I've come hundreds of miles to tell you how I feel...'

'Perhaps you should have told her before you got engaged to someone else,' said Logan. 'Or before you made her redundant because you couldn't cope with your *confusing feelings*.'

'She can speak for herself,' snapped Oliver. 'I'm telling you, mate, this one's the feistiest little kitten in Britain.'

Something in me curled like an endive and wilted. 'This one' and 'little kitten' had killed any residual fondness I may have felt stone dead.

'I *am* speaking for myself.' I glared at him. 'I agree with everything Logan's said, and if you're not here to invest in Iolair, you're wasting your time.'

'Oh, I see you're making me work for it.' Oliver grabbed my arm and pulled me towards him. 'Come on, Cat, enough of the games now. We both know how we feel about each other.'

'I don't feel that way any more,' I insisted, pulling away, but his fingers were tight around my wrist.

Guests were still thundering round the floor to the waves of music coming from above us, and the caller was bellowing, 'Form a circle! Step in!' Rory belted past with Mel, whose hair was flying from its clips. She was laughing hysterically, and I saw Ishbel whisking by on Ryan Clough's arm, while Agatha was now dancing cheerfully with Darko Bix. Jack Campbell and his father weren't dancing – they were still at their table, seemingly deep in discussion.

'She's told you she's not interested.' Logan leaned in, with the stony expression I'd come to know so well. 'I suggest you find someone else to dance with.'

'It's not up to you, mate.'

Oliver bent to speak directly into my ear. 'I've got a suite at the hotel. Why don't you pack your things and come with me? We can make up for lost time. Obviously, you can have your job back.'

'I shag you and I get my job back?'

Oliver chuckled. 'I wouldn't put it that way. But I'd love to explore our connection.'

Who *was* this preening LinkedIn post?

'No,' I said. 'I made a mistake. I'm not coming with you.'

'There's playing hard to get and then there's being a prick-tease,' Oliver shouted, his face crimson.

'Don't you ever speak to her like that!' Logan said, ice in his voice.

Oliver stepped forward. 'She's not yours, *mate,*' he said, and jabbed Logan in the chest.

'Get your bloody hands off me,' spat Logan, and Oliver threw a flailing, drunken punch that went wide and whacked me in the ribs. I screamed in shock.

Logan drew back his arm and punched Oliver in the nose. My ex-boss fell to the floor at my feet like a sack of cement.

Eighteenth-century gentleman dueller that he was, Logan offered a hand to Oliver to pull him back up, but he swore and rolled away into a foetal position, a hand clamped to his face. Bo'nita ran over, screaming, and behind her, a tide of drunken rubber-neckers rushed to witness the drama.

'He's a danger!' Oliver shouted, finally struggling to his feet. 'He's a bloody lunatic!' It came out 'bubby loomtic' as his hand was still pressed to his face.

'Let's have a look, babe,' said Bo'nita, gently easing his hand away. There was a small red mark on his cheek.

'Ow!' Oliver screamed as she experimentally pressed a finger to it. 'I need to get this looked at!'

'Who by, a Swiss watchmaker?' Logan asked. 'You'd need a magnifying glass to find it.'

As Oliver drew breath to reply, I grasped Logan's wrist and dragged him through the teeming, exclaiming crowd. Over their heads, I spotted Rory waving frantically at me and mouthing, '*What's happened?*' I shook my head. I didn't want to stop and explain – I needed to get Logan out of there before anything else kicked off. From the corner of my eye, I saw Jack Campbell raise his phone and point it at Oliver. *He'd better not put that on Instagram*, I thought.

'Do you often punch people?' I asked Logan, as we emerged into the pleasantly cool corridor, after the humid scrum of the Grand Hall.

'Not since school, when Malachy Burridge called me a sneak.'

'What had you done?'

'Told the Head that Malachy and his horrible sidekicks

were relentlessly bullying a terrified first year. I don't regret it. He was expelled.'

'Good. But punching Oliver... Logan, if he tells people, or God forbid, presses charges, it could be very bad for Iolair.'

'Don't give a monkey's. He deserved it.'

'You might not, but your dad and Rory will.'

Logan shrugged. 'He was being utterly disrespectful and abusive to you, Cat. You can argue with a man like that till you're blue in the face, but trust me, he won't listen. So... it felt necessary.'

Part of me was thinking, *For Christ's sake, Logan, it's not the bloody Stone Age.* The other, more treacherous part was wondering if he had a point – and whether, in fact, Oliver had had it coming for years.

'Sorry,' Logan said, as we leaned against the wall, side by side. 'I know you can look after yourself, I wasn't trying to say "hands off my little lady" or anything. I just thought he needed telling.'

'He did.' We looked at each other, and I started to laugh.

'His tiny scratch,' Logan snorted.

'*Bubby loomtic,*' I said, and guffawed.

'I hope someone invests, though,' I added when we stopped laughing. 'The evening hasn't gone quite as I planned.'

'Well, if Agatha can't get the money, nobody can,' said Logan. 'She was magnificent.'

'Not sure Rory thought so.'

Logan smiled. 'I love my little brother, but he's become a bit staid in his old age. Sometimes, you need to shake things up and see what emerges. Dad would just have droned on about historical battles. Aggie got straight to the point.'

I was seized with a desire to know the worst.

'Logan, if we do get investment... will you really still go to New Zealand? You wouldn't consider staying to advise, help your dad deal with it all?'

His smile fell away. 'Cat, I know it makes me seem awful,' he said. 'Of course I'll help Dad as much as I can. But now it looks like Rory's staying put, he can do all the number crunching. You know how much I love this place, but I can't loom around like a ghost who won't accept he's dead, sneering at jolly tourists and lurking round my old veg patch.' He sighed. 'It's all going to change, and I'd rather not have to witness it.'

There was a roar of noise behind us, and I peered round the corner to see an exodus of VIPs. Someone was stabbing at their phone trying to summon an Uber, clearly unaware of the 'Morag's cousin's son' local cab situation, while a tipsy Californian blonde wailed, 'I can't walk the lawn in these heels, Cole!'

'Stay there,' I said, mindful of Oliver's wrath. 'I'm going to see what's happening – why are they all leaving? They're supposed to be here till midnight!'

I made my way to the edge of the crowd that was milling towards the entrance hall, and spotted a tall figure.

'Rory!'

He looked distressed. 'Everyone's leaving because Oliver yelled that he was calling the police. I managed to talk him out of actually doing it, but it was too late...'

He gestured helplessly at the guests streaming out into the night.

Oliver was standing with Bo'nita, gesturing furiously. She was rummaging in her bag, presumably looking for her silver hip flask.

'Oliver,' I said, tapping him firmly on the shoulder. 'There was no need to threaten us with the police.'

'*Us?*' He looked at me. Something was off, and I realised that his eyes were no longer a shimmering Pacific turquoise, but an indeterminate blue-grey. His coloured lenses had apparently been dislodged by the fight.

'Yes, *us*.' I glared at him. 'If the police turn up, no doubt it'll be all over the media in five minutes – *megastar Bo'nita in shock castle raid* – and we can wave goodbye to any chance of investment.'

'I was *assaulted*,' began Oliver, when Agatha's shriek cut across the rumble of conversation.

'The party bags!'

She was shoving her way through the crowd, carrying an armful of our little gift bags with the smart Castle Apothecary stamp.

'Hey!' she shouted, 'All of you! Take them!' She thrust them into the hands of bleary VIPs. 'Rory, get more!'

He hurried off, and I ran after him to help, returning behung with the little blue bags and handing them out.

'Well, doesn't that smell divine?' cried a woman, marvelling at the glorious scent coming from the bags.

'Bog myrtle,' Agatha said. 'There's a whole lot of bogs in Iolair.'

Bo'nita snapped one up. 'Oh my God,' she said, inhaling. Her eyelids fluttered closed in ecstasy. 'Girl, that is *major*.'

'Sweet to do something home-made,' said Jack Campbell as he passed. 'Rich people get so bored of Tiffany freebies.'

Agatha's face fell. I didn't dignify his remark with a reply, but my loathing of him rose another notch.

Soon, the last of the guests was stumbling down the lawn, lit by the flicker of burned-down torches on the steps, and Rory was quite literally paying the piper, who had evidently been at the whisky cocktails.

'Stonking night, pal,' he was saying. 'Food, booze and a fight, right enough. Like Sauchiehall Street on a Saturday night. Belter.'

Rory's face was somewhat less flushed with delight, and as we finally closed the doors and heard the distant parp of Harwood's foghorn, he groaned aloud.

'Well, that was an unmitigated disaster,' he said. 'I'm going to bloody kill Logan.'

'Why? Oliver started it!'

'It's not *school*!' Rory shouted. 'Oliver was a guest! Even if he was being a bit annoying...'

'Try "massively offensive".'

'Either way! Cat, do you honestly think that in business, I don't have to deal with utter fools every day? These are the money people – that's what they're like! Who's going to invest in us after that amateurish debacle? Edam sauce! Fights! Midges!'

As an advert, I had to admit, it wasn't going to get the punters in.

'Hey.' I turned. Mel had a firm hand on Rory's arm. 'Listen, everyone loved it. They had a great time. Come on, let's go and have a drink. I'll hang on to help with the clear-up. Belle's staying with Mum tonight.'

I gave her a very grateful smile. 'You must be knackered, Cat,' she added. 'You've not stopped. Come and have a glass with us. And Agatha,' Mel put an arm around her shoulders, 'you deserve a giant shot of whisky if anyone does.'

'I'll join you soon,' I promised. 'I just need to find Logan.'

I slipped away, back down the corridor, but there was no sign of him. Had he gone to bed? It was still only ten o'clock. Perhaps he was in the sitting room.

The door was ajar, and the cosy room was lit by a single lamp. At first, I thought it was empty, but as my eyes adjusted to the murk, I saw a still figure in the wing-backed armchair, holding a framed photograph.

'Logan?'

'Cat. I'm glad it's you. I'd rather avoid the inevitable row with Rory until tomorrow.'

'He's just upset that it went wrong.' I sighed. 'I know it wasn't your doing.' I crossed to the enormous sofa and subsided. It occurred to me that it was the first time I'd sat down all night.

'Oliver was being obnoxious,' I added. 'I feel such an idiot for ever looking twice at him.'

'Love makes idiots of us all.'

I looked at the photograph Logan was holding, and realised it was the picture of his mum, holding on to him and Rory and beaming with pride.

'Sorry. Being sentimental,' said Logan. 'I just... She was so happy here. Mum would have had all kinds of plans to save Iolair, she'd have cheerfully opened it up to the public and shared it all. Dad was always the worrier, she was the doer. You remind me a bit of her.'

'Really?' I felt immensely flattered.

He nodded. 'Maybe that's one of the many reasons why I like you so much.'

I opened my mouth to reply, but he stood and went to put the photograph back. 'I'm off to bed,' he said. 'Bracing myself for the inevitable fall-out tomorrow. You did a fantastic job, Cat. Sorry I screwed it up for you. I meant to help.'

He squeezed my shoulder, and left the room. I heard his footsteps echoing down the corridor, and longed to follow. But what good would that do? We'd both soon be gone from here, back to our separate lives, thousands of miles apart. The castle would be sold off at auction, and I'd never have any reason to come here again.

The door creaked, and I sat up, heart racing, hoping that Logan had returned.

Sir Alastair stood in the doorway, swaying, Hannay at his side.

'Good evening to you both,' he said, blinking at me in puzzlement. 'I suppose it must be almost time for my speech.'

47

I woke early, soft light filtering through the curtains, and it took me a moment to understand that there was no more preparation to do, no more worrying about food or staff or bagpipes.

It was all over, and so were our hopes of saving the castle. We'd spent thousands of Sir Alastair's remaining money on a night everyone would remember for all the wrong reasons, and it had made no difference. If anything, it had only hastened the demise of Iolair.

I'd offer to leave tomorrow, get out of their way as they faced the inevitable. My heart felt like a lump of iron. Logan was in my blood. I thought of him constantly, was drawn to him magnetically, and no matter how many times I forced myself to look at the facts – his bad temper, his plans to emigrate, my future in London, the fact that we had nothing in common apart from a fondness for animals – all rationality was on hold. I just wanted to be near him, touching him, laughing with him. Breathing him in.

'Get a bloody grip, Cat,' I said to my reflection. '*Move on.*'

To rally myself, I opened my WhatsApp chat with Alice

and typed a brief update on last night's disasters. *You were right about Oliver.* I added, *I'll be back home soon.*

Almost immediately, a reply pinged in.

THIS IS AMAZING!!! Also, was Logan punching him extremely hot?

I snorted out loud, and sent a flame emoji.

Alice: *Then stay! Fight for your man.*

Me: *Can't. He's going to New Zealand.*

Alice: *What?! No way! I'm messaging Cameron right now & telling him to intervene.*

Me: *Alice, don't! I mean it!*

Though I waited several minutes to see the ticks turn blue, my last message remained distressingly unread.

Downstairs, everyone was draped round the kitchen in various shades of exhaustion. Rory was frantically tapping at his phone, Agatha was muttering, 'Tiffany bracelets! Audrey Hepburn herself couldnae afford them,' as she stirred porridge, and Sir Alastair was looking very pale and robotically feeding scrambled egg to Hannay. There was no sign of Logan.

'I've been up since five, sending apology texts,' said Rory bleakly. 'Nobody's even replied.'

'Because they'll all still be asleep!' I said. 'Not everyone gets up at dawn.'

'I'm wondering if I should go down to the hotel,' he went on. 'Grab a few of them over breakfast, apologise in person.'

'Appalling idea,' said Agatha testily. 'Leave them be.'

I was inclined to agree with her.

'I'm so terribly sorry,' murmured Sir Alastair. I had the sense that this was not the first time he'd said it today. 'I was just so damned nervous, and that lovely Bonnie girl gave me a drink... awfully strong. Not used to it.'

'We'd better send her hip flask back,' I said, helping myself to toast. 'It's solid silver and was a gift from J-Lo, apparently.'

The door opened, and Logan appeared, back in his usual jeans and checked shirt. I rather missed the kilt.

'Good morning,' he said, sitting opposite me.

I smiled at him. Somehow, the events of last night had intensified my feelings.

I felt a giant clock was hovering above me, ticking down our time together. Another breakfast gone, another afternoon... Oliver's fumbled declaration had only shone light on Logan's genuine decency and moral core. What I'd once felt for my old boss had been physical attraction, the allure of forbidden fruit, a lazy infatuation born from lack of options. I now knew I could meet a thousand men in future, and they'd all be a disappointment to me – because none of them would be Logan.

'You've a rare cheek,' Rory snapped at him. 'It's not a good morning for some of us, Logan, actually. I don't know how we're going to patch up the damage to our reputation after that fiasco, and I need a serious word with you after breakfast...'

'I did my best,' said Agatha sulkily.

'Your speech was great,' Logan assured her. 'They'd never heard anything like it.'

The rarely used landline began to ring. Rory, who was nearest, stood and snatched up the receiver.

'Complaints, no doubt,' he muttered. 'Castle Iolair, Rory speaking. Oh, hi there.' He listened. 'No.' His voice took on an ominous tone. 'No, I did not know. That's not been mentioned.' He paused. 'I see... Well, thanks for telling me. We must have that drink when you're back.'

He put the phone down, and when he turned back to the room, it was clear that Rory was clenching his teeth.

'That was Cameron.'

Bloody Alice.

'Anything you'd like to tell us, Logan?' he asked tightly. 'Any big plans you'd like to share with your family at all?'

'I don't know what you...'

'Oh, don't play the bloody innocent.' Rory slammed a fist on the table, making us all jump. 'New Zealand!' he roared. 'When were you going to drop that little bombshell?'

'When the big event was over,' said Logan calmly. 'When an investor made an offer, and I knew you were all safe.'

'And then you'll just trot off to the other side of the globe and abandon us to deal with it all? Is that it?'

'I don't really see I've much choice,' Logan said. 'If the castle's under new management, what am I going to do with my life? Work at the Falls of GlennIolair forever and live in the flat above the post office with Ewan?'

'You could stay *here*! You pig-headed, selfish git!'

'I could not,' said Logan. 'I presented all my ideas to Dad, he didn't believe they could work, so here we are. I'll be off in a couple of weeks. I didn't want to tell you until we knew what was happening with Iolair. I suppose now it'll be sold.'

'Thanks to *you*!' bellowed Rory, pink-faced. 'Because you couldn't keep your fists to yourself!'

'That's not fair,' I interrupted. 'Oliver tried to hit him first.'

'Oh, for crying out loud.' Rory banged his forehead lightly against a watercolour painting of a small boat.

Sir Alastair put his spoon down. 'Did you just say you're going to New Zealand?' he asked faintly.

Logan looked uncharacteristically upset. 'Dad, I was going to tell you when things were clearer...'

'You've made up your mind?'

Logan nodded. 'I'm afraid so. There's a good life waiting for me out there.'

'You sound like the bloody Pilgrim Fathers,' snapped Rory. 'Will you be rolling across the fields in a covered wagon, singing hymns?'

'Stop it,' I said. 'Logan's right – at least there he'll have a good job and a future. Even if we – you – wish he wasn't going.'

'A good job is everything,' intoned Agatha mournfully. 'Now, my poor mother cannae—'

She was interrupted by the doorbell. I wondered if one of Bo'nita's minions had been sent to collect the flask.

Agatha went to answer, and when she reappeared, her lips were pressed into a thin line. Two men stepped past her into the kitchen.

'Morning,' said Jack Campbell, grinning round at us all. His father gave a narrow smile, and nodded at Sir Alastair. 'We bring good news.'

'I very much doubt that,' said Logan, ice in his tone.

'Hear us out,' said Jack. 'I think you'll be pleased. After much discussion, we've decided to go for it.' He paused.

'Go for *what?*' snarled Logan. 'I've no idea what you're talking about, and I don't know why you're in our kitchen.'

'The reason we're in *the* kitchen, that's yours at this particular moment,' said Jack, 'is because if you're buying a house, it makes sense to have a look round. And that's what we've decided to do. We're buying Castle Iolair.'

48

There was uproar.

The dogs launched into a deafening chorus of barking at the mean strangers who were not paying them attention, just as Logan stood up.

'Over my dead body!' he snarled, brandishing a piece of toast. Rory shouted, 'This castle is not for sale!' and Sir Alastair sagged in his chair, brokenly murmuring, 'How have I let it come to this?' Agatha, meanwhile, looked ready to throw the entire pot of porridge over the two smirking interlopers.

I swiftly nipped in front of her, and said, 'You can't buy something that's not available.'

'Oh, it *is*, though,' said Jack. His father nodded, like every dumb movie henchman.

Jack pulled out a chair and threw himself into it, carelessly clipping Dougie's tail with his boot.

Agatha flew across the kitchen and snatched the little dog to her. 'Do *not* touch that puppy!' she yelled. 'You great brute!'

'Chill, guys,' crooned Jack, taking a gulp of Rory's abandoned coffee. 'Everyone take a beat, yeah?' God, he was despicable. 'Look, we know you've no cash. This one made that pretty clear.' He nodded at Agatha, who was still clutching Dougie to herself like a precious parcel while he nibbled her hair.

'Nobody's going to invest after that pantomime,' he went on. 'Besides, it's not worth it to them – the land slopes down, it won't make a golf course, there's no infrastructure here and all the tattered old crap needs ripping out.'

By 'tattered old crap' I assumed he meant the priceless historical art and artefacts.

'But we've a plan,' said Jack. 'Hand it over for the going rate – around £700k, which we think is more than fair, given the work that needs doing... obviously, that includes the land and the gatehouse,'

Logan laughed out loud.

'And we'll do the rest,' Jack went on.

'What "rest"?' Logan spat.

'Making it habitable! You can't think this leaky old shell is worth much? People expect luxury these days, pal, they want monsoon showers and walk-in wardrobes with under-lit handbag shelves in their hotel suite, they want a glass-walled gym full of shiny Pelotons, not a faded historical re-enactment that smells of wet dog.'

'A hotel?' repeated Sir Alastair. He'd been pale to begin with, now he looked like wet putty. I wondered if he should be led back to bed.

'Haggis Hotels,' said Jack proudly. 'Scottish-themed. Luxe with a twist. Big, graffiti-style paintings of Highland cows on the walls, ironic battered Mars bar and Irn Bru sauce on the menu, neon signs that say HASTE YE BACK... they're going to love it. Iolair will be the flagship, then we'll roll out a full Haggis Hotels chain across the Highlands.'

The three McAskills were staring at him, their faces rigid with horror.

'No,' Sir Alastair confirmed. He seemed to have woken up at last. 'Iolair is not for sale.'

Bran Campbell looked over at Jack, and grinned.

'What's so funny, Bran?' Logan asked.

'I'm just impressed with my son's brains,' the older man said. 'Proof a private education is no match for a sharp mind.'

'What are you talking about?' Logan snapped. 'Jack's mind is about as sharp as a snapped crayon.'

Jack was holding up his phone. 'Oops,' he said. 'Tabloid stories can really do some damage.'

A close-up image of Oliver last night, the red mark clearly visible on his face, appeared on the small screen, and Jack jabbed his thumb to play the recording.

'Tonight, I was invited to an event at Castle Iolair, on Scotland's West Coast,' intoned Oliver, like an earnest news reporter. 'The owners are urgently looking for investment, and threw a party to charm hedge fund managers and highflyers such as myself.'

I experienced a small, inner shudder at the pomposity of that 'myself'.

'Unfortunately,' Oliver paused heavily. 'The heir to the castle, Logan McAskill, brutally insulted me, then punched me during the course of a small disagreement. I sustained a facial injury, which may permanently scar, and fell to the floor. He walked away.' Oliver looked solemnly into the camera. 'I'm considering whether to press charges. I've received no apology, and it's clear that Clan McAskill believes they're above the law. Not only that, we were also assailed by biting insects due to a lack of forward planning, the basic food offering was severely below par, and the cleaner stood up and made a frankly bizarre speech, begging for money, while the incumbent laird had staggered away, drunk.'

He smiled sadly. 'I'm a high-end events organiser, working with celebrities and royalty, and believe me, this is not how it's done. I'm just sorry that this family, custodians of an ancient building desperately in need of help, have so recklessly thrown away their one chance of rescue.'

The video ended, on a still of Oliver looking nobly sorrowful.

'Cleaner?' whispered Agatha. '*Cleaner?*'

'*May permanently scar?*' I cried. 'I've had bigger wounds from midge bites.'

'What exactly do you propose to do with that travesty?' Logan demanded.

Jack smirked. 'There's this thing called "the internet", and sometimes – I know this will be a new concept to an ancient family such as yourselves – videos "go viral". There's plenty of news outlets who'd be interested, too, I imagine. Once it's clear that Oliver knows Bo'nita.' He pressed the screen, and another video popped up – this time, of Oliver laughing with Bo'nita, his arm around her shoulders, standing on the castle porch, evidently before the fight. She must have gone out to vape. '*Megastar in posh boy fight showdown,*' said Jack. '*Who is pop princess's mystery man?*' They're going to love it. So, either we buy the castle – because we *do* have investment – or I press "post". I'll leave it with you for a few hours.'

He nodded at Bran Campbell, and they left the room.

'Dear God,' said Sir Alastair. 'Over my dead *body* will those wide boys snatch Iolair from us!'

'It's blackmail, pure and simple!' stormed Rory. 'I've a mind to call the police.'

'It's Oliver,' I realised, horrified. 'He's got the money to do this. He's made a fortune, and he's going to get the Campbells to buy Iolair to punish *me* for rejecting him. The narcissism is off the scale,' I added. 'I'm so sorry. I brought that selfish monster to your door.'

'Don't be ludicrous,' said Logan. 'If anyone's to blame, it's Rory for inviting him.'

'I didn't know he was Cat's ex-boyfriend!'

'He *isn't!*' Logan and I chorused.

Rory sat down at the table again, and Agatha subsided into a chair. Dougie was now wriggling, so she gently put him down and allowed him to play with Arran's plumy tail.

It occurred to me how happy I felt here with these people. They had welcomed me and fed me and confided in me, and in Logan's case, a great deal more. They had trusted me, and in that moment, I felt I'd let them down terribly. I thought of Agatha's mum, and the care home her children couldn't afford, and of Sir Alastair's cosy turret. I remembered Rory had quit his glamorous Manhattan career to come back, and that Donald and Ishbel would be turfed out of their lovely home, which the Campbells would probably knock down and replace with a car park.

As for Logan... he'd be far away, his family scattered. He may never come back.

49

I looked at Logan across the table, emanating rage and despair, and I yearned to put my arms around him.

'So, what do we do?' asked Rory. 'Sell up?' He glanced at his phone in despair. 'We've had no offers at all. Nothing but a few half-hearted thank yous, and Darko Bix asking for tips on infected midge bites.'

'Give it time,' said Sir Alastair hopefully. 'Someone might come through.'

Rory shook his head. 'I didn't get any sense of... eagerness,' he said flatly. 'I think once the VIPs realised how much work was needed, they backed off. They're more Silicon Valley start-up than Scottish castle renovation, I guess.'

'It's my fault.' Agatha gazed hopelessly at the teapot. 'I was too honest.'

'You did a great speech,' I told her, whilst silently agreeing.

'Should we wait a few days?' I ventured. 'See if *anyone* bites?'

'Even if they do, one won't be enough,' said Logan. 'To turn the castle into a functioning events venue would cost hundreds of thousands. The state of the drive alone...'

Rory was nodding. 'I don't see that we have much choice,' he said grimly. 'It's either sell to the Campbells at a knock-down price, or wait for the bailiffs to come and chuck us out. And if we refuse the Campbells, Jack'll send that video to the *Daily Mail*, and we'll be a laughing stock.'

'Oh, boys,' said Sir Alastair. 'I'm so very sorry. And Agatha...' He looked on the verge of tears.

'I'll be okay,' she said gruffly. 'I'll get a job as a cleaner, like they said. Sooner scrub lavvies than work for *Haggis Hotels*.'

I felt sick with guilt that all my attempts had led only to this bleak moment. As I gazed down at the table, the WhatsApp chat pinged. I was going to have serious words with Alice later, I thought, glancing at it.

OMG, she'd written. *Have you seen this?*

She had attached a link to Instagram, and, my heart fluttering unpleasantly – had Jack already made good on his threat? – I opened it.

The link sent me straight to Bo'nita's account. She had... I read it again. *Seventy-one million followers*. And she had just posted a beautifully styled image of her Castle Apothecary gift bag, soap, bath bomb and candle in a hotel bathroom with a copper bathtub and terrazzo tiles.

She had captioned it:

Check out this incredible beauty range from @castle_iolair – loving it!! The smell is un-beee-lievable. #gifted #westhighlands #socute #sniffdatting

The post had – I gasped out loud, and everyone looked up – 382,000 likes and 4,328 comments, all, judging by my brief scroll, versions of 'Love it Kween! Where can I buy?', 'Link please!', 'Gorgeous!! Want it so bad. Where from?!', 'Do they ship to US?'

I found that my hand was trembling. Even as I watched, the

likes and positive comments rolled on in real time. Bo'nita had tagged the account I'd set up – I'd been posting photos of the castle and the loch, mostly for the delight of Alice and my mum. We now had over 40,000 followers.

'Cat?' Logan was staring at me. 'What is it? Has Jack bloody Campbell...?'

I shook my head, unable to speak, and held out the phone to Agatha. She peered miserably at it, expecting bad news – viral criticism of her Edam sauce, or mockery of her speech. It took her a moment.

'My God.' She put a shaking hand on Alba's head, and turned to me, her eyes filling with tears.

'Cat, I think we did it,' she said. 'You, me, Bo'nita. I think... maybe we've saved Castle Iolair?'

It took a while to explain to Sir Alastair what had happened. 'That lovely woman I was talking to?' he kept saying. 'Seventy million? My great-grandmother's old teacups?'

Rory looked shell-shocked. 'I can't believe it,' he said. 'All that effort. Pies. Ceilidhs. Yachts. All we needed was one post from a pop star.'

Logan's face broke into a smile. 'So,' he said. 'We should convert the barns properly, so Agatha can do her thing.'

'You overlook the fact that we have no money left,' said Rory. 'That party pretty much cleaned us out.'

'Ah,' said Logan. 'But this is something we could get funding for. With instant results. Even the bank might stump up for it.'

'I'll draw up a business plan,' Rory said thoughtfully. 'Even if Bo'nita never posts again, millions of people will know about Castle Iolair now.'

My phone pinged again. Alice had attached a link to an online tabloid story: 'Hunt is on for Bo's Beloved Boutique Beauty Brand'.

Hopeful shoppers were 'going wild', apparently, and 'The

Castle Apothecary is the new buzz phrase in beauty – here's everything we know about this under-the-radar bombshell brand that oozes authenticity.' It wasn't much – a blurred picture of the castle and a reprint of Bo'nita's post.

'Cat, can you make a web page, fast?' Rory asked, when I showed him. 'We can start taking pre-orders.'

'We'll send gift packages out to other stars, too,' I said. 'The more buzz the better. I've still got my old contacts book.'

'Hold on.' Logan leaned across the table. 'Agatha, do you actually want to do this? Be in charge of a beauty brand? Come up with the recipes? Because if you don't, it's absolutely fine. Don't feel pressured.'

Agatha laughed. Today she was wearing a Ramones-style black T-shirt reading, 'Emmeline, Sylvia, Christabel, Emily'.

'Logan,' she said firmly. 'It's everything I ever wanted. Of course. But who'll look after the castle?'

'Mel's mum, Lorna, told me yesterday that she's looking for a job,' I said thoughtfully. 'And her cranachan was amazing...'

'Lovely Lorna,' said Sir Alastair dreamily, his hangover forgotten. 'I knew her long ago, in our teens...'

Rory and Logan exchanged a horrified glance.

'So this is definitely happening?' I clarified. 'Because there's a small problem.'

Everyone looked at me.

'Logan,' I said quietly. 'If he's not here, how will you get the ingredients for all the soaps and things? Who will run the market garden? If you buy them elsewhere, it'll eat into any profits straight away.'

The table fell silent.

'Logan,' said Sir Alastair quietly. 'Must you really go? Now there's this new plan?'

My heart raced as we waited for him to answer. I felt a treacherous spark of hope. He sighed heavily, reaching under the table to scratch the spaniels' heads – always his 'tell' when he felt particularly stressed.

'Look, I've already taken the job,' he said. 'I've booked my flights and applied for a visa. Jamie and his wife Kendra have got accommodation in a wooden cabin by the shore waiting for me.'

It sounded the perfect life for Logan. Rustic, simple, immersed in nature, growing good things... Perhaps it wouldn't be Marina running down the wooden steps to join him, as she had in my vision, but it certainly wouldn't be me. I felt a deep ache in my chest. He was right in front of me holding a striped mug of tea, his hair ruffled, dark stubble on his chin because he hadn't shaved yet... and I'd already lost him.

'I'll work on the website and the social media this after-noon,' I said, as briskly as I could manage. 'I can set up a holding page for a shop, to allow pre-orders before we launch. Then I suppose I'll think about heading back to London in a couple of days. Better check the train times.'

I longed to reach across the table and grab Logan's hand. I wanted to shout, 'What are we doing?', make him see the poten-tial of a future here – one that involved us being together. London felt far away, too busy, too noisy. I didn't want to wake up to sirens and bin lorries, or wait for a bus wreathed in other people's bubblegum vape smoke, listening to their tinny music. I didn't feel enthused by slaving over boutique events so C-list celebrities could yell at me about flower walls and ice sculptures.

I had fallen in love with Iolair; its peace and beauty, the sense of history in every stone, the glimpse of the loch each morning that told me the weather before I looked at the sky, the ever-present dogs. I had fallen in love with the people. And, I finally admitted to myself, with Logan.

Sir Alastair looked worriedly at me. 'Cat, there's no need to rush away, you know. You've done wonders here, and we all think the world of you. You could stay on, run the new business?'

'He's right,' Rory chimed in. 'This new brand needs a manager, and you're proven yourself more than capable. We could pay you a salary, it wouldn't be much at first, but...'

'Stay, Cat.' Agatha's pale eyes blazed. 'We need you, lassie.'

I thought of it – the chance to stay at Iolair, a new job, helping to make something real and affordable that people would love, rather than trying to translate the idiotic fantasies of millionaires into reality. I had friends here, a purpose, a beautiful place to live...

But without Logan, it would feel as though the heart of Iolair had been ripped out. Every time I passed the veg patch, or glanced uphill towards the bothy, or glimpsed his little garden shed, or had a drink in the pub, I'd miss him. Without Logan here, staying would hurt too much to bear.

'I don't think I can,' I said eventually. 'I know you'll all do brilliantly, and I'll visit, I promise. But...'

'Your life is in London.' Sir Alastair nodded, and patted my hand gently. 'We understand. But you'll be very much missed by all of us.'

The lump in my throat was too big to speak, but I glanced up, and finally, Logan looked back at me.

His expression was wretched – and I knew it reflected my own.

50

I spent the afternoon in a frenzy of activity, working on a simple website, checking the ever-increasing comments on Bo'nita's Instagram post and jotting down ideas for the new business. Keeping busy was always how I held back a tide of misery, but despite my attempts, the grief of imminent loss hovered close by.

By five, I'd had enough. I still hadn't booked a train, but if I left on Tuesday, I'd have time to pack and say my goodbyes to everyone tomorrow. I wondered if Rory and Mel might make a go of things – although she needed to tell him the truth about Belle first. I'd have a word with her, I decided. Rory deserved to get to know his daughter.

I also wasn't sure what Logan would do about Jack Campbell's threat. The castle may not be for sale, but would Oliver's video scupper our fledgling business before it had begun?

One more day near Logan. I closed my heavy bedroom door, and descended to the hall. *This is one of the last times I'll go down these stairs*, I thought, like a child counting the hours to the end of a wonderful holiday. *This is the last time I'll touch the bust of the seventh laird for luck as I pass...*

As if to emphasise what I was losing, the weather was glorious, late-afternoon sun illuminating the garden and transforming the loch to a gleaming silver blade. Rather than going straight to the kitchen, I allowed myself a final tour of the places I had come to love.

I walked the long corridors, feeling a nostalgic fondness for the miserable Victorian cattle and their crumbling bridges. I even had a pang for the glowering portrait of the fourth laird, as I turned towards the Queen's Room. I wanted to breathe in the lavender and beeswax one last time, see the lozenges of gold light falling onto the polished wooden floorboards. I hoped to transform my feelings of deep loss into deep gratitude for the time I'd spent here. I opened the door quietly, and closed it behind me.

'Cat!' Logan was once again standing by the long, mullioned windows and he turned as I entered. He looked tired and pale. 'I was just taking a moment,' he said. 'Having a think.'

'Funny,' I smiled at him. 'I was about to do the same.'

'I'll leave you to it,' Logan said. 'I need to go and speak to Dad, anyway.'

'Things okay?'

'Yes, the Campbell threat has been neutralised.'

'How come?'

'Actually, thanks to Marina,' said Logan. 'I messaged her for advice.'

A shadow must have crossed my face.

'She studied law,' he added quickly. 'I told her what Jack said about sending the clip to the media, and she says it's libellous, so no reputable outlet will touch it. Same law applies to social media.' He shrugged. 'I'm sure Oliver's beauty won't be affected long-term.'

I laughed, and subsided to sit on the bed. It had been remade since Alice's stay, with a beautifully embroidered pale green bedspread.

'That's been in the family for centuries,' said Logan, nodding at it. 'It was made for the fifth laird's wedding by local craftswomen. It's supposed to bring luck to any couple that sleeps beneath it.'

'Did it?' I stroked a hand across the fine old silk.

'Apparently. They were married for seventy-three years.'

'And then the laird's wife ran off with the farmer,' I joked.

Logan sat down alongside me, stretching out his long legs, gazing at the dust motes dancing in the thick shaft of sunlight filtering through the window.

'What I love most about this room,' he said quietly, 'is that in here, we could be living in any era over the last five hundred years. It feels like a place out of time. I've always loved coming in here to think.'

'What were you thinking about?' I asked boldly. What did it matter now? We'd both be gone soon.

Logan was silent for a moment.

'I was thinking of all the things I'll miss about Iolair,' he said. 'Seeing the loch when I open the shutters first thing, not knowing if there'll be rain clouds misting the view of Ben Iolair, or a deep blue sky reflected in the water, and the mountain bright and sharp in the morning sun. Walking the dogs up the forest tracks, everything scented with pine and bog myrtle, seeing the red squirrels darting away through the branches. Watching the waterfalls crashing down over the rocks after a deluge, knowing they'll still be running long after I'm gone. Walking back up the drive in the gloaming, seeing the deer herd in the distance and light glowing from the porch, knowing I'll soon be in front of the fire with a whisky, chatting to Dad about this and that. And...'

He stopped.

'Go on.'

'I'm not sure if it's wise to say it.'

I waited, the blood fizzing in my veins. I felt as though we were standing on the edge of a cliff, the sea churning beneath us.

'Please say it.'

Logan looked at me. I saw the golds and greens in his brown eyes, the colours of an autumn hillside.

'It's you I'll miss the most,' he said. He picked up my cold hand and laced his fingers through mine. 'I know you're going home soon, and I don't mean to make you feel guilty, or as if I won't cope without you. I just... I wanted to tell you, before it's too late and I'm nearly twelve thousand miles away.'

'I'll miss you the most, too,' I said. The desire to tell him the truth was too strong to fight. I took a steadying breath. 'Logan, the only reason I'm going home is because you're leaving. I'll go back, pick up my life in London, hang out with my friends and family, probably start a little events company. I'll be all right – I might be better than all right, in the end. I might meet someone lovely, and one day, we'll get married and have children, and I'll think back to these few weeks at Iolair as a sort of wonderful daydream – a room out of time.'

He was looking at me with such tenderness, I suddenly wanted to cry.

'Cat.' Logan touched my face. 'Catrina, as your mum called you when you came here all those years ago. It suits you.'

'You remember that?'

He breathed a laugh. 'It took me bloody years to try and forget you. In fact, I didn't. I kept you in my mind, in a room out of time. And then a few weeks ago, there you were, on the doorstep, with a big, glamorous London life, in love with your boss, flying round the world... I was certain you wouldn't look twice at the skint, grumpy gardener who never leaves Iolair. I tried to keep away from you. Stop me *catching feelings*, as the kids say nowadays.'

'And all the time, it was me catching feelings,' I said, stroking his wrist with my thumb.

'It was both of us.'

Logan moved closer, and put his arm around me. 'If I did stay,' he said, his voice low and uncertain, 'would you stay, too? With me?'

'As in, together?'

'Cat, I've fallen in love with you,' he said quietly. 'I don't want to be without you. I don't want to emigrate to New Zealand and think about you every single day, wondering where you are and what you're doing. Yes, as a couple. But only if you feel the same way.'

I leaned forward and rested my forehead against his. 'Of course I feel the same way,' I said. 'Deep down, I've felt the same way since I was sixteen years old. But what about your friend in New Zealand?'

'He'll understand,' said Logan. 'He only moved out there because he fell in love.'

Our lips were a hair's breadth apart. One of us moved slightly, and then we were kissing. There was love and wonder and passion and hope in that kiss. I never wanted it to end. I had lost all sense of time, but Logan pulled away briefly.

'Stand up,' he said.

Puzzled, I did. He pulled the silk bedspread from the mattress and wrapped it round us both, then took my hand and led me gently back to the bed.

'There,' he said. 'Seventy-three years of luck for the sixteenth laird and his love. Guaranteed.'

We resumed our kiss, under the silk that was scented with dried herbs and centuries of sunlight. As I raised my arms to remove my top, desperate to be closer to Logan's warm skin, I heard a scrabbling noise in the corridor, followed by the click of the door. Arran and Alba leapt onto the bed, wriggling and licking our faces, doing their best to insert themselves between us.

'This comes with the territory, I suppose,' Logan sighed.

'Get *down*, Alba! Cat, can you honestly deal with all the ongoing nonsense of Castle Iolair?'

I looked at Logan, one arm restraining Arran from knocking over the medieval candlestick, the other still tightly around me. I reached up and kissed him again.

'Logan, my darling love,' I said, 'I don't ever want to deal with anything else.'

51

MAY BANK HOLIDAY WEEKEND, FIFTEEN YEARS EARLIER

The trip back to shore is almost silent.

I can't think of a single thing to say that won't embarrass me further, and after a few game attempts at conversation – 'When are you back at school?' and 'That's a buzzard circling up there, they make a weird noise like a scream,' – Logan gives up. The only sounds are the oars splashing through the water, and the occasional cry of a bird. I'm holding back tears of embarrassment, and all I want to do is get back to the B&B, put on a brave face for Mum and Dad, and get the hell out of the West Highlands.

At last, Logan pulls the boat alongside the little jetty, springs up and ties its rope to a weathered post. He offers a hand to help me out. I almost refuse through pride, but the boat wobbles alarmingly as I stand up, and I grab his fingers. He pulls me up to stand alongside him, and releases my hand.

'I'd better get back,' I say. 'They'll be wondering where I am.'

Nice, Cat, remind him one more time that you're a child whose parents monitor your every move.

'Shall I walk you back to the village?'

I shake my head. 'I'm fine. Thanks, though. And for the boat trip.'

We walk down to the pebbly shore, and he raises a hand.

'I probably won't see you before you leave,' says Logan. 'Have a safe journey back.'

Despair washes over me at the bland emptiness of the middle-aged phrases we're politely exchanging.

'Look,' I say in a hectic rush. 'I'm sorry about... you know. Before.'

'It's okay,' says Logan, 'don't give it a thought.'

Now, I wish I'd kept quiet. I'm about to turn away, when Logan steps forward.

'Cat,' he says quietly. 'Listen, I'm sorry, too. I'd have kissed you if it wasn't for...'

'Your girlfriend.'

'Yes. It wouldn't be fair on her.'

He leans forward and kisses me on the cheek, a fleeting brush that sends a rush of exploding little stars through my skin.

'One day, perhaps you'll come back to Iolair,' he says. 'Things might be different, then.'

'Perhaps,' I say, knowing I never will.

We turn and go our separate ways.

EPILOGUE
ONE YEAR LATER

The bluebells were beginning to turn the south lawn into a soft sea of flowers, and the breeze was just strong enough to ensure nobody would be bothered by midges.

Sir Alastair was already seated in a wicker chair by the picnic area, a panama hat tipped over his eyes, Hannay resting beside him. His Scotch eggs were still in Tupperware – Lorna had a never-ending stack that now lived in Dougie's old cupboard. He was too big to fit in there now, and had taken to sleeping on the rug in front of the Aga.

As I watched from the castle steps, Agatha strode into view. She was chatting to a couple of the new Castle Apothecary staff, who lived above the rebuilt stables, and carrying a plate of mini pork pies. Agatha had just returned from visiting her mum, who was now fully ensconced at Strathan View Lodge, and known among the other residents for her astonishing Dolly Parton impersonation.

Ishbel and Donald arrived next, with Arran and Alba dancing at their heels. I waved at them, and Donald lifted his six-pack of Tennent's in greeting. They opened up their folding chairs, exclaiming at all the food, and the white-clothed trestle table that held wine and a couple of buckets of champagne. We'd decided against serving whisky cocktails this time.

I ran down the steps to greet Mel and Belle. Belle had shot up over the past few months, and as she flung her arms around me, her head almost reached my shoulder. 'Auntie Cat,' she said, 'Mummy says we can get a puppy!'

I glanced quizzically at Mel, who was rolling her eyes. '*When* we move in,' she said. 'Not before. It'll be a few months yet, chick.'

'But when we do!'

'Aye, but you're not naming it Marina.'

'It's such a pretty name, though!'

Mel winked at me, and I laughed. 'There's other pretty names,' she said.

The human Marina was back in Edinburgh, tentatively dating a law professor at the university. We kept in touch warmly and sporadically, though I wasn't sure we'd ever be best friends. To the relief of everyone at the castle, Jack had also moved away, leaving Bran to run the chandlery alone. He was too busy to retain his seat on the council, and now preferred to drink alone at the Kincherrell Arms rather than risk running into any of us at the Falls of GlennIolair.

As I showed Belle the little strawberry cakes that her Granny Lorna had made, whisking one away from Alba's hopeful jaws, Rory emerged from the main doors, chatting animatedly to Alice. Dougie was trotting adoringly after them – he had taken a great shine to my best friend during her regular visits to Iolair. As I waved, Cameron appeared behind them, carting a large box of grilled langoustines – it seemed that over their year of long-distance love, Alice had overcome her seafood aversion. They were now talking about her moving up here, which, naturally, I was thrilled about.

'I can work from home,' she'd said. 'It doesn't matter where I am, and I can rent out the Kilburn flat.'

'But what about when Cam's away? Won't you miss him?'

She'd looked at me, eyes sparkling with excitement. 'Don't tell anyone,' she said, 'It's early days, but we're thinking of opening a little restaurant on the shore. He's had enough of crewing for millionaires.'

It would be perfect, I thought – and of course, they'd have access to the very best fruit and vegetables.

Rory came over to where we were standing, and kissed Mel's cheek.

'Not long now,' he said. They stood side by side, watching Belle throw a tennis ball for Arran. They looked as though they'd been together for years.

Soon after the ceilidh, at my gentle urging, Mel had invited Rory round and told him the truth. He had been truly shocked at first, and devastated that he had missed so much of his daughter's infancy. Mel had confessed to me that it happened one Christmas – Rory paid a flying visit to the castle, they'd met for a reunion drink in the Falls of GlennIolair and stumbled back to hers for a drunken night of passion.

'He flew back to New York the next day,' she said. 'I felt awful about Stacey, and when I found out I was pregnant, I knew he'd do the decent thing and tell her – I didn't want to ruin his relationship. And I had Mum, and Belle.'

Now, she deeply regretted not having told him. Rory was a wonderful dad, though until recently, they hadn't felt ready to live together.

'Belle needs to get to know me,' he'd said. 'And so does Mel.'

As time went by, though, it was clear the two of them were meant for each other. Mel was going to put her little cottage up for sale, and she and Rory would live in the castle's west wing. We'd finally had it insulated and made habitable, and their new turret apartment was painted a dazzling white, ready for them to make their own mark on it. I couldn't wait to have them all living at Iolair – Sir Alastair was thrilled to have a granddaughter, and was full of plans for teaching her to fish, and run an estate. 'It's important,' he said, when we queried this. 'One day, after I'm gone, she'll need to know.'

It was a relief, Rory had admitted, that Lorna was not keen to rekindle her teenage romance with Sir Alastair – 'Because that would make me and Mel... no, I don't want to know what it would make us.'

They were, however, the greatest of friends – she made a wonderful housekeeper for the castle now that Agatha was otherwise occupied, and she and Sir A both looked forward to their daily catch-ups over a cup of tea. I often saw them wandering down to the pub together for Hannay's daily Scotch egg.

Agatha was fully occupied in the stable block, now a highly professional workshop, making Castle Apothecary products to send all over the world. Bo'nita had been to visit, and flooded Instagram with gorgeous shots of herself sitting in rowing boats holding soap, or – memorably – lying in the heather, wearing a gold bikini and clutching a bath bomb.

My next project, as brand manager, was to open a shop on the estate. It wouldn't be up and running for months, but I had plans to sell the food we produced, alongside the bath and beauty ranges. Agatha had been interviewed in *Scottish Life Magazine*, about our rags-to-riches tale. It was safe to say she'd been as honest as ever, given that the piece was entitled 'Bats, Midges and a Punch-Up Led to My Soapy Success'. She had framed it and hung it on the stable wall.

Ross the fish man often popped in for a cup of tea with her, when he'd finished his rounds. I'd noticed she didn't wear her slogan sweatshirts quite so often, and she now drank her tea out of a mug with a lobster on it.

As we arranged ourselves on chairs and rugs, and filled our glasses to toast the first anniversary of The Castle Apothecary, the business that had saved Iolair, Alice nudged me.

'Where is he?' she asked. 'Everyone's here, but I can't see Himself.'

I pointed. Logan had been for a shower after a hard morning's digging, and he was now making his way down the lawns towards us. As he came closer, I squinted in disbelief.

'Is he wearing a *kilt?*' murmured Mel.

I nodded slowly. 'Looks like it.'

Logan was, in fact, wearing the full McAskill regalia, tweed jacket, white cravat, woollen socks...

I stood up. By contrast, I was wearing jeans and a floral top, with my hair in a ponytail to stop Dougie chewing it. He'd taken to sleeping on our bed with Arran and Alba, so I'd often wake up in Logan's arms roasting hot, with Dougie nibbling on the ends of my hair.

The past year, living at Iolair with Logan, had been the happiest of my life. Even my dad had come around to the idea, once he'd been to visit and had a long, whisky-fuelled discussion with Sir Alastair about the state of the nation.

'Quite a sensible bloke,' he'd said the next morning, which was high praise from my dad with a stonking hangover.

'Good afternoon, all of you,' Logan said, raising a hand. Everyone had fallen silent with surprise – even Belle was staring at her uncle Logie with narrowed eyes.

'Sorry to hijack the picnic,' he added. He made his way over to me, and I stared up at him.

He was still ridiculously handsome. Sometimes, I'd find myself gazing at him, marvelling at how a human could be so perfectly crafted. Of course, he always claimed to feel the same way about me. 'Love makes fools of us all,' I'd say, and kiss him on his rough, spiced-sandalwood cheek.

Now, he took my hand.

'It's been a year since we got together, Catrina.' He looked into my eyes. 'And I wanted to ask you something I... well, I've been wanting to ask for a while.'

Alice gasped, and Mel clasped her hands together in excitement.

My heart galloped, as Logan dropped to one knee and held up a small velvet box.

'I know I'm grumpy and difficult,' he began. 'Although I can safely say I'm no longer in a permanent state of angry misery about every single thing...'

I blushed, remembering what I'd said to him.

'That's thanks to you,' he added. 'Cat, you've changed my life, you've saved Iolair, I'm hopelessly in love with you... Will you...'

'Yes!' I cried, before he'd finished the sentence. 'Yes! I'd marry you right now if I could.'

'... marry me?' he finished, deadpan, then broke into a smile that could have lit the entire castle.

The others cheered and applauded as he extracted his great grandmother's diamond ring from its little box and slipped it onto my finger.

'There,' he murmured, bending to kiss me. 'Herself of Iolair at last.'

'You'll make a perfect laird,' I whispered, before our lips met. 'But Cat of Iolair will do just fine.'

A LETTER FROM F.L. EVERETT

Hello,

Thank you so much for reading *Dreams of the Scottish Highlands*. As an author, it's always wonderful to know that readers have made it right through the book – and, I hope, enjoyed the journey. Please do sign up to my newsletter for more information on my books. Your email address will never be shared and you can unsubscribe at any time.

www.bookouture.com/f-l-everett

I genuinely loved writing about Cat and Logan, partly because in some ways, the story reflects my own life.

Over ten years ago now, I went on a trip to Scotland with a friend, at a time when my life was emotionally unravelling. While there, I met a man who lived by a loch. He loved dogs, was extremely comfortable in his own company and did not suffer fools. He could be a bit grumpy, and he cared deeply about rivers and forests and rewilding and ecology. Like Logan, he was also a great cook and had a lovely dad.

I fell in love with him, moved to the West Highlands to be with him and now we're happily married. So hello, Andy – and thanks for inspiring much of the character of Logan.

We don't, however, live in a castle (try a two-bedroom cottage), and the bothy is sadly fictional. But we do have two spaniels and a cat. Arran, Alba and Tortoise are entirely based on Ellroy, Larkin and Marlowe. It's Larkin who likes to chase ducks across the loch. His middle name is trouble, but we love him.

Falling in love with a place has much in common with falling in love with a person – and I fell hard for the West Highlands. It was a joy to experience it all over again through Cat's urban eyes. I still feel the same way about it now, even if I'm not waking up in the four-poster that might have belonged to Mary, Queen of Scots.

I already miss Iolair – perhaps you do, too. But the beauty of Scotland is always here, and I can only encourage you to come and visit. Though if you're planning to swim in the loch, please do pack a wetsuit. We're not all as hardy as Mel.

Thank you again for reading. If you enjoyed your romantic trip to Iolair, please do write a review if you can. It helps new readers to discover my books, and I'm always so grateful when people take the time to share their thoughts.

You can also get in touch via Goodreads, X, Instagram or Facebook.

Until the next book...

Flic x

x.com/fliceverett

instagram.com/fliceverett

ACKNOWLEDGEMENTS

Unlike my historical Edie York novels, writing about Iolair required less research – as I already live by a loch just as beautiful as Loch Iolair, and of course, I've had my heart broken and mended, much like Cat.

So while I may have fewer people to thank directly for this one, I must say a huge, grateful thank you to Susannah Hamilton – we finally got there! – and enormous gratitude also goes to Jess Whitlum-Cooper, whose hand-holding, ideas and editing have been exemplary throughout the process. It's a far better book, thanks to your insights.

I must also send big thanks to Kim Nash, Jess Readett and the whole team at Bookouture, who are the friendliest people in publishing, and who give the best parties.

Thanks also to Stef and Simon and Georgie and Malcolm, dear friends who have over the years given me an exclusive look at what living in a castle or a Scottish stately home really entails (number one, 'being very cold'). I'm also full of gratitude to my friend Diana, for our bolstering writers' lunches and the Corryvreckan swimming anecdotes, and to Simone and Ian for the beautiful boat trips. In fact, I'm grateful to all my Scottish friends and family who have welcomed me so warmly and helped me to feel so at home in our gorgeous, remote part of the world.

Thanks to my lovely family for everlasting support and jokes. Thanks to Andy, who is always on the front line of dog-walking, making tea and listening to my hair-tearing anguish over tricky chapters.

And most of all, thanks to the readers – without whom I wouldn't be able to do what I love most.

PUBLISHING TEAM

Printed in Great Britain
by Amazon

58522388R00184